DISCONNECT

A SAINT SQUAD NOVEL

OTHER BOOKS AND AUDIOBOOKS
BY TRACI HUNTER ABRAMSON

DISCONNECT

A SAINT SQUAD NOVEL

TRACI HUNTER ABRAMSON

Covenant Communications, Inc.

For Lauryn Blume

Inscription: Classified

Cover images: *Military Helicopter* © BoJack, shutterstock.com; *Portrait of Woman Working* © Roman Samborskyi, shutterstock.com; *Soldiers in Camouflag*e © Gorodenkoff, shutterstock.com; *Fully Equipped Soldiers Wearing Camouflage* © Gorodenkoff, shutterstock.com

Cover design by Julie Olson
Cover design copyright © 2024 by Covenant Communications, Inc.

Published by Covenant Communications, Inc.
American Fork, Utah

Library of Congress Cataloging-in-Publication Data

Name: Traci Hunter Abramson
Title: Disconnect / Traci Hunter Abramson
Description: American Fork, UT : Covenant Communications, Inc. [2024]
Identifiers: Library of Congress Control Number 2023947873 | 9781524422523
LC record available at https://lccn.loc.gov/2023947873

Printed in the United States of America
First Printing: June 2024

30 29 28 27 26 25 24   10 9 8 7 6 5 4 3 2 1

PRAISE FOR TRACI HUNTER ABRAMSON

"The story's tension-packed plot had me hooked from the start to the end. I loved the blend of romance and suspense and enjoyed the twists. Combing a wedding, a presidential election, and an overseas terrorist threat, *Covert Ops* contains many captivating scenes. It is led by likable lead characters who I felt were all well fleshed out. The dialogue was also entertaining and authentic. There are a couple of mysteries included as well, which are solved by the end of the book. As part of a series, the novel can be read by itself. *Covert Ops*, a Saint Squad novel by Traci Hunter Abramson, is a compelling read with many gripping scenes. It skilfully combines different genres, delivering an absorbing, riveting story. Fans of romance and suspense will love it."

—Readers' Favorite five-star review

"The daughter of a congressman with a flair for baking + a young man destined for politics = the perfect recipe for romance! Katherine's feelings get twisted like her famous cinnamon rolls when she learns that Jim wants to go into politics. She's tired of that world, but she can't let him go. And together they unravel a political plot! A wholesome Christian romance with strong family connections, prayer, and sweet kisses. Like a gooey cinnamon roll, you'll devour this delicious story!"

—Samantha Hastings, author of *By Any Other Name*

"Traci Hunter Abramson weaves her magic again, and we get the delightful story of Jim and Katherine's courtship. Jim's honesty is unfailing, and Katherine stalwartly supports him while discovering her own path. With Abramson's knack for intrigue, suspense, and heartwarming romance, Jim and Katherine is a book you won't want to put down."

—Chalon Linton, author of the Flying in Love series

"Traci Hunter Abramson's thriller *On the Run* is an intense spy novel of epic proportions. She has created a plausible and almost frightening scenario and woven a plot that will have the reader on the edge from beginning to end. The characters, settings, and situations are well described and very believable. The plot is electrified with energy and motivates the story ever forward. In an era of almost palpable global disaster around every hidden corner, this plot speaks volumes for the unethical situations projected by evil minds. With good and evil on a crash course headed directly toward the protagonist, the plot is driven with considerable action as the reader follows the line of thought that similarly leads the main characters toward their ultimate goal: the evil force that threatens world stability. A powerful story. I couldn't put it down."

—Readers' Favorite five-star review

"Abramson always delivers a fast-paced and action-packed novel, and *Sanctuary* is no exception!"

—Books Are Sanity

"*Not Dead Yet* is a heart-pounding suspenseful adventure that you won't want to put down!"

—*InD'tale* Magazine

ACKNOWLEDGMENTS

THANK YOU TO THE MANY readers who have encouraged me to continue this series. And thank you to Samantha Millburn for making my words the best they can be. Thanks to Sian Bessey, Amy Miller, and Tracy Bentley for your constant encouragement throughout this project. Thank you to Shara Meredith and the amazing marketing team at Covenant as well as the rest of the Covenant family, who continue to support my career.

Thanks also to the many critique partners and beta readers who helped me polish this story in its early stages: Lara Abramson, Scott Abramson, Kyle Beecroft, Paige Edwards, and Ellie Whitney.

Thank you to the CIA Publication Classification Review Board for your continued support. And finally, thank you to my family for sharing me with my fictional worlds.

1

Brent's heart raced, and he clawed at consciousness as he fought to free himself from the tangled images of the dream. He'd been here before. It wasn't real. This wasn't now.

The thick trees of the jungle, the gunshots flying through the air, the pungent smell of leaves rotting mixed with the scent of the ocean.

Perspiration beaded on his forehead. His memories and the nightmare combined—a cry of pain, a man falling to the jungle floor.

Brent grunted, his legs moving restlessly as gunshots echoed through his mind.

A hand caressed his shoulder. "Shh. It's okay."

Amy's soothing voice cut through his semiconsciousness and pulled him into the present.

Brent's body stilled, and he concentrated on breathing. A deep breath in, a slow breath out. He forced his eyes open and lifted his free hand to cover hers. Her smooth skin beneath his touch, her auburn hair spilling onto her pillow, her blue eyes filled with concern. Love swamped through him and chased away the worst of what he'd just experienced.

"Where were you just now?" his wife asked.

"Nicaragua."

"The night Kel was shot."

Even though she didn't phrase it as a question, he responded with a simple, "Yeah."

Not for the first time, gratitude filled him for the fact that Amy worked with his Navy SEAL unit. As the intelligence officer for the Saint Squad, she was privy to all his operations and had been an integral part of many of them.

"You've been dreaming about that a lot lately, ever since Kel announced his retirement," Amy said. "Are you worried about working with his replacement? Or is it the recent missions looking for Morenta that have you on edge?"

Leave it to his wife to cut straight to the heart of the problem. "It's never sat well with me that we didn't take Morenta down when we had the chance."

Amy propped herself up on her elbow. "And?"

"I don't know. I still can't believe Kel is going from commanding SEAL Team Eight to being the Secretary of Veteran Affairs. Not exactly a typical career path."

"Honestly, I can't think of anyone better to fill that position. He suffered through a career-altering injury; he knows what it's like to be behind enemy lines. Vets don't always have someone looking out for them who understands them so well," Amy said. "Besides, Dad has said a number of times that he doesn't want to fill his cabinet with a bunch of politicians."

President-elect James Whitmore. His father-in-law.

"Has it sunk in yet that your dad is going to be the next president of the United States?" Brent asked. "It still doesn't seem real to me."

Her lips curved into a smile. "It's about to become very real. His inauguration is only a week away."

"At least we've managed to stay out of the limelight."

"So far. I promised to be on stage with him for the swearing-in ceremony," Amy said. "You're invited to be up there too."

"I think it's best if I stay in the audience with the rest of the squad, especially since the press only knows you by your maiden name." Even though it was in his father-in-law's official bio that Amy was married, Jim had been able to classify Brent's name because of Brent's role in the military. So far, the press had left them largely alone.

Amy ran her fingers along his beard, sending a shiver of attraction through him. "I think it's about time for you to shave this off and get a haircut."

"My squad is still active for a few more days." Brent and his fellow SEALs often let their hair grow out when they expected to be working in the field. With the news that Morenta was expanding his empire throughout Central America and Mexico, his squad had already been activated for surveillance missions three times in the last few weeks.

Amy lowered her hand to his chest. "We should try to get some more sleep. Kel's replacement reports tomorrow."

"I still can't believe they brought in someone from California." Brent could have lobbied for the position, but he didn't want to leave the Saint Squad any more than he wanted Kel to retire.

"Everything will work out." Amy settled her head on his chest and snuggled beside him. "It always does."

Everything *had* always worked out since he'd been part of the team. Brent attributed his squad's high success rate and lack of casualties to a combination of training and inspiration. Would his new commander allow them the same flexibility to follow inspiration in the future? Or would he assume the Saint Squad relied too much on luck?

Brent wrapped his arm around his wife and pressed a kiss to her forehead. Grasping at her optimism, he forced himself to close his eyes. Amy was right. Everything would work out.

* * *

A whimper carried through the stillness of the night. Seth quieted his breathing, his eyes peeking open just enough to take in his surroundings. The whimper repeated, red lights illuminating on the baby monitor beside his bed. He was home.

The mattress shifted beside him. Seth rolled over and put his hand on his wife's arm before she could climb out of bed. "You sleep. I'll get her."

Vanessa flopped back onto her pillow. "I really love you right now."

Seth's lips quirked up. He pressed a kiss to his wife's forehead. Even after four years of marriage, he couldn't believe Vanessa was his. Six years of dating in high school and college. Then six years apart before they'd reconnected and found their happily ever after.

Little Talia began to fuss in earnest.

Seth swung his long legs over the side of the bed and moved into the baby's room. As soon as he walked in, Talia craned her head toward him.

"Hey there. What are you doing awake?"

Talia rolled over and pushed to a stand, using the bars of the crib to steady herself.

"Come on. Let's see if we can rock you back to sleep."

Even though their daughter's middle-of-the-night demands had reduced over the past several months, Seth didn't know how Vanessa managed to keep up with taking care of Talia and working part-time, especially when he was deployed and she had to do it all on her own. Though Vanessa frequently traded babysitting with some of the other wives in his SEAL unit, her organizational skills had been stretched to the point of breaking.

Seth settled into the rocking chair in the living room. Talia snuggled against him, her little hand gripping his finger.

A wave of love hit Seth as he stroked his daughter's head. Already a year old. Where had the time gone?

As Talia's body relaxed, the first rays of sunlight filtered through the window. Only another hour or so until Seth would need to get up for work. He should put the baby down and go back to bed. But he quickly discarded that thought.

He leaned his head back against the chair and closed his eyes. Deployments had already cost him too many precious moments with his wife and daughter. He was going to enjoy this one for as long as he could.

* * *

Amy shuffled the papers on her desk in search of today's duty roster, pausing when she uncovered the baby shower invitation for two of the squad members' wives. After spending their teenage years living in the same house, Tristan Crowther and Quinn Lambert were like brothers. When the two men married the Palmetta sisters, Riley and Taylor, their family status had become official. A few months ago, both families had been blessed with new babies, but with the squad's schedule over the fall and winter, the baby shower had been postponed three times already.

The event had expanded to include Carina, Jay's wife, who was due with her first child in another month.

Envy coursed through Amy along with an ache that pierced her heart and sank deep into her core. Her sister-in-law, Kendra, had announced her pregnancy only last week. No doubt the news would create a whirlwind of excitement. Besides being the daughter-in-law of the future president, Kendra was a famous singer and the daughter of an iconic actor. Kendra and Charlie would be parents by the year's end, and Amy and Brent would celebrate their sixth wedding anniversary childless.

With some effort, Amy fought back the negativity. She didn't begrudge her friends their good fortune, but after so many years of trying to have a child of her own, every time a squad member announced a new baby, it reminded her of what she didn't have, what she might never have.

Determined to keep her personal problems at bay, Amy checked her email. Great. She hadn't been in the office fifteen minutes and already the new commanding officer of SEAL Team Eight was requesting a meeting with her as well as a summary of the squad's missions and training exercises for the past three months.

She supposed it made sense that he wanted to review personnel on his first day, but she had expected Commander Gardner to meet with Brent rather than her. After all, Brent was the commanding officer of the squad. Amy was the lone civilian assigned to them. Maybe the commander had seen that the squad was training this morning and had been unwilling to wait.

Amy gathered her reports and headed to Kel's old office. As much as she was excited for Kel to take on his new position in her father's presidential cabinet, she was going to miss having someone in their chain of command who understood the Saint Squad so intimately.

Amy was halfway down the hall when Seth Johnson, all six feet seven inches of him, rounded the corner. Sweat glistened on his dark skin, and his quick pace suggested he was late for something.

"Hey, do you have the training schedule for this morning?" Seth asked with his typical Southern drawl. "The shooting range said we aren't on their list."

"I scheduled you last week."

"The petty officer said he didn't get it."

Amy fought her rising frustration. Mix-ups like this had been constant since Kel had retired. "There's a copy of the verification on my desk. It's in the green folder."

"Thanks."

Amy continued to Commander Gardner's office and greeted the secretary. "Hey, Mei Lien. How's everything going with the new boss?"

Mei Lien looked up, her expression much like a new recruit reporting for her first day of boot camp. Amy's eyebrows lifted. Though Mei Lien was only in her early twenties, she had proven repeatedly that she was exceptional at her job. She'd also become a trusted friend.

An angry voice echoed from behind the commander's closed door. "Did you even read our file before you started changing everything?"

Amy lowered her voice to a whisper. "Who's in there?"

"Lieutenant Commander Webb." Mei Lien leaned closer. "I think Commander Gardner is planning to reorganize his squad."

"Why would he do that on his first day?" Amy asked. "Come to think of it, why would he do that at all?"

"I have no idea."

The door flew open, and Lt. Commander Webb stormed out. "This isn't over."

Commander Gardner didn't respond, but he appeared in the doorway. He was younger than Amy had expected, maybe thirty, and his eyes were nearly as dark as his hair.

"Amy Miller?" he asked.

"Yes, sir."

"Commander Kirk Gardner." He extended his hand, and Amy shook it. "It's good to meet you."

"Please come in." Commander Gardner motioned her inside and shut the door. "Do you have the reports I asked for?"

"Yes, sir." Amy handed them over. As soon as he indicated that she should sit, she took the seat across from him.

He settled behind his desk and flipped through the reports. His eyebrows furrowed. "How in the world did a squad of seven men end up with three officers in it? The standard is to only have one in a unit this size."

Though Amy was fully aware that the unit had been created with the squad members' religious and moral compatibility in mind as much as their other strengths, she said, "Varying language skills and compatible specialties were the key factors when it was formed. If you look at the squad's success rate, you'll see that the dynamics have worked exceptionally well."

"I would expect it to, considering they have their own intel officer." Commander Gardner picked up a pen and scribbled a few notes. "I'm in the process of reallocating resources in this unit."

Amy squelched the urge to squirm. "Begging your pardon, sir, but wouldn't it be wise to take some time to assess your men's strengths before making changes?"

"I've been looking through personnel files since I was assigned this command."

"I'm sure you have, but you can learn only so much from a person's file. Personalities, compatibility, trust—all those things have a significant impact on a squad's success."

His eyes flashed, and the muscle in his jaw twitched. "I'll be the judge of what's best for this unit."

"I'm sorry, sir. I didn't mean to imply otherwise." The *but* on her tongue nearly spilled out. Where had this man come from? Could he be this clueless, to think he shouldn't assess the emotional, psychological, and intellectual strengths of his men in person before making sweeping changes?

The commander made another note on the duty roster. "From now on, you'll be supporting the entire second platoon, not just one squad."

Acid rose up her throat. She swallowed the burning sensation. "When will that change take effect?"

"Today. The intel officers for Alpha and Gamma squads report this afternoon to their new assignments."

Amy blinked. No one ever processed reassignments that quickly. She pushed her questions about the new commander's methods to the back of her mind and focused on the real issue at hand. "What about deployments? I routinely accompany the Saint Squad into the field, particularly when they're working off a vessel."

"That isn't necessary. The squad can receive adequate support from the various ships' intelligence officers."

"Respectfully, sir, I disagree." This man was making changes that could endanger the lives of her squad members, endanger her husband's life. "I am an integral part of the squad's success as well as their nonexistent casualty rate."

"This isn't up for negotiation. I also want your recommendation for who would be the best candidate to take over command of the Saint Squad: Lieutenant Johnson or Lieutenant Wellman."

Seth or Jay? Amy swallowed hard. "Why would you need to replace Commander Miller?"

"The promotion list comes out this week," Commander Gardner said. "I prefer not to have subordinates who are equal in rank to me."

Amy read between the lines. Her husband was getting promoted. What should be cause for celebration had turned into a nightmare. "Even if that's the case, it doesn't change the command structure of the unit."

"Be that as it may, Commander Miller is being reassigned."

"Reassigned where?"

"It depends on if he's selected as the ball carrier position at the White House."

The White House? Amy's jaw clenched. Was her father behind this? Could he be trying to keep Brent out of harm's way in an effort to minimize security risks to their family?

"The military aide position doesn't change over until April," he continued. "That will give the commander plenty of time to train his replacement."

Amy gripped the arms of her chair and fought against the anger simmering inside her. Eager to get out of this man's office, she stood. "Would you like me to set up a meeting with you and Commander Miller?"

"My secretary has already sent him a meeting invitation." He looked down at the duty roster again. "Wait, you and the commander have the same last name? Any relation?"

"Like I said, sir, you can learn a lot when you look beyond the personnel file." Without another word, Amy left the commander's office and headed for her own. She wasn't going to let anyone endanger the Saint Squad, not if she could help it.

2

PRESIDENT-ELECT JIM WHITMORE SETTLED BEHIND the desk in his temporary office and reviewed the daily intelligence report, automatically making a mental list of which of his contacts in the intelligence community would be able to provide clarity if needed. It wasn't his job to lead the military and intelligence community in protecting the United States yet, but it would be soon. Very soon.

He still couldn't believe he'd won. Despite multiple assassination attempts and political ploys to undermine his integrity, the Lord had allowed this miracle to happen. In six days, Jim would be sworn in as the next president of the United States.

A knock sounded on his office door.

"Come in."

Doug Valdez, Jim's newly appointed secretary of Homeland Security, poked his head inside. "Do you have a minute?"

"Yes, come on in." Jim set the secure iPad aside.

Doug held out a folder. "Here's the latest security report for Inauguration Day."

"Anything of concern?"

"There's some chatter about a potential car bomb outside the Capitol building, but the FBI and Secret Service have the area under surveillance. They're also conducting regular sweeps with the bomb-sniffing dogs."

"Sounds like they have the situation under control."

"As much as possible."

Jim leaned back in his chair. "How is our FBI director handling the idea that he'll be working for you now instead of the other way around?"

"He seems to be settling into the idea." Doug flashed him a wicked grin. "I think he kind of likes that you nominated someone who understands field-work."

"I'm sure I'll benefit from your experience working for the FBI, but the main reason I want you in this job is because I trust you and I believe you'll help make this country safer."

"I appreciate the vote of confidence." Jim's personal cell phone rang. "I'll let you get that."

"Thanks, Doug." Jim checked the caller ID as Doug left the room. Jim's smile was instant when he saw Amy's name. "Hi, sweetie. How are you doing?"

"I'm not sure," Amy said. "Did you ask for Brent to be reassigned as your military aide?"

Jim replayed the question in his mind again to make sure he'd heard her right. He had anticipated this call, but Brent's name wasn't the one he'd expected to hear. "Brent?"

"Yes, your son-in-law," Amy said. "I just met with our new commanding officer. He said he's reassigning Brent and that he's up for the military aide position at the White House."

"I did have a talk with the secretary of the navy about who I would like to have in that position, but it wasn't Brent."

"Wait, why would you get involved in the navy's personnel decisions?" Amy asked.

"Because it would help with another position I need to fill."

"Dad?" The suspicion in her voice thickened. "What aren't you telling me?"

"I want Seth as my military aide."

Understanding carried over the line. "You want Vanessa to work for you."

"I do." The girl always was quick. "If Seth is willing to work at the White House, his wife will be more open to accepting the position I have in mind for her."

"You know there are nepotism laws in place for a reason."

"I'm not related to Seth or Vanessa."

"You might as well be. The Saint Squad is practically family to you."

"Which is why I want to surround myself with them, people I trust, people who have proven themselves to be invested in the protection of this country and her citizens."

"I can't blame you there," Amy said, the accusation in her tone falling away.

"I don't know why your new commander would try to send me Brent instead of Seth."

"I do. He said he doesn't want to have subordinates who are equal in rank. It looks like Brent's name is on the promotion list to commander."

"That's great."

"It's great, except that Commander Gardner has only been here one day, and he's already reorganizing squads and adjusting duties," Amy said, her exasperation obvious. "He's having me support an entire platoon, and he doesn't see the need for me to deploy with the Saint Squad." Her voice went up an octave. "He has no understanding of the role I play in keeping these men safe."

As the former Senate intelligence committee chair, Jim was well aware of the danger his son-in-law often faced and the many times Amy had deployed with the navy. "I'm sorry, honey. Maybe this is something you need to take up the chain of command."

"Or I could wait until next week and jump straight to the top."

"You could, but I'm not sure you want your relationship with me to impact your job," Jim said. "You've made a point of keeping your family life separate from your work."

"I know." Amy's sigh carried over the line. "You're right."

"Give the new commander a chance before you start stirring the pot," Jim suggested. "Once this Commander Gardner finds out he's losing Seth instead of Brent, maybe he'll let things go back to the way they were."

"You're assuming Seth will apply for the job."

"I'm hoping he will," Jim admitted. "It will be far easier to have you call him when you need my interference than to have you try to get through to me."

Amy's laughter rang over the line. "You may have a point."

* * *

Brent waited impatiently at the outdoor firing range while another unit practiced during his squad's time slot. This was the third time in the last two weeks that his squad had been either double booked with another unit for a training site or hadn't been on the schedule at all.

"What do you think the chances are that we can get Kel to come back?" Tristan asked, his lazy Texan drawl verbalizing Brent's thoughts.

"I don't see that happening." Quinn nodded at the man beside him. "You sure Jay didn't pay someone off so he wouldn't have to lose to me again today?"

"Not a chance." Jay straightened before glaring down at Quinn. "You still owe me lunch from the last time I beat you."

"That's not true. I gave you that chicken alfredo last week."

"Wait." Craig stepped forward. "You're the one who took it? My wife sent that in for me."

"Sienna should know by now that food isn't safe if it's left out in the open." Unrepentant, Quinn shrugged.

Craig's eyes narrowed. "Sienna said she hid it in my desk drawer."

"Your *unlocked* desk drawer." Quinn held up a finger to punctuate his words.

"This proves my point that you still owe me lunch," Jay said. "The deal was that you had to buy me lunch, not steal lunch from Craig."

The squad continued to bicker over whether their general policy of sharing included food. Brent shook his head.

In the field, the tight bond between his squadmates made them a formidable force. When left with too much time on their hands, they were like unruly brothers looking for a fight. They needed something to do or a common enemy to battle to keep them from turning on each other.

Brent went to the best option available, the petty officer overseeing the shooting range. "Sarge, can't you let us take those last few spots on the end there?"

"I'm sorry, sir, but I need authorization before I can let your squad on the range."

Seth jogged toward them and held up a single paper. "Got it."

"Thank goodness," Brent muttered under his breath.

Seth handed the paper to the petty officer.

The petty officer skimmed over the paperwork. He motioned to open stations at the far end of the range. "Your men can take those for now. Unfortunately, you only have fifteen minutes before the next unit gets here."

"Craig, Damian, Jay, you go first." Brent stepped closer to the petty officer. "Which unit comes in next?"

"Gamma Squad."

Webb's unit. With anyone else, Brent could have simply explained the mix-up, but Webb wasn't one who tolerated excuses, even if they were justified.

"I'll talk to the commander," Brent said.

The petty officer lifted his eyebrows skeptically. "Good luck, sir."

"Thanks, Petty Officer." Brent turned to Seth, Tristan, and Quinn. "The three of you go next. Alternate with the others until I get this resolved."

The three men started toward the rest of their squad before Brent added, "And, Quinn, give Craig some space."

Quinn glanced at Craig, who was currently glaring at him while he loaded his rifle. "Craig will cool down if Amy orders lunch in for us."

"I'll text her." Brent waited until a spark of victory filled Quinn's eyes before he added, "But you're buying."

"What? I only owed Jay—"

That was as far as Quinn got before Seth grabbed his arm and dragged him forward. "Come on, Quinn. You can take out your frustration on the target."

"Here comes the commander now," the petty officer said.

Brent swept his gaze over the path leading to the parking lot. Sure enough, Lt. Commander Webb was heading their way as though preparing to do battle, seven men following behind him.

"Miller, we need to talk." Webb turned to his men. "Check your weapons. We start in ten minutes."

"I wanted to talk to you too," Brent said, his tone deliberately civil. "There was a mix-up on the schedule. Our units will need to share the range."

"We'll let our second-in-commands handle that. We have bigger problems."

"Seth!" Brent called out. As soon as Seth turned his way, Brent said, "You're in charge."

Webb issued a similar order to his senior chief before leading Brent across the grass to the edge of some trees.

"What's going on?" Brent asked.

"Commander Gardner is what's going on." Webb waved a hand toward the range. "He's transferring a third of my squad, reassigning my intel officer, changing our training schedule. And that's just to start."

"Why all the changes?"

"I asked him that." Derision filled his voice. "He said our team is going to be the model for how SEAL teams operate in the future."

Brent shifted his weight. "I didn't hear anything about the navy revamping how the teams operate."

"Me neither, but our new commander thinks our units could run more efficiently with less personnel."

"What do you know about him?"

"Nothing, except he transferred from Coronado," Webb said. "With the changes he's making, my guess is he's bucking for stars on his shoulder."

Great. An officer looking to make a name for himself. That was the last thing Brent's squad or SEAL Team Eight needed. "He should worry about making his next rank before he looks forward to admiral."

"I don't care what rank he is; we have to do something. He can't switch up personnel on a whim and expect us to maintain operational readiness."

"I'll have Amy do some digging."

"She had a firsthand view of what the man's up to this morning," Webb said.

"What are you talking about?"

"The commander met with her right after he got finished with me."

Brent's cell phone buzzed with an incoming text. He read the message from his wife. "Looks like Amy's way ahead of us. She wants my squad to meet off base for a lunch meeting."

"Keep me and my men in mind when you formulate your plan of attack."

Brent nodded. "I'll do that."

3

Amy settled at the head of the long table in the banquet room of her squad's favorite Italian restaurant. A private room was critical for today's meeting, but she hadn't dared hold it on base. She couldn't risk Commander Gardner getting wind of it.

Ideas circled through her mind, and her emotions tangled. She hadn't expected that anyone would be able to step into Kel's position without a few bumps, but her meeting with Gardner had been so unnerving, she needed the whole Saint Squad family involved to protect their unique bond.

Her talk with her dad had offered one idea for a temporary solution, but she couldn't help mourning what would be lost with the coming changes. The Saint Squad was her family. They had saved her when she had been taken hostage in Abolstan, and it hadn't taken long for Brent to capture her heart. Brent was her everything, and his men were her brothers. She prayed their union could weather the coming storm.

Vanessa rushed through the door. "I got here as fast as I could. What's wrong?"

"The squad is fine," Amy reassured her.

Vanessa lowered her purse to the floor and slipped into the chair beside Amy. "They'd better be fine. Seth knows he'll have to deal with me if he goes off and gets himself injured or worse."

Amy's lips twitched into the beginnings of a smile. The woman beside her might be petite, but none of the squad members would want to cross her in this life or the next. As one of the top intelligence officers in the CIA, she was someone the squad often relied on for her expertise when faced with serious threats.

"Maybe I should rephrase," Amy said. "The squad is physically fine." That was as far as Amy got before her husband walked in, followed by his men.

Seth spotted his wife and rounded the table to sit beside her. "What are you doing here?"

"We're about to find out." Vanessa tilted her chin up and leaned in for a quick kiss.

The rest of the squad settled into their seats.

Brent closed the door and, like a second parent preparing to control his unruly children, opted to sit at the foot of the table. He lifted a hand to silence the friendly chatter at the table, and his dark eyes met Amy's. "What happened in your meeting this morning?"

How her husband knew about her meeting with Commander Gardner when he'd been on the shooting range was beyond her, but Amy had learned long ago not to be surprised by his ability to absorb knowledge wherever he was.

"I'll apologize now for sharing information that some of you should be receiving through different channels later, but this can't wait," Amy began. "Our new commanding officer seems determined to reorganize personnel within SEAL Team Eight, including in the Saint Squad."

Quinn leaned forward and gripped the edge of the table. "He's breaking us up?"

"He can't do that," Craig insisted. Despite being the newest member on the squad, he was every bit as much a part of the Saint Squad family as any of the others.

Damian rattled something off in Spanish. Amy didn't need a translation. The man was clearly as upset as everyone else at the table.

"Let her finish," Brent said. His eerily calm voice signaled that his anger was simmering.

The men quieted. None of them wanted to be on the receiving end if the volcano of his emotions spewed over.

"First, a small bit of good news." Amy focused on her husband, love and pride welling up inside her. She couldn't keep her smile from forming. "Brent made the promotion list."

Congratulations sounded around the table. Excitement flashed in Brent's expression before he sobered. He held his hand up to silence them.

Sympathy rose within Amy. Keeping her eyes on Brent, she forced herself to continue. "Because of Brent's promotion, Commander Gardner wants to transfer Brent out of the unit. He doesn't want any subordinates who equal him in rank."

"Now, that's just stupid," Seth said.

"Way to spoil the good news," Tristan said.

Brent's brown eyes darkened. "Where's he sending me?"

"His plan is to put you in for the military aide position at the White House." Before Brent could jump to the same conclusion she had, Amy quickly added, "No, my father didn't have anything to do with it."

"That's a competitive position. Why would he put me in for it?" Brent asked. "Does he know I'm related to our president-elect?"

"I doubt it," Amy said. "Even though Commander Gardner said he's been reviewing personnel files since receiving this assignment, he didn't go beyond the basics. He doesn't even know we're married."

"What other changes is he planning?" Brent asked.

"The main one so far is to have me support our whole platoon. Looks like he's reassigning some of the other intel officers and trying to reduce his civilian staff."

"He's setting you up to fail," Seth said.

"Why?" Amy asked. She hadn't considered that as one of Gardner's possible motives.

"Military officers have less control over civilians within their command. If this guy wants to make changes, he'll clean house of as many civilians as he can, especially ones who might challenge his authority."

"We've all seen this kind of thing before," Brent said.

"He's going to have to try a lot harder if he expects me to mess up."

"I don't think you understand." The typical soothing rhythm of Seth's words faded beneath his rising anger. "Gardner will overwork you until you won't be able to keep up."

"Seth's right, honey." Brent's use of an endearment in an office setting punctuated the concern in his voice. "If you manage to keep up, he'll create more work for you until you either quit or he can get you fired or transferred for not meeting the needs of the unit."

"That's evil," Vanessa said.

Evil was right. Amy looked from Brent to Seth. Did they really believe Gardner would do such a thing? She shook that question away. Of course they did. These men didn't lie unless it was necessary to complete a mission, and even then, it was rare.

"You need to document everything he's doing," Seth said. "I guarantee the time will come when you'll need to defend yourself against this guy."

"I'm already making notes."

"Store them away from the office," Vanessa said. "And not on your work computer."

Amy took a moment to process this latest suggestion before she retrieved a file from her purse and set it on the table. "I have a plan to slow Gardner down, but it does still involve some changes to our squad."

"How so?"

"Again, sorry for spoiling news." Amy turned her attention to Seth and Vanessa. "My dad wants Seth to apply to be his military aide."

Seth straightened to his full height of enormous. "Me? Why me?"

"Two reasons. First, my father is surrounding himself with people he can trust implicitly, especially as he's beginning his presidency."

"And second?" Seth asked.

"He wants Vanessa to fill a position at the White House."

Vanessa's eyebrows rose. "What kind of position?"

"He didn't say, but knowing your background, I assume it's some kind of intelligence adviser," Amy said. "I know you'll need to talk it over, but if you do want to consider a two-year break from the Saint Squad, I have a plan to interrupt Gardner's personnel transfers."

"What are you thinking?" Brent asked.

"The new military aide won't report until April. Brent, I say we have you apply so Gardner thinks that's how he's getting rid of you. Seth, if you're interested in the position, you can interview for the job while we're in DC next week for the inauguration."

"So, Seth would already have the job, but I would pretend to want it," Brent said.

"Yes. Come April when the winning candidate is announced, the Saint Squad will have what most would deem an appropriate number of officers, and Gardner will have to look for a new way to transfer you."

"It's a start, but in the short term, we need to find out everything we can about Gardner. We aren't the only unit he's messing with, and none of us are willing to sit by and watch this guy unravel the safeguards that prevent us from getting ourselves killed."

Tristan nodded. "Amen to that."

* * *

Jim hadn't planned on talking to Vanessa Johnson about his job offer until she came to his inauguration, but after speaking to Amy, he couldn't wait until then. In truth, he wasn't sure he was prepared to begin his role as the president of the United States without her in place.

After spending the past two years overseeing the highly classified guardian program, he was uneasy with his new position cutting him off from the steady flow of information from the operatives who few people knew existed. The guardians had saved his life. In return, he had ensured they would have sufficient funding and resources to protect US intelligence assets around the world. The guardians were crucial in keeping information flowing when red tape got in the way of efficiency.

Jim picked up the secure phone one of the guardians had given him and dialed the number for Vanessa's office at the CIA training facility. No time like the present.

"This is Vanessa."

"Vanessa, it's Jim Whitmore."

"You'll have to start introducing yourself as President Whitmore pretty soon."

"That's still a few days away."

"It'll be here before you know it," Vanessa said. "I assume you're calling to tell me about the job offer Amy mentioned."

"Yes." Jim had suspected his daughter would speak with Vanessa before he finished with his morning meetings. "I'm sure Amy told you I asked for Seth as my military aide."

"She did. We had lunch with the squad today to talk about the challenges their new commander is throwing at them," Vanessa said. "I haven't spoken to Seth yet about whether he's interested, but I would like to have a full picture of what you have in mind for me before we talk tonight."

"The short version is I want to create a new intelligence advisory position, and I want you in it."

"I appreciate you thinking of me, but after Talia was born, I cut my hours to part-time so I can be home more."

"This would be a full-time position, but with what I have in mind, I believe you would be able to work from home most of the time."

"An intel job that can be done at home? Now I'm intrigued."

"I hoped you might be." Jim smiled. No better way to hook an intel officer than to dangle a mystery in front of them. "As you may be aware, as soon as I'm sworn into the office of president, one of the luxuries I'll be giving up is the ability to keep my private cell phone."

"I'd never thought about that, but it makes sense. From an intelligence standpoint, no one wants your private phone conversations intercepted regardless of what's said."

"It's a minor inconvenience for my family and friends to have to go through, but it isn't my personal cell phone I'm worried about." Jim lowered his voice before he added, "It's the cell phone Ghost gave me that I'm reluctant to part with."

"Ghost?"

Jim had to give her credit. If he didn't know any better, he would have believed Vanessa had no idea what he was talking about.

"When I spoke to our mutual friend about my concerns, he suggested I bring in an intermediary, someone he can contact who has easy access to me," Jim said. "Your name is at the top of our list."

"Assuming we do have a mutual friend, what role would this intermediary serve?"

"For the past couple years, I've been the sole member of Congress who has known of the guardians' existence. I'm also the person who managed their funding needs."

"I'm not sure I'm following," Vanessa said. "It sounds like the guardians would need to recruit another senator to replace you."

"We talked about that possibility, but the truth is, it's no longer necessary," Jim said. "Within the next few years, the guardians will be funded out of a perpetual fund we started two years ago."

"And as president, you can make sure Congress doesn't cut that out."

"Correct," Jim said, grateful Vanessa grasped his plans so quickly. "What I need is a liaison between me and the guardians."

"It sounds like an interesting challenge, but to be of any good to you, I would need to be at the White House every day. That doesn't sound like working at home to me."

"You would be issued a secure phone that would have direct access to my personal assistant as well as your husband, assuming he agrees to come on as one of my military aides."

"Even if Seth agrees, the transfers don't happen until late spring or early summer," Vanessa said.

"Yes, but Ghost can help set you up with a secure computer there in Virginia Beach," Jim said. "I know you and Seth already have a solid security system in place in your home."

"If I can do this new job from my home in Virginia Beach, why have me move to Washington?"

"Two reasons. First, I do want Seth as one of my military aides. It's an opportunity that will bode well for him the next time he comes up for promotion. Plus, I want people I can trust surrounding me."

"I can't fault that logic. What's the other reason?"

"Because I guarantee a day will come when the flow of information doesn't get to me fast enough. I want to make sure you're close enough to the White House to come knock on my door when it's necessary."

"And you know I will, even at the White House."

"I do know that, which is why you're perfect for the job," Jim said. "My question for you is, Is this a job you want?"

"It would be hard to be away from the Saint Squad and their families, but I have always loved being in the inner circle."

Satisfied that he was halfway to accomplishing his goal, Jim said, "Talk to Seth tonight. If he's agreeable, I want you to start working for me on Inauguration Day."

"Don't you think I should give my current employer at least two weeks' notice?"

"Typically yes, but in this situation, I think the agency will forgive you for your speedy departure."

"I suppose you're right."

"You have my number. Give me a call when you decide, but I would like to have your answer by the end of the week."

"We'll talk soon," Vanessa said. "And Mr. President-Elect?"

"Yes?"

"Thank you for the offer."

"You're welcome. I hope to work with you very soon." Jim hung up the phone. After a brief moment, he picked it up again. No point in doing anything halfway. He pulled up Seth's number and dialed. The sooner he could get his key staff in place, the better.

4

THIS WAS NOT BRENT'S DAY. First the mix-up at the shooting range, then the news about Gardner, and now his afternoon dive—it had been canceled right as they'd been about to enter the water. Brent didn't generally believe in bad luck, but at the moment, it was feeling like the universe was against him and his squad.

Water splashed up over the side of the inflatable boat that had taken them from base to their intended dive site.

Damian said something, his words lost in the wind. Whether those words were in English or Spanish, Brent had no idea, but since Brent was sitting next to Craig, it could have been either. The two often forgot that not everyone on the squad spoke Damian's native language.

Craig settled his dive tank in front of him and balanced it between his knees. "The higher-ups must know something is on the horizon if they didn't want us diving today."

Brent had come to the same conclusion. They couldn't safely fly for at least eighteen hours after a dive. He wouldn't be surprised if they had travel orders when they got back to base.

"They could have told us before we went out," Quinn grumbled.

"For all we know, the word came down but didn't get to us," Tristan said.

Brent tried to give their new commander the benefit of the doubt. "We have to get used to the fact that Kel isn't in command anymore."

"Doesn't mean we have to like it," Quinn said.

Jay stretched his long legs in front of him. "If Gardner's already got Amy riled, who knows how long this guy will last."

"You don't think she's going to have her dad get him relieved of duty, do you?" Brent asked.

"Nah." Jay shook his head. "She's not the type to need her dad's help. I think she'll take care of him on her own."

The surety of Jay's statement and the rest of the squad's acceptance of it eased some of the tension that had been building inside Brent all day. If anyone could take on an overeager commander and win, it was Amy.

"You said a bunch of Webb's men were getting transferred," Seth said. "Do you think Gardner will go deeper than trying to get rid of just you from our squad?"

"I don't know. We're the smallest squad on our team," Brent said.

"Yeah, but we started with only five men," Seth said as they reached the dock. "He could try to knock us down to our original size."

"He'd better not." Damian stepped onto the deck and tied off the boat. A cell phone rang.

"Sounds like we really are shipping out," Jay said.

Brent grabbed the waterproof case where his squad had stored their phones when they'd boarded. "Only one phone is ringing, and it isn't mine."

Brent opened the case and located the ringing phone. It stopped the moment he plucked it out of the pile. "Damian, I think it was yours."

Damian extended his hand and took it from Brent.

They all disembarked and reclaimed their phones once on the dock. Damian pushed several buttons on the screen.

"*¿Fue importante?*" Craig asked.

Damian shrugged and lifted the phone to his ear.

"You're as bad as him," Quinn told Craig. "We don't all speak Spanish, remember?"

"If you can't figure out what *importante* means, you need serious help," Craig said.

Damian's jaw clenched, and Brent held up a hand to silence the squabbling.

"What's wrong?" Brent asked Damian.

Anger flashed in his eyes. "Looks like I'm the one Gardner is getting rid of."

"Why do you say that?" Jay asked.

"That was the housing office. They wanted to confirm that they'd taken me off the list for base housing."

"You're kidding," Tristan said. "You were supposed to move on base next month."

"I know. Paige and I have to be out of our townhouse by the end of February."

Brent's hand fisted around his cell phone. When Damian and his wife had learned their landlord planned to sell their townhouse, they'd been assured a spot would open up for them to live on base before then.

"Did the housing office say who took you off the list?" Brent asked.

"No. She thought I requested it, but she called to confirm when they couldn't find an email or call log."

"Did she put you back on the list?" Craig asked. "Maybe this was just a mistake."

"Even if it was a mistake, she said I have to go to the back of the line on the waiting list." Damian lifted both hands in an exasperated gesture. "She doesn't think anything will open up in time though."

Seth put his hand on Damian's shoulder. "Everything will work out."

"It doesn't feel like it today."

Brent let out a sigh. "I know what you mean."

* * *

Seth hit the button to open his garage door, both pleased and irritated that his wife had beaten him home from work. He loved every moment he could spend with Vanessa and Talia, but trying to pull into the garage after Vanessa had already parked was a challenge he hadn't wanted to entertain today. How the woman could weave through traffic at breakneck speeds without an accident was a mystery in itself, but her parking at an angle—almost like she was testing him—was next-level driving. With a frost expected overnight, Seth parked on the far side of the driveway, then proceeded to repark his wife's car so he could get his inside too.

Once he hit the button to close the garage door, he headed into the house.

Vanessa sat at the kitchen table, her laptop open in front of her while their daughter played with plastic dishes on the floor beside the table.

Talia turned her head when the door closed, and she squealed the moment she saw him. Seth grinned. She pushed to a stand, her little legs not quite steady as she toddled toward him.

"Hey there, baby girl." He leaned down and lifted Talia into his arms. He planted a kiss on her cheek before he repeated the gesture with Vanessa. "How was the rest of your day?"

"Enlightening."

"You talked to Senator Whitmore?"

"I did." Vanessa leaned back in her chair.

"And?"

"It could be a great opportunity, but that isn't really important unless you want to work at the White House." Vanessa's direct gaze met his. "Do you want to work at the White House?"

"It's hard to imagine." Seth leaned back against the counter and snuggled Talia close. "Even the idea that we're personally acquainted with the future president is hard to believe. Working there, having access, it's beyond anything I ever thought possible."

"You don't have to imagine it." Vanessa kept her expression neutral. The fact that she was hiding her expression spoke volumes. If she didn't care about the job, she would say so. The job Jim Whitmore had in mind for Seth's wife was something she was very interested in.

"Tell me about Whitmore's offer."

Vanessa glanced around as though someone might overhear her. "You remember my friend Ghost."

"Hard to forget a man who shot at us."

"That was one of his friends," Vanessa corrected.

"Either way." Seth hadn't appreciated the guardian's little test of readiness at the time it happened, but the man had a way of coming through when help was needed. "What does Ghost have to do with your job offer?"

"In a way, Ghost is the job offer," Vanessa said. "Our president-elect wants me to be the intermediary between him and the guardians. Basically, I would be the person who would make sure intel gets to the president when the regular channels don't work the way they're supposed to."

Seth wasn't sure what to think about the idea of his wife working with people who couldn't even tell her their names. Yet despite his reservations, he couldn't miss the spark of excitement that peeked out behind her carefully constructed expression of neutrality. "You want the job."

"Even if I do, I have a good job now," Vanessa said. "I don't want you to have to make a change unless you want to."

Talia squirmed in his arms, and Seth settled her back down on the floor beside her toys. "With the way things are going with this new commander, I'm torn. Part of me wants to take the couple years away from the teams so I don't have to deal with him, but I also feel like I'm abandoning my squad if I leave them to face this guy alone."

"They won't be alone. They have each other." Vanessa stood and closed the distance between them. She put both of her hands on his arms. "For a minute, don't think about the rest of your squad. Assume they'll be okay without you. What do you want?"

Seth wrestled with the question. Talia let out another squeal. "I want to watch our daughter grow up."

"Being the military aide to the president isn't exactly a nine-to-five job," Vanessa said.

"No, but I would have two years knowing that I wouldn't have any long deployments."

"That's true," Vanessa conceded. "What about the work? Playing in the political fishbowl is a lot different from facing armed men."

"Not that different," Seth muttered.

"Look at the next two years. What do you want it to look like?"

Anticipation tangled with a sense of loss. His slipped his hands around her waist. "I'll miss the squad, but it's hard to pass up the chance to work for the president of the United States. Especially when it's someone I respect."

"Does that mean we're moving to Washington?"

He couldn't help the excitement that rushed through him. "I'd have to get the job first, but if you're good with changing jobs, so am I."

Vanessa leaned in and kissed him. He drew her closer, savoring the moment.

When she pulled away, she took his hand. "Come on. You can help me look at apartments."

"You're already looking for a place to live?"

"Just weighing our options." Vanessa smiled.

"I'm surprised you haven't already picked out a place."

"If there were a rental house in our price range, I probably would have, but everything is ridiculously expensive," Vanessa said.

"It's going to be hard going from a house to an apartment."

"I know, but it's only for two years," Vanessa said. "Besides, if you want to spend more time with Talia, you aren't going to want a long commute."

"You've got that right."

5

BRENT SAT IN THE PASSENGER seat of his wife's SUV, his thoughts racing. The nightmares that plagued him were nothing compared to the reality he was facing today. His bad luck had continued into the morning when his car wouldn't start, which had forced Amy to leave for work an hour earlier than she'd planned. It was a minor inconvenience he'd solve by buying a new battery. He wished a simple purchase could fix the challenges Amy had outlined yesterday at lunch.

"You okay?" Amy asked as she pulled up to the gate of the navy base.

Brent flashed his badge at the guard as Amy did the same. "I'm having a hard time imagining the Saint Squad without Seth there."

"I know." She glanced sideways at Brent, compassion and understanding reflecting on her face. "He's been your swim buddy for a long time."

His swim buddy, his partner, his protection. He and Seth were brothers-in-arms, and for the past seven years, they'd had each other's backs. They fought together. They laughed together. They pretended not to cry together. He was the one friend Brent could confide in about anything, even his and Amy's difficulty in conceiving a child.

The pang from that struggle fought its way to the forefront of his mind. The doctors still weren't entirely sure what had prevented them from getting pregnant, but the most recent school of thought was that Amy's health might be the cause. She hadn't even been aware of her gene mutation until a few years ago or that one of the side effects could be infertility. Now that knowledge was complicated by the guilt she experienced every time the subject of children came up. The hardest part for him was standing beside her as she yearned for what they would likely never have.

He fought against the ache that settled in his chest and grasped for a distraction. Work. Seth transferring. A difficult commanding officer. All three served to mask the deep-seated anguish.

"You said Commander Gardner sent me a meeting request?" he asked.

"Yes." Amy reached out and put her hand on his. "My guess is he's going to break the bad news that he's planning to transfer you."

"I don't know whether I should grab my guys and head out to the obstacle course so I can avoid him or go to his office now and get it over with."

"After seeing Commander Webb go after Gardner, I can tell you that our new CO doesn't seem concerned about upsetting the balance around here."

"Maybe it's time to throw him a curve ball."

"How so?" Amy asked.

"I have to think he's expecting me to fight the transfer."

"That would be my assumption." Amy pulled into a parking space outside the building.

"Being the aide to the president is a huge honor. I'm curious to see how he reacts if someone doesn't fight back," Brent said. "Webb already told me his meeting didn't go well yesterday."

"That's an understatement." Amy turned off the ignition and turned toward him. "Webb was furious, but Gardner didn't back down."

"Gardner isn't going to back down, but maybe by playing along, I can figure out his end game."

Humor lit her eyes. "I'm sorry, but I'm having a hard time picturing you as the brownnosing type."

"I'm not going to brownnose." Brent caught the raised eyebrows and disbelief in Amy's expression and her inherent sense of fun that he so loved. His lips quirked up. "I'm just going to do a little psych profiling."

"Maybe you should wait until I have time to dig into his background." Amy gave Brent's hand a squeeze. "With all of my meetings yesterday afternoon, I never had more than five minutes with my computer."

"We'll consider this field research." Brent leaned in and kissed her. The familiar spark ignited in the brief contact, but he forced himself to pull back. The last thing he needed was for Gardner to see him kissing his intel officer, even if she was his wife. "Try to make some time to do some digging today."

"I will. Good luck." Amy leaned in for another quick kiss before she climbed out of the vehicle. She waited for Brent to join her, and together they headed into their building. "While you talk to Gardner, I have to check in with the other squad commanders to evaluate their intel needs."

He opened the door and waited for her to walk through. "Sounds like you need luck as much as I do."

"You're probably right."

Brent put his hand on her arm. "I'll see you later." Turning away from his office, he headed for the SEAL team commander's office.

He already missed the days when Kel was the person occupying that particular space. Then again, he also missed his early days as a SEAL when Kel had been his commanding officer. Kel had moved on. Now Seth could be leaving. If Gardner had his way, Brent would be on his way out sooner rather than later. Possibly Damian too. His squad was disintegrating.

Even though Brent understood that someday he would find a life beyond the teams, he didn't want that time to be now.

He willed the tension out of his body as he turned the corner and approached the secretary's desk. "Hi, Mei Lien. Is Commander Gardner available? Amy mentioned he wanted to meet with me."

Mei Lien cast a warning glance his way, but she nodded.

"Can you let him know I'm available now if he is?"

Mei Lien leaned forward and whispered, "Are you sure you want to meet with him today?"

Brent lowered his voice. "Can't avoid him forever."

"Okay." Disapproval hung in her voice, but she picked up the phone on her desk and called the commander. As soon as she hung up, she motioned to his closed door. "He said to send you right in."

"Thanks." Brent knocked twice before opening the door.

The commander pushed back from his desk and stood. Average height, average build, average looks. If it weren't for the gleam of ambition in his brown eyes and the air of determination in his posture, Gardner would make a good intelligence officer. No one would ever notice him.

A single file lay open on the desk; the rest of the space was bare, except for a computer monitor and a wire vertical file holder.

Gardner waved at the chair across from him. "Take a seat, Commander."

Brent complied. "How are you settling into the new office?"

"Well enough." He closed the yellow file folder in front of him and exchanged it for a blue one. "I met with your intelligence officer yesterday."

"Yes, she told me."

"How is it that you've been allowed to have your wife work for you?"

Brent had suspected the commander would do his research after meeting with Amy. All he had to do was look as far as the emergency contact form in his personnel file to discover their connection. "Amy wasn't my wife when she joined my unit, and as a civilian, she isn't in my chain of command."

"Regardless, I don't feel comfortable with spouses working together." He opened the blue file. "I put in the request for personnel to transfer her to one of the other teams."

Brent stiffened. He had mentally prepared for the news of his transfer, but pulling Amy from the Saint Squad? *That* was asking for a revolt. "I would advise against it, sir," Brent said. "She is an integral member of my squad."

"If transfers go as expected, she would likely request a change in a few months anyway."

"How's that?" Brent asked.

"You've been selected as a candidate to be the military aide for the president."

"That's quite an honor."

"Yes, it is." Gardner retrieved a paper from the file and held it out. "This is the information on the application and interview process. I'd like your application complete by the end of the week."

"I go on leave on Friday."

"Then I suggest you make this a priority."

Brent bristled and reminded himself not to allow anger to overshadow his overall objective: to protect his squad. He scanned the paper the commander had given him. "This says the assignment wouldn't begin until April. Does that mean Amy and I will stay in place until then?"

"You will, but your wife's transfer is already in progress."

"What's the point of sending her to one of the other teams? None of them are located in DC," Brent said. "It makes more sense to keep her in place and allow her to request a position at the Pentagon or at the navy yard when I move, assuming I get the position."

"Like I said, I don't want family members working together."

The muscle in Brent's jaw twitched. "Will there be anything else?"

"I'll need a recommendation on your replacement as squad commander."

"Logically, it would be Lieutenant Johnson. He's been with the teams longer, and he's up for promotion."

"That was my thought as well." Commander Gardner jotted down a note before looking up again. "Thank you, Commander Miller. That's all."

Brent stood. Without a word, he left the room and closed the office door behind him. He stopped at Mei Lien's desk and lowered his voice. "Have you already put the transfer order in for Amy?"

Mei Lien motioned to her overflowing inbox. "It's somewhere in there."

Damian's housing issue came to mind. "Do you have one for Damian Schmitt too?"

"Yes."

"Can you do me a favor and slide both of them to the bottom of the stack?" Brent asked.

A flicker of defiance danced in her eyes. "I'm happy to."

"How long do you think we have before it gets to the top of your pile?"

"At the rate he's generating transfer requests, at least a few days."

"Great. Thanks." Brent headed for his office. Time to make a few calls. Whether Gardner realized it or not, he was about to have mutiny on his hands.

6

Amy's plan to dig into Commander Gardner's background took a backseat to the latest intel report on Morenta. Not only had he created a new base of operations in central Mexico, but he'd also taken over the fortress one of his former colleagues had built in Nicaragua, the same fortress that was home to Brent's nightmares.

Amy submitted a request to her contact at the CIA who worked in the South American division. She'd barely hit the Send button when her secure phone rang.

She answered, surprised that the man she had just emailed was on the other end. "Clark, I just sent you an email."

"I saw it, but it'll be easier to talk to you about my intel rather than explain it in writing."

"What do you know?" Amy asked. "Is Morenta really in Nicaragua?"

"We don't have a visual, but Morenta's private helicopter was spotted at the fortress," Clark said. "Not only that, but we've been picking up chatter that he's stockpiling weapons again."

"Last time he did that, he nearly took out half the state of Arizona." Amy shuddered at the memory of the attempted terrorist attack on the Hoover Dam. "Any idea what his target is this time?"

"Not yet. I'm sending you the latest images for you and your squad to go over."

"Why do you want us involved?"

"Because your squad is the only one to ever breach the fortress and come out alive," Clark said.

Clark's words weren't entirely correct. Vanessa had also spent the better part of a week living inside the fortress, but few had access to that particular detail.

"It's only a matter of time before the navy sends them back in," Clark continued.

"For what? Do you think the government will authorize us going after Morenta?"

"We're hoping our new director of intelligence will plead our case. Morenta is evil. If we don't shut him down, we might as well announce to the public that we're going to have another 9/11 on our hands."

"That's the last thing we need, especially with a brand-new president."

"You know as well as I do that it's often during those first few weeks after a presidential inauguration that our enemies attack. They know our government moves slowly to get the political appointees approved."

"Which leaves the president shorthanded as he's settling into his new job." Amy had discussed this very thing with her father. She'd even helped him formulate the order in which his appointees would go before congress to ensure he would get his intelligence operations up to speed as quickly as possible. She suspected Vanessa's job offer was part of her father's overall plan to keep their country safe.

"Any idea when the Saint Squad will be sent in?" Amy asked.

"Admiral Singer sent a request for the latest intel on the fortress less than a half hour ago. Looks like he's gearing up for another sneak and peek."

"My squad is standing down Friday and will be on leave for a week."

"If the admiral knows that, your boys are likely heading out tonight."

"Thanks for the heads-up."

"Let me know if you turn up anything that's not already in our intel reports on the fortress."

"I will." Amy hung up the phone and sighed. Only three days before the Saint Squad would be in the clear for a much-needed break, but if Clark was right, they would be working right up until their leave started. And that work wasn't going to happen here on the base. It would be in Nicaragua.

* * *

Seth's mind wouldn't settle no matter how hard he tried to distract himself. A job at the White House. Never in his wildest dreams had he considered the possibility, certainly not during his early childhood when he'd been living in the drug-infested hovel his mother had called home. He'd been fortunate to ultimately have his uncle raise him. Patrick had been the one person who had given him what he'd needed most: love and support. The familiar pang pricked his heart when he thought of the man who had died only two weeks after Seth had graduated from high school. Patrick had believed in him. His uncle's incredible sense of patriotism and his expectation that Seth would graduate from college had pushed Seth to become the man he was now.

Yet despite his college degree and numerous recognitions during his time as a SEAL, the truth remained that he hailed from the part of New Orleans people didn't go to after dark.

The White House. Did Seth even want the job? He'd told Vanessa he would apply, but the Saint Squad had been his family since its creation eight years ago. His fellow teammates were his brothers, their wives and children as close as any extended family could be.

As family, they would also want what was best for him. He wished he knew what that was.

Brent walked into his office, tension rolling off him.

Seth's sympathy stirred. Brent had never been a fan of politics, ironic considering his father-in-law's profession, but he played the game well when he needed to. Judging from the expression on Brent's face, he wasn't happy with the hand he'd been dealt.

"What happened with Gardner?" Seth asked.

Brent closed the office door. "This guy's a piece of work. He's not only trying to get rid of me and Damian; now he's transferring Amy."

Seth straightened. "What? He can't do that."

"Mei Lien said she'd put the transfer request at the bottom of the pile, but if we don't do something, Amy will be out of here by the time we get back from the inauguration."

"Amy's a civilian," Seth said. "Gardner can't issue transfer orders without personnel agreeing."

"You're right. If we can find out who Amy's personnel officer is, we might be able to stop the transfer from going through."

Knuckles rapped against the closed office door.

"Come in," Seth called out.

Amy pushed the door open and walked in, bringing with her an air of professionalism and urgency. "I just received new intel. It looks like Morenta has taken over Akil Ramir's fortress in Nicaragua."

Seth's chest tightened. He had lived within the walls of the fortress with Vanessa for several days, both of them operating under aliases. When the time had come to escape the confines of the fortress, they'd barely made it out alive, and Kel Bennett, their former commanding officer, had been shot.

"Any idea what he's doing there?" Seth pushed to a stand. "The Ramir family hasn't been functioning since we shut them down. That was years ago."

"Yes, but from the reports I'm getting, Morenta has a new flow of money coming in from somewhere." Amy's businesslike demeanor dropped away, replaced by concern. "There's been chatter about a possible terrorist strike against the US."

"You think we're shipping out," Brent said.

"I do." Worry flashed on Amy's face but was quickly banked. She glanced at the clock on the wall. "Best guess is you have an hour, two tops, before the order comes in. My source at the agency said it's another sneak and peek."

"When did this intel pop the first time?" Brent asked.

"A couple hours ago." Amy's eyebrows drew together. "Why?"

Suspicion hummed through Seth. His eyes met Brent's. "Maybe yesterday wasn't about being ready to deploy. Maybe it was about our new commander wanting to see if we'd follow orders."

Amy looked from Seth to Brent and back again. "You think Gardner canceled your dive just because he could?"

Seth nodded. "That's exactly what I think."

"We can look into that later." The muscle in Brent's jaw twitched briefly before he waved the irritation away with his hand. "While we're waiting for the official word, we have another problem we need to deal with," Brent said.

"What's that?" Amy asked.

"Who's your personnel officer?" Seth circled to the front of his desk.

"Rose Christiansen. Why?"

"How well do you know her?" Seth asked.

"I've only dealt with her through email." Amy looked from Seth to Brent. "What's going on?"

Brent put his hand on Amy's back. "You need to meet with your personnel officer. Gardner is trying to transfer you."

"Since when? This morning, he was planning to get rid of you."

"Yeah, but now he knows we're married," Brent said.

"Next thing you know, he'll find out Tristan and Quinn are brothers-in-law." Seth leaned back against the front of his desk. "This guy is dangerous."

"Sounds like we need to make some adjustments to our battle plan." Determination sparked in Amy's eyes. "I'll talk to my personnel officer, and you two should see if you can find anyone who worked with Gardner in Coronado."

"I'll do that," Brent said. "Seth, you work with Tristan and Quinn on the logistics of a sneak and peek at the fortress. You three know the area as well as anyone."

"What about the rest of the squad?" Seth asked.

"Put Craig and Damian on the intel reports for Morenta since they both speak Spanish."

Seth nodded. "And Jay?"

"He can help me research our new commander," Brent said.

Seth cocked his head to one side. "Don't you have a job you need to apply for?"

Brent grimaced. "Right. Jay will have to start on that research without me."

"I guess we'll all have to see how much we can get done in an hour." Seth reached for his phone and tried not to regret that he likely wouldn't see his family tonight.

7

BRENT SLAMMED HIS OFFICE PHONE down when he hung up with yet another member of Commander Gardner's former SEAL team. Three conversations so far, and each one could have been a repeat of the one before. They didn't know much about him, and not one of the men Brent had served with previously had ever interacted with Gardner. How had the man risen through the ranks if no one knew who he was?

Jay knocked on Brent's open door. "Got a sec?"

"Yeah. What did you find?"

Jay closed the door behind him and moved to the chair across from Brent, then dropped into it. "This guy is bad news."

"How so?"

"I managed to track down a friend who works in his former unit," Jay said. "According to him, Gardner presented a proposal to the higher-ups about how the SEAL teams could run more efficiently."

Brent leaned back in his chair and shook his head. "It's hard to believe this guy is a SEAL."

"He barely was."

"Come again?"

"He made it through BUDS, but he was only on his second mission when he took a bullet to the shoulder," Jay said. "He hasn't been on a mission since."

"Then how in the world did he get command of a SEAL unit?" Brent's voice rose. He had to remind himself that this conversation wasn't for public consumption. He took a deep breath and asked the more telling question. "Who does he know?"

"His uncle is Admiral Roger Moss."

"The vice chief of naval operations." The second-in-command in the US Navy. Great.

"There's more." Jay held up the folder in his hand.

"I'm not sure I can handle anything else."

"From what my buddy in Coronado told me, if command likes what they see, Gardner's changes could be implemented in all the teams."

A well of panic bubbled inside Brent. He'd rather face a dozen armed men than an overeager, uneducated bureaucrat. "He isn't trying to increase efficiency. He's trying to get noticed."

"You aren't wrong." Jay slid the file he held onto Brent's desk. "That's the first few pages of his proposal from last year."

"Only a few pages?"

"I got the impression that someone made an extra copy when the commander started drafting it."

Brent opened the file and skimmed the first page. "He's trying to cut costs. Culling extra officers out of the teams lowers the payroll."

"So does reducing the number of intelligence officers on our team." Jay lifted both hands in frustration. "Under his proposal, we rely heavily on the CIA for our operational intel."

"That's fine as long as we have someone on our side of things to process their reports," Brent said. "We don't have time in the middle of an op to call the agency and hope someone picks up."

"It's not exactly like our ops happen during their business hours anyway," Jay said. "And there's no way the navy is going to inform the CIA every time we're sending a SEAL team in somewhere."

"I agree. This whole idea creates too much red tape."

"And inefficiency," Jay added. "Exactly the opposite of what the commander is claiming."

"I agree."

"So what are we going to do about it?"

"I hate to say it, but we may have to go over Admiral Moss's head."

"Are you really going to involve your father-in-law his first week in office?" Jay asked.

"Not yet. And I'm not saying we should jump right now, but I'm keeping it in mind. I say we try Admiral Rivera first," Brent said, referring to an admiral in their direct chain of command, directly above Commander Gardner. "Maybe we can get the issues with Gardner handled in-house."

Knuckles rapped against Brent's door, and it opened a second later. Amy poked her head through, and his heart lifted.

"Sorry to interrupt, but your orders just came in. You fly out in an hour," she said.

Brent closed the file and gave her a wry smile. "You're full of good news today."

"Sorry about that."

Brent stood and handed the file to Amy. "I want to take this with me, but you'll need a copy first."

Amy took it from him. "What is this?"

"Intel on our current problem. See if you can find any ammunition in there."

Amy glanced at the contents and lifted her eyes to meet his. A spark of determination shone in the deep brown. "I can do that."

* * *

Though Amy itched to delve into the report Brent had given her, she locked it in her drawer. Before she could deal with battling office politics, she needed to make sure the Saint Squad had everything they needed for their mission.

She glanced at the time on her laptop. Thirty minutes until her husband and his unit shipped out. Thirty minutes to verify the latest intel on Morenta and the fortress.

Footsteps approached and stopped outside her office door. Amy looked up, expecting to see Brent or another Saint Squad member. Instead, it was Lt. Commander Webb.

"Hello, Commander. What can I do for you?"

He stepped inside and held out a stack of papers. "I hate to do this to you, but Commander Gardner had the training sites clear their schedules. We need to rebook everything for the rest of the month."

Amy's heart sank. Redoing the training schedule would take hours.

"I also need the latest intel on terrorist activity in north Africa," Webb said.

Another commander appeared behind Webb, a folder in his hand and a scowl on his face.

Webb turned and acknowledged the newcomer. "Kaminski."

"Sorry to interrupt." Kaminski stepped past Webb and set the folder on Amy's desk. "Just heard from our new commander that he cleared all our training ops. My squad had a jump scheduled for tomorrow night."

Amy suppressed a sigh. "I'll see what I can do to get it back on the schedule."

"This is mission critical," Kaminski said, his voice tense.

"So are the intel reports for the Saint Squad," Amy replied.

A knock on her door jamb interrupted her words. Brent stepped inside. "Amy, have you pulled the last satellite photos?"

"I was about to."

Kaminski glared at Brent. "I need my op put back on the schedule, or we aren't going to be ready for our next mission."

"I was here first," Webb countered.

Brent pulled the door closed. He opened his mouth, but before he could speak, Amy held up a hand. "Gentlemen, all of us know that you each need your own intel officer," Amy said in as calm a voice as she could manage. "I'm going to do my best to fix these problems, but you have to work with me."

"She's right." Brent dropped into one of the chairs across from Amy's desk. "Gardner's already trying to transfer Amy because we're married."

Kaminski sat beside him. "Why didn't he transfer her already, then, and keep one of our intel officers?"

"Gardner didn't know Amy and I are married until today."

Webb folded his arms and glowered. "If he transfers Amy, too, we'll all be dead in the water until a replacement shows up."

"That could take weeks," Kaminski said.

"If not longer," Brent agreed.

Satisfied that the men were no longer fighting over her time, at least for the moment, Amy opened the classified program she needed to access the satellite photos.

"What are we going to do about Gardner?" Kaminski lifted his hands in a gesture of exasperation. "We can't operate like this for long without something falling through the cracks."

"I know." Brent stood. "I'm not happy Amy is staying behind tonight."

Amy selected the satellite photos she needed and hit Print.

"When do you hop?" Webb asked Brent.

"Thirty minutes."

"Brent, your photos are on the printer."

"Thanks." He scooped them up. "I'd love to stay and help you plan, but Amy will let me know if you come up with any ideas."

"Be safe," Amy said, wishing she had a moment alone with her husband before he left.

"Always." Brent opened the door and stepped into the hall.

As soon as he walked out, Webb pulled the door closed again. "What are we going to do about Gardner?"

"I don't know." Amy debated how much to confide in these two men. Trusting her instincts, she said, "He's obviously trying to thin out the civilian staff."

"Wouldn't be the first time an officer did that after taking command." Webb took Brent's vacated seat.

"How do we make this work?" Kaminski asked. "No offense, Amy, but you can't keep up with three squads, especially after Gardner wiped out everything our intel officers did before they were transferred."

"I can't believe he already got them transferred out." Amy shook her head. "The navy never moves this quickly."

Kaminski leaned forward and lowered his voice. "I heard Gardner submitted the transfers right after he found out he got this post."

"This is a nightmare." Webb ran his fingers through his hair.

"It is, but for now, let's get you and your squads taken care of." Amy put the two sets of paperwork side by side. "Commander Kaminski, would you have any objection to Webb's unit joining you on your jump tomorrow?"

"I don't see why it would be a problem."

Amy focused on Webb. "Would that work for your training tomorrow?"

"I was planning on a dive, but we could do a jump instead."

"Great." Amy made a note. "If you're both willing, I'm going to give you similar schedules so I can simplify my workload until I get us caught up."

"At this point, we'll take whatever you can give us," Webb said.

"Thanks." Amy went over the timeline in her head of how long it would take to accomplish the basics for both squads. It was going to be a late night.

Webb turned to Kaminski. "Let's have the three of us meet tomorrow at eleven hundred to compare notes on how to function until we can get some of our support staff back."

"Works for me." Kaminski stood. "I'm sending a complaint up the chain of command about Gardner's actions."

"I sent mine in this morning," Webb said.

Relieved that both commanders were willing to work together to resolve their current nightmare, Amy leaned back in her chair. "We'll talk tomorrow. And I'll email you the new training schedule as soon as I get it set."

Both men expressed their thanks and left her office.

Amy looked at the clock on her computer again. Twelve minutes until the plane carrying the Saint Squad to the aircraft carrier would depart. If she hurried, she might just make it.

Despite the mountain of work on her desk, she couldn't resist. She grabbed her purse and headed for the door. It would be worth working late tonight if she could steal a moment with Brent before he left. Besides, they both deserved a proper goodbye.

8

JIM SAT BEHIND HIS DESK in his temporary office and read the daily brief. He paused when he reached the update about Morenta's possible activity. Though no details were given on military action, he had little doubt that the Saint Squad would be involved. He also didn't put it past the drug-lord-turned-terrorist to use the early days in Jim's presidency to try to create havoc in the US.

Vice President Elect Nathan Jameson walked in and held up the iPad in his hand. "Have you seen the latest on Morenta?"

"I was just looking at that." Jim motioned at one of the chairs across from his desk and waited for the retired general to take a seat. "I imagine the navy will send someone in to scout out what he's up to."

"You think they're sending in your boys?"

"That's my guess," Jim said. "I talked to Amy yesterday, but this intel came out after that."

"Does Amy usually tell you when the squad ships out?"

"I typically figure it out when I don't hear from her, but from what she said, the new team commander isn't letting her deploy with them anymore."

"Some parents would be relieved to get that kind of news," Nate said.

"Part of me is, but I worry that Amy not being with her squad in the field could compromise their safety." Jim set his iPad on his desk and leaned back. "I wouldn't want to be in that commander's shoes if the Saint Squad suffers a casualty under his command."

"Who is the new commander?"

"I think she said his name is Gardner."

"Kirk Gardner?" Nate asked. "Roger Moss's nephew?"

"She didn't mention the commander's first name."

"Roger said something about his nephew taking a new command in Virginia Beach. That must be him." Nate scowled. "From what I've heard, Gardner is already looking forward to stars on his shoulders."

"I hope he doesn't try to use his association with my daughter to boost his career."

"This guy plays the game well. My guess is he'll use anyone to boost his career." Nate shrugged. "Of course, you're assuming he knows who Amy is. I worked with the Saint Squad before I retired, and I never made the connection that you had a daughter working with them until you introduced me to her."

"Amy can be discreet." Jim motioned to the iPad on his desk. "What do you make of this Morenta business?"

"Looks like he's up to something, but without someone inside his organization, tracking his movements and communication may be the only thing intel can do for now."

Nate was right. If Vanessa didn't have a child, Jim would have seriously considered asking her to go undercover again as Lina Ramir so she could infiltrate Morenta's organization.

The thought of sending anyone in chilled his blood. He had no doubt the hardest part of being president would be risking people's lives through intelligence-gathering endeavors and military action. Having friends in those positions only served as a constant reminder of how precious each life was, especially to the families of those who served.

Nate understood this as well. Not only had he spent more than thirty years serving in the military, but his niece had also married a guardian only a few months ago.

Jim straightened in his seat. "I reached out to Vanessa Johnson yesterday."

"The one you want to act as our go-between with the guardians?" Nate asked.

"Yes."

"It's pretty crazy that we need someone to filter information to us when we have family who can give it to us firsthand."

"I've had the same thought more times than I can count," Jim said. "Having Vanessa work as our liaison for the next two years will help us determine how critical her position is and also whether we need her in DC or if she can operate out of Virginia Beach."

"Do you think she'll take the job?"

"She's intrigued. I'm hoping that will lead to a yes."

"Keep me in the loop." Nate pushed to a stand. "In the meantime, I'm going to give my niece a call to see if her husband knows anything about Morenta."

"Thanks. Let me know if you find anything."

"You know I will." Nate left Jim's office.

An unexpected sense of comfort washed over Jim. He did know Nate would share whatever new intel he discovered.

With Nate serving as his VP and with the other qualified and upstanding men and women he planned to place in his cabinet, Jim prayed he would be successful in keeping the United States safe for as long as the American people entrusted him to lead their country.

* * *

Amy settled on her couch and flipped through Commander Gardner's file. Not exactly the evening activity she would have preferred, but at the moment, anything she could do to introduce their new commander to reality was a step in the right direction. Besides, having something to focus on would help her keep her mind off the ache that always settled in her heart when Brent was away.

Her gaze landed on the framed photo hanging on the wall across the room. She could almost taste the salty air from that day when she and Brent had been on board the USS *Harry S. Truman* for a mission several months ago.

She should be with him now. Gardner had no idea how much keeping her stateside could jeopardize the flow of information to the Saint Squad, and she couldn't shake the uneasy feeling that had been hanging over her since the moment Brent had stepped onto the transport plane that had taken him away.

Tears welled up in her eyes as an unexpected wave of emotions flooded through her. At least she'd been able to kiss him goodbye before he'd left. Good thing Gardner hadn't been at the airstrip at that particular moment.

She shook her head and cleared her thoughts. She wasn't the weepy sort, someone who couldn't handle it when her husband was deployed. A tear spilled over. So why was she crying?

She pressed her fingers against her eyes and wiped away the few tears that had escaped. The best thing she could do for her husband and her team was to find out everything she could about their new commanding officer. She flipped open the file and read: Kirk Gardner. Naval Academy graduate. BUDs training. A short stint with the SEALs before an injury sidelined him. Several years working at the Pentagon in logistics and policy before he moved back to Coronado to rejoin the SEALs.

The doorbell rang. Amy set the file aside and made her way to the entryway. She pulled open the front door. "Vanessa. Come on in." Amy waved her inside and closed the door. "I didn't expect to see you tonight. Where's Talia?"

"Carina is watching her," Vanessa said.

"I'm surprised she's up for that. She's due in less than a month." Amy tried to keep her envy from surfacing.

"She said she wants the practice."

"Come on in and sit down." Amy led the way to the living room. "I was just looking over Commander Gardner's file."

"I was thinking about what the guys were saying about Gardner setting you up to fail."

"If today was any indication, they're probably right." Amy sat and waited for Vanessa to settle beside her. "Not only did Gardner pull the intel officers out of the two other squads in our platoon, but he canceled a bunch of training exercises so I would have to do work that had already been done."

"Not exactly the ideal when you're trying to prep our guys to deploy."

Amy had no idea how Vanessa had ascertained that everything had happened at the same time, but she had learned long ago that the woman had sources everywhere. Although this time, the source was likely her husband.

"Have you heard anything from the guys?" Amy asked.

"Nothing yet, but I know they made it to the carrier."

"Yeah, I got that update too." Amy flipped open the file. "Brent gave this to me to look at. We're hoping if we can figure out why Gardner is making all these changes, we can head him off before he damages our operational readiness."

"He's already damaged the Saint Squad's operational readiness by keeping you on the sidelines," Vanessa said. "I can tell you, none of the wives are happy that you're here when the squad isn't."

"It's not like they've never deployed without me before."

"I know, but I personally feel a lot better when you're out there keeping the intel flowing."

"Me too."

The doorbell rang again.

"That must be Paige." Vanessa got up and went to answer the door herself. She returned a moment later with Damian's wife, who also worked with Vanessa at the CIA training facility.

"Hi, Amy." Paige set her purse down on the kitchen table. "I hope you don't mind me dropping by. Vanessa said you might want some help with a psych profile on the new commander."

"That would be amazing." Amy led them into the kitchen and set the file in the center of the table. "It'll probably be easier to work in here."

"What's that?" Vanessa motioned to the file.

"The background we managed to dig up on Gardner's career and the first section of the proposal he made to change how SEAL teams operate."

"He wants to get noticed." Paige sat down and opened the file. "He only went on two missions?"

"Yeah, just two," Amy said.

"A wannabe who wants to get noticed," Vanessa said. "I'm not liking this."

"Neither am I." Paige skimmed through the information.

"What can you tell us about the mission the guys are on?" Vanessa asked.

In the past, Kel had approved Amy and the Saint Squad's bringing Vanessa and Paige into their circle of need-to-know. Though she doubted Gardner would grant his approval, Amy trusted her instincts and followed her past protocols. "They're going into Nicaragua. A sneak and peek."

"Nicaragua?" Vanessa straightened. "Morenta?"

"Yes. Intel has him at the fortress."

Vanessa shuddered. "I hate that Seth has to go back there, that any of them have to go back there."

"With any luck, Brent will email me their mission plan tomorrow so I can still provide support," Amy said.

"Maybe Paige and I can come in and help."

"That would be great, but I doubt Gardner would let you," Amy said.

"I wasn't going to ask permission," Vanessa said dryly.

Amy's grinned. "I'd love to see you go toe-to-toe with the commander."

"We'll save that for after Seth has the job in DC."

"Is he really going to apply?" Amy asked.

"He is." Vanessa nodded. "I'm not sure if he's applying because he knows I want the job your dad offered or if it's because he's really interested in it, but we'll have some time to figure it out after we meet with your dad."

"What is the job he offered you anyway?" Amy asked.

"He wants an intel officer who isn't afraid to wake him up in the middle of the night," Vanessa said.

Amy laughed. "You qualify."

"She really does," Paige agreed. "Though I don't know what I'm going to do if she actually leaves."

"You'll be fine," Vanessa said. "For now, let's make sure our guys have everything they need to get home safely."

"Where do you want to start?" Paige asked.

"Paige, you look over the personnel file. Amy, you can read over Gardner's proposal and note what won't work."

"And you?" Amy asked.

"I'm going to pull up everything I have on the fortress so you have all the latest intel."

"Won't you have to go into your office for that?" Amy asked.

"No. I saw a ghost on the way here. He gave me a secure laptop to help us out."

"I really like your friends," Amy said.

Vanessa pulled her laptop from her oversized purse. "So do I."

9

JIM ROLLED OVER IN BED and reached out his arm. When he found nothing but a cold spot beside him instead of his wife, he forced his eyes open. Had he overslept?

A quick glance at the clock on his bedside table revealed it wasn't quite six. He sat up. "Katherine?"

No response.

He climbed out of bed and headed downstairs. The scent of bread dough hung in the air.

A spoon clattered against the counter.

Jim reached the kitchen and stopped in the doorway. Katherine stood beside the far counter, an apron over her pajamas and thick socks on her feet. Her dark hair was pulled back with one of those clip things she used when she was cooking.

His heart did a slow roll in his chest. Even after all these years, he still didn't know how he'd gotten so lucky. He might have been elected president, but the country was getting a huge bonus in the first-lady department.

Katherine opened the cabinet beside the stove and pulled out a spice jar. Cinnamon.

"Are you making cinnamon rolls?" Jim asked.

"Maybe." She glanced over her shoulder. "You're up early."

"I woke up, and you weren't there." He closed the distance between them and kissed her cheek. "I missed you."

"I wanted to make something for the agents outside," Katherine said. "It won't be long before this won't be my kitchen anymore."

So many years spent in politics, so much of his life dreaming of the unlikely goal of becoming president, and they were only days away from changing their address to 1600 Pennsylvania Avenue. A wave of nostalgia swept through him. This had been his home for so long. This was where his memories lived.

"Any regrets that we're leaving this behind?" Jim asked.

"No, of course not." She leaned over and kissed him. "I knew when I married you that we would eventually live in the White House."

Jim's heart warmed. Katherine had never doubted he would achieve his dreams, not even when they'd first been dating. "Only three more days. I can hardly believe it's almost here."

Katherine mixed sugar and cinnamon in a bowl. She may not have directly answered his question about cinnamon rolls, but the evidence spoke for itself.

Jim stepped behind her and wrapped his arms around her waist. "You're going to let me have one, too, aren't you?"

"I might be persuaded."

Persuaded. "What do you want me to do?"

"The horses need to be fed, and the trash needs to go out."

"How long do you think it will take the White House staff to know who's really running this country?" Jim asked.

Katherine laughed. "I'll leave running the country to you."

"You're just saying that so I'll have something to do." Jim pulled the full trash bag out of the garbage can.

"It's always best to stay busy. You're good at that."

Jim chuckled. "I'll be right back." He walked into the mud room and slipped on a pair of shoes, then shrugged on the coat he kept on the rack mounted to the wall. He flipped on the outside light and opened the back door.

Instantly, a man wearing a long trench coat, a hat, gloves, and the telltale earpiece of a Secret Service agent stepped forward. "Can I help you, sir?"

Jim took a moment to identify the man. "Good morning, Gray." He held up the trash bag. "Just doing some morning chores."

Gray held out a hand. "I can throw that away for you, sir."

"I've got it." Jim kept the bag at his side. "I need to feed the horses too."

"We'll take care of that too."

Jim should have been relieved to have someone else deal with those mundane tasks, but the lack of freedom rankled. "I know it sounds silly, but I'd prefer to do it myself. I'd like to keep my routine for as long as I can."

Gray's eyebrows rose. "Even taking out the trash?"

"Okay, fine. You can take out the trash, but I get to feed the horses."

Gray smiled. "Yes, sir."

* * *

Amy headed straight for the personnel office when she arrived on base. With how yesterday afternoon had gone, she suspected the minute she walked into her office, she would get slammed with intel and training requests for her two additional squads.

Thankfully, Vanessa had passed the latest intel on to the Saint Squad so Amy's most critical need for the day was largely behind her.

She tried not to resent the fact that she was in Virginia instead of on an aircraft carrier. At least she was able to sleep in her own bed. And truth be told, she hadn't slept the greatest last night. Maybe it was a good thing she wasn't aboard ship right now. She was exhausted.

She was nearly to the personnel office door when Mei Lien rounded the corner, her body stiff and her lips pressed together in a firm line.

"Mei Lien, what are you doing down here?"

Mei Lien held up a stack of transfer orders. "Same thing I've been doing since Commander Gardner got here." She looked at the empty hall behind her and lowered her voice. "Someone has to do something. I can't get any real work done because all I do is answer the phone and listen to complaints."

"I'm so sorry." Sympathy rose, and with it came a new flood of anger. "Do you have any idea why he's doing all this?"

"It looks like he's trying to bring a bunch of his buddies from Coronado out here to work with him."

Now things were making sense. "He's transferring people out to make room for the ones he trusts."

Mei Lien nodded.

Amy took a half step closer to her friend and whispered, "Any chance you can get me a list of the transfers?"

"In or out?"

"I'd love both, but especially the ones coming in."

"I need to make some copies in about an hour." Mei Lien stepped back. "Maybe I'll see you later."

Amy nodded. She checked her watch, noted the time, and headed into the personnel office.

A receptionist sat behind a utilitarian desk. "May I help you?"

"Yes. I need to see my personnel officer."

"Sign in here, please." She handed a clipboard to Amy.

Amy hesitated briefly. She hated leaving a paper trail that she had been here, but today, she didn't have a choice. She printed her name and gave the clipboard back.

After a short wait, the receptionist showed Amy back to a private office.

The middle-aged woman inside stood and extended her hand. "I'm Rose Christiansen."

"Amy Miller."

"Nice to meet you." She waved Amy inside and closed the door. After they were both seated, Rose asked, "What brings you in today?"

"I need to block a transfer."

Rose leaned back in her chair and let out an exasperated sigh. "You work in Gardner's unit?"

"I guess I'm not the first to come in."

"No."

Rose's hard answer and the derision vibrating through the single syllable gave Amy courage. "I know this sounds crazy, but I think Commander Gardner is trying to get rid of all the civilians in his unit."

"You aren't crazy. I received his request to reclassify four out of five of his civilian positions to military billets." She paused and met Amy's gaze. "Including yours."

"Is there a way to stop it?" Amy asked. "The reason so many intel officers are civilians is to ensure information can't be influenced by the chain of command."

"I made the same argument, but my boss is a people pleaser. He doesn't want to rock the boat with the new commander."

"Even when he's jeopardizing the safety of our men and potentially our country?"

"He doesn't see it that way." Rose leaned forward as though to say something else but stopped.

"I'm trusting you to keep this conversation between the two of us," Amy said. "You can trust me to do the same."

"I'm sorry, Amy, but there's really nothing I can do."

"Would it do me any good to talk to your boss?"

"I doubt it." Again, Amy sensed Rose was holding something back.

"Commander Wilkins knows who Gardner's related to, doesn't he?"

"Most people in this office do," Rose said.

"Which is why all the transfers are getting approved, even when they shouldn't."

Rose fell silent.

"Have the reclassification requests already been sent up the chain?" Amy asked.

"They should be hitting Admiral Rivera's desk today or tomorrow."

"Thanks for the information." Amy stood. "Oh, one more thing. If I manage to keep my position from getting reclassified, is it possible to block my transfer?"

"You want to keep working for Gardner?"

"I want to make sure our SEALs have every shred of intelligence that will bring them home safely," Amy said firmly. "Office politics should never get in the way of that."

"I agree." Rose stood as well and squared her shoulders. "If you manage to protect your position, I'll do everything I can to keep you in your job."

"Thanks, Rose." Amy shook her hand. "It was nice to finally meet you in person."

"You too."

Amy left the personnel office and headed down the hall. One more stop to make before she reported to work for the day.

10

SETH PUSHED BACK FROM ONE of the three computers lining the side of the board room the Saint Squad had been assigned when they'd reached the USS *Harry S. Truman*. The television in the corner had been muted, the closed captioning informing them of the latest weather forecast. Seth joined the rest of his squad at the worktable in the back of the room and pulled one of the satellite photos closer, his gut clenching at the thought of going back to this isolated spot in Nicaragua.

"Seth, you know the fortress better than the rest of us," Brent said. "Is there another way to breach the perimeter besides going in through the jungle?"

"No." Seth tapped on a photo. "This shows a guard on the beach, and I'm sure they still have patrols by the gate and along the exterior walls."

"So, even if we can get in that way, we'd have to neutralize guards to do it," Brent said.

"Yeah." Seth nodded. "Not exactly what we want if we don't want these guys to know we've been there."

Brent spread out the photos and plucked one out of the group. "This may be our best option."

Seth leaned forward. In the photo, trees crowded a small inlet, the dense foliage around the cove making it difficult for anyone to see them coming from their potential insertion point to the fortress. His eyes narrowed. Was this the same spot where his squad had inserted when they'd rescued him and Vanessa?

"You're thinking about using the same landing zone as last time?" Tristan asked, confirming Seth's suspicions.

"It makes sense," Brent said. "Morenta had already left the fortress when we inserted last time, and Ramir was arrested a short time later."

"You're banking on Morenta not knowing about our last visit?" Seth asked.

"What do you think?" Brent asked in return. "Is it possible Ramir would have told Morenta about us breaching the fortress?"

"Not likely," Seth said. "Ramir and his men had a healthy dose of fear when it came to dealing with Morenta."

Jay leaned back in his chair. "Even if that's the case, last time you guys went in there, Kel was shot."

The familiar guilt rose within Seth. "That happened because the guards were coming after me and Vanessa. Had the squad been going in for a look, no one would have known they were there."

"What other options do we have?" Craig asked.

"There's another spot over here." Brent rearranged the satellite images and tapped on another inlet that was much wider that the first. "It's about five miles farther down the coast."

"Which means more time on the ground," Quinn said.

"And fewer hours of darkness to spy on Morenta," Seth added.

"You can always send Jay up a tree to spy on them from above," Quinn suggested.

"Can we please go on one mission where someone doesn't send me up a tree?" Jay asked. "Seems like the enlisted guys should have to do that."

Seth fought back a smile. "They would . . . if you weren't the best spotter in the squad."

"I hate to break it to you, Jay, but there are a lot of trees where we're going," Craig said.

"Thanks a lot." Jay let out a heavy sigh.

Ignoring the interaction of his teammates, Seth motioned to the photo with the preferred landing site. "I say we stick with this one for our primary insertion point and make the other a backup."

"I agree." Brent scanned the faces of the rest of the men. "Jay, work with Damian and Craig on the backup plan. Seth, you work with Tristan and Quinn on the primary."

"Got it."

"I'm going to get a message to Amy to see if she has confirmation on who is really inside the fortress," Brent said.

"You're assuming intel will know who's there," Tristan said. "They've never been able to get anyone in undercover since Vanessa."

"I'll take whatever they've got," Brent said.

"Probably should also see if intel has anything on changes to the security systems."

"Yes. That too."

* * *

Amy juggled calls and intel reports all morning, adding a deliberate trip to the copy room to meet Mei Lien. A dropped file, a few mixed up papers, and Amy had the information she needed. And though they had been friends since Mei Lien had first been assigned to work for Kel, the ease with which Mei Lien made the handoff without alerting anyone else nearby made Amy suspect the commander's secretary had done at least some intelligence work in her past. That could come in handy if Mei Lien was willing to help her overcome their current challenges. Assuming Amy would be able to stay long enough to be part of the stop-Gardner-before-he-gets-someone-killed campaign.

Amy's attempt to meet with Admiral Rivera had failed, but his aide had promised to give the admiral the message that Amy had stopped by to see him.

A knock sounded on her open door, and Lt. Commander Kaminski stepped inside. "Sorry I'm a couple minutes early, but do you have my surveillance photos yet?"

"I do." Thanks to Vanessa's help last night. Amy retrieved the photos from her desk and handed them to the commander. "Today's feed hasn't come through yet, but this is everything as of nineteen hundred yesterday."

"Thanks."

Webb walked in and closed the door behind him. "Any luck with personnel?"

"No, but I'm going to try to see Admiral Rivera again later today." Amy gestured for Webb to sit in one of the two chairs by her desk. "I did confirm that Gardner requested that all but one of the civilian positions be converted to military billets."

"We suspected that was going on." Rather than sit, Webb gripped the back of the empty chair in front of him. "I'm surprised he didn't try for all of them."

"The only one he didn't mess with was Mei Lien," Amy said.

"She's not a threat since he's the one writing her evals," Kaminski said.

Amy didn't correct Kaminski's assumption. If anyone was a threat to Gardner right now, it was Mei Lien. She plucked the latest information off her desk and handed both men a copy of the details Mei Lien had shared with her. "This is a list of the transfers in progress."

"He's weeding people out and making room for people who are already in his pocket." Kaminski tapped the top page. "I've had dealings with Bachman before. He's a paper pusher who toes the party line. No originality whatsoever."

"Looks like he also spent the last two years working under Gardner," Webb said.

"Now that we know what Gardner is doing, how do we stop him?" Amy asked.

"Great question." Webb circled the chair in front of him and sat down.

Knuckles rapped against Amy's door.

"Come in."

The door opened, and Admiral Rivera stepped inside.

Everyone stood.

"Admiral." Amy barely resisted glancing at the two commanders as she fought back a surge of guilt. They might be planning a mutiny of sorts but only for the very best reasons. "I didn't expect to see you here."

"My aide said you stopped by this morning."

"Yes, I did." Amy lifted her chin and forged on. "I need you to deny the reclassification of my position."

"I haven't seen anything on that." Admiral waved at everyone. "At ease." He grabbed a chair from the corner of the room and sat. Everyone else reclaimed their seats.

"The request should hit your office today or tomorrow," Amy said. "It's to reclassify all the intel officer positions."

"And you think it's a bad idea?"

"Yes, I do. Civilian intel officers are intended to enhance our intelligence gathering and administrative support of our teams. Putting those positions in the typical chain of command takes away their purpose."

"You two agree with her?"

"Yes, sir," Webb said.

Kaminski nodded. "We do, sir."

"It just so happens, I do as well." Admiral Rivera focused on Amy. "You've proven yourself a valuable asset to your squad. Making procedural changes just for the sake of mixing things up doesn't make any sense to me."

Amy let out a relieved breath. "Does that mean you'll support me when Commander Gardner tries to push through my transfer?" Amy asked.

"You aren't going anywhere."

"Thank you, sir."

The admiral stood, prompting everyone to follow suit.

"What about our intel officers who have already been transferred?" Commander Kaminski asked. "Amy can't be expected to support the whole platoon."

"I'll kick the reclassification back to personnel," Admiral Rivera said. "As soon as they know it was rejected, they can fill those positions again."

"Thank you, sir," Kaminski said.

"Yes, thank you," Webb added.

The admiral nodded and left the room.

Commander Webb turned to Amy. "At least we know you aren't going anywhere."

"Let's hope we can get your intel officers back quickly," Amy said.

Deliberate footsteps thudded in the hall. Commander Gardner stormed into Amy's office. "What was Admiral Rivera doing in here?"

Amy forced herself to face Gardner. "He was here to see me."

"Why?"

She tried to swallow the news of her victory but didn't quite manage it. Gardner would find out soon enough that his attempt to get rid of her had failed. "We had some personnel matters to discuss."

Fury erupted on Gardner's face. "You went over my head?"

"Yes, sir."

Gardner charged forward until barely a foot of space separated him and Amy. He leaned in. Amy started to back up, but something inside her snapped. This man had no right to push her or anyone else around. She straightened her shoulders and held her ground.

"If you think you can play politics in my unit, think again. I don't tolerate anyone undermining my authority."

"And I don't tolerate anyone putting our SEALs in danger," Amy shot back. "Limiting our platoon's resources is too risky."

Gardner turned and took several steps toward the door before waving mockingly toward Amy. "And this is why I don't want married couples in my command."

"Whether it's my husband or someone I barely know, I'm not going to stand by and let politics result in this unit having anything less than optimum readiness." She took a step forward and looked him in the eye. "SEALs coming home in body bags is not an option."

"This isn't the end of this," Gardner said.

"You're right," Amy agreed. "These commanders need their intel officers back."

"That's not going to happen," Gardner growled. He turned on his heel and stormed out of her office.

Amy waited a full ten seconds before she let out the breath she was holding.

"Well, he knows where we all stand now," Webb said.

Kaminski nodded. "The question is, What's he going to do about it?"

11

BRENT FACED THE FAMILIAR SCENERY as he fought back the images of his most recent nightmare. The low hum of the inflatable boat currently carrying his squad off the coast of Nicaragua blended with the roar of the surf. Water sprayed onto Brent's face as he judged the distance to shore. He signaled Craig to cut the engine.

Behind him, his men extended their paddles into the water and rowed forward.

They reached the cove where they had hidden their boats when they'd liberated Seth and Vanessa. Working in tandem, Craig and Damian secured their boat. Brent stepped onto solid ground, his night-vision goggles in place, his weapon raised in preparation for any possible threats.

Using hand signals, Brent commanded them to move forward. They fanned out, with Seth taking point. The thought invaded Brent's mind that Seth might not be with the squad much longer. Brent pushed it aside, along with the clawing panic that tried to surface. No distractions. Focus on the mission.

Tonight, that included gathering as much information as they could while remaining undetected.

Seth stopped and signaled the presence of an obstacle. Brent's gaze dropped to where Seth indicated. A motion detector. That hadn't been here the last time they'd breached the fortress.

His squad moved forward, avoiding the security measure as well as the one that lay beyond. When they reached the trailhead that opened to the vast grassy area surrounding the fortress, Brent signaled everyone to stop.

The building in the center stretched ten stories high. Had it not been for the guards patrolling the grounds, it could have passed for a luxury resort, with the beach stretching out on one side and the main structure boasting concrete and wrought-iron balconies for every room on the upper floors.

It was the occupants of the upper floors they were interested in tonight.

Brent signaled for his men to take their positions. Jay immediately selected his perch for the night up in a tree that overlooked both the trailhead and the fortress grounds. Quinn and Tristan disappeared into the depths of the jungle in search of a spot where they could provide cover for everyone else. Craig and Damian followed. Trusting them to conduct the recon assigned to them on the ground, Brent turned to Seth.

A simple nod of Seth's head was all it took to communicate everything Brent needed to know. He was ready. It was time to make their climb and find out if Morenta was really here and collect any intel they could to uncover his objective.

*　*　*

Amy walked past the security guards and turned down the deserted hallway to her office. It was well after midnight. She should be home in bed rather than on base, but every time she'd lain down to sleep, her body had revolted. After her run-in with Gardner this morning, her whole system had been off. The adrenaline rush from standing up to her overeager boss had faded into a tangle of nausea that hovered just beneath the surface.

All afternoon, she had braced for some kind of backlash from Gardner. It hadn't come, but that didn't take away the tension the expectation had burdened her with.

Despite her discomfort, Amy had waited until after the evening intel reports had posted to go home. She hated that Brent was going into the field without her. She hated not being by his side. And she hated the worry gnawing at her that her absence on the ship might prevent her from making a difference in keeping them safe. It was that worry that had brought her back to work tonight.

She glanced at the photo beside her computer of her with the entire squad, and a smile touched her lips. In it, she was pictured in the center of the group, both Brent and Seth with their arms slung around her shoulders. She and Brent made every effort to keep a professional air at work, but that photo had been an easy way to have him with her all day even when he was in the field, whether he was on a training exercise or absent on a mission she wasn't allowed to be on. She should be used to the separation by now, but it didn't change the simple fact that she missed him every time they were apart.

She also missed his cooking. A bowl of chicken noodle soup and some saltine crackers had been the extent of her dinner tonight. And she had barely finished eating when an overwhelming fatigue had led to a long nap on the couch. Now here she was at one in the morning, sitting at her desk, scrolling through intel reports, wishing her husband were beside her. At least she didn't have to worry about Gardner interrupting her at this time of night.

Amy bypassed the reports she had already reviewed, relieved that nothing new had posted for Nicaragua. With nothing better to do, she expanded her search and browsed the updates from the rest of the region. Gang problems in Honduras, an incident with illegal immigrants on the New Mexico border, an arms deal in Belize.

She scrolled to the next one, a resource concern for Morenta. She read the report that had posted five hours ago. Morenta had acquired another Z-10 helicopter, the same model he had used in a previous attack against the US. The CIA operative who had detailed the transaction also expressed concern that the attack helicopter was not currently visible at Morenta's compound in Colombia.

Amy clicked on the latest satellite photos. The most recent images popped up on her screen, but they weren't the original ones she had printed for Brent. These had updated only three hours ago.

She quickly retrieved the original images and compared the two sets. The photos of the beach didn't show any changes other than a guard present in the first photo and not in the second. The squad would have assumed guards were patrolling even without visible evidence.

She scrolled to the next photo and the next, relieved that she found no other noticeable differences. When she reached the fourth image, her body stiffened. In the open space a short distance from the fortress's main structure, trees suddenly appeared. Unless Morenta's men had planted a good section of jungle between the time the photos had been taken, the only explanation was that those trees were some sort of camouflage covering.

Amy plucked up her desk phone and dialed the comm center to ensure her squad had seen the updated intel. She waited after she finished dialing, but nothing happened. She hung up to try again. No dial tone.

Amy quickly checked beneath her desk. The phone was plugged in. She unplugged it and plugged it in again, but when she picked up the phone, she received the same results. What was going on? Her eyes narrowed. This couldn't be a coincidence.

With the rest of the offices locked for the night, she grabbed her cell phone and dialed Vanessa's number.

"Is everything okay?" Vanessa asked in lieu of a greeting.

"I don't know." Amy described the updated images and the problem with her phone, carefully wording the information since she wasn't on a secure line.

"Is the space big enough to be a camouflage tent hiding a helicopter?" Vanessa asked.

"Yes, it is."

"Hold on." Vanessa went silent for a moment before speaking again, but this time, her voice was barely audible. "I need you to get a message to the USS *Harry S. Truman*. We have new intel on the fortress, and I'm not sure if the Saint Squad has the update."

Vanessa paused. "I'll wait."

"Who did you call?" Amy asked.

"A friend," Vanessa said.

Her friend. Vanessa-speak for Ghost. "Does your friend have access to the navy's communication system?" Amy asked. She had met the guardian only a handful of times and knew little about his resources.

"We're about to find out." Vanessa fell silent.

Amy fought against her helplessness and the rising panic that accompanied it. Words didn't need to be spoken for her to know Vanessa was experiencing similar emotions.

Several minutes stretched out, each one feeling like an hour. Finally, Vanessa spoke again, first thanking Ghost before speaking to Amy once more. "My friend sent the intel to the ship, and they're relaying it to the squad."

"They didn't get the update before they inserted, did they?"

Vanessa's voice carried both fury and fear when she spoke. "No, they didn't."

* * *

Seth ducked behind a palm tree and trusted his dark skin, dark clothing, and the dark of night to hide him from the passing guard. Tension rolled off him as a sense of foreboding filled his gut. He and Vanessa had escaped here once, but not without a cost. The near failure and Kel's injury haunted Seth, and he had no doubt the memories burned brightly in the other squad members who had been there.

And while their familiarity with the fortress gave them some advantage, the latest security enhancements had slowed them down considerably. The already tight window for collecting intel was closing fast.

Seth visualized the guard passing by as well as Brent's position beside him. He couldn't see his teammate, but he didn't have to. Instinct and experience filled in the information his vision couldn't give him.

He counted off a few extra seconds beyond what the guard should have needed to pass by. His muscles tensed as he edged forward. He'd barely moved when Jay's voice came over his communication headset.

"Hold your position," Jay said. "The guard is still there."

Seth froze. And waited.

Two minutes passed before Jay spoke again. "Clear."

Moving as one, Seth and Brent crossed the open lawn, moving quickly to the near wall of the fortress. With a silent nod, Brent found his first hand-hold in the bricks and began his climb up the side of the building. Using the bricks and balconies on each floor, Seth followed.

Light spilled out of the fourth-floor windows. Seth paused and listened for any sign of life inside. Though none came, he retrieved a listening device from his combat vest and planted it at the edge of the window, where it would pick up the sound from inside without being noticed.

He continued upward, planting three more devices, one on each floor.

Brent followed a parallel path, but his listening devices were each attached to the bottom edge of the balconies. While those weren't as likely to pick up sound, if the ones by the window were discovered, at least they would still have a chance of gathering some intelligence, even if it required people to be outside to be heard.

Seth grabbed the railing of the next balcony and pulled himself upward. Only two more floors until they reached the penthouse. If his internal clock was right, they would just barely make it out of here before the first light of dawn.

Craig's voice interrupted his thoughts. "We have a problem."

That was as far as Craig got before the rumble of a helicopter engine broke over the surf and sounds of the jungle.

Seth judged the direction of the aircraft, adrenaline and irritation merging together. He fought against both.

Speaking low, Seth said, "It's coming from the helicopter pad on the gate side."

"I see it," Quinn said.

"Take cover, and hold your positions," Brent commanded.

Fully exposed to the view of an aircraft, Seth continued upward until he reached the spot between the tenth and eleventh floors. He folded his body up beneath the eleventh-floor balcony and used the top of the tenth-floor french door to help keep him in place. He'd barely ducked out of sight before a spotlight swept up the side of the building.

"Morenta's paranoia has reached new heights," Tristan said through the comm set.

Seth agreed, but he didn't say so. At the moment, he was too busy praying no one would walk out on the balcony below.

The search concluded on his side of the building, but Seth didn't dare move. Sure enough, the helicopter circled and started a second search.

An unfamiliar voice broke through Seth's comm set. "Be advised, possible Z-10 helicopter on site at the fortress."

"Confirmed," Jay said. "The Z-10 is here."

* * *

A Z-10, complete with heat sensors and a full complement of weaponry. Great.

Brent waited until the helicopter cleared the building before he lowered his leg and rested his foot on the side of the eleventh-floor balcony, the same balcony that led to Vanessa's former living quarters when she'd been undercover for the CIA. The presence of people in the building and whatever lights and electronics they had running inside should protect him from the sensors, but if the spotlight passed over him while he was climbing down, he'd be an easy target.

He tried to bank his fury that intel had neglected to share the detail about the helicopter's presence until it had been too late. He suspected that had Amy been on board the carrier, this wouldn't have happened.

Keeping his breathing steady and silent, he retrieved a listening device from his combat vest and pressed it to the underside of the balcony; the gray color would blend into the concrete it was now attached to.

Once satisfied that he had accomplished his mission to the best of his ability, he positioned his toe and started his downward climb. When he reached the spot where Seth was still hiding, he paused. A nod of Brent's head was all it took for Seth to slip out of his hiding place and follow Brent downward.

They made it two floors before the helicopter reappeared, the beam of light now sweeping the dense foliage where Tristan, Quinn, and Jay were currently positioned.

Brent opened his mouth to issue an order for his men to fall back to their transport, but a window slid open on the floor above him, preventing him from speaking without giving himself away.

As though reading his intentions, Jay spoke. "Craig, Damian, fall back to the boat."

"I'll cover Seth and Brent," Quinn said.

"I have the best vantage point," Jay countered. "You and Tristan can cover us from the trailhead."

Brent clicked once into his mic to communicate his agreement with Jay's assessment.

The comm went silent, and Brent prayed his men would be able to slip through the jungle undetected.

The beam of light from the chopper crept up the side of the building. Brent and Seth took cover again, this time beneath the eighth- and ninth-floor balconies.

As soon as the helicopter cleared, they went into motion again. They reached the ground level an instant before the guard rounded the corner. Both men froze, using the shadows to hide their presence.

A walkie-talkie buzzed before rapid Spanish carried through it. The guard spoke just as quickly before hurrying toward the trailhead.

"Tristan, Quinn, you have guards heading your way," Jay said. "Get out of there."

"Get to the boat," Brent ordered. "Jay, you too."

"Roger."

"What about you and Seth?" Damian asked.

"We'll meet you at our alternate landing site." Brent checked the space between him and the trees. A quick glance at Seth and a nod in agreement and both men sprinted from the building to the jungle's edge and took cover in the trees.

The guard reappeared, this time with another man. They spoke rapidly as the helicopter flew overhead once more.

Brent and Seth held their position. The two guards came to a stop a short distance away, their conversation continuing as soon as the helicopter started another wide circle. Several minutes passed.

"We're clear," Jay announced. An instant later, he spoke to one of the other men. "Stay close to the shore. The Z-10 is still out there."

Brent lifted his eyes upward as the spotlight filtered through the trees, then he crouched low in the hope that the heat sensors would mistake him for wildlife.

The Z-10 was still out there. Brent drew a deep breath. And so was Morenta.

12

Seth huddled beside Brent until the helicopter passed by for the eighth time. They had made it nearly a mile before they'd given up trying to evade the helicopter and its advanced tracking capabilities. By staying still, they could pass for a couple of deer rather than predators someone might want to take a shot at.

The Z-10's spotlight filtered through the trees in the predawn light. The beam swept wide, circling away from them once more.

"Status?" Brent said into his headset, but nothing came through Seth's earpiece.

"I'm not getting anything," Brent said. "You try."

Seth complied. "Sit rep?" He waited a moment, but he, too, didn't hear anything beyond his own voice. "Comm must be down."

"If the chopper is still up there, either they know we're here or Morenta really is paranoid."

"Morenta might be paranoid, but using a helicopter as a watch tool is overkill, even for him."

"Someone must have tripped a sensor." Brent reached into his combat vest and retrieved a protein bar.

Seth followed suit. Had someone on their squad messed up? Or was there another reason for the helicopter's diligence?

Brent rested his arms on his knees. "You want to pray today, or should I?"

"I will." Seth bowed his head and offered a blessing on their meager meal. He also asked for protection and guidance for their squad as well as a blessing on their loved ones back home. He was about to close the prayer when another thought popped into his head, and he added, "And bless Vanessa and Amy that they will be guided in what they should do."

After he said amen, Brent looked up. "This isn't going to be a simple extraction, is it?"

"I don't know, but I'm ready to meet up with the rest of our squad."

"Me too." Brent took a bite of his breakfast.

As soon as they'd both finished eating and had tucked the wrappers back into their vests, they stood.

"I don't hear the helicopter," Seth said.

"Daylight is breaking. It may have gone back to the fortress."

"Let's hope." Seth started forward, changing direction when he reached a motion sensor.

Together they zigzagged through the jungle, evading several more. Seth's brow furrowed. They had to be nearly two miles from the fortress now. Why were they still encountering so many surveillance devices?

They continued, the motion sensors increasing in number.

Uneasy, Seth readied his weapon. Brent's hand went up to signal him to stop at the same time a twig snapped nearby. They weren't alone, but what or who was out there?

Seth and Brent took cover, both listening for any other sign of movement. The deer in the area where the jungle gave way to forest would be feeding this time of day. It was also possible someone in their squad had come looking for them when they'd lost contact.

The faint scent of cigarette smoke carried toward them. Not wildlife and not one of their squadmates.

Questions burned inside Seth. They were still on fortress land and would be for another mile, yet when Seth had gone undercover here, no one had ever gone beyond the outer marker of the security zone, which extended a mile in every direction. Why had security increased in this part of the woods? And who had ventured this far from the main compound?

A minute passed and then two.

Leaves rustled, followed by muted footsteps against the soft forest floor.

Brent signaled again, but this time, it wasn't for them to hide but rather to pursue.

Moving silently, Seth and Brent picked their way through the motion detectors and followed the retreating footsteps. They went only a few hundred yards before voices carried to them. The conversation lasted but a moment before the woods went quiet again.

Seth stopped at the edge of a clearing, or almost a clearing. A long, narrow building stretched through the center, but the trees on either side of it created a canopy that filtered the morning light. The color of the roof matched the foliage, and Seth doubted it would be seen as anything other than fauna from the sky.

The structure itself could have been mistaken for a house, except for the lack of windows on the front half. Only one door was visible on the narrow side of the building. He also doubted a house would have need for the guard who was currently patrolling the perimeter of the clearing.

Another guard stepped into view.

They needed to know what was going on inside that building, but with two guards, they wouldn't be able to get through while the sun was up. Should they meet up with their squad and regroup? Or should they hunker down here and wait for night?

Moving during daylight was risky in the best of circumstances. With no clue of how many other people might be around here, their likelihood of making it out without being seen reduced significantly.

Yet would staying in place result in their squadmates coming to look for them? Their mission safeguards gave them until an hour before daylight tomorrow to regroup. After that, their squad would be obligated to return to the ship.

Seth shifted his gaze to meet Brent's. A brief flash of indecision shone in his eyes, followed by determination. He signaled to some dense foliage. They were staying.

* * *

Amy rubbed at the ache in her back, which was now a constant reminder that the little sleep she had managed during the night had come while dozing in her office chair.

She should have gone home and tried to sleep in her own bed, but the possibility of an update had kept her glued to her desk.

For the hundredth time, she checked for any new mission reports for the Saint Squad, but so far, nothing had posted. She checked the time. Six fifty. Logically, the squad should have arrived on the ship already. She hated not being right there to welcome them back and to know exactly when they cleared the danger zone.

Shoes squeaked against the tile floor in the hall, growing louder and then fading. Amy used her fingers to comb her hair back from her face. Go home and shower? Or stay here and take her lunch hour to freshen up?

Kaminski appeared in her doorway. His gaze landed on the scatter of files on her desk. "Any word from your boys?"

Amy shook her head. "Their after-action report should post anytime now."

"It'll probably be slower than usual since you're here."

"Probably."

"I hate to throw something else on your plate, but can you call and get someone to check out the phone in my office? It isn't working."

"Mine isn't either."

"That son—"

Amy held a hand up to stop him. "You can think whatever you want, but I don't need to hear it."

Kaminski clamped his jaw shut, and the muscle jumped as he glared in the direction of Gardner's office.

"It's probably a system failure." She hoped, although she understood perfectly why Kaminski was casting blame so quickly.

"Then why is Mei Lien's phone working?" Kaminski asked. "She was using it when I walked in."

Amy's own fury erupted. Gardner really had disabled their phones to punish them for not falling in line.

Kaminski unclenched his jaw and huffed out a breath. "He's making sure we can't communicate without monitoring us."

"You think he's reading our emails?" Amy asked incredulously.

"I wouldn't put it past him."

"How can sabotaging us be to his advantage?"

"If he can show us underperforming, he can get rid of us."

"All of us?"

"Yes, all of us."

Thoughts raced through Amy's mind. Gardner was a more formidable foe that she had anticipated. Protecting her position was one thing, but if Gardner could prove her incapable of performing her duties, he would have grounds to fire her.

"Is your phone the only one not working for your unit?" Amy asked.

"I haven't checked."

"Find out." Amy motioned to her computer. "I'll send in a service request for both of us once we know which lines are affected," Amy said.

"And if Gardner intercepts it?"

"I'll go over to the comm building at lunchtime to follow up." Amy picked up her cell phone. "In the meantime, I'm going to bring in some outside help."

Webb walked into Amy's office. He spared a glance and nod of greeting to Kaminski before focusing on Amy. "Can I borrow your phone? Mine isn't working."

Amy blew out a frustrated breath. "Of course it isn't."

* * *

Amy went through the motions of sending her email to the service tech about the nonfunctioning phones as well as stopping by Mei Lien's desk to inform her of the problem. At least Commander Gardner had remained in his office, though Amy suspected he had listened in on their conversation through his open office door.

Fighting fatigue, Amy took an early lunch and made the trip to the communications building. She needed this resolved soon, especially since she was prohibited from using her personal cell phone for official business.

The young ensign working the reception desk was on the phone when Amy approached.

As soon as he ended his call, he asked, "Can I help you?"

"Yes. I'm here to follow up about a service request I emailed this morning," Amy said. "We have a number of phones that stopped working sometime last night."

"Let's see what we have." He tapped on his keyboard. "When did you send in the request?"

"A little before oh seven hundred."

"I don't see anything." A line of concentration appeared on his brow. "Let me try something else." He clicked on his mouse and started typing again. He repeated the process several times before he looked up. "I'm sorry, but I don't see a service request."

Amy fought back a sigh. "I need to put one in now, then."

"Of course." He printed off a form and handed it to her. "Fill this out. In the meantime, can you give me one of the numbers that isn't working? I can run a quick check and see if it's something easy to fix."

Amy recited her number and filled out the top line of the form.

"Well, here's the problem."

"What?" Amy leaned forward.

"There was a service request yesterday afternoon to put all of the numbers in the offices for platoon bravo on hold."

"You can't be serious."

"This often happens when a unit is going out to sea. We deactivate the current numbers while the unit is gone in case that office space is temporarily reassigned to other personnel."

"How do I get those numbers reinstated? We're dealing with SEALs here. They need to be operational at all times."

"I'll contact the phone company right now."

"How long does it usually take to get the phones turned back on?" Amy asked.

"A few days, maybe a week," he said. "It probably won't be until Tuesday at the earliest."

"Tuesday?" Amy's voice rose, and she had to remind herself that the ensign was only the bearer of the bad news, not the cause. "Please let the phone company know that this is a priority."

"Yes, ma'am. I will."

"Thank you." Amy held up the service request form. "Do you still need me to fill this out?"

"Just the top part. Since I can't call you in your office, if you want, you can put a personal cell phone number down so I can keep you updated."

Amy filled out the designated section and added her personal cell phone number to the form. "One more thing. Can you tell me who put the request in for the cancellation of our phones?"

"Yes. I have it right here." The ensign scrolled down the screen. "Commander Kirk Gardner."

"That's what I thought."

13

JIM SCOURED THE DAILY REPORT for any updates on the Morenta situation, but "mission in progress" was the only note. What was that supposed to mean? According to yesterday's report, the mission had been in progress then too. Surely the SEALs weren't inserting into Nicaragua for a lengthy stay.

His eyebrows drew together. He'd tried calling Amy at her office for an update, but for some reason, the call had repeatedly said the number was no longer connected. He was starting to wonder if something was wrong with his office phones, but they were clearly still working.

Nate knocked on Jim's open door. "Got a sec?"

Jim nodded. "What's up?"

"The chatter about a potential terrorist attack has picked up again."

Jim had been receiving the daily reports for only two months now, and this was already the eighth threat of a terrorist attack. "Do you have any details?"

"It's originating out of Central America, but that's all we have so far."

"Central America?" Jim glanced at the report in front of him. "Any chance Morenta is involved?"

"One of our CIA analysts listed him as a potential contributor to the plans," Nate said. "The details are still sketchy."

"What do we know?"

"Not much. I'm supposed to be meeting with Admiral Rivera tomorrow morning. He should be flying up from Virginia Beach tonight," Nate said.

"Rivera? He's with the SEAL teams, isn't he?"

"Yes. When I found out he's giving a briefing tomorrow, I finagled an invite."

"Taking advantage of your military ties."

"You know it," Nate said. "Until we all have access to secure phones, it's hard to function."

Jim slid his iPad toward Nate. "What do you make of this?"

Nate skimmed the page. "The 'mission in progress'?"

"Yeah. It said the same thing yesterday," Jim said. "I thought we were sending men in to plant surveillance devices and that was it."

"The mission must have changed."

"After the SEALs were already in Nicaragua?"

Nate nodded. "I gather you haven't heard from your daughter?"

"She isn't answering her cell, and when I try calling her office line, it keeps telling me her phone has been disconnected."

"You sure you have the right number?"

Jim's eyebrows winged up. "Amy's been working in the same office for five years. I know her phone number."

"I'll ask Rivera for an update." Nate handed the iPad back to Jim. "As for the phone problem, you'll see Amy in a couple days anyway. You can ask her about it then."

"I'm not going to wait that long," Jim said. "She should be home in a few hours. I'll call her tonight."

Nate stepped back. "I'll let you know tomorrow what I found out. We can compare notes."

"Sounds good. Thanks, Nate."

Nate nodded and left the room.

Jim picked up his phone and tried Amy's office again. The same error message rang through the line. What was going on in Virginia Beach?

Only two more days, he reminded himself. Two more days and he would have the resources necessary to access whatever information he needed to analyze the threats against his country. Maybe those resources would also give him the ability to get his daughter on the phone.

* * *

Amy couldn't stand it anymore. All day, she had searched for any information on her squad's missions, but so far, nothing had popped up in her email or in the updated reports. With her phone out of commission, she couldn't place a secure call to the ship to get an update.

She'd even stopped at Admiral Rivera's office in search of information, but his secretary had informed her the admiral was in meetings and likely wouldn't return to his office until Monday.

With no other alternative within her chain of command, Amy forced herself to walk down the hall to Commander Gardner's office. Fatigue, worry, and dread combined to add weight to each step. When Amy arrived at Mei Lien's desk, the commander's door was closed.

"Is he available?" Amy motioned to Gardner's office.

Mei Lien shook her head. "He's in a meeting with Admiral Rivera. I doubt he'll be back today."

"Any chance you can help me make a call to the *Truman*?" Amy asked. "I need an update on my squad. Nothing has hit the system yet."

"Sure. I can do that." Mei Lien picked up her phone.

Gardner's voice cut through the air. "Hang up the phone."

Mei Lien's eyes darted up to where Gardner had appeared in the hall, and she complied. "Sir, I was just calling for an update on the Saint Squad."

"You don't need to do Ms. Miller's job for her."

Amy stiffened. "Had you not disconnected my phone, I wouldn't need her help."

Commander Gardner pressed his lips together briefly before he spoke again to Mei Lien. "Lieutenant Vanderhoff will report in the morning. Make sure his housing is squared away."

"Yes, sir."

Gardner spared Amy a glance. "As for you, Kaminski's squad is due to ship out in two days." He took a step toward his office before adding, "And I don't have to remind you that the use of personal cell phones to conduct classified business is grounds for dismissal."

"No, sir." Amy glared. "You don't."

"Mei Lien, I need you in my office, please."

Mei Lien stood, an unspoken apology on her face.

Amy waited for Mei Lien and Gardner to disappear into Gardner's office. She'd planned to use Mei Lien's phone while she was away from her desk, but Gardner took up position in his doorway and waited for Amy to leave.

She moved down the hall, her insides turning to lead. Gardner was making sure she failed, and if her suspicions were correct, someone coming home in a body bag would be the exclamation point on his insistence that she shouldn't be working with the SEALs.

She clenched her teeth. Not while she could help it. Admiral Rivera might not be in his office, but his phone was. Amy headed to the admiral's office.

With both squads here at home currently out on training exercises, she had time to make a few phone calls before they returned.

She reached the admiral's outer office, and the secretary looked up.

"I'm sorry, but he isn't back yet."

"Actually, I was hoping for another favor," Amy said. "The phones are messed up for my whole platoon. Is there an empty office somewhere that has a phone I can use? I have one unit out in the field and another one heading there within a couple days. I really need to make sure they're covered."

"I'd love to help, but the only office open is the admiral's."

"Would it be possible for me to use his phone? It'll only be for twenty minutes or so."

"I don't know . . ."

Admiral Rivera walked in.

"Admiral." The secretary stood. "I didn't expect you back today."

"I got out to my car and didn't have my keys." He glanced at Amy. "Don't tell me personnel processed your transfer."

"No, sir. Worse."

"Come into my office." Admiral Rivera escorted her inside and promptly opened his desk drawer to retrieve a set of keys. He pocketed them and looked up. "Close the door and have a seat."

Amy did as he asked. As soon as she sat, he took the seat beside her. "What's the problem now? And why am I getting so many complaints about Commander Gardner?"

Amy swallowed. If she confided in the admiral, would that yield results or add gasoline to the office politics already igniting around her? Honesty first. That had always served her well. "I have strong evidence that the commander has plans to reinvent the way SEALs operate, and he's shuffling personnel all over the place to gear it toward what he wants."

"This kind of thing happens from time to time," Admiral Rivera said. "Growing pains can be difficult, but sometimes they are necessary."

"Does necessary include canceling crucial training exercises?"

"It's certainly his prerogative to change training to maximize our resources."

"What about disconnecting my platoon's phones?"

His eyebrows shot up. "Your phones?"

"That's why I'm here. I hoped to be able to use your phone while you were out of the office. Kaminski's unit is due to ship out on Sunday, but none of us have the ability to confirm flights or mission details because our phone lines are down."

"And you're blaming that on Commander Gardner?"

"I am," Amy said. "And before you tell me I'm wrong and that it was some administrative mistake, I already went by the communications office. Commander Gardner is the one who ordered the phones disconnected."

"Did you ask him why?"

"I spoke to him briefly when I asked his secretary to help me make some calls."

"And?"

Frustrated that this conversation had reduced her to a tattletale, Amy forced herself to continue. "He told Mei Lien that she wasn't to do my job for me. Then he reminded me that using my personal phone for navy business was grounds for dismissal."

Admiral Rivera's eyebrows lifted. "Do we have a war on our hands?"

"I'm afraid so."

"For this afternoon, you can use my office," he said.

"I appreciate that, sir, but the phone company doesn't expect to have the situation sorted out for at least a couple days."

"I'll ask my secretary to find you a temporary desk. If she can't find somewhere else for you to work, you can use my desk again. I'll be out of town for the next few days."

"Thank you, sir."

The phone on the desk rang. The admiral snatched it up. "Yes?" He listened for a moment, and his body tensed. "Put him through."

A man's voice came over the line, but Amy couldn't make out the words.

"What's the contingency window?" he asked. Another pause. "Keep me informed."

Amy waited until he hung up before she spoke. "Thank you again for letting me use your office."

"Amy, that was about the Saint Squad."

A tightness formed in her chest and shot through her body. "What's wrong?"

"They didn't make their extraction last night, and no one has heard from them since they forwarded a message about an attack helicopter on site."

"I'm the one who sent that message," Amy said. "Or rather, a friend at the CIA did since my phone wasn't working."

Admiral Rivera's jaw set. "Are you telling me you couldn't get intel to our men because your commanding officer turned off your phone?"

"Yes, sir."

Admiral Rivera glanced at his watch. "I have a flight to catch. I have a meeting at the Pentagon tomorrow, but I'll be having a nice chat with the commander when I get back."

Amy couldn't celebrate her new ally when her thoughts were so consumed with her husband's and the rest of the squad's safety. "What about the Saint Squad? What else do you know?"

"The contingency is for an extraction at oh four hundred tomorrow."

"Thank you, sir."

He stepped forward and put his hand on her shoulder. "We'll get them back."

Amy nodded. "Yes, sir. We will."

14

JIM PULLED INTO HIS DRIVEWAY, a wave of nostalgia flowing over him. Only two more days and this would no longer be his home. His house, yes, but once he moved into the White House, the stately home he had shared with Katherine throughout most of their marriage would become a place to visit rather than a place to live.

He waited until his security detail pulled in behind him before he hit the button to open the garage door and parked in his usual spot. Rakes and shovels hung from a rack on one wall, and a long workbench lined the space in the far corner of the third bay. He couldn't count how many projects he'd helped his boys with from that exact spot over the years. Amy too. She never wanted to be left out when it came to building something.

Jim climbed out of his car and headed through the door into the warmth of the kitchen. The scent of something baking wafted over him. Was that chicken pot pie?

Jim set his briefcase down on a kitchen chair and peeked into the oven to see that it was indeed a pot pie baking inside. His stomach grumbled, and he checked the timer on the oven. Fifteen minutes. He wasn't sure he could last that long.

He took the lid off the cookie jar, plucked out two chocolate chip cookies, and ate the first before heading into the living room.

Katherine sat on the floor beside the bookshelf, a box beside her. She glanced up, and her gaze zeroed in on the cookie in his hand. "You're going to ruin your dinner."

"You should know better than that." Jim crossed to her and greeted her with a kiss. "What are you doing?"

"Cleaning a few things out."

"I thought you'd already packed everything you wanted to take with us." Jim took a bite of the second cookie.

"I did, but I wanted to clear some space out in here."

"Why?" The word was barely out of his mouth when he caught the gleam in his wife's eyes. "What's going on?"

"I had an idea."

"Uh-oh."

Katherine leaned back on her heels. "I was just thinking what a waste it is to have this house sitting here empty for the next four years."

"We talked about this. Neither of us wanted to have strangers live in our house." His eyes narrowed. "You aren't thinking about selling, are you?"

"No. This is our home," Katherine said. "I can't imagine living anywhere else."

"Except in the White House."

"Well, yes. Except there." She grinned. "What do you think about seeing if Seth and Vanessa want to stay here?"

Jim tried to imagine it, someone else living in his house. "The main reason we didn't want to rent our place is so we wouldn't have to deal with putting everything in storage."

"Yes, and we wanted to make sure we could come back here whenever we needed a break from the White House."

"If Seth and Vanessa move in, we would still have to put everything in storage, and we wouldn't have access to our home anymore," Jim pointed out.

"Not necessarily. I'm sure Seth and Vanessa would let us come visit, and our basement storage room is big enough to store some of our furniture. Or theirs."

Jim weighed the idea of having someone in his home against the challenges of leaving it empty. "If they were living here, maybe we could leave the horses instead of boarding them."

"I had the same thought," Katherine said. "If they pay for the utilities, we would actually save money having them here. Plus, we wouldn't need to hire an extra security service to keep an eye on the place."

"And it isn't that bad of a commute into the city," Jim said, warming up to the idea.

"What do you think?" Katherine asked.

"Already having a place to live would make life a lot easier on them, but maybe we should wait on this until after we're settled at the White House."

"I know you said Vanessa could work from Virginia Beach for the next couple months, but isn't it worth a little chaos now if it helps you put your team in place right away?"

"Probably."

Katherine gave him that smile she always used when she knew she'd already won. "Do you want to call them, or shall I?"

"Either way. I would call tonight, but I'm not sure if Seth is in town." Jim stroked his chin. "Have you talked to Amy today?"

"No, why?"

"Just curious." Jim sniffed the air. Another ten minutes until dinner. "I'm going to give her a call."

"Give her my love."

"I will."

* * *

Amy grasped for reasons why her squad hadn't made their rendezvous point. An unexpected obstacle, an opportunity for new intel, an injury, a death. Her chest seized. Was this what the other wives went through when their husbands were in the field? The leap from everything being okay to two men showing up on her doorstep offering condolences had taken less than a second. How did the other wives stand this?

Her call to the carrier hadn't revealed much information other than the confirmation that her squad had received the intel about the Z-10 helicopter and that they were already aware of the situation.

The latest satellite photos hadn't shown any changes from the day before, but what had happened during the hours between images, no one knew.

Comm had cut out with the Saint Squad shortly after that last exchange, and all the ship's executive officer could tell her was that another attempt would be made to retrieve them in the morning.

With her exhaustion catching up to her, Amy drove home with the intent of hiding in sleep. The craving for a hamburger slipped into her mind, a reminder of the number of hours that had passed since she'd snacked on a granola bar at lunchtime. She debated going the long way home to pick something up, but even that little effort was beyond her.

If she really wanted a hamburger badly enough, she could figure out how to make one. It couldn't be that hard. Or she could use DoorDash.

Her stomach growled in protest. Definitely DoorDash.

She was nearly home when her cell phone rang. She hit the button on her steering wheel to answer.

"Hello?"

"Hi, honey." Her dad's voice carried over the phone. "I haven't talked to you in the last day or two and wanted to touch base. Are you still at the office?"

"No." She turned into her driveway and hit the button to open the garage. "I just got home."

"Is Brent home too?"

Amy translated her father's meaning. Was Brent deployed? "He had to work late, unexpectedly."

"Sorry to hear that." The concern in his voice left no doubt that her father had read between the lines. "Is his work going to keep you from coming home early?"

"I'm afraid so," Amy said. She and Brent should have been leaving for her parents' house tomorrow morning, but the weekend they'd planned to spend together as a family was clearly not going to happen the way they'd hoped.

"Your brothers fly in tomorrow. I'm sure one of them would be happy to come down and drive with you if you want."

Amy didn't want to consider the possibility that Brent might not return before her father's inauguration, but she forced herself to face it. "Thanks, Dad, but I can always catch a ride with one of my friends if I need to."

She parked in the garage and grabbed her cell phone so she could use it after she turned off the car. "How is everything going at home? Has Mom already got the Secret Service agents hooked on her chocolate chip cookies?"

"Her cinnamon rolls, actually." Her father's dry tone chased some of her stress away.

"I'm sure Brent and his friends wouldn't mind if she had a batch waiting for them too."

"She already mentioned something about that, although how she can even think about baking when we're in the middle of a move is beyond me."

Amy closed the garage door and made her way inside. "Mom is one of the most organized people I know. Besides, she loves baking."

"I know. She's already a bit worried she won't get to do that as often as she likes once we move."

"It'll all work out." A wave of dizziness washed over Amy, and she gripped the door frame until it eased. She must be hungrier than she'd thought.

"Is there anything we can do for you?" her dad asked.

"I wish there were," Amy said, unable to keep the worry out of her voice.

"Your mom and I will be sending you lots of prayers."

"Thanks, Dad."

Amy's doorbell rang.

"Someone's at the door. I'll talk to you later."

"Okay, honey. Love you."

"Love you too." Amy hung up and pocketed her phone. When she opened the door, Paige stood on her doorstep, a takeout bag in her hand and the scent of hamburger wafting in the air.

"I thought you might want some company." Paige held up the bag. "And some dinner."

"Bless you." Amy waved her inside. "I'm starving."

"I figured you didn't get much time to eat today." Paige walked in and headed for the kitchen table. "Vanessa and I both tried calling you, and neither one of us could get through."

"Gardner disconnected my office phone."

"He did what?" Paige's normally calm voice rose.

"Yeah." Amy dug the food out of the bag, placing a Styrofoam container in front of each of them. Not fast-food hamburgers. Paige had stopped at a restaurant for these.

Amy settled into her seat. "Gardner tipped his hand today. He cut off my phone to trap me into using my cell phone to do my work."

"You could get fired for doing that."

"Exactly."

Awareness lit Paige's face. "If he can't transfer you, he's going to find grounds to dismiss you."

"That's his plan."

"So, did you use one of the guys' offices to work?"

"I couldn't. Gardner cut off all the phones for my entire platoon."

"How can he get away with that?"

"I don't think he's going to for much longer," Amy said. "Admiral Rivera said he'll deal with the problems when he gets back."

"How long is he going to be gone?"

"My guess is he'll stay in DC through the weekend so he can attend the inauguration," Amy said.

Paige joined her at the table, and they blessed the food, adding a special prayer for the safety of their husbands.

After the amens were said, Amy took a bite of her burger and let out a satisfied sigh. "I can't remember the last real meal I ate."

"Best guess, when Vanessa met you for lunch."

"Probably."

"What do you know about the squad?" Paige opened her takeout container. "When Vanessa tried to pull up the mission report, she couldn't find anything."

Technically, Amy could pull out the need-to-know card to keep from answering, but the truth was she needed to talk to someone with clearance. "Vanessa didn't find anything because they aren't back yet."

The french fry Paige had lifted to her mouth lowered. "I thought it was a quick sneak and peek."

"So did I," Amy said. "Their extraction should happen sometime early tomorrow morning."

"Can you let me know when you hear something?"

"I'll text you an okay as soon as I hear," Amy said. "I'm afraid that's the best I can do with my phones down."

"I'm really not liking this new commander."

"That makes two of us," Amy said. "Let's talk about something else. Any luck with the housing office?"

"Maybe we shouldn't talk about that either," Paige said. "It's another annoyance I don't want to face."

"How soon do you have to move out?"

"February 24," Paige said. "I know five weeks sounds like a lot of time, but we have so much to do. And with Damian not wanting me to lift anything heavy . . ." Paige trailed off as though she were trying to find a way to take her words back.

Amy caught the sympathy on her face that overrode an underlying excitement. "You're pregnant?"

Her eyebrows lifted, and she nodded. "Sorry. I didn't mean to bring up another painful subject. We aren't even telling people yet."

Amy reached out and put her hand on Paige's. "I'm happy for you. Really, I am. I don't want you to feel like you have to keep your good news to yourself. I just . . ."

"You just wish you could have the same news for yourself too."

Amy let out a sigh. "Yeah, I do."

"Well, you're the first to know besides our families."

"I'm honored."

"Well, and Vanessa. I haven't told her, but . . ."

"Vanessa always sees everything," Amy finished for her.

"Yes, she does."

15

FROM HIS POSITION BEHIND A fallen tree, Brent timed the guard's path in his mind. Over the past twenty hours, he and Seth had taken turns sleeping and watching. They both watched now.

Three sets of guards, each on eight-hour shifts. The most recent pair were the same men who had been on duty early this morning when Brent and Seth had first spotted the guard taking a smoke break.

Except for the rotating guards, not once had anyone else come outside. Whether anyone else was in the building or not, they couldn't tell.

Throughout the day, lights had illuminated the windows, but as the hours had passed, they'd turned off one by one. Now only a single light burned in the far window.

Could he and Seth wait for it to turn dark? They still had five more miles to traverse tonight to meet up with their squad and only four hours to plant their surveillance equipment and pick their way through the remaining defenses Morenta had placed in their path.

Brent should be home right now, his arm wrapped around his wife as they slept in their quiet home.

The guard nearest Seth angled away from them, and Brent's hand tightened on his assault rifle. An instant later, the flame from a lighter preceded the glow from the end of a cigarette.

If the guard's pattern held, Brent and Seth could go now. Or they could wait two hours until the guard's next cigarette break.

Brent weighed the two options. They couldn't wait.

Using hand signals, he communicated his intentions. He would create a diversion. Seth would plant the bugs.

Seth nodded and held up one finger. One minute for him to get into position.

Brent checked the position of the second guard and started the count-down in his head. Silently, he crept backward until he could use a nearby tree for cover. He shouldered his rifle and grabbed one of the rocks he had collected earlier in anticipation of this moment.

Fifty-one, fifty-two, fifty-three. The seconds counted off in his mind. He chose his target and lifted his arm. Fifty-nine. Sixty.

Brent hurled the rock in the general direction of the nonsmoking guard. The rock thudded against the base of a tree several yards into the woods. A bird took flight. The guard's rifle came up, and he charged toward the source of the sound.

Brent retrieved another rock from the pile at his feet. He hurled it, this one thudding deeper in the woods.

The first guard called to the second. The cigarette dropped to the ground, a heel grinding it into the dirt. The smoker sauntered across the narrow clear-ing, his voice indicating irritation instead of concern.

Silently, Seth darted from the woods to the side of the building.

Brent sent another rock flying. This time, something scampered across the forest floor. One guard shook his head and grumbled something. Then he drew out a fresh cigarette and lit it. With another muttered complaint, he strolled toward the back of the structure where the light spilled into the night and Seth now crouched trapped in the shadows.

* * *

Seth twitched his nose. Why was it always when he needed to remain silent that he had to sneeze?

Over the past two hours, he had used the brief gaps in the guards' patrol patterns to plant listening devices at the edge of all the windows. Unfortunately, the two men had yet to give him a large enough opening to escape back to the safety of the trees.

Under normal circumstances, it would have been easy enough to disable one of the guards and disappear into the darkness before the other knew what had happened. Unfortunately, the need for their presence to go undetected removed that option. He needed one of the guards to break their patrol pat-tern so he could move. Before he sneezed.

Seth sent up a silent prayer. He wasn't sure the Lord would appreciate him asking for another man to smoke a cigarette, not when Seth was personally against smoking, but surely the situation warranted the unconventional request. If his internal clock was right, he and Brent were running out of time.

Had their comm gear still been working, he would have told Brent to go without him and plan a later rendezvous for himself. Not the ideal situation, but it was better than putting the whole squad at risk. Then again, if they could communicate with the rest of their squad, Brent would undoubtedly opt to stay with him and send the others back to the ship.

The guard nearest him reached into his pocket and moved to the edge of the woods. Seth checked the position of the second guard, who was now on the far side of the building. The man disappeared behind it.

Seth checked the other man's position again. He had already lit his cigarette, but he was facing the general direction of the structure. Could Seth risk making a run for it?

A thud reverberated from the woods.

The guard turned.

Seth sprinted. He reached the nearest tree and froze. Had he been spotted?

When silence returned, he peeked out. The guard had fixated on the building once more, the glow of the tip of his cigarette lifting and then lowering.

Deliberately, Seth sidestepped a motion sensor and moved to the next tree. A moment later, he continued deeper into the jungle. When he reached the outcropping of rocks where he and Brent had taken turns sleeping, he listened for any sign of movement.

Less than a minute passed before he sensed another presence. An instant later, his teammate emerged from a nearby copse of trees.

A hand signal was all it took for the two men to move away from the structure and make their way toward their objective.

Motion detectors, security cameras, tripwires. The defensive measures around the building in the woods didn't decrease until they were more than a mile away from it.

When they finally made it a quarter mile without any more man-made obstacles, Seth checked his watch. Less than an hour until their extraction. It wasn't enough time.

Beside him, Brent glanced at his compass. He made a course correction, motioned to Seth, and broke into a jog.

The rumble of a helicopter vibrated through the thick trees. Would it search this area of the woods, or would it go only as far as the hidden structure?

Seth increased his speed. Brent matched him stride for stride. They cleared another half mile before the sound grew louder and Brent motioned for him to take cover.

Seth stopped beside Brent, both men squatting to disguise themselves as wildlife.

Brent checked their location on his GPS. Seth checked the time.

"Forty-three minutes," Seth whispered.

"It's going to be tight," Brent said, his voice low.

The helicopter buzzed overhead, a spotlight filtering through the foliage. As soon as it moved on, Brent tapped Seth's arm.

In an instant, they both sprinted forward. They traversed a good mile before they emerged onto a stretch of beach. Seth calculated the risk they were taking even as he increased his speed. Running on the beach would allow them to move faster, but it also left them exposed if the Z-10 returned.

They were over halfway to the spot where the beach disappeared into a tangle of trees and rocks when the helicopter engines rumbled toward them again.

Brent didn't deviate his path. Neither did Seth. If they didn't use the open space to their advantage, they would miss their transport, but how far could they go before they would be seen?

The rumble grew louder. The spotlight swept over the beach in front of them.

Brent and Seth both dove into the trees, their breathing rapid, Seth's pulse racing.

Brent did another quick check of their location. "Two more miles."

"Two miles in sixteen minutes," Seth muttered. "This guy needs to move on."

"We can't wait." Brent craned his head so he could see the helicopter. "As soon as it turns back, we're moving."

One precious minute ticked by, followed by another. The spotlight swept over their location, both men ducking their heads and letting their camo protect them.

Then the light faded, and the vibration in the air changed.

Seth glanced up at the now-retreating helicopter.

He and Brent both leaped to their feet and started forward, this time sticking to the edge of the beach where the trees would shield them from view. As soon as the helicopter disappeared, they both moved onto the sand and increased their speed.

* * *

Brent didn't dare look at the time. They were less than a half mile from their destination and had less than four minutes to get there. His lungs burned, and his muscles strained as he raced forward. Had they not encountered so many obstacles, he might have considered ditching his body armor, but that hadn't been an option, not with the Z-10 making regular passes overhead.

Seth hurdled a fallen tree, and Brent followed.

Brent's internal compass said they should be close. If only they'd been able to follow the water's edge the whole way. An outcropping of rocks and cliffs interrupted the terrain and had forced them to fight their way inland for a quarter mile before they'd been able to correct their course.

The seconds ticked by. He did a quick check of his watch. They were already a minute late. Would their squad still be waiting?

Only once since joining the SEALs had his squad been separated, and he'd been the one left behind. He didn't want to repeat that experience, even though it had resulted in him getting to know Amy.

Two steps in front of him, Seth burst through the trees and onto the sand. Immediately, Seth lifted his arms and waved both hands.

Brent followed him onto a secluded beach that stretched along a quiet cove. Twenty yards out, his squad was headed out to sea in their inflatable boat.

Brent whistled and followed Seth's example of waving his arms.

The boat came about, making a tight half circle to head back to shore.

The familiar rumble echoed toward them, and Brent looked skyward. The spotlight from the Z-10 wasn't yet visible, but he doubted it would be long before it strafed across the beach.

Could his men get back to shore and take cover before they were seen? Could they hear the helicopter over the boat's motor?

Brent waved them forward, willing them to move faster. The helicopter appeared over the water, the beam sweeping over the coastline.

The boat reached the beach, and Brent and Seth both leaned down to pull it beneath the canopy of trees that bent over the cove.

Jay jumped out of the boat first. "Take cover."

The rest of the squad followed, all of them clustering at the edge of the trees, their bodies close together, their heads low.

The beam of the spotlight searched the water's edge, coming within inches of the boat.

It passed over where the squad had taken cover without slowing. Twice, the helicopter circled, the light coming uncomfortably close to them each time.

When it finally moved off, Brent stood. "Let's go."

They all took their positions in the boat, and Craig started the motor again. The boat fought against the incoming waves, lifting and falling until it finally broke through the cresting waves.

"What happened to you two?" Jay asked as soon as they reached the open water.

"We found a new problem," Brent said. "Is your comm working?"

"No." Jay shook his head. "I don't know if our comm unit isn't working or if there's a dampening field nearby."

"I hope it's the former, otherwise we may not be able to get any readings from the bugs we planted."

Seth leaned forward. "If they have a dampening field up, they can't communicate either."

"We need to find out what's going on in that building," Brent said.

"First we need to find a way to signal our ride," Jay said. "We're twelve minutes late."

"Let's hope they're looking for us when we get to the extraction zone."

"I'm past hoping," Seth drawled. "It's time to pray."

Brent blew out a breath, and a warmth spread through his chest. "I agree."

16

STILL NO WORD. AMY HAD hoped Brent would find a way to email her when he returned to the ship, but so far, she hadn't received any kind of communication from him.

Worry shimmered around her heart, and a layer of tension enveloped her when Commander Gardner approached, his jaw set.

Amy swallowed her pride and asked, "Sir, have you heard any updates on the Saint Squad?"

"You'll hear their status with all the other wives."

Amy jolted back, and an unexpected surge of tears threatened. She clenched her teeth and fought the rising emotions. She would not let this man make her cry.

Without the least bit of concern or sympathy, Gardner continued past her.

Needing a minute to regain her composure, she made her way to her office. As soon as she entered, she picked up the phone on her desk. Still no dial tone.

A new surge of emotions churned inside her. She focused on the anger. At least being mad wouldn't make her cry.

She turned on her computer. Maybe she could at least access the after-action report by now. Assuming the squad had made it out of Nicaragua.

She shook away the possibility that they hadn't. Positive thoughts. Worrying about the what-ifs was making her crazy.

Her computer screen came to life, and she typed in her log-in credentials. She missed a letter in her password and had to input it a second time. When she was finally in, she accessed the correct database, and her heart sank. Still nothing. No after-action report. No mission updates.

Amy swallowed hard.

"Amy?" Vanessa walked in. "You okay?"

Amy took a shaky breath and willed her fears to settle. The squad could be perfectly fine and en route to the carrier. She focused on Vanessa. "What are you doing here?"

"Paige told me you had an issue with your phones yesterday."

"Yeah. Looks like they won't be working until next week sometime."

Vanessa fished a cell phone out of her purse. "Here you go."

"What's this for?"

"You need a secure phone." Vanessa handed the cell to her. "This is a secure phone."

Amy knew secure cell phones were issued to some intelligence personnel, but that had never been a piece of equipment she'd been privy to. "Where did this come from?"

"I had a nice chat with Ghost this morning. He agrees that you need to have more support than you're receiving."

"Admiral Rivera said I could use his office today," Amy said.

"I'm not sure it's a good idea to be away from your desk when your boss is trying to fire you."

"You may have a point." Amy held up the phone. "Thank you for this. Any chance Ghost has any updates?"

"No. He checked right before I met him."

Amy motioned to her computer. "There's nothing on the system either."

"They must have run into some unexpected obstacles." Vanessa spoke calmly, but Amy didn't miss the worry beneath the cool exterior.

A brief knock sounded on Amy's door before it swung open.

"Excuse me. I'm sorry to interrupt." Mei Lien walked in and glanced at Vanessa. Recognition flashed in her eyes for a brief moment and was quickly banked. Mei Lien held out a note. "A storm is moving in. Kaminski's transport for this afternoon was moved up an hour."

"Kaminski can't have been happy about that."

"He doesn't know."

"Gardner didn't let you tell him?"

Mei Lien shook her head. "I'm on a bathroom break."

"Better get out of here," Amy said. "He's trying to find out if you'll tell me."

"Watch your back," Mei Lien said in a low voice. Then she disappeared the way she had come.

Vanessa followed her to the door and closed it again. "He's testing her loyalty."

"Where do you know her from?" Amy asked. When Vanessa's face went blank in her standard I-don't-know-what-you're-talking-about look, Amy shook her head. "And don't tell me you don't know her. Mei Lien isn't as skilled as you are at hiding surprise."

One of Vanessa's shoulders lifted briefly. "I had her in class."

Amy's eyebrows shot up. The only reason navy personnel would ever be in one of Vanessa's classes was if they were receiving additional training from the CIA. And that meant intel officer. "She's intel?"

"She was going to be. I'm not sure what happened to change her mind, but my guess is her fiancé didn't want to be married to an intel officer," Vanessa said. "It's too bad. She had a lot of promise."

Amy couldn't recall a single time Mei Lien had mentioned a fiancé. Maybe they weren't as good of friends as she thought. "She's not setting me up, is she?"

"I seriously doubt it. Everything in her psych profile and her actions indicate she's as loyal as they come, and I guarantee she wouldn't pledge her loyalty to someone like Gardner." Vanessa motioned to Amy's new phone. "You'd better call and check on that transport."

"Want to watch for Gardner for me?" Amy asked. "If he comes to my office and my door is closed, he'll suspect I'm using my personal cell phone to make calls."

"You got it." Vanessa opened the door and stepped out into the hall.

Amy made the call, and a brief conversation confirmed the information Mei Lien had passed along to her. Amy quickly pulled up Kaminski's number.

Vanessa's voice carried to her. "Excuse me, sir, but can you tell me how to find the personnel office?"

"No." The single syllable wasn't enough to identify Gardner, but Amy's suspicions prevented her from making the next call.

She sat at her desk and pulled up the latest intel reports.

Footsteps approached her office, paused briefly, and then passed by. A minute later, Vanessa stepped back into Amy's office.

"Was it Gardner?" Amy asked.

"That's what his uniform said." Vanessa glanced over her shoulder before she added, "I'd better get out of here so he doesn't know I was here to see you. Make your call. And let me know when you hear from our guys."

"I will."

"Oh, one more thing: my secure cell is programed into your new one. So is Ghost's."

Amy wasn't sure what to think about this newest declaration. "You're giving me a guardian?"

"Something like that," Vanessa said. "If you get in trouble, he's usually close by."

"Thanks, Vanessa."

Vanessa nodded and disappeared into the hall.

Amy used her new phone to call Kaminski's cell. Once she relayed the change in his departure time, she settled back at her computer to continue her search for her husband.

Where was the Saint Squad? And why hadn't anyone heard from them?

* * *

Seth examined the battery of yet another comm set. He had checked five so far, and the battery had died in every one. What were the odds?

He placed it next to the others on the worktable in the ready room the Saint Squad had been assigned on the USS *Harry S. Truman*. This wasn't the first time they'd experienced equipment failure on a mission, but never had it expanded to the entire squad like this. At least their meet-up with their ship had gone according to plan despite their tardy arrival at the rendezvous point.

Across the room, Jay's fingers tapped on the keyboard of one of the three computers lining the wall. He muttered under his breath, the cadence of the tapping stopping, interrupted by what Seth assumed was the delete key.

"Aren't you done with that yet?" Seth asked. "Amy would have had the after-action report submitted a half hour ago."

"Amy is better at this job than I am." Jay rolled his head from side to side. "And my hands are still sore from spending most of the night in a tree. Holding on to branches isn't my idea of a good time."

"You were in command. Why didn't you make Quinn and Tristan do it?"

"They both took a turn, but I swear they don't see half of what's out there."

Seth smothered a grin. Without meaning to, Jay had just condemned himself to the truth: he was the best lookout on the squad. "Better get that finished up. I'm sure our wives are waiting for Amy to give them an update."

"I'm going as fast as I can."

Brent walked in, followed by Craig and Damian. "You two, see if you can pick up anything on those listening devices we planted."

"And if we can?" Craig asked. "Please tell me you aren't going to make us sit surveillance on this."

"If you can, turn it over to intel so they can track it." Brent crossed to Seth and picked up one of the disassembled communication headsets. "Find anything?"

"All of the batteries are dead." Seth checked the sixth unit. "This one too."

"All of them?" Brent asked. "How is that possible?"

Seth checked the last battery. "I don't know. Maybe we got a bad batch."

"Report it to logistics. They'll need to run an equipment check for any other units that might be affected." Brent picked up one of the batteries and turned it over in his hand until he located the serial number. "Have you checked to see if these numbers are sequential?"

"They're all within a few digits," Seth said. "Our equipment report said they were all changed out last week."

"And with our training mix-ups, we hardly used them." Brent's jaw clenched.

"What?" Damian asked in Spanish, swiveling in his seat and switching to English. "If Gardner let us train properly, we would have checked our comm sets."

"You don't think he switched out good batteries for bad ones, do you?" Craig asked.

"I would hope not, but, at this point, I wouldn't put anything past him," Brent said.

Damian changed back to Spanish. "I really hate that guy."

Craig automatically gave a translation, even though it was no longer needed. Brent had understood the comment in Spanish, which demonstrated how frequently Damian had shared the sentiment.

Jay stood and let out a sigh of victory. "Done."

Brent turned to him. "Are you just now sending the after-action report?"

"It's harder than it looks," Jay said. "It's in now though."

The hatch opened, and Tristan and Quinn passed through.

"What's going on?" Tristan asked.

"We're talking about how much we hate our new commanding officer," Craig offered.

"And how Jay needs typing lessons," Seth said, the Southern in his voice thickening.

"I'd rather sit up in a tree all night than write a report," Jay grumbled.

"Well, lucky you," Quinn said. "On this mission, you got to do both."

Seth didn't miss the light of challenge that flared in Jay's eyes. He stepped between the two men. "Quinn, wait until we've all had some sleep before you start picking fights."

"He's right." Brent nodded. "Let's focus our energy on defeating a common enemy."

"Morenta?" Craig asked.

"Him too," Brent said. "But I was thinking of Gardner."

17

AMY CURLED BOTH HANDS INTO fists and took several deep breaths. The urge to pound on her keyboard or, even better, throw it across the room, didn't fade. How could Gardner do this?

The error message on her screen continued to flash. Access denied.

After a day and a half of waiting, the Saint Squad's after-action report was finally in the system, but someone had revoked her access to the database where the information—where the fate of her husband and their friends—was stored.

Gardner.

No one else up her chain of command would stoop to such a low.

Amy pushed away from her desk, paced across the room, and swallowed the scream trying to erupt from deep inside her. She clenched her fists tighter, her fingernails digging into her palms.

She couldn't do this anymore. The man was a tyrant, a more formidable foe than she had given him credit for. More than that, in the short week he had been with SEAL Team Eight, he had demonstrated his complete disregard for the well-being of the personnel in his command.

She drew another deep breath, worry competing with her fury. The worry dominated now and gnawed at her.

She had hoped to drive to her parents' home after work today to prepare for the momentous events of tomorrow. Her father was becoming the commander in chief, and his daughter was falling victim to a military bully.

The Whitmore competitive streak whipped through her. Amy straightened her shoulders. No one was going to push her around. She might not have her older brothers or the Saint Squad here to guard her back, but she had Vanessa and the other wives. They were smart and resourceful. And three of them had security clearances.

Security clearances. A new resource popped into her mind. She reached into her pocket and retrieved her cell phone, then pulled up the contacts. Vanessa's name flashed on the screen, but she hit the number for the name at the top: Ghost.

The phone rang twice before a man answered with a terse greeting. "What?"

Maybe it wasn't a greeting. "This is Amy Miller. I could use some help."

"Are you safe?"

"Physically, yes." Amy let out a little sigh. She hated asking for help. "It looks like my commander has restricted my access to my squad's after-action reports. I was hoping you might be able to help me at least find out what's in the latest one."

"Hold on." The rustle of movement carried over the phone, and then there was a murmur of voices, Ghost's and a woman's. A minute passed. "I've got it. They made their rendezvous this morning. Looks like their comm was out when they were in Nicaragua."

Amy grabbed the back of her chair as relief flowed through her. "That explains why no one heard from them yesterday."

"Are you able to retrieve your reports?" Ghost asked.

"No. I'm locked out of the program I need to track their comm."

"Give me a second." The faint tapping of computer keys carried over the line. "Okay, you're all set."

"All set with what?"

"I'm granting you access to the system on your new cell phone," Ghost said. "It won't be as easy to use as if you were on your laptop, but this will keep you in the loop."

"You can do that?"

"I just did."

Amy lowered into her chair. "Thank you."

"Watch your back," Ghost said, his irritation obvious. "I don't like what I'm seeing with this commander."

"Me neither." Amy ended the call a moment before Mei Lien walked into her office.

"Do you have lunch plans?"

"No, I don't."

"I've heard Lin Garden is pretty good." She glanced behind her. "I think I'll head over there around eleven thirty."

Amy wasn't sure why Mei Lien had opted to avoid making specific plans with her, but if cryptic was what she wanted, Amy could play along. "I'm going to go off base for lunch today too."

"We could both use a change." Mei Lien nodded once and then turned and left the room.

Amy leaned back and checked the time on her computer. Two hours until she would meet up with Mei Lien. Plenty of time to make sure Webb's unit had what they needed for the day and to catch up on the intel reports Gardner was determined to keep from her.

* * *

Relief rushed through Jim when he received the update on the Saint Squad. The information hadn't been in the daily brief, but Ghost had been kind enough to call and give him the good news. His son-in-law was safe and so was the rest of the Saint Squad. As to when they would return home, Jim didn't know.

The possibility of Brent and his squad missing Jim's inauguration rankled. These men were among the select few who had ensured his safety long before this election, who had protected him and his family and helped make tomorrow possible.

Three of the guardians would also be in attendance, but they would remain in the shadows of the proceedings to ensure they wouldn't be caught on camera. Dead men couldn't stay dead if someone knew they were walking among the living.

Jim pushed back from the desk in his home office. He'd made the decision to work from home for his last day as president-elect as much so he could savor his last hours here with his family as for security reasons.

He walked into the living room, where his youngest son stood with Doug Valdez.

"It's not going to happen." Charlie waved his hand in a circle in front of Doug. "Do whatever you have to, but I'm not going through tomorrow unarmed."

"I'll talk to Secret Service again, but you know we have protocols to follow."

"I know, and I'm telling you that there has to be a way around this."

"What's going on?" Jim asked.

"The Secret Service has a policy that no one in their area of protection can be armed. That includes the White House," Doug said.

"So, Charlie can have his gun with him through the inauguration but not when we get to the White House?" Jim asked.

"I could live with that," Charlie said, "but they're telling me I can't even have it when we're out in front of the Capitol."

"That doesn't make sense." Jim's eyebrows furrowed. "Other law enforcement officers will be there, and they'll all be armed."

"Exactly." Charlie motioned to Jim. "That's what I said."

"The problem is that Charlie isn't on the security detail," Doug explained.

"Then put him on the security detail." Jim shrugged. "Problem solved."

"You want one of your own children to be listed as security?"

"Sure. Why not?" Even after thirty years in public service, he still didn't know how so many people could manage to wrap simple solutions inside so much red tape. "Tell the head of the Secret Service detail that Charlie is going to be part of the security for the first family. You know he's going to be scanning the crowd the whole time he's on stage anyway."

"That's true." Doug's lips quirked up. "I'll put him on the list, but, Charlie, you're going to have to check in your weapon when you enter the White House."

"Fine. As long as Secret Service takes it after we walk through the front doors," Charlie said. "I'm not going to do anything to mess with my dad's image on his first day in office."

"Good point." Doug nodded. "I'll take care of it."

"Thanks, Doug."

"Any word yet on Brent and his boys?" Doug asked.

"Just heard. They're back aboard their ship."

"Wait." A crease formed between Charlie's eyebrows. "I thought Brent was already on leave."

Jim wished his son-in-law were already on leave. "He was supposed to start leave today, but a mission went longer than expected."

"Is that why Amy didn't come up last night?" Charlie asked.

"Yeah."

"Let me know if you need me to go down and get her." Charlie grinned. "I have a gun, and I know how to use it."

Jim laughed. "Thanks, but I'd rather not have my children kidnapping each other this week."

Charlie let out an exaggerated sigh. "Fine."

* * *

Amy followed the beckoning scents into the Chinese-food restaurant. Mei Lien already waited inside at a table in the far corner.

A hostess hurried forward from what appeared to be the door to the kitchen. "Table for one?" she asked with a thick Chinese accent.

"No. I'm meeting a friend." Amy motioned to Mei Lien.

"Very good." The hostess nodded and step aside to let Amy pass.

Amy's gaze swept over the other patrons in the restaurant. Two women in business attire across from them, a group of enlisted men and women at a large, round table by the window. The tables nearest where Mei Lien sat were all empty.

Amy reached Mei Lien and slid into the seat across from her. She lowered her voice and asked, "What's going on?"

"First, your squad is safe."

Amy feigned relief so Mei Lien wouldn't know Amy had already received that information through another source. "Thanks for telling me. My computer access was changed so I couldn't retrieve the reports myself."

"I know." Mei Lien glanced around the room before continuing. "I don't know exactly what you did to tick Gardner off, but he has a vendetta against you. Big-time."

"What else do you know?" Amy asked.

"Personnel denied the reclassification requests, but Gardner is refusing to fill the intel spots until you're gone."

"What? He would just leave all of our squads shorthanded?"

"He's convinced that intel officers aren't necessary." Mei Lien lowered her voice. "He says that SEALs should be checking intel reports themselves so they don't miss something important."

An alarm bell rang inside her head. "When Gardner was injured, was it due to bad intel?"

"I don't know, but it would make sense."

Amy leaned forward. "What else have you heard?"

"He tried to revoke your squad's leave, but Admiral Singer overrode him."

"How did Admiral Singer get involved?" Amy asked.

"I may have said that the approval was granted by him and that to revoke it, he would need the admiral's permission."

"Thank you." Relieved that she wouldn't have to go over Gardner's head again, she picked up her menu.

"He really has no idea who you are, does he?" Mei Lien asked.

Amy's gaze whipped up to meet Mei Lien's. "What?"

"I follow politics," Mei Lien said. "You may not use the same name or wear your hair the same way as when you're with your dad, but I'd have to be hiding under a rock not to make the connection."

"And you don't think Commander Gardner knows who I am?" Amy asked.

"He follows politics but only the kind attached to how many stars are on an admiral's shoulders."

"You know who his uncle is?" Amy asked.

She nodded. "I did a bit of digging when he was named Commander Bennett's replacement."

"I hope Kel likes his new job, because I'm already missing him here."

Mei Ling sighed. "We all are."

The waitress arrived, a Chinese woman who moved with the ease of someone half her age. "May I take your order?"

Mei Lien said something in Cantonese, but Amy wasn't able to discern what she had ordered.

After the woman took Amy's order, she bustled back to the kitchen door.

"I didn't know you spoke Cantonese."

Mei Lien's eyebrows lifted. "You know Cantonese too? I'm impressed."

"Don't be. The only phrase I know in any Chinese language is *xièxiè*."

"That's the Mandarin version, but being able to say 'thanks' is appreciated in any language."

"Maybe you should also teach me how to say 'thank you' in Cantonese, then, because I want to ask a favor," Amy said.

"What's that?"

"Can you keep an eye on my squads for me while I'm gone? I know it's a lot to ask, but I wouldn't put it past Gardner to sabotage them to make it look like I did something wrong."

"I already planned on it," Mei Lien said. "I don't want to see any of them hurt any more than you do."

"Thank you."

"*M-goi*," Mei Lien said. "That's how you say 'thank you' in Cantonese."

"*M-goi*," Amy repeated.

"*Shĭ wú gāi*." Mei Lien smiled. "You're welcome."

"How did you end up working as an admin assistant instead of in intelligence?" Amy asked, her voice low.

"My fiancé wasn't a fan of being married to an intel officer."

"I didn't realize you're engaged."

"I'm not." Mei Lien shrugged. "Turns out my career choice wasn't the only thing my fiancé had a problem with."

"Sorry."

"It was for the best. I'm better in a support role anyway." Mei Lien shrugged. "At least, I was."

"We'll get through this," Amy said. "Together."

18

BRENT READ THROUGH THE ROUGH translation Damian had given him from the recordings from the fortress. So far, their listening devices had caught only snippets of conversations but nothing useful. The audio feed from the structure in the woods had provided a bit more, but talk of food and work rotations had been the main topics.

The whole squad had congregated in their board room to wait for word of when they would be able to transport home. Jay was the only one missing, having been tasked with sorting out the details with the higher-ups. If Amy were on board, they'd probably already be halfway home.

Brent had tried calling her to enlist her help, but he hadn't been able to get a good connection. Email had been his second option, but she hadn't replied to that either. So strange. Even though, technically, they were all supposed to go on leave today, he had expected Amy to keep working until they got home, or at least until she received word from them. Why wasn't she responding?

Maybe her dad had convinced her to go up to northern Virginia early. He likely received updates on their mission and could pass information on to Amy. Still, this wasn't like her to go silent.

Regardless, without the extra admin support, Brent had moved to his next best option. Who better than the man with a pregnant wife at home to get them stateside as soon as possible?

Brent glanced at his watch. They were barely going to make it back in time to drive from Virginia Beach to DC for the inauguration.

Brent set the translations on the worktable in front of him. "Damian, how many different voices did you hear at the building in the woods?"

"*Siete. Más o menos.*"

Seven. Give or take. Having Damian on the squad was going to teach Brent Spanish whether he wanted to add another language to his arsenal or not.

"That's three sets of guards, two each, and at least one other person," Seth said. He pushed back from the computer station he'd been working at and crossed to the worktable. "Who could be so important that he would warrant a hideaway and a full contingent of guards?"

"I don't know that it's so much who it is as what he's doing there."

"Intel will figure it out," Brent said. He hoped.

Jay walked in, ducking to keep his head from hitting the top of the hatch. When he straightened, the frustration on his face brought with it a sense of dread.

"What's wrong?"

"Our transport has been deemed nonessential," Jay said, the muscle in his jaw jumping. "We've been bumped until Tuesday."

"What?" Quinn shot to a stand.

"Four days?" Tristan asked as well.

Craig shook his head. "My wife is not going to be happy."

"None of our wives will be happy. Neither will Brent's in-laws," Seth said in his slow, methodical way. "More importantly, who classified us as nonessential?"

"I'll give you one guess," Jay said.

Brent gritted his teeth and fought for control. "Gardner."

"Brent, you can't miss tomorrow," Quinn insisted. "Especially not because of some red tape."

"He's right," Craig said. "This is a once-in-a-lifetime event."

"I haven't been able to get through to Amy," Brent said. "Seth, see if you can get in touch with Vanessa. Damian, you try calling Paige. Let them know what's going on, and see if they can work with Amy to cut through the red tape."

Brent stood and headed for the hatch.

"¿Adónde vas?" Damian asked.

"I need to talk to the XO to see what we can do to change our status without involving Gardner."

"Are you going to tell him why we need to get back?" Jay asked.

"I'd prefer to avoid that unless we don't have another option."

"If it comes down to it, we may have to call Jim," Seth said.

"I know." Brent opened the hatch. "Do what you can without bringing my father-in-law into this."

"Yes, sir."

* * *

Enough was enough. Amy was supposed to be the person who knew what was going on, the person who communicated with the other wives and shared the latest updates.

She stormed into her closet and grabbed her suitcase, her jaw tense. Today alone, she had received more information from her friends without security clearances than she had through official navy communication channels.

Carina had been the first to share the news that the squad had been bumped off the next available transport. Vanessa had confirmed the news within minutes of Carina's call.

Taylor had called next, followed by Sienna. A clothing designer, an artist, and an actress. Really? As much as she loved her friends, they couldn't be more civilian if they tried.

Gardner shouldn't have been able to get in the way of Amy's ability to communicate with her husband and his men. And Amy had no doubt the commander was at the heart of why she was the only wife who hadn't received an email from her husband.

Amy set her suitcase on her bed and moved to her dresser. She packed the essentials before retrieving the clothes Carina had made for her for tomorrow's festivities. The elegant pantsuit would be paired with a long wool coat for the inauguration itself, with the flowing bright-red gown for the inauguration ball.

Carina had included two other options for additional events, a business suit and an elegant dress, in case the need arose for more wardrobe changes than Amy anticipated.

She could hardly believe it. Her father was going to be president. She tried to focus on that instead of her own mess.

She finished packing her clothes and moved back to her walk-in closet. Was it even possible for Brent to make it to her father's inauguration?

Helpless to use official channels to get her husband home, she pulled out her new cell phone and called Ghost.

"What?"

The terse greeting matched the one she'd received with her last call. Was this man always impatient?

"Sorry to bother you. This is Amy Miller. Or maybe I should say Amy Whitmore."

"Jim's daughter. I know who you are."

Amy's eyes widened. Only a select few called her father by his first name. The fact that *Jim* rolled off this man's tongue with such ease communicated more than any assurances could have. This man was a friend. At least, he was a friend to her father.

"I'm having a transportation emergency. Well, it's an emergency for my husband."

"Vanessa already called me. I'm working on a solution now."

"Can you tell me what that solution is?"

"I'm still debating if it will be faster to try to cut through the navy's bureaucracy or send a Coast Guard helicopter in to retrieve them."

"Either way, you're going to have to deal with getting clearance from the captain of the ship."

"What do you know about the captain?"

"I know his name, but that's about it," Amy said. "I usually deal directly with the XO, Commander Chang."

"Will he want to help?"

"He's a good man, but he won't disobey orders."

"That's what I needed to know. I'll be in touch."

The call clicked off.

Amy pocketed her phone. A few more details of Ghost's plan would have been nice.

She set her suitcase on the floor and flopped onto her bed. Her eyes drooped closed. It would be so easy right now to drift into sleep and pretend everything was as it was supposed to be.

Maybe a nap would be a good idea. She could hide in her dreams instead of her nightmares for an hour before facing the four-hour drive to her father's house.

Her personal cell phone rang, foiling that plan. "Hello?"

Sienna's voice carried over the line. "Are you about ready to leave for your dad's?"

"I've packed my suitcase."

"Great. I'm picking you up in fifteen minutes."

"Why?"

"Because Kendra said you might want someone to ride up with." Kendra. Amy's sister-in-law, Sienna's sister.

"Is Charlie behind this?"

"He wanted to come down and pick you up himself. Kendra intervened."

"I owe her."

"Finish packing your things. And don't forget to pack a bag for Brent," Sienna said. "Craig called a few minutes ago and said they're fighting to get a transport straight to DC."

"Craig called?"

"Well, one of the communication guys called and then let me talk to him."

"Craig's using the I'm-married-to-a-famous-actress card again, huh?"

"Works every time." Sienna laughed. "Although it's really the I-know-a-famous-actress card."

"Whatever works," Amy said.

"It'll work, and our guys are going to be there tomorrow," Sienna said. "You can count on it."

Amy's stomach flipped in a combination of anticipation and discomfort. "I hope so."

19

BRENT FOUGHT TO KEEP HIS breathing steady as Commander Chang explained in detail why he and his squad couldn't leave.

"I'd love to help you. Really, I would." Commander Chang settled behind his desk. "Had it not been for this last-minute training exercise, we could have sent you back to Virginia Beach on a chopper."

Brent paced to the single chair opposite Commander Chang's desk. He gripped the back of it. "Get us as far as Miami. We can grab a commercial flight from there," Brent said.

"We don't have any aircraft available," Chang said.

"We're on an aircraft carrier. There's got to be something," Brent said. "All of my men are qualified pilots. We'll fly ourselves if you lend us a ride."

"I'm under orders. No navy aircraft that isn't mission required can fly out of here."

Brent's fingers dug into the wooden back of the chair. "There has to be a way."

The phone on the commander's desk rang, and he snatched it up. "Chang."

He listened for a brief moment, and then he held up a finger to signal Brent to remain where he was. "I have him right here." Chang paused. "He'll be relieved to hear that. They'll be ready."

After another brief pause, Chang hung up the phone. "Your squad must be living right because your prayers were just answered. A Coast Guard cutter is sending a helicopter to pick you up."

"Can the Coast Guard get us as far as Virginia Beach?" Brent asked. Traveling by chopper wouldn't be as fast as if they could take a transport flight, especially with refueling requirements, but anything that would get his squad stateside was a step in the right direction.

"It'll take a few refueling stops, but according to what the captain just told me, the helicopter is taking you to DC. You'll have to find your way home from there."

Brent fought back a grin. "That won't be a problem."

"Better get your squad moving. The chopper is already en route," Chang said. "ETA twenty minutes."

"We'll be ready." Brent left the XO's office and hurried to his squad's ready room. The moment he opened the door, everyone looked his direction.

Jay paced across the room. "Any luck?"

"Grab your gear. We're shipping out in twelve minutes."

"How did you get Chang to change his mind?"

"I didn't," Brent said. "The Coast Guard is sending a chopper for us."

"How did the Coast Guard get involved with helping us?" Seth asked.

"I have no idea." Brent shrugged. "But I'm not going to pass up a free ride."

* * *

Jim's secure cell phone rang. He held it up enough for his oldest son to see. "Sorry, Matt, I've got to take this."

"Go ahead. I've got them." Matt motioned to his two oldest children, who were currently riding in circles on their respective horses. Aiden, the youngest of Matt's three children, rested on his hip, with his arms clinging to Matt's neck.

Jim left his son and grandchildren and stepped into the barn, where he would have some privacy, before he answered. "Hello?"

Ghost's voice came over the line. "It's Kade."

"It's so weird to hear you tell me your name."

"Get used to it, Mr. President. You're one of the privileged few who gets that information."

"I've told you before, you've earned the right to call me Jim," he said. "What's the latest? Any luck getting Brent and his squad home?"

"The Coast Guard is giving them a lift," Kade said.

"The Coast Guard? Why are they involved?"

"Because the navy blocked all our usual channels." Kade's voice tightened. "That new commander of SEAL Team Eight is a problem."

"I should have given Amy more credit when she complained about him."

"After tomorrow, you'll be in a position to override military politics."

"I wouldn't count on it, but I'll try," Jim said. "Where is the Coast Guard going to drop them off? Will they have time to make it to DC before the inauguration?"

"Troy is heading to Georgia to meet up with them now," Kade said, referring to the guardian who was currently residing in Maine. Thankfully, Troy had already flown to DC a couple of days ago to provide additional security.

"Any idea when they'll get here?"

"With the refueling stops, it probably won't be until late tonight," Kade said. "Since you want to keep Brent out of the spotlight, it would be best to keep them in DC tonight instead of bringing them to your house."

Jim debated briefly. "I hear what you're saying, but it will be easier on everyone if they can meet up with their wives. None of them are going to have clothes for tomorrow without going out and buying something."

"I hadn't thought about that." Kade grew silent for a moment. "If you're okay with me parking my rig behind your house, I'll pick up anyone who is staying at your place and bring them over."

"That will be Brent, Craig, Seth, and Jay. Everyone else is staying with family or friends."

"Just do me a favor and let Secret Service know I'm coming," Kade said. "I'll put in the authorization, but it would be best if they didn't think I'm trying to hack my way in."

"I'll take care of it. Thanks."

After Jim ended the call, he returned to Matt's side and leaned on the split-rail fence. Kailey held the reins exactly as she had been taught, her face a study in concentration. In contrast, her younger brother was grinning, his hands gripping the reins like a cowboy getting ready to urge his mount to a gallop.

Jim reached out and ruffled little Aiden's hair. "It won't be long before he's out there with his brother and sister."

"I can't believe Spencer is already riding on his own," Matt said. "I don't think I rode nearly that well when I was four."

"You were too busy throwing baseballs through your mother's kitchen window."

Matt cast a sideways glance at him. "That only happened twice."

"Which was twice too many." Jim laughed. "Not many kids could throw a ball with enough force at that age to break a window."

"Seems to me you were the one who was supposed to catch the ball to keep it from hitting the window."

"You mother clued in on that pretty fast." Jim remembered his scolding well.

"Spencer, tighten up on the reins," Matt called out to his son before turning his attention back to Jim. "Have you figured out what you're going to do with the horses yet?"

"Maybe." Jim mulled over his plans for a moment before sharing them. "How do you think the family would feel about me letting someone else live here for the next four years?"

"I don't know. It would be weird, but as much as the kids love to ride the horses, we come to visit you and Mom, not the animals."

"I think we could arrange to have the kids still ride if they want to," Jim said. "I'm trying to get one of the men from Brent's unit to work for me. If he takes the job, he would be up here for a couple years."

"And you want him to live here?"

"Seth and Vanessa have been good friends to Brent and Amy, and by having someone we know staying here, we would be able to avoid boarding the horses or getting rid of them altogether."

"I don't think my kids would forgive you if you sold the horses."

"You're probably right." Jim chuckled. "I need to head back down to the house. Do you want me to take Aiden with me?"

"Sure." Matt shifted the two-year-old in his arms. "Aiden, go with Grandpa."

Jim reached out for his grandson. "Come on, kiddo. Let's go see if Grandma has any cookies."

"Cookies." Aiden immediately reached for Jim.

"Works every time," Jim said.

* * *

A flood of memories swept through Amy when Sienna pulled into her parents' driveway. The home of her youth really had given her an idyllic childhood, complete with playing basketball in the driveway with her older brothers and riding horses at every opportunity.

The spotlight that came from her father's career choice had been difficult at times, but since college, it had faded to almost nonexistent. She didn't know how her father's PR team had done such a great job shielding her from the constant scrutiny of the press, but her lack of exposure to social settings within the DC crowd hadn't hurt.

"It's hard to believe this is your parents' last night here for the next four years," Sienna said.

"Or eight." Amy pushed open the door. "Knowing how quickly my father gains people's respect, the country will probably beg him to run for reelection."

Sienna climbed out of the car, and they both moved to the back to retrieve their suitcases. "All I can say is he's going to be a hard act to follow."

"That's the truth." Amy pulled out her suitcase and hanging bags that held her formal wear and Brent's best suit.

"Are you ready for the spotlight tomorrow?" Sienna asked.

"Maybe I should stand with you and your family," Amy said. Besides Sienna's and Kendra's personal fame, their father was one of the most well-known actors of his generation. "Everyone would focus on you, your sister, and your dad. I could just fade into the background."

"That wouldn't work." Sienna laughed as she closed the trunk. "People would want to know who our friend is."

"You're probably right." Amy led the way inside. She barely had the door closed when Charlie appeared and scooped her into a hug.

"It's about time you got here." He released her and repeated the gesture with his sister-in-law. "Sienna, thanks for giving Amy a ride."

"No problem." Sienna stepped out of his embrace. "Where's Kendra?"

The notes of a guitar rang out at the same time she heard Kendra's pure voice.

Charlie's face instantly lit up. "Does that answer your question?"

"Go say hi to your sister." Amy motioned to their bags. "Charlie can help me put your things in the guest room."

"Which one am I in?" Sienna asked.

"The one upstairs." Charlie picked up Sienna's bags and jutted his chin in the direction of the long downstairs hall. "Kendra is in the library."

"Thanks."

Charlie led the way up the sweeping staircase.

Amy followed and deposited her suitcase by her bed before she opened her closet door. A basketball rolled out. She nudged it aside with her foot and hung her clothes on the rod. She smoothed out the sleeve of Brent's suit jacket before leaning down to retrieve the ball.

"You want to shoot some hoops?" Charlie asked from her doorway.

"You really want to lose?"

"Those are fighting words." Charlie waved her forward. "Come on. Let's see what you've got."

Amy's eyes lowered to her brother's pant leg, the faint bulge there barely noticeable. "Better secure your weapon first."

His eyebrows lifted. "You're getting good at spotting those."

"I've been working with the Saint Squad for a long time."

"Any word from them yet?" Charlie asked.

Amy pulled her personal cell phone from her pocket. "Nothing yet. Last I heard, they were trying to find a transport off an aircraft carrier."

"The navy isn't seriously going to keep the new president's son-in-law from being at the inauguration, are they?"

"This is one time when I wish we had let our chain of command know we're related to Dad."

"It's a tough spot for both of us." Charlie led the way outside. "Working for the government while your dad is a senator is tough enough, but the president?" Charlie shrugged. "I don't want everyone using me to advance their agendas."

"Or their careers." Amy pushed aside the image of Gardner that popped into her mind.

"What's going on?"

"We're dealing with a command problem." Amy bounced the basketball as she walked down the sidewalk to the driveway.

"Dad said something about your new commanding officer being a challenge."

"He's elevated himself from challenge to nightmare." She stopped at the faded paint that marked the three-point line. She lifted the ball in front of her, eyed the basket at the edge of driveway, and sent the basketball flying. The ball swooshed through the net. Amy cocked an eyebrow. "That's three nothing."

"I wasn't ready yet."

"That's what you always say."

Footsteps approached. "Amy. You made it."

She turned at the sound of her father's voice. "Hi, Dad." She crossed to him and gave him a hug.

She breathed in the familiar scent of his cologne and hay dust. "You've been up in the barn."

"Matt and the kids are up there," he said. "Well, Aiden is now eating cookies in the kitchen with your mom, but Kailey is turning into quite the little rider." Her dad put his arm around Amy's shoulders and gave her a squeeze. "She reminds me of you."

"I wish we had time to ride down to the falls today."

"You and Brent can stay for a couple extra days if you want," her dad said. "He's on his way here."

Amy pulled away so she could face her father fully. "He is?"

"The Coast Guard picked him up," he said. "A friend will bring him, Craig, Seth, and Jay here to the house as soon as they land."

"Wait. Are Vanessa and Carina here?"

"They arrived a couple hours ago. Carina is making some last-minute adjustments to your mom's dress. Vanessa is in the kitchen with CJ," her dad said, referring to Matt's wife.

"Are you sure you want such a full house right now?" Amy asked. "Some of us can get hotel rooms."

"No need for that. Matt and CJ are staying in the basement with their family. With Matt's old room and the two guest rooms available, we have plenty of space."

Charlie retrieved the basketball and held it up. "You want to play a round?"

Her dad grinned and shook his head. "And let your sister beat up on me? No thanks."

Charlie lifted the ball as though to shoot, and Amy swatted it free. It bounced twice before she scooped it up, turned, and shot. It went off the backboard and into the hoop.

"That's five nothing."

Her dad chuckled. "Good luck."

Some of the tension of the past week dropped away, and Amy grinned. "He's going to need it."

20

SETH GRABBED HIS PACK AND climbed out of the Coast Guard helicopter as the pilot cut the engines.

"Your next ride is over there." The pilot pointed to a rescue helicopter parked a short distance away.

"Let's go." Brent started walking in that direction. His eyes narrowed when they reached the aircraft, and he opened the front. "Where's your copilot?"

"I'm flying solo," the new pilot said.

"Seth, take the copilot's spot."

Before the pilot could reject the offer, Seth said, "I'm qualified on helicopters."

The man nodded and offered Seth a helmet.

Seth settled into his seat and glanced at the man next to him. Ghost? Not the ghost whom Vanessa sometimes worked with in Virginia Beach but the man the Saint Squad had worked with in Europe a couple years ago. "I know you."

He shook his head. "No one knows me."

The faint Scandinavian accent in the man's voice confirmed his identity.

Seth didn't counter his claim. In truth, no one did know him. "Thanks for picking us up," Seth said instead.

Ghost nodded and fired up the engines as the rest of the squad climbed aboard. "Let's get you all where you're supposed to be."

Seth twisted in his seat to confirm the rest of his teammates had strapped themselves in. Brent gave him a thumbs-up, and Seth relayed the signal.

As soon as they were airborne and Ghost checked in with air traffic control, he switched to another frequency. Seth noted it and followed suit.

"We'll stop in Norfolk to refuel before continuing on to DC."

"How did you get roped into flying us?" Seth asked.

"One of my colleagues got a message that you ran into a transportation problem," Ghost said. "I was already stateside to provide support for tomorrow."

"If you need any help, our squad is ready and able," Seth offered.

"Your wife already made that offer, and we accepted."

"We've got a couple hours together. Want to fill us in?"

"Might as well."

Seth used hand signals to communicate with Brent which frequency they were on.

As soon as his squad switched over, Brent asked, "Status?"

"Our pilot here is part of your father-in-law's security team for tomorrow," Seth said. "He's going to fill us in on what we can do to help."

"As long as you keep me away from the cameras, I'll fill in wherever you want," Brent said.

"Same here," Craig said.

Seth couldn't count the number of times the paparazzi had caught a glimpse of Craig on the edge of their screen, but so far, he and Sienna had managed to keep their marriage under wraps. If Seth had any question whether or not miracles existed, that was one example. He supposed his squad's liberation from the carrier was another.

His hands fisted briefly. His squad was used to calling upon the Lord for guidance, but it grated on him that they would need His intervention because of someone who was supposed to be fighting on the same side as them.

If Seth's interview on Monday went well, Gardner wouldn't be his problem much longer, but he hated that he would be abandoning his squad to deal with the man on their own. Not that he could do much to combat a power-hungry bureaucrat. How did anyone win against this kind of adversary?

Even though Brent and Amy seemed determined to keep Jim Whitmore out of their work drama, if the situation didn't resolve itself soon, Seth would have to choose between overstepping the boundary of his friendship and involving their new president or risking his squad's safety. At this point, he'd rather have Brent mad at him if it would help ensure that Brent and the rest of the squad would stay alive.

* * *

Brent leaned forward as the guardian beside him made the turn into the narrow drive that ran the length of his father's property. The ease with which he navigated the dark road indicated this wasn't his first time visiting his in-laws' home.

How his squad had ended up being escorted by not one guardian but two was still beyond him. The Saint Squad were supposed to be the people who went in and rescued others, not the ones who needed to be rescued.

The ghost who had flown them to DC had taken on the task of driving Tristan, Quinn, and Damian to Quinn's childhood home, where the three men would meet up with their wives. The rest of his squad currently sat on the bunks that lined the back of the extended cab in the tractor trailer.

Brent had finally managed to send a quick text message to Amy when they were in Savannah, but other than that, he hadn't spoken to her.

He was almost afraid to find out what had happened on base during their absence. For all he knew, Gardner might have succeeded in transferring Amy out of his unit by now.

Ghost pulled to a stop along the back of the Whitmores' property, not far from the barn. He pulled out his phone and made a call. After a brief conversation, he hung up and swiveled in his seat to speak to the men still sitting in the space behind him. "You're good to go. Secret Service is expecting you."

Brent turned to the three men behind him. "Let's go."

Seth unfolded himself from the lower bunk and climbed out. Jay followed. Craig lay on the top bunk and didn't move other than the steady rise and fall of his chest.

"Jay, wake him up," Brent said. "We're not leaving him."

"Fine." Jay shook Craig's shoulder.

Craig shot up and bumped his head on the top of the cab. "Ow."

"We're here," Jay said.

Still rubbing his head, Craig exited the cab behind them.

Ghost joined them.

"Thanks for the ride," Brent said.

Ghost nodded. "I'll see you in the morning."

"You sleeping out here tonight?" Seth asked.

"I am," Ghost said. "Never hurts to have an extra set of eyes on the perimeter."

"I agree." Brent thanked him again and led the way down the long trail between the barn and the house. After checking in with Secret Service, they went inside.

"I have no idea which rooms you guys are staying in," Brent said.

"Sienna texted me," Craig said. "Seth is in the downstairs guest room. Jay's in Matt's room, and I'm in the upstairs guest room."

"Come on." Brent motioned toward the living room. "I'll show you which one is which."

"I know the way to mine." Seth headed out of the kitchen.

Craig scanned the countertops. "No cinnamon rolls?"

"Katherine is moving tomorrow. I doubt she had time to make any." Brent would have laughed at Craig's crestfallen expression if he hadn't been so tired. "Check the cookie jar."

Craig lifted the top of the ceramic apple. "Oh yeah." He pulled out two cookies the size of his palm. "Snickerdoodles."

"Come on. We need to get some sleep," Brent said. "And I want to see my wife."

Jay retrieved a couple of cookies for himself before leaving the kitchen.

After pointing his squadmates in the direction of their rooms, Brent reached his wife's childhood bedroom and slipped inside.

His wife's auburn hair spilled onto her pillow, and her skin glowed in the moonlight that flooded the room.

Brent set down his pack and toed off his boots. The moment he sat on the bed, Amy's eyes fluttered open.

Her dazed look cleared quickly, and she reached out her hand to take his. "You're home."

"I'm home." He leaned down and captured her mouth with his, his arms encircling her and drawing her closer. "I missed you."

"I missed you too."

"How did things go with Gardner after we shipped out?"

"I don't want to talk about him right now. We're both on leave."

"You're right." He kissed her again. "Thanks for helping us get home."

"I didn't have anything to do with that."

"You didn't?" Brent straightened. "Was it Vanessa?"

"Technically, we both called a friend, asking for a favor," Amy said. "Next thing I heard was that the Coast Guard was getting you home."

"Not just the Coast Guard. The guardians."

"Ghost came through, then."

"Two of them actually." Brent glanced in the direction of his in-laws' bedroom. "I get the feeling your dad knows a lot more about those guys than he lets on."

"He's about to become the president of the United States," Amy said. "I imagine he'll be privy to a lot of secrets in the coming years."

"You're right, but it's kind of nice to know we aren't the only ones watching his back."

"It really is."

21

SURREAL. THERE WAS NO OTHER word to describe it. Jim stood on the stage on the lawn of the Capitol building, Katherine at his side and their children and their spouses behind them. Brent was the sole exception, but he currently sat right behind Jim's parents and extended family.

Close friends filled the space behind Brent, with his teammates and the guardians interspersed through the front section of the crowd.

And what a crowd. Jim had never seen anything like it.

Waves of people flowing from the Capitol grounds and onto the mall.

The events leading to this moment passed by in a blur: the armored limousine that carried him away from his home of the past thirty years, the crowds waving flags along their route as they approached the Capitol.

Katherine's hand found his, a reminder of what was most important. The breeze whipped over them and brought with it an additional chill to the already cool day. At least there wasn't any snow.

Jim fought back a shiver.

Then it was time. He stepped forward with Katherine by his side. He placed his hand on the Bible that the Chief Justice of the Supreme Court held.

The moment his hand made contact with the worn leather, a new understanding seeped through him: the Lord had brought him here, had allowed him to fulfill this childhood dream.

Jim focused on the Chief Justice and fought to keep his voice steady as he repeated the oath. Despite his efforts, his voice wavered when he recited the final words, "Defend the Constitution of the United States."

Deafening cheers swallowed up the moments that followed.

Jim's gaze swept over his extended family and friends and then continued to the people who clapped and waved. His throat clogged up. He was theirs now. For the next four years, his actions didn't affect only him and his family. They affected an entire nation and rippled into the rest of the world.

The words of his carefully crafted speech jumbled in his mind as he stepped toward the microphone. Despite the many hours he had spent with his speech writer, carefully crafting each word, despite the repeated rehearsals and the teleprompter in front of him, the opening line wouldn't pass his lips.

Jim experienced a brief flash of panic and then a new clarity and calm.

Following inspiration rather than preparation, Jim said, "Faith is what brought us all here today. Your faith that I will lead and guide you to the best of my ability, and my faith that the Lord will guide me through every moment of every day that I serve the people of the United States of America."

Like a calm after a storm, the wind stilled, and the words of Jim's prepared speech merged with others that went beyond his own understanding.

An unexpected warmth enveloped him as he continued, a reverent hush falling over the crowd. When he concluded, everyone seated rose to their feet, and the applause roared.

Jim swallowed hard and savored the moment. His life had irrevocably changed over the past few minutes, and it would never again be the same. He uttered a silent prayer that these next four years would bring his country peace and prosperity and that the Lord would carry his family through whatever the future held.

The applause increased in volume.

He amended his prayer, changing four years to eight.

* * *

Amy peered out the bedroom window and took in the White House grounds below. How the White House staff had managed to move her parents into the historic home in only a few hours' time boggled her mind. The little touches in her White House bedroom added to her amazement.

A dish of her favorite butter mints beckoned from the accent table beside the love seat that stretched on the far side of the room. Beside it, a vase full of white and pink roses scented the air.

Amy turned in a circle, the skirt of her gown swishing around her ankles. She had a bedroom in the White House.

Brent emerged from the bathroom, still fiddling with his bow tie. He lowered his hands, but his tie was still slightly askew. "Are you sure about me escorting you tonight?"

"I'm sure." Amy crossed to him and reached up for a kiss. "I've missed you. Besides, there's no one I would rather dance with."

"Even though we'll have the world watching?"

"Dad already talked to his press secretary. She's approving all the still photos, and she's working with the video crew to make sure any shots of us with your face visible will be edited out," Amy said. "Besides, you're here as a civilian tonight. Without the dress uniform, no one will know you're navy unless you tell them."

"Sounds like your dad is taking charge already."

"He's been ready for this for a long time." Amy straightened his tie.

Brent's hand reached for hers. He stepped back and studied her. "You're stunning."

"Thank you." She squeezed his hand. "You look rather dapper yourself."

"Ready?" Brent asked.

Amy nodded. They left their room at the same time Charlie stepped into the hall.

"Where's Kendra?" Amy asked.

"She's already downstairs getting ready," Charlie said. "Dad has her performing first so she can join the family for the rest of the night."

Amy shook her head. "Putting his daughter-in-law to work already."

"Kendra is thrilled to be performing," Charlie said. "As she says, this is a dream."

Amy smiled. "It's kind of funny how past presidents have bragged about what famous people would be in attendance, and with Dad, the majority of them are family and personal friends."

"The stars will definitely be out tonight," Charlie said. When Matt and CJ appeared at the end of the hall, he added, "Here come a couple of stars now."

"Not me." CJ smoothed the pale-pink fabric of her dress and tilted her head toward her husband. "Matt's the only star in this relationship."

Charlie laughed. "Yeah, like winning an Olympic gold medal doesn't make you famous."

"CJ is just catering to Matt's ego." Amy grinned. "You know how he likes the spotlight."

"He can have it," Charlie said.

"Knock it off." Matt shook his head even as he fought back a grin. "We all know Dad's the star of the show."

"We should let him enjoy it while it lasts," Charlie said. "Once the country gets to know mom better, she's going to be running this place."

"Looks like she already is." Amy waved at the doorway that led to her parents' new bedroom. Her mother had stepped into the hall to speak with the Secret Service agent stationed there.

She gave a satisfied nod before turning to them. "Oh good, you're all here." She focused on CJ. "Are the kids okay?"

"Yes. They're having a wonderful time playing with the babysitter in Kailey's room upstairs."

"Is Dad ready?" Amy asked.

"He'll be right out." Her mom put her hand on Amy's back, and her other hand on Charlie's arm. Her eyes focused on Matt as though to make sure everyone received her attention at the same time. "Are you all ready for this?"

"As ready as we'll ever be," Matt said.

Amy's dad walked into the hall, both of his hands lifted to straighten his bow tie.

Her mom turned and shook her head. "Your tie was just fine before you started playing with it again."

"This sounds familiar," Brent said under his breath.

Amy lifted an eyebrow. "I didn't say anything about your tie."

"No, you just fixed it for me."

In a replay of the scene that had just occurred in Amy and Brent's bedroom, her mom straightened her dad's tie.

They all gathered around their parents and waited for the signal that it was time for their grand entrance.

"Okay. This is it." Her dad took her mom's hand and tucked it into the crook of his arm.

They all fell into step behind the new president and first lady.

When they neared the elevator, Matt glanced over his shoulder. "I heard there's a basketball court somewhere here at the White House. Maybe we can slip out early and play a game or two."

"Charlie's still recovering from the last game," Amy said.

"We'll play two on two," Charlie said. "I get Brent on my team."

"Oh, no." Brent shook his head. "If you think I'm going to play against my wife, you have another thing coming."

"You aren't afraid of her, are you?"

"Charlie, the big difference between you and me is that I'm intelligent enough to be afraid of her."

Amy slipped her hand around Brent's waist. "You are such a smart man."

Brent nodded. "It's why you married me."

Amy reached up and kissed his cheek. "It's one of many reasons."

"I'll see you down there." Brent pressed the button for the elevator. As soon as the doors slid open, he stepped inside so he could avoid the crowd at the base of the stairs.

Charlie offered Amy his arm. "Looks like you're stuck with me."

"Worse things could happen." Amy tucked her hand through the crook of her brother's arm.

"You sure you don't want to shoot some hoops tonight?"

"It's January."

"So?"

Amy broke the bad news. "The basketball court is outside."

Charlie hesitated a half second before he gave her a definitive nod of his head. "Then we'll play tomorrow."

She laughed. "Fine. We'll play tomorrow."

* * *

The hotel ballroom glittered, from the chandeliers overhead to the shimmering ballgowns and sleek tuxedos the occupants wore.

Brent's hand found Amy's, and he nodded to the already crowded dance floor. "Shall we?"

Her face radiated when she tilted her head to look at him. "I'd like that."

Brent led her to an open space and slipped his arms around her. Cameras flashed, and he fought the urge to duck out of sight. He had to trust Jim's press secretary to keep the spotlight where it belonged, which was anywhere but on him and his men. His gaze swept the room, and he caught sight of the guardian who had driven them to Jim's house last night. Maybe he wasn't the only one staying out of the limelight tonight.

The heir to the throne of Meridia waltzed past, his wife in his arms. Directly beyond him was actor Reed Forrester and his wife. A short distance away, Matt and CJ chatted with a recent Baseball Hall of Fame inductee.

Brent couldn't help but smile. With the star power in this room, the likelihood that the photographers would zero in on him fell into the less-than-average category. Only his association with Amy would put him on anyone's radar.

Amy tilted her head, and an inquisitive spark lit her eyes. "What are you smiling at?"

"Just thinking that unless someone is taking a photo of you, I don't need to worry about being noticed."

"That's funny."

"What is?"

She trailed her hand up to his neck to bring his head closer to hers. Then she lowered her voice and whispered in his ear, "These people have no idea that you're the most important man here."

The familiar jolt of attraction shot through him. "I think your dad gets that distinction tonight."

"Okay, you're one of the top two," Amy conceded. "Don't tell my brothers I said that."

"Afraid they'll take it out on you on the basketball court?"

"No. I'm afraid Charlie will march down to the national zoo and find some ridiculously ugly toad to put in my bed."

"I would think he's outgrown such pranks."

"One would hope."

The song ended, and Brent reluctantly released Amy, his hand linking with hers once more.

A short distance away, Jim stood with the secretary of the navy and Admiral Moss.

Jim waved for Brent and Amy to join them.

"We're being summoned," Amy said.

Together they crossed the short distance to join the three men.

"Have the two of you met my daughter?" Jim asked his companions.

"I don't think so." The secretary extended his hand. "Connor Hartley."

"Amy Whitmore." Amy shook his hand before motioning to Brent. "And this is Commander Brent Miller."

The introductions and handshakes were repeated with Admiral Moss.

"I'm surprised you're not in uniform this evening," Admiral Moss said.

"The president and I decided it would be best if I didn't draw attention to myself tonight," Brent said.

"Brent and my daughter actually work for the two of you in a roundabout way," Jim said.

"Oh, really?" Secretary Hartley asked.

"We're both with SEAL Team Eight," Brent said.

"You're a SEAL?" Admiral Moss asked Brent.

"Yes, sir."

Admiral Moss shifted his focus to Amy. "And what is your role?"

"I'm the intelligence officer for Commander Miller's unit."

"Then you must have already met my nephew. He took over command of SEAL Team Eight just this past week."

"Yes, sir." Amy's dry tone did little to hide her sarcasm. "We are well-acquainted."

"How's he doing down there?" Admiral Moss asked. "I know he has some big plans with shaking things up in the teams."

"Well, sir, there's a word for his performance so far." Amy paused and leaned closer. "But I'm afraid I don't use that kind of language."

Jim reached out and put his hand on Amy's arm. "Honey, there are a few more people you need to meet." Jim nodded at the secretary of the navy. "We'll chat later."

Jim whisked Amy away to speak with a cluster of women who were all dripping in diamonds.

"Am I to infer Miss Whitmore doesn't approve of my nephew's changes?"

"Yes, sir." Brent forced himself to speak the truth. "I'm afraid none of us do."

Before Admiral Moss could respond, Secretary Hartley asked, "How is it that you were invited tonight? Are you and Miss Whitmore dating?"

Brent glanced in Amy's direction, not sure how to answer.

Admiral Moss saved him from making a response. "I can only imagine your friendship with the president's daughter will complicate your role as a SEAL."

"Amy is worth the effort."

"I thought I heard somewhere that all the president's children were married," Secretary Hartley said.

Brent could sidestep the truth, but he wasn't prone to lying unless it was mission-essential. "All his children are married." Brent lifted his left hand, where his wedding band encircled his ring finger. "I'm Amy's husband."

The secretary's eyebrows lifted. "The president's son-in-law is a navy SEAL?"

"Yes, sir."

"This really could complicate things," Secretary Hartley said.

"It doesn't have to," Brent said. "Very few people take the time to learn Amy is married, much less who she's married to."

"It's only a matter of time," Admiral Moss said. "Your association with the president makes you a potential hostage risk."

Brent understood the concern, but he couldn't take the time to dwell on what might happen when he was behind enemy lines. More often than not, positive thoughts and diligent preparation led to positive outcomes. "Any navy SEAL is a potential hostage risk when we're outside our borders."

"Yes, but if the world knows your face. . ." Admiral Moss trailed off when Craig and Sienna approached.

"Sorry to interrupt." Sienna put a hand on Brent's arm. "We're getting ready to leave for the next party."

"You're Sienna Blake." Admiral Moss opened his mouth, closed it, and stumbled to speak again. "I'm a huge fan."

"Thank you so much, Admiral." Sienna graciously extended her hand. "It's a pleasure to meet you."

Brent introduced Sienna to the secretary of the navy and turned to Craig. "This is Petty Officer Simmons. He's a member of my squad."

"Wait." Admiral Moss held up a hand. "You're married to the first daughter." He shifted his gaze from Brent to Craig. "And you're dating the star of *Beachfront?*"

"Guilty," Craig said, playing along with the assumption. He lowered his voice and added, "But that information is still need-to-know."

"How is it that I didn't know this?" Admiral Moss asked.

Secretary Hartley chuckled. "Admiral, you of all people should know our SEALs are trained in many disciplines, including intelligence. Clearly, these men excel in the art of keeping a secret."

Brent couldn't have said it better himself. "It was nice meeting both of you." Brent nodded at both men and stepped back. "Enjoy the rest of your evening."

Sienna led the way to where the rest of their squad hovered near Jim and Katherine.

"I guess it's only a matter of time before Gardner finds out he missed the boat," Craig said. "If he wanted to advance his career, staying on Amy's good side could have worked wonders for him. Assuming he knew how to do his job well."

"Gardner didn't miss the boat," Brent countered. "He was never on it."

22

Jim fastened his cuff links and slipped on his suit jacket. His first full day of being president and he was going to church. *Keep the Sabbath Day holy.* The words replayed through his mind and battled against his doubts.

Katherine emerged from the bathroom. Their bathroom. This was their house now.

She picked up her purse and asked, "Are you ready to go?"

"Am I going to get blasted by the media for demonstrating that our religion is our top priority so soon after taking office?"

"I can't think of a better way to begin this journey," Katherine said. "The Lord put us here. Seems to me, going to church and expressing our gratitude is exactly how we should start this presidency."

"When you put it that way . . ."

She leaned in and kissed him. "Come on. We have new friends to meet."

"Too bad we can't have the guardians sneak us into a ward in some obscure part of the city where no one knows us."

"We can do that next week," Katherine said. "I doubt the Secret Service will approve of us going to the same place every week."

"This is going to take a lot of getting used to."

"Yes, it is." She moved to the door and opened it. A Secret Service agent stood just outside the room. "Good morning. I don't think I've met you yet."

"I'm Dylan, ma'am."

"It's nice to meet you, Dylan." Katherine continued into the hall.

Jim followed.

Dylan lifted his arm and spoke into the microphone at his wrist. "Valiant is moving."

"Do you want me to check on the kids?" Katherine asked Jim.

The thud of footsteps on stairs preceded Kailey rushing into the hallway followed by Spencer and Aiden.

"The grandchildren are ready," Jim said.

By the time Matt and CJ caught up to their children, Spencer had reached Charlie and Kendra's door. He lifted his little fist and pounded. "Uncle Charlie!"

The door swung open, but it was Kendra who stood on the other side of the threshold, not Charlie.

"Hey there, kiddo." Kendra squatted so she was on Spencer's level. "Do you want to help Uncle Charlie get ready?"

Spencer nodded.

"Great. Go get him." Kendra stepped aside and let Spencer into her room. She came out into the hall. "I've been telling him for ten minutes that it's time to go. Maybe a four-year-old will have better luck getting him out the door."

Jim laughed. "Charlie never has been a fan of early church."

"Which is crazy because he has no problem getting up early for work," Kendra said.

Matt reached Charlie's doorway. "I don't think Mom and Dad ever should have told him that Sunday is supposed to be a day of rest. He takes it way too literally."

"I'm coming, I'm coming." Charlie appeared in the doorway, one shoe on his foot, the other under his arm, and his hand caught firmly in his nephew's as Spencer dragged him into the hall.

"Spencer's good," Katherine said.

"That he is." Matt ruffled his oldest son's hair.

Vanessa and Seth emerged from the stairwell with their baby in tow at the same time Brent and Amy came out of their room.

"Is everyone ready?" Katherine asked.

"Let me put my shoe on." Charlie dropped his shoe and worked his foot into it.

After Charlie finished tying his laces, Jim turned to Dylan. "I assume we're good to go."

"Yes, Mr. President."

The formal address struck Jim, a jarring reminder of his new reality. "This new title is going to take some getting used to."

Amy stepped forward and put her hand on his arm. "Don't worry. We won't forget to call you Dad."

"That's a relief." Jim noted the lack of color in his daughter's face. "Are you feeling okay?"

"Just tired after last night," Amy said.

"I think everyone is wiped out after so many parties," Matt said. "Ten inauguration balls? That was crazy."

"I agree." Jim headed for the stairwell.

Following the path dictated by his Secret Service detail, he and Katherine walked to one of the many exits and climbed into the back of the limo with Charlie and Kendra.

As soon as the others were safely in their vehicles, the agent in the front seat gave the okay for the motorcade to proceed.

"How far is the church building from here?" Kendra asked.

"About twenty minutes."

"Has anyone warned the bishop that we're coming?" Kendra asked.

"I asked our old bishop to give him a call, but with everything going on, I didn't follow up on that," Jim said.

"We spoke with him," Dylan said from the front seat. "He asked to meet with you immediately after church."

"Good. It will be nice to get to know him," Jim said.

"You sure this is just a meet and greet?" Charlie asked. "Maybe the bishop wants you to teach Sunday School or something."

Teaching a bunch of teenagers about the scriptures while a couple of Secret Service agents stood in the back of the classroom didn't sound like Jim's idea of a good time. "Church is going to be very interesting over the next few years."

Katherine put her hand on his knee. "Yes, it is."

* * *

Seth wanted this. Over the past several days, the wonder of interviewing for a position at the White House had faded into a deep desire to work with the president. And not just any president. Jim Whitmore had the potential to be the greatest president of his era. Seth wanted to enjoy a front-row seat as the man made history.

The fact that Seth and Vanessa had been invited to stay at the White House for the past two nights drove home how surreal their lives had already become.

In the crib on the far side of their third-floor guest room, Talia babbled happily while her chubby little hands squeezed her favorite doll.

Seth buttoned up his uniform and turned to face Vanessa.

"Are you ready?" She smoothed the lapels of his uniform.

"I hope so."

Vanessa stepped back, and her gaze met his. "You aren't just doing this for me, are you?"

"No. I'm doing this for me too." Seth leaned down and kissed her. "We can both help Jim make a difference."

"That's exactly how I feel." Vanessa smiled. "Maybe tomorrow we can start looking at houses up here."

"I don't know."

"We can rent," Vanessa said quickly.

"I'm not crazy about renting out our place," Seth said. "We've put so much effort into building a top security system. We let someone else live there, and we have to tip our hand as to what we have in place."

"Not necessarily."

Seth caught the gleam in his wife's eyes. "What are you thinking?"

"Damian and Paige still need a place to live. We could rent our house to them," Vanessa said. "That would give them two more years to save up for a house of their own."

"They have to be out of their place by the end of February. We probably wouldn't move until at least April."

"So we let them take the basement until then," Vanessa suggested.

"That would take the pressure off them to find a new place, especially since we'll likely have to deploy again in the next few weeks."

"Morenta?"

Seth nodded. "I don't know what he's up to, but it can't be good."

"With that man, it never is."

A knock sounded on their door.

Seth opened it to find Matt standing in the hall.

"CJ and I are taking the kids out to explore the grounds a bit. We thought you might want to join us."

"I have an interview to get to, but Vanessa might want to come."

"It sounds like fun." Vanessa stepped forward. "How cold is it outside?"

"Way warmer than yesterday." Matt pretended to shiver. "I was missing Florida during my dad's speech Saturday."

"At least he kept it short," Seth said.

"Let me get a blanket for Talia and put her coat on." Vanessa moved deeper into the room and returned a moment later holding the baby and a blanket.

"I'd better get going," Seth said. "If my interview doesn't take too long, I'll catch up with you afterward."

"Sounds good." Vanessa leaned in for a kiss. "Good luck."

"Thanks." Seth pressed his lips to the top of Talia's head before taking the stairs.

He had to stop and ask directions only twice before he found his way to the Secret Service agent who guarded the entrance by the East Reception Room.

"I'm Seth Johnson. I'm here for an interview with Commander Engel."

The agent's eyes swept over Seth's uniform. "Where's your badge?"

Seth reached into his pocket and withdrew the visitor badge that allowed him to move about the White House without an escort.

The agent took the badge, examined it, and handed it back. "You can either wait in the reception room or in the hall outside the military aides' office. They're interviewing someone else right now."

"I'll just wait by the office."

The agent granted him entrance through the door by his desk, and Seth stepped into the long hallway. The door closed behind him, and he took a moment to settle the nerves and excitement battling inside him. He drew a deep breath. He was in a part of the White House few people ever saw. He had stayed the night in a guest room where only a select few had ever slept.

A silent prayer rose within him. He wanted this job that only a few people ever held.

23

BRENT STRETCHED OUT HIS ARM only to find the space in bed beside him empty and cold. He forced his eyes open and pushed up on his elbow.

Sunlight streamed through the tall windows on the far side of the room, and Amy sat at the antique writing desk beneath the closest one.

"What time is it?" Brent rubbed a hand over his face to clear the sleep from his brain.

"Twenty after nine."

Brent sat up. "Seriously?"

"You needed the sleep."

He swung his legs over the side of the bed and crossed to her. He settled his hands on her shoulders and began kneading. "What are you working on?"

"I'm doing an analysis of Gardner's proposed changes in the SEAL teams. Ghost managed to email me the full report."

"We're supposed to be on vacation."

"Only for a few more days," Amy said. "I want this analysis in Admiral Rivera's hands the minute I report back to work."

"What really happened while I was gone?" Brent asked.

"I don't want to ruin your leave by talking about it."

"Don't let it ruin your vacation either."

"I'm not."

"Amy, you're doing an analysis when you could be exploring your parents' new home. And not just any new home." Brent squeezed her shoulders one last time and stepped to her side so he could see her better. "We're in the White House. Your whole family is here. Let's enjoy this time together."

"I know, but I won't have time to do this once we get back to the office."

Brent leaned against the wall beside her. "Tell me what happened while I was gone."

Amy sighed. "Gardner is worse than I thought." She relayed the events at work, including the disconnected telephones and the limited access to intelligence reports.

"I'm so sorry," Brent said. "Even I didn't think he would stoop low enough to impact our operational readiness."

"I've never been so frustrated in my life as when I got the intel on the Z-10 helicopter at the fortress and couldn't call to tell anyone."

Brent pushed away from the wall. "You're the one who sent that intel?"

"Yeah. I had to call Vanessa on my cell phone and have her pass the intel to you since I didn't have any other way to get it out."

"When did you find it?"

"You were already midmission," Amy said, "but if I hadn't been taking care of Kaminski and Webb, I would have gone over that report hours earlier."

"This guy could have gotten us killed."

"I know." Amy stood and slipped her arms around him as though reaffirming that he was indeed alive and here. "I had a couple restless nights waiting for word."

"Waiting for word without a work phone or full intel access."

"Yes."

Brent pulled her tight. "I'm sorry."

"I'm sorry you went in underprepared."

"Once we report this up the chain of command, Gardner won't be able to mess with us anymore. No one is going to stand for this kind of deliberate sabotage against our own personnel."

"I hope you're right," Amy said.

"If we have to, we'll pull your dad into it." He pressed a kiss to her forehead. "For now, we're on vacation. It's time to relax a bit."

Amy's lips curved. "Charlie did mention something about basketball."

"I say we can take him and Matt."

"Oh yeah."

* * *

Seth waited outside the room where his interview would be held. He tried to remember the last time he had sat across from a potential employer, his memory stretching all the way back to his job at a grocery store during college.

The store manager had asked, "Can you lift at least fifty pounds?" Seth had merely nodded, which had resulted in the manager immediately declaring, "You're hired."

Was it too much to hope this interview would follow a similar pattern?

The office door opened, and two naval officers walked out. Seth fought the urge to bristle when he identified the one wearing a red visitor badge as Commander Bailey. The man had crossed paths with Seth only twice, but both times, the other man's arrogance had caused problems for the Saint Squad, the most recent of which had nearly come to blows when Seth had learned Bailey had neglected to pass updated satellite images to the squad.

The commander Seth didn't know stepped forward. "I'm Ted Engel. You must be Lieutenant Johnson."

Seth nodded. "Yes, sir."

"Johnson." Commander Bailey gave him a terse nod. "I didn't expect to see you here."

Seth ignored the sneer in the other man's voice and chose not to respond.

"Go on in," Commander Engel said. "I need to walk Commander Bailey out to security."

Bailey shot Seth a condescending look, but the purpose behind it eluded Seth. Did this guy think he had nailed his interview and already had the job? Or did he assume his higher rank would make him a better fit?

The two men continued down the hall, and Seth knocked on the open door.

"Come on in." Someone called from inside.

Seth stepped through the doorway. He had expected his interview to be conducted in a conference room or a traditional office. This cramped space with desks pushed against every available wall shattered that image.

Four of the five current military aides sat in the room, all of their office chairs situated loosely in a circle in the limited space in the center of the room.

All four men rose and introduced themselves. Captain Lance Howarth, US Army, Captain Kendrick Guevera, US Marines, Commander Preston Davies, US Coast Guard, and Lieutenant Commander Heath Warren, US Air Force.

The Marine captain motioned to one of the two empty chairs. "Have a seat, Lieutenant."

Seth nodded and lowered himself into his chair as the others reclaimed their seats.

"Where are you currently serving?" Captain Guevera reached out and retrieved a file off the desk behind him.

"Virginia Beach. SEAL Team Eight."

As Guevera opened Seth's personnel file, Commander Engel walked in and closed the door behind him. He rolled the only empty chair closer to him. "It seemed as though you knew Commander Bailey."

Seth kept his voice neutral. "We've crossed paths."

"What do you think of him as an officer?" Lt. Commander Warren asked.

"Like I said, we've crossed paths." Seth met Warren's gaze. "I've never served with him."

The other five men exchanged a look that appeared to have meaning, but Seth didn't have the context to translate what it was.

"Tell us about yourself," Guevera said.

"Not much to tell beyond what's in my file."

Commander Engel leaned back in his chair and laughed. "Told you."

Seth's eyebrows drew together as he continued to miss out on what was clearly a private joke.

Captain Howarth waved a hand at Engel. "Ted said you weren't the type to blow your own horn."

"No point in telling you what you already know."

"Then, tell us something we don't know," Engel suggested. "You've been with your squad for most of your naval career. Why are you looking to change?"

"I wasn't," Seth admitted. "I love my squad, but the chance to support this president, to aid in positive history unfolding, that's something worth making a detour for."

"A detour," Howarth said. "Does that mean you intend to return to your squad after you finish your tour here?"

Seth couldn't imagine going anywhere else. Despite the ripple of uncertainty that tangled in his gut, he nodded. "That would be my preference."

"You realize that serving as the military aide to the president opens doors, right?" Commander Davies asked.

"He's right," Engel said. "I've practically been given my choice of assignments."

"Where are you going next?" Seth asked.

"I'll be working with the joint chiefs."

The interview continued, the questions shifting from probing to conversational.

As minutes passed, the roles reversed, and instead of answering questions, Seth asked them. What were their days like? What did their duties entail? Did they have time to maintain their training and military qualifications?

The last question brought a grin to Engel's face. Engel looked around the room, his eyes asking a silent question. Each man nodded.

"Looks like you're in," Engel said.

"I'm in?" Seth repeated. "I got the job?"

"We've conducted nineteen interviews so far, and you're the first person who is as concerned about maintaining your operational readiness as you are in understanding the job."

"You do want the job, don't you?" Warren asked.

A fleeting doubt shot through Seth only to dissipate beneath the certainty that this was where he was supposed to be. Seth nodded. "Yes. I want the job."

"Great." Warren closed Seth's file. "Normally, we don't have our new guys report until late spring or early summer, but Engel over there is anxious to start in his new job. How would you feel about starting in two weeks?"

"Two weeks?" Seth's eyebrows rose. "That's not a lot of time to find housing."

"I know it's quick, but we should be able to get you temporary lodging for a few weeks if you need it," Engel said. "With the new administration coming on board, the joint chiefs want me in place as soon as possible."

Seth's mind spun through his housing options. Under normal circumstances, he could have asked to stay with the Whitmores, but he wasn't sure that was the best plan now that their address had changed. Then again, Jim did want Vanessa working for him as soon as possible. Maybe he would be okay with Seth and Vanessa staying at their old house for a couple of weeks.

"What do you say?" Engel asked.

"I can make that happen."

Engel's posture relaxed. "Excellent."

Howarth stood and extended his hand. "Welcome aboard."

"Thank you, sir."

"We're going to be spending a lot of time together. Call me Lance," he said. "Oh, and one more thing."

"What's that?" Seth asked.

"We took a sneak peek at the promotion list." Lance grinned. "Congratulations, Lieutenant Commander Johnson."

A new job *and* a promotion. "I made the list?"

"That you did." Engel picked up a stack of papers. "Come on. Let's get the paperwork out of the way. You can use my desk. It'll be yours soon enough."

Seth accepted the paperwork and stood. "Anything else I need to do to put the transfer in motion?"

"Not from the administrative end," Engel said, "but you'd better prepare yourself for when you start this job."

"How so?" Seth asked.

"Everyone you've ever known will want a tour of the White House."

Seth fought back a grin. "Somehow, I don't think that will be a problem."

24

Jim settled behind his desk in the Oval Office and soaked in the moment. He was here, in the White House, and he was the president of the United States.

This morning, he had already gone through his daily briefing with his transitional staff members. Congress would begin the confirmation hearings today for his cabinet members, but he suspected those would move more quickly than even Congress expected. The men and women Jim had selected with the help of his vice president and trusted advisers were individuals above reproach. In most cases, he had steered clear of politicians, choosing instead individuals he knew and trusted personally.

His office door opened, and his personal aide popped her head inside. "Sir, Mr. Valdez is here to see you."

Doug? He was supposed to be sitting in front of the Homeland Security and Governmental Affairs Committee this morning. "Thank you, Sarah," Jim said. "Please show him in."

Sarah pushed the door wide, and Doug stepped inside.

"I thought your confirmation hearing was supposed to be today. What happened?"

"I'm already done."

"You're done?" Jim glanced at the grandfather clock across the room. "It's only one o'clock."

"I guess they ran out of questions."

"It went well, then." Jim motioned to the seat across from him.

"I think so. Their questions were all pretty predictable," Doug said. "And you were right. They did ask about my daughters."

"I thought they might," Jim said.

Though Doug had two teenage daughters, one had been adopted after she had fallen under Doug's protection. The other, while Doug and his wife technically had only parental rights, had joined their family under similar circumstances.

"Did the committee give you any indication of when they're starting their deliberations?" Jim asked.

"After lunch."

"That's good. With any luck, we'll have you in place by the end of the week."

"Let's hope," Doug said. "The sooner we get out of this transitional phase, the better."

"I agree. Right now, I'm feeling a bit defenseless."

"Hopefully your appointee for secretary of defense will cruise through as easily as I did."

"I wouldn't count on it. No one makes it through as fast as you just did."

"Assuming fast means good, I brought this for you." Doug handed a file folder to Jim. "These are the appointees I have in mind for the Department of Homeland Security."

Jim scanned the list. "We've already talked about most of these."

"I shuffled a few around, but only a couple of the names have changed."

"I assume you've vetted everyone on this list."

"Absolutely."

"I'll give this to Sawyer," Jim said, referring to his chief of staff. "As soon as you're confirmed, he can start working on getting these approved."

"Thank you." Doug stood. His gaze drifted to the windows leading onto the south lawn. "Looks like the grandkids are making themselves at home."

Jim turned, and his smile was instant. Matt crossed the lawn with Aiden on his shoulders. CJ walked beside him while their older two kids raced around the fountain.

Vanessa pushed Talia in the stroller Jim and Katherine always kept in the garage at home. His wife had made the right choice in adding that to the items to bring with them to the White House.

Doug motioned to the french door that led outside. "Do you mind if I go out that way? I'd love to say hi to Matt and CJ."

"Go ahead." Jim focused on Vanessa. "While you're at it, can you ask Vanessa if she has a minute to chat with me? I'm sure CJ can watch her baby for a few minutes."

"No problem." Doug walked outside, a blast of cool air entering during the brief time the door was open.

A short conversation ensued between Vanessa and CJ before Vanessa leaned over the stroller and tucked a blanket more firmly around her daughter. Then Vanessa made her way to the Oval Office.

Jim stood and opened the door for her.

"Mr. President." Her lips quirked up as she greeted him.

"Did you all enjoy checking out our new yard?"

"We did."

Jim closed the door and motioned her to the center of the room. He waited for her to sit on one of the couches before he sat on the one across from her.

"Have you given any more thought to my offer?"

"I have. If Seth gets the position as your military aide, I want the job."

"Has he already had his interview?" Jim asked.

Vanessa glanced at the grandfather clock on the far wall. "I thought he would be done by now."

Jim's eyes strayed to the lawn where CJ was now pushing the stroller. As though on cue, Seth appeared from the mansion and started across the lawn. "There he is now."

Jim stood and opened the door leading outside. He motioned to the Secret Service agent stationed nearby. "Can you please let Lieutenant Johnson know I need to speak with him?"

"Yes, Mr. President."

Trusting the message to get passed to Seth, Jim closed the door and returned to his seat.

"Looks like you're settling into the new job well enough."

"I'll feel better when all of our key personnel are in place." Jim settled back on the couch. "Including you."

Knuckles rapped against glass. Jim waved at Seth, who now stood on the other side of the door.

He walked inside. "You wanted to see me, sir?"

"It's just us. You can call me Jim."

"It may be best if I practice calling you sir or Mr. President," Seth said.

Vanessa's eyebrows lifted. "You got the job?"

"I did." Seth grinned. "And I made the promotion list."

Vanessa jumped up and hugged him. "Congratulations."

"Thanks." Seth returned his wife's embrace before releasing her.

Jim stood and shook Seth's hand. "Congratulations, Seth. I can't tell you how happy I am that I'll have the two of you working with me." Jim waved at the couch. "Please, sit down." They all took their seats. "I'm surprised you already found out you got the position."

"I am too," Seth said, "but I think one reason for the quick decision is that the man I'm replacing wants to rotate out early."

"How soon do you report?" Vanessa asked.

"Two weeks." Seth's eyes lit with apology. "I'm sorry. I know that's way faster than we expected."

"We'll make it work," Vanessa said. "Housing is going to be a challenge, but we'll figure something out."

"Interesting you should bring that up," Jim said. "I have a proposition for you."

"What's that?" Vanessa asked.

"How would you feel about house-sitting for us for the next couple years?"

Vanessa's eyes widened. "Live at your house?"

"That's right." Jim leaned forward. "Katherine and I don't want to rent it out, and we really aren't crazy about having to board our horses."

"We can't just live there for free." Seth shook his head. "That's too much."

"It wouldn't exactly be for free. You would pay all the utilities, and we would ask you to care for the horses as part of our agreement to let you stay there," Jim said. "We also don't want to have to store our furniture, so you can decide if you want to use ours and store what you have or if you would rather move some of ours down to our basement while you're living there."

"This sounds too good to be true," Vanessa said.

"We were talking about letting Damian and Paige rent our place if we got the jobs up here," Seth said. "Maybe we can store our furniture in our basement and only bring what we need for Talia."

"I'll let you work out the details with Katherine," Jim said. "Assuming you want to take us up on our offer."

Vanessa and Seth exchanged a look before they both nodded and answered in unison. "Yes."

* * *

Seth unlocked the front door and walked into Jim and Katherine's home. Despite the lack of the usual occupants, the house looked and felt the same. Granted, the smell wasn't quite right, but a batch of those refrigerated cinnamon rolls would come in as a close second to the scents that normally wafted through the air here.

Vanessa juggled Talia in her arms, and Seth closed the door behind them. They made it only a few steps inside before a voice rang out from the living room.

"You cheated!" Damian broke into a string of Spanish before he reverted back to English again. "I saw you mess with the dice."

"Can you prove it?" Jay asked.

Paige's calm voice cut through the tension. "Why did we agree to play with them again?"

"Because we were trying to keep them from using the Whitmores' backyard for shooting practice," Carina said.

Seth stepped forward. "Do you need a referee?"

"No," Jay said.

"Yes," Damian insisted at the same time.

Paige and Carina looked at each other. "Maybe."

"What are you playing anyway?" Vanessa asked.

"Parcheesi."

"He's been blocking me the whole game." Damian waved at Jay with an irritated gesture.

"It's part of the game."

Seth debated how Brent would handle the typical squabbling. He opted for the distraction technique. "What are all of you doing over here anyway? Damian, I thought you were staying at Quinn's parents' house."

"We were, but the president said we could stay here once everyone moved over to the White House. More room."

"Enjoy it while we can," Paige said. "Starting tomorrow, you have to help me start looking at rentals."

Damian groaned.

"We wanted to talk to you about that." Vanessa set down her baby bag and retrieved a blanket.

"About what?" Paige asked.

"Your housing situation." Vanessa spread the blanket out one-handed and set Talia on top of it. She dug a few toys from the baby bag and set them beside their daughter. "How would you feel about staying at our house?"

"Where are you going to be living?" Carina asked.

"Seth and I both got jobs up here."

"You're the new military aide to the president?" Jay asked.

"I am," Seth said.

Vanessa's face lit up with a smile. "And he made Lieutenant Commander."

"I can't believe it." Jay pushed to his feet and slapped Seth on the back. "Congrats, man."

"Thanks." Some of the tension that had built inside him eased. Leaving the squad wouldn't be easy, but he hoped the rest of his teammates would be as encouraging as Jay.

"It's not going to be the same without you," Damian said. "*Buena suerte.*"

"Thanks."

"How soon are you moving?" Paige asked.

"Two weeks."

Paige's eyebrows lifted. "That's fast. Are you going to try for some kind of military housing up here?"

"Actually, we'll be living here."

Damian let out a whistle. "I knew the Whitmores were good people, but wow."

"Wow is right," Seth agreed. "So, what do you think? Do you want to house-sit our place while we're up here?"

They chatted about details, what to do with their excess furniture and which expenses Damian and Paige would cover while living in Seth and Vanessa's house.

Talia stood and took several steps. Vanessa reached out and grabbed their daughter around the stomach to keep her from toddling away.

"Babyproofing this house is going to be an adventure," Vanessa said.

Seth stood. "Let's go decide which room is going to be our daughter's."

"You go explore," Paige said. "We can watch Talia."

"You sure?"

"There are four of us," Jay said. "I think we can handle one baby."

Vanessa simply cocked an eyebrow.

Carina shooed them toward the stairs. "We'll be fine. I'll babysit the men. Paige will watch Talia."

Seth chuckled and put his hand on Vanessa's back. They reached the stairs, and Vanessa walked into Jim's office.

"I could work from here most of the time."

"There's enough room to put a playpen in the corner," Seth said.

Vanessa turned back to face him. "Is this real? Are we really going to be living here?"

"It feels like we stepped into someone else's lives, doesn't it?"

"It really does." Vanessa slipped her arms around his waist. "Are you sure about all this?"

"Every time I pray about it, it feels right."

"I know." Vanessa pulled him closer. "It's going to be hard being away from our friends."

"Do you think Jim already told Brent?"

"We'll find out soon enough," Vanessa said. "We're all invited to the White House for a movie night."

"Somehow, I don't think Talia is going to care about watching a movie."

"Maybe not, but how many people can say that their first visit to a movie theater was in the White House?"

"I believe our daughter will be one of a very select few."

"Yes, she will."

* * *

Basketball against her brothers. A walk around the grounds with Brent. Lunch with her mom. A tour of the West Wing. An impromptu promotion ceremony for Seth in the Oval Office. Now a movie night with the rest of the Saint Squad and their families. Amy rather liked her father's current situation.

She settled back in her seat beside Brent and took in her surroundings. Red walls broken up by strips of paneling. Plush chairs arranged on risers so everyone in the miniature theater would have a clear view and be comfortable while enjoying whatever was playing on the screen.

Her niece and nephews had opted for front-row seats with her mom and dad. They were one seat short, but Aiden had remedied that problem by crawling onto her mom's lap.

Amy glanced behind her, where a Secret Service agent currently stood. Tristan's son, Dixon, stood up on his seat, and Riley put a hand out to hold him in place. A baby whimpered, but Amy couldn't tell if it was Riley's little one or Taylor's. The two sisters had opted to sit in the back in the event that their babies wouldn't let them sit through the whole movie.

Vanessa and Seth approached, Talia snuggled in Seth's arms, her eyes closed.

Brent moved over, and Amy followed suit so Seth could claim the aisle seat. Vanessa took the spot beside Amy.

"Where have you been today?" Amy asked. "I haven't seen you at all."

"After Seth's interview this morning, we went over to your parents' house."

"Making sure Jay and Damian are playing nice?" Amy asked.

"That too," Vanessa said, "but mostly we wanted to look around. Your parents offered to let us live there for the next two years."

"What?" Amy leaned forward to look at Seth. "You got the job?"

"We both did," Seth said, his drawl slow and thick. "Are you okay with us living in your old house?"

Vanessa cooking in her mother's kitchen. Seth tending to the horses. By spring, little Talia could be out playing in the yard. Amy smiled. "I'm glad someone will be able to enjoy it while Mom and Dad are here. It's a great place to raise a family."

"What are you doing about your place?" Brent asked.

"Damian and Paige are going to house sit for us," Vanessa said.

"I hope they can find someplace to live short-term until you move up here," Amy said.

"That's the other thing." Seth glanced at Amy before settling his gaze on Brent. "I report to the White House in two weeks."

Brent fell silent for a moment, and Amy didn't doubt he was fighting his emotions. She laid her hand on his knee.

Brent cleared his throat. "You'll be missed."

The muscle in Seth's jaw twitched in a rare show of emotion. He swallowed hard, but rather than speak, he simply nodded.

A new churning worked through Amy. The plan to keep Brent with the Saint Squad had worked, at least for now. They had outwitted Gardner on this particular front. So why did she feel like they had all just lost?

25

BRENT SETTLED INTO THE OFFICE chair by the bedroom window and stared at the peaceful setting beyond. The wide lawn, the circular fountain, the wrought-iron fence in the distance. He was sitting inside the bedroom that would be his and Amy's anytime they came to visit the White House. His father-in-law was president, and life would never be the same.

When Amy had talked about Seth's working here, Brent's focus had been on preserving his squad to the best of his ability. With Seth's announcement last night, Brent had to face the facts: Seth was the heart of the Saint Squad. His loss couldn't be calculated in the operational skills he possessed. His worth went so much deeper than that. Seth was the first to suggest praying before every mission. He was the listening ear, the voice of reason. He was more than Brent's swim buddy. He was his best friend.

Brent's breath backed up in his lungs, a burning sensation spiraling up his throat. He closed his eyes, straightened his back, and drew a slow, steady breath. The numbers one through four echoed through his mind as he breathed in; he repeated the numbers as he held the breath, and then he slowly breathed out. A minute passed into two and then three.

When he opened his eyes, he lowered his gaze to the file Amy had left there. Gardner's plan.

Even though Brent had insisted Amy ignore work during their time off, he couldn't resist flipping open the folder. He had skimmed through the first few pages before his last mission but hadn't had access to go beyond that. He read the report in earnest now.

Reduced civilian personnel, naval officers in intelligence roles, reorganized squads with specialized training. With the exception of shifting civilian positions to military billets, nothing in the report was terribly groundbreaking. Many of the SEAL teams already specialized in either a certain discipline or a certain region of the world. Then there were squads like his who could plug gaps wherever they were needed. Over the years, the Saint Squad had assisted other units with counterterrorism efforts as often as it had worked with its own team. Was that one of the situations Gardner was trying to eliminate?

Someone knocked on the bedroom door.

"Come in." Brent swiveled in his chair, expecting to see one of his in-laws or a niece or nephew. Instead, Seth walked in.

"I'm headed to the gym to work out. Want to come?"

"Sure, but want to help me with something first?" Brent waved at the chair angled in the corner of the room beside the desk.

"What are you working on?" Seth sat and stretched out his long legs.

"I'm reading through Gardner's report. I don't get why he would think this plan of his is so revolutionary."

"There has to be something in there to cause so many personnel changes." Seth reached out his hand. "You're reading the first part. Hand me the last half."

Brent divided the remaining pages of the forty-three-page report into two parts and gave Seth the second section.

The two read in silence for several minutes. Details of unit sizes, officer-to-enlisted ratios, deployment rotations. Nothing pointed at any major changes.

When Seth straightened, Brent looked up. "Did you find something?"

"I think so." Seth stood and set page thirty-eight on the desk. He pointed at the section heading "Reduction of Duties." "He's proposing that the SEALs reduce not only their squad sizes but also the number of platoons."

"Why would he suggest that?"

"On the surface, it looks like it's to save money, but there's got to be more to it than that."

Brent skimmed through the section, the shift in procedures and policies downright terrifying. "He has the SEALs turning all hostage rescue over to the FBI? That means any American taken hostage overseas has no one to help them."

"It's like he doesn't know our job is to protect Americans overseas and make sure threats don't make it past us."

"This isn't just changing policy." Brent held up his half of the report. "This is putting American lives at risk."

"Not only that. He's also advocating for a consolidation of the units under JSOC," Seth said, referring to the Joint Special Operations Command. "He wants to get rid of SEAL Team Ten."

"What?" First, Gardner wanted to take away the SEALs' ability to protect American lives, and now he was suggesting an entire team of SEALs was altogether unnecessary? Did he not understand their role, that SEALs were trained to go into situations when all hope was lost? They were the last line of defense, the men who eliminated deadly situations when the politicians couldn't succeed through diplomatic channels.

"He makes the argument that Delta Force can do everything SEAL Team Ten can do, and by integrating some of the SEALs into Delta Force, they can reduce training and operational costs."

"And significantly cut our response capability."

"I know." Seth dropped back into his chair. "If there's a way to save money and weaken a nation at the same time, this is it."

"It's the saving money that he's banking on. This proposal would save millions in the long run."

"On paper," Seth countered. "It's not cheaper when you're losing American lives because you can't cover all the necessary missions."

"I can't imagine the joint chiefs signing off on this. The secretary of the navy would never agree."

"Unless he listens to his second in command," Seth said. "Gardner's uncle has the secretary's ear."

"That's a scary thought."

"Maybe it's time to make sure our new president knows about this," Seth suggested.

As much as Brent hated to involve Jim, he nodded. "You could be right."

* * *

Jim had received Brent's meeting request hours ago, but with the constant barrage of tasks in his overly full schedule, he hadn't managed a spare minute. A dinnertime conversation hadn't been possible with the grandchildren demanding his attention, and Jim suspected Brent's desired conversation was of the classified variety.

Katherine's schedule must have been equally full because she had requested that the White House chef prepare their meal for tonight. Having that option would be an interesting adjustment for his wife, who always took great joy in creating food for others to enjoy.

With the family now congregating in the living room to play board games, Jim approached Brent. "Sorry I didn't get back to you earlier. It's been quite a day."

"I figured as much." Brent glanced at Seth, who stood near the living room entrance. "Do you have a minute to meet with us now?"

"This may be the best chance we have to chat," Jim said. He headed into the West Reception Room, the living room of sorts located outside his new bedroom. He took in the half-moon window on the far side of the room, only darkness and a few scattered city lights visible now, then sat in an armchair that was more comfortable than it looked.

Seth and Brent positioned themselves on the couch opposite him.

"I really hate to bring my work into your home, but Seth and I came across something concerning today that you need to be aware of," Brent said.

"I'm listening."

"We've had some difficulties with our new commanding officer."

"Amy mentioned something about that," Jim said. "It sounded like he was butting heads with a quite a few people."

"He's doing more than butting heads," Seth said. "He's trying to rewrite how special ops teams function."

"This is a navy commander we're talking about? I seriously doubt he could have much influence in the way the military does business."

"He might not be able to on his own, but with the support of his uncle, it's possible his plans could slip through without everyone recognizing the true impact of what he's doing."

"What is he doing?"

Brent and Seth described the overarching plans Commander Gardner had created, many of them including common-sense, cost-cutting methods. But then Brent said, "It's what's buried inside all of these cost-cutting ideas that we're worried about. He proposes cutting out SEAL Team Ten in addition to eliminating all hostage rescue from the teams."

"The FBI would take over hostage rescue," Seth said, "but Delta Force would be the only one left in the military with that capability."

"That's the one under JSOC, right?" Jim asked.

"Yes. Gardner's logic is that it's rare to need more than one hostage rescue at a time, so we could reduce our costs by only using Delta Force."

"Which is fine as long as we don't have two problems at the same time." Jim said.

"Yes, but we can't count on that. We would be seriously underprepared, and all of our resources would be clustered in one location and in one unit."

"What happens to the SEALs who are on the team he plans to eliminate?" Jim asked. "We'd still need to put them somewhere."

"Since Delta Force accepts members from all the military disciplines, some would likely transfer over there, but most would be reassigned into units that have SEALs who are older than average."

"Like the Saint Squad."

"Yes." Brent nodded. "Even though Seth and I both just hit thirty, most of our squad is in striking distance of it."

"Under Gardner's plan, people like us would be phased out of active combat and start serving as either boat operators or intelligence officers."

"So instead of making the decisions based on the individual's capability, age would become a determining factor." Jim didn't want to think about what the press would do if they got ahold of that tidbit.

"He's prioritizing youth over experience," Brent said. "But more concerning than that, he's proposing to take away one of this country's most effective tools against terrorism."

"Explain to me the differences between Delta Force and the SEAL Teams."

"In many ways, the two have a lot of similarities." Seth slowly offered his explanation. "They can both go into hostile situations, they are trained in hostage rescue and counterterrorism measures, but while the SEALs rely on a unified training regimen to qualify candidates, Delta Force relies on the diversity of its members."

"Sounds like both scenarios could be useful depending on the situation," Jim said.

"Yes. When you need a unit on the high seas, you want the SEALs to be there. We train rigorously for situations in and on the water," Brent said. "On land, it often comes down to which special skills are needed."

"And you're convinced reducing the number of SEAL teams is a bad idea."

"A very bad idea," Brent said.

"Right now, we have units stationed all over the world. We have the ability to insert into multiple hot spots at the same time."

"There's also a huge advantage in training in smaller units," Brent added. "You know your men. You anticipate their actions. You have each other's backs and can make sure you all get out alive."

"You have me convinced, but as much as I'd like to help, I'm not sure inserting myself into military operations during my first week on the job will bode well, especially since I've never served in the armed forces." Jim leaned back in his chair. "I think we need to see how the secretary of the navy reacts when this plan of Gardner's makes it to the top of command. I have to think he will shut it down regardless of who Gardner is related to."

"We hope that's the case, but I don't think we can take the chance," Brent said.

"Let's give the situation a couple weeks to settle. If you get wind that this report is getting approved, let me know, and I'll intervene." Jim pushed to a stand.

Brent and Seth stood as well.

"Thanks, Jim," Brent said. "Or I should say, thank you, Mr. President."

"I'm still not used to being called that."

Seth grinned. "In eight years, you'll have to get used to not being called that."

"Eight years," Jim repeated. "That would be something."

26

AMY APPROACHED HER OFFICE WITH a sense of dread. Her stomach roiled in the same way it did every time she thought of working with Commander Gardner. Even during her time in DC, the mildly nauseous feeling never completely went away. The stress of the changes at work must be affecting her more than she realized.

Too bad she didn't have the guys with her this morning to back her up.

Unfortunately for her, Brent and the rest of his squad had reported first at oh six hundred hours. Thanks to Mei Lien's efforts, they were able to go straight to work on the obstacle course. A session on the shooting range would follow.

For Amy, it was business as usual. At least, she hoped it was. She had no idea if anyone at work had caught sight of her on TV during the inauguration, but she doubted she had managed to go completely unnoticed.

Had Gardner seen her? And if so, would his behavior change for the better or for the worse?

He couldn't get much worse.

Amy reached her office and uttered a silent prayer that her phones and computer access would be available to her today. She dropped her purse on her desk and picked up the phone. A dial tone. Hallelujah!

Amy turned on her computer. Nothing happened.

She leaned down to ensure the computer was plugged into the surge protector. The green light on the surge protector saved her from checking to see if it was plugged into the wall. The power cord was still attached to the back of the computer, but Amy pulled it out and pushed it back in just to be sure. She pressed the Power button again. Still nothing.

Amy dropped into her seat and let out a sigh. She picked up her desk phone and dialed Mei Lien's number. "Hey, Mei Lien, it's Amy."

"Let me guess. Your computer doesn't work."

"Yes." Amy fought back another sigh. "What do you know about it?"

"One of the new transfers had one that crashed on Monday, but he had a new one within a few minutes. It had to come from somewhere."

"So, this isn't even my computer?" Panic rose within her. "I have classified material on my hard drive."

"I'm sorry. It didn't dawn on me where the new computer came from until I heard your voice."

Ideas and solutions competed with Amy's exasperation. "I'll call you back."

"Do you want me to put a work order in for you?"

"That would be great. Thanks."

"I'm really sorry."

"You don't have anything to be sorry about," Amy said. "I appreciate you covering for me while I was gone."

Amy ended the call and retrieved the cell phone Vanessa had given her. She dialed Ghost's number.

He answered on the second ring. "Don't tell me your phone isn't working again."

"It's not my phone. It's my computer." Amy explained what had happened.

"Mishandling classified information, dereliction of duty—this guy is a piece of work."

"I'm not sure I can prove the dereliction of duty, but the piece-of-work part is spot on."

"Hang tight," Ghost said.

"What are you going to do?"

"You'll see."

The phone went dead, and Amy set it down. Resigned to using the tools available to her, she accessed her government email account on her secure cell phone. Time to see what had happened in the world while she had been living at the White House.

* * *

Seth raced toward the next obstacle on the outdoor course. He gripped the knotted rope hanging from the top of the twenty-foot-high wall and planted his first foot. Using a combination of strength and technique, he scaled the wall and then rappelled down the other side.

Brent dropped down beside him. Together they sprinted toward the rope swing. The double row of tires came next.

In front of him, Tristan caught a toe on the edge of a tire, and Quinn reached out to keep him upright. The gesture was so instinctive, the result so expected that Seth doubted either man registered what had just happened. A member of their squad could have gone down, but he didn't because they all worked together to keep each other up.

One challenge after another, he and his teammates worked in tandem.

Seth would miss this.

Tristan and Jay sprinted toward the end of the course, Jay leaning forward so he would cross the finish line first.

The other team members all finished a few steps behind them.

Quinn stopped beside Tristan and leaned over to catch his breath. "Tristan, you're slacking."

"He barely beat me."

"Doesn't matter," Jay puffed out. "I won. You have to pick up lunch today."

"No way. If you hadn't cut me off on the rope swing, I would have beat you."

"Doesn't matter," Jay repeated and shrugged unrepentantly. "You still have to make the lunch run."

The bickering continued. Okay, maybe Seth wouldn't miss *everything* about his squad.

Brent stepped beside him. "Did the mil aides say anything about how soon they were going to cut your new orders?"

"They started the process right after my interview on Monday." Seth caught the look in Brent's eye, the quiet calm that often preceded a storm. "You gearing up for a run-in with Gardner?"

"It's bound to happen," Brent said.

"Assuming Amy hasn't already been called out on the switch we made," Seth said. "I'm sure she's in the office by now."

"We spent a lot of time on our knees last night, asking for guidance on how to deal with Gardner." Brent stretched both arms above him, his hands together as though posed to dive into a pool.

Seth grabbed his ankle and pulled his leg up behind him to stretch out his quad. "You're going to have to put some of that prayer time into deciding what to do about a replacement for me."

"Assuming they give us a replacement. I still haven't seen the final transfer order on Damian either."

Quinn called out, his voice rising over the continued banter going on with the rest of the squad. "Brent, doesn't Tristan have to pick up lunch today?"

"Pick up, yes. Pay for, no." Brent turned back to Seth. "Let's get to the shooting range. We need to give them something else to do."

"Maybe we need to schedule a dive tomorrow," Seth suggested. "It's harder for them to argue underwater."

"Harder." Brent glanced at Jay, who currently had Tristan in a headlock. "But not impossible."

* * *

Amy lowered her phone into her lap when footsteps sounded outside her door. Even though the secure phone would alleviate her from being in violation of security protocols, she didn't want to explain to Commander Gardner how she had come to be in possession of the device.

A man's voice called out, "Delivery for Amy Miller."

Amy swiveled in her chair. A navy commander stood in the doorway. Her jaw dropped when her gaze lifted from the rank insignia on the uniform to the man's face. Ghost.

Before she could ask why he was here, he held out a rectangular box. "You needed a new secure computer?" He phrased the words like a question, as though they hadn't already had this conversation before.

"Yes. I'm surprised you were able to get me one so quickly."

Ghost set the computer on the open space on Amy's desk. He lowered his voice. "Who ended up with your computer?"

"I'm not sure," she whispered.

"Find out."

Amy nodded. She raised her voice to a normal volume. "Can you set it up for me?"

"Sure."

While Ghost opened the box, Amy picked up her phone and called Mei Lien. "I'm sorry to bother you, but can you tell me who ended up with my computer?"

Mei Lien lowered her voice and gave her the name. "Don't go looking for it though. If you do, Gardner will know I'm the one who told you."

"Don't worry," Amy assured her. "I always protect my sources."

As soon as she hung up, Ghost asked, "Did you get it?"

"Yeah." Amy wrote the name on a piece of paper and held it up. "This can't come back to my source."

"It won't." Ghost snatched the paper from her fingers. "Trust me."

He started for the door.

"Where are you going?" Amy asked.

"I'll be back." He motioned to the laptop. "It's all set up. Your password is your dad's birthday. You'll need to change it as soon as you log in and set the biometrics."

"Biometrics?"

Ghost didn't explain any further. He disappeared into the hall, his footsteps fading.

Amy opened the sleek laptop that now lay on her desk. After moving through the setup screen, the biometrics comment explained itself—facial recognition through the webcam, her fingerprint on the mouse pad. Ghost had taken security to a whole new level. No one was going to be able to use this new computer without her help.

Anxious to put her office in order, Amy unhooked the broken computer from the monitor and set the CPU aside for disposal; then she shifted the monitor so it was beside the laptop. She had been asking for a second monitor for months. Maybe Ghost had inadvertently fulfilled that request as well.

She was nearly done setting everything up when Ghost reappeared.

He motioned to her desk. "Let me get in there for a minute."

Amy stood and moved aside.

Ghost pulled a small portable hard drive from his pocket and hooked it to the laptop.

"What is that?"

"All of your files from your old computer."

"How did you get those?"

"Don't ask." He started the file transfer and glanced up. "And if Lieutenant Hopper asks why his computer's hard drive was wiped clean, you don't know anything about it."

"I *don't* know anything about it."

"Good." Ghost finished his task. After he unhooked the portable drive, he stood and pocketed it. "Vanessa has already started her new job, but if you need any backup, give Paige a call."

"As well as you've gotten to know my squad and their families, it feels like we should be on a first-name basis."

"We are." Ghost shrugged. "Kind of."

"Thanks for your help, Ghost." Amy smiled and waved at the laptop. "This is way more than I expected."

"Just make sure you secure it when you're not here." He nodded at the four-drawer safe in the corner. "You don't want it to grow legs and walk away."

"That's good advice."

"One more thing," Ghost said.

"What's that?"

"When personnel informs you that you've received a promotion, turn it down."

"A promotion?"

He moved to the door. "Things aren't always what they seem."

27

UNSETTLED. THAT WAS ONE OF the many words Brent could use to describe the myriad feelings churning inside him. Like the first hint of color in the fall, his world was changing, but he didn't know how to adjust to it.

Had a transfer occurred under Kel, Brent would have sat across from his commanding officer and discussed the best course of action. To do so with Commander Gardner would require a certain degree of trust. It would also require admitting Seth's transfer was imminent. But Brent didn't trust Gardner, and he couldn't muster the appropriate emotions when dealing with the man who had hindered the flow of information during their last mission. He doubted the commander even knew of the significance of his actions or the nearly catastrophic results.

With his squad trailing behind him, Brent headed for Amy's office. He needed to talk out options with a neutral party. At least she was more likely to be objective than his squadmates at the moment.

Brent cast a glance behind him when the grumbling from Tristan started about lunch.

"Just deal with it," Quinn said in his irritated-brother tone.

"You're supposed to be on my side," Tristan shot back.

Brent's lips quirked up. If he didn't know better, he'd swear the two were blood relatives rather than in-laws.

Seth interrupted the fight. "Tristan, go pick up lunch. Quinn, stop stirring the pot."

"He started it," Quinn grumbled.

"What are you? Ten?" Craig asked.

Brent turned and held up his hand before the next battle could begin. "Craig, Damian, check on the surveillance from the fortress and the hideout. Jay and Quinn, I want a new analysis of the surveillance photos from the area. We need to be ready in case we have to insert again."

Tristan headed for the door before Brent could give him another task.

"You don't really think they'll send us back in, do you?" Quinn asked.

"We're going to be prepared if they do." Brent's stomach curled at the possibility—never a good sign. "I'm going to check in with Amy. Let me know when Tristan gets back."

Seth nodded. "Will do."

Trusting Seth to play referee, Brent crossed to Amy's office. Inside, she sat at her desk, typing on a laptop, a second computer monitor angled so it wasn't visible to anyone but her.

"Where did that come from?"

"A friend." Amy motioned for him to close the door.

Brent caught the evasion and the little half smile that flashed on her face. "What kind of friend?" He closed the door. "Should I be jealous?"

She smiled fully and stood. "Never."

Though he rarely had a moment alone with his wife at work, he took advantage of this one. He settled his hand on her waist and leaned down to kiss her.

He had intended to keep the kiss brief, but when her hand slid up his back, he couldn't resist. He drew her closer and deepened the kiss. The spark that he had come to expect ignited inside him, that connection that reaffirmed he would never be alone.

He drew back and ran his hand down her arm. "I'm really glad you have a private office."

"Me too." She eased out of his arms. "Although, with the rate Gardner's going, he may try to take that away too."

"What did he do now?" Brent asked.

"He took my computer."

"What?" He stepped back so he could see her more clearly. "You had classified material on there. Mission data, intelligence reports . . ."

Amy held up a hand to stop him. "I know, and I already have it all back."

"How?"

"Ghost." Amy set her hand on the top of the laptop. "This was a gift from him after I told him what happened."

"He got your files from your hard drive?"

Amy nodded and leaned closer. "And he wiped it so no one could access them."

"Good." A thread of relief surfaced. "Since you're operational again, do you have a minute to talk shop?"

"Sure. What's up?"

"Seth. I need to decide whether to ask for a replacement or adjust to working with a smaller squad."

"That's a tough call." Amy sat down. "You've had seven for a while now."

Brent lowered into the seat beside her desk. "I know, but what happens if I request someone new and they're not a good fit?"

"It's always a gamble." Amy reached out and took his hand. "Have you prayed about it?"

"A bit, but I haven't gotten any answers."

"It'll come. Just have faith."

"Right now, I'd prefer that my faith translate into answers."

"I know what you mean." Amy released his hand and retrieved an oversized photo from her desk. "For now, though, I have something you need to see. Based on the intel from your last sneak and peek, the Air Force did a surveillance run over the fortress."

"And?"

Amy handed him the photo. "This is from the thermal scan."

Brent lowered his gaze to the image where a significant heat signature interrupted the dense woods. "What is this?"

"The analysts don't know. They're guessing the heat is from computers, maybe a data-mining operation."

"There's got to be more to it than that," Brent said. "Two guards rotating at all hours of the day, a helicopter patrolling at night. That's overkill if all they're doing is going after personal information."

"I think so, too, but I don't have a clue what else it might be."

"I'll run this by the guys and see if they have any ideas." Brent stood. "Has this already gone to the CIA for analysis?"

"It was supposed to, but I'm going to check with Paige to make sure it's put in as a priority."

"Thanks." Brent leaned down and kissed her. "I'll see you later."

"Love you."

Brent kissed her again. "Love you too."

* * *

Rarely did the navy move fast when it came to personnel changes, but someone was making things happen. Seth had barely finished lunch when the call came for him to report to personnel. Whoever wanted Commander Engel at the pentagon must have some serious sway to get orders cut in less than a week.

With his new orders in hand now and his report date set, Seth headed for his office. He needed to call his wife.

"Lieutenant Johnson."

Though the new oak leaf on Seth's uniform contradicted the rank Commander Gardner had just addressed him with, Seth turned.

The commander stood in the doorway leading to his office. "A word, please." Commander Gardner waited by his door.

"Yes, sir." Seth walked into the commander's office.

Gardner closed the door with more force than necessary and turned on Seth. "Would you like to explain how you were selected for the military aide position at the White House?" His gaze landed on Seth's rank insignia. "And how you were promoted without my knowledge?"

Seth had anticipated this conversation, but he had expected it to be relayed to him after Brent had had a showdown with Gardner. "I was asked to interview for the mil aide position when I was on leave in DC earlier this week. I learned of my promotion at that time."

"And your new rank was already processed?"

"Yes, sir. My promotion ceremony was held in DC on Wednesday."

"How did your name even end up in the applicant pool?"

"I'm still not quite sure why I was offered an interview." Other than his friendship with the president. Still, Seth's words were true. Jim could have requested Jay or Brent instead of him.

"You're telling me that out of all the qualified officers, you just happened to get a phone call requesting you to interview for one of the most prestigious jobs in the navy?"

"Yes, sir."

"What happened with Commander Miller? He was supposed to interview for that position." Gardner's voice tightened. "Did he?"

"I did see him at the White House when I was there for my interview."

"He's a higher rank and has more command experience. Yet they chose you." Gardner stormed to his desk and picked up a file. He shook it in the air. "That's what you're telling me?"

Seth shrugged. "I guess they liked me better."

Gardner's fury boiled over into full-blown rage. "Don't get cute with me."

"I wouldn't dream of it, sir."

Gardner slammed the folder back onto his desk. "I have half a mind to disband your entire unit."

"I would advise against that, sir."

"Oh, you would, would you?" Gardner closed the distance between them and took a combative stance despite the seven inches Seth had over him. "You listen to me. I'm going to streamline this SEAL team into the top unit in the navy. No more civilians screwing things up or officers going off on tangents on how things should be done."

Seth straightened his shoulders and tilted his head enough to make eye contact with the shorter man. "Will there be anything else, sir?"

Gardner's face reddened. Seth had the sudden image of an old cartoon in which the character's anger caused steam to blow out his ears.

"Tell Commander Miller I want to see him." Gardner took a step back. "Now."

"Yes, sir." Seth opened the door. As an afterthought, he turned back. "Sir, by any chance, did you watch the inauguration last weekend?"

"What does that have to do with anything?"

"Nothing." Seth gave a subtle nod to the commander. "Nothing at all."

* * *

Brent uttered a silent prayer as he approached Gardner's office. He was sick and tired of this man and his ridiculous power plays getting in the way of more important matters, like getting to the bottom of Morenta's plans.

Mei Lien looked up from her desk, a look of pity crossing her face.

"That bad?" Brent whispered.

She nodded.

Resigned, Brent let out a sigh. "Better call and let him know I'm here."

Webb approached and veered toward Brent. "I was on my way to your office. Do you have the layout for the fortress? Looks like we may be teaming up on a snatch and grab."

"Check with Commander Johnson. He's our expert on that."

"Thanks." Webb jutted his chin toward Gardner's office. "You getting called out on something?"

"Looks that way."

"Meet me at the officers' club after work, and I'll buy you a beer."

"I don't drink."

"Right. A root beer, then. Seventeen thirty." Webb lowered his voice. "It's time we compare notes."

Brent nodded. "I'll text Amy. She'll want to be part of the conversation."

"Sounds good."

As soon as Webb moved down the hall, Mei Lien picked up the phone and informed Gardner of Brent's presence.

"Yes, sir." Mei Lien hung up. "He said for you to take a seat. He'll be with you in a minute."

Not about to spend his time idle, Brent asked, "Any updates on personnel changes?"

She leaned forward and dropped her voice to a whisper. "Damian's transfer orders got canceled."

"Damian is staying?" At least that was a piece of good news. "Any idea why it got canceled?"

Mei Lien glanced down the empty hallway in front of her. "I know this sounds terrible, but I think he was listed as a transfer so it would open up a housing spot for one of the new guys."

"You can't be serious."

She nodded toward Gardner's door. "I heard him talking to someone at housing last week. He asked for one of the California transfers to take Damian's spot on the list."

"That's low."

"I've been working with housing to see if I can get Damian back to the top of the list," Mei Lien said. "I'll let you know if I have any luck."

"Actually, that's no longer necessary. He found a place, but I really appreciate your efforts."

"Someone has to play fair around here."

The door swung open, and Mei Lien leaned down to open a desk drawer. The movement was so smooth, Brent doubted Gardner would know his secretary had just been gossiping about him.

"Commander Miller," Gardener said, his voice tight.

Brent nodded in greeting and waited to be invited into Gardner's office. Once they were inside, he stood opposite the commander's desk while Gardner circled behind it.

"I received orders for Lieutenant Commander Johnson's transfer to DC this morning."

"Yes. Seth informed me of the upcoming change."

"I understand you interviewed for the position too."

Brent didn't respond. Technically, he hadn't interviewed. Luckily, Gardner didn't wait for Brent to answer.

"Care to explain how Johnson was even in the running?"

"I didn't put him up for it, if that's what you're asking." A stretch of the truth but the truth nonetheless. Jim had asked for Seth, and Amy had facilitated that communication.

"I certainly didn't put his name forward," Gardner growled.

"Maybe Commander Bennett submitted Seth's name before he retired," Brent said. The likelihood of Gardner having access to check with Kel was slim, at best.

"That's your story."

"I don't know what you're implying," Brent said. "Seth and I were both at the White House. He was offered the job. I wasn't."

"Fine. Have it your way." Gardner sat at his desk. "I tried to give you a leg up on your way out of here, but since you didn't take that opportunity, it looks like you'll be heading over to SEAL Team Ten."

Brent crossed his arms over his chest. "The team you're trying to get rid of."

Surprise flickered in Gardner's eyes. "Where did you hear that?"

"You aren't as subtle about your plans as you think you are." Brent took a step forward. "Tell you what: I'll agree to a transfer to SEAL Team Ten, but I have one condition."

"You aren't in a position to ask for conditions."

Brent ignored him. "Transfer my whole squad."

"What?"

"If you're so determined to downsize this team, then we'll make it easy for you." Brent gestured toward the door. "You can get rid of your problem children in one fell swoop."

"You really want to risk your men getting downsized into teaching or intel positions?"

"I'm willing to take that risk if I can keep my squad together."

"Deal," Gardner spat out.

Brent opened the door before he turned back. "And one more thing."

Gardner's eyebrows lifted.

"Amy comes with us."

28

JIM STOOD AND CIRCLED HIS desk as Doug walked in the door. "Congratulations, Mr. Secretary."

Doug chuckled and shook Jim's outstretched hand. "I still can't believe it."

"I have to say, it's not often you see a cabinet member get confirmed in only three days."

"I doubt I'll be the only one," Doug said. "Rumor has it the Senate is going to vote on your secretary of defense this afternoon."

"Good. I need him in place soon." Jim picked up the latest update on Morenta and handed it to Doug. "Take a look at this."

Jim sat in a chair in the center of the room and waited for Doug to sit beside him. "Morenta's up to something, and if these reports are any indication, whatever his plans are, they're going to happen soon."

Doug scanned over the top sheet before flipping to the photo and the attached analysis. "CIA thinks Morenta is planning a cyberattack?"

"That's their best guess." Jim blew out a breath. "I'll be honest with you, Doug. I always knew there was a possibility of some kind of terrorist activity trying to disrupt the American way of life during the transition between presidents, but I didn't expect this."

"The heat signature on the thermal photos could be anything. People, heat-generating equipment, even a fire in a fireplace." Doug flipped to the next page. "But paired with these transcripts from the conversations they picked up, I have to agree with the agency. This looks like a cyberattack."

Jim tensed. "But we have no idea when or where it will occur."

"I'm afraid not. Unless someone discusses it near one of the listening devices, we may not know until it's too late."

"I'm not willing to take that chance." Jim tapped his fingers together. As much as he hated to send anyone into harm's way, he didn't have a choice. "I need options on how to stop this."

"I suggest you have your chief of staff call in your joint chiefs. We need to rely on the expertise of all your top advisers."

Jim stood and crossed to his office door. He pushed it open and spoke to his aide. "Sarah, can you tell Sawyer Gaines I need to see him?"

"Yes, Mr. President."

Jim closed the door again. "Is there a way out of this, short of a full-on raid?"

"If we send a special ops team in to get Morenta, that could stop his plans."

"Or it could accelerate them."

"It's a gamble either way." Doug leaned forward and lowered his voice. "Listen to what the joint chiefs have to say. Then pray about what to do next."

"Thanks, Doug." The churning eased slightly. "That's good advice."

A knock sounded at the door, and it immediately opened. His chief of staff poked his head in. "You asked to see me, sir?"

"Yes." Jim pressed forward. "We have a situation."

* * *

Amy walked into the officers' club, her gaze sweeping over the scatter of occupants enjoying happy hour after work. Buffalo wings, taquitos, and cheesy nachos scented the air.

Amy didn't want any of them. She hadn't even seen Gardner today, so why were her nerves still wreaking havoc on her appetite?

Brent's text message to meet him here after work hadn't given her any details, and a video conference this afternoon had prevented her from seeking him out.

"Hey, hon," Brent called from behind her.

She turned and resisted the urge to greet him with a kiss. Too many people around.

"I don't see Commander Webb here yet," Amy said. "What happened today anyway?"

"I'll tell you when Webb gets here." Brent signaled to the hostess that they wanted a table. "No point in replaying it twice."

Amy motioned toward the entrance. "There he is now."

Webb approached them from one direction as the hostess approached from the other.

"Will there be anyone else joining you?" the hostess asked.

"Just the three of us." Brent pointed at some empty tables away from the bar. "Can we take one of those?"

"Of course, sir." She led them to a table in the corner. "Can I get you started with some drinks?"

Webb gave his order, and Brent requested his typical root beer.

"And for you, ma'am?"

The scent of fried meat carried to her but did nothing to stir her appetite. "Just water for me, please."

The hostess nodded and moved to the bar.

"What happened with Gardner today?" Webb asked.

"He's still trying to get rid of me, so I gave him a solution," Brent said.

An uncomfortable sensation prickled up Amy's spine. "What kind of solution?"

"I offered to take a transfer to SEAL Team Ten if he'll send my whole squad with me." Brent put his hand on Amy's. "You too."

"That takes care of your problem," Webb said, "but it leaves me and Kaminski in one heck of a bind."

"With any luck, Admiral Rivera will set Gardner straight before anything else changes," Amy said. "There's no reason for the Saint Squad to move if Gardner is on his way out anyway."

"I saw Rivera talking to Gardner on Tuesday, and it didn't seem like there were any changes coming."

Amy shook her head. "That can't be right. Rivera knows Gardner cut off our phones."

"Yeah. Mei Lien was not very happy when she told me Gardner passed the whole thing off as an administrative error."

"Rivera believed that?"

"Looked like it."

"Maybe we do want to transfer, then," Amy said.

"That still leaves my squad high and dry," Webb complained. "Without Amy, we won't have any direct access to intel reports."

"Sorry, but with the roadblocks Gardner is putting up for Amy, you won't be that much better if she stays."

Irritation flashed on Webb's face. "What happened now?"

"I came back from leave to a broken computer," Amy said.

"He broke your computer?"

"Not exactly." Amy chose her words carefully. "Let's just say my computer didn't work and he was responsible for the problem."

Now anger flared. "Who does this guy think he is?"

"I don't know who he thinks he is," Amy said, "but my guess is he's a certifiable narcissist."

"How he got through the psych eval to get into the teams is beyond me," Brent said.

Webb shook his head. "Some guys get a taste of power, and they can't handle it."

"He likely falls into that category," Brent said. "Not only is he messing with our squads, but he's also sending up a proposal for cost-cutting measures within the teams, including getting rid of SEAL Team Ten."

"Wait. You're volunteering to get transferred to a team that could get axed?"

"I took my concerns up the chain of command to prevent that from happening." Brent fell silent when a waiter approached to take their order.

Amy scanned the menu, but nothing sounded good. Opting for simplicity, she asked, "What's your soup of the day?"

"Minestrone and chicken noodle."

"I'll have the chicken noodle."

"Don't you want anything else?" Brent asked.

"I'm not that hungry."

"I am." Webb ordered an appetizer along with a burger, and Brent followed suit.

As soon as the waiter left them alone, Webb said, "I doubt taking your concerns up the chain of command will do any good, not with Gardner's uncle being the vice chief of naval operations." He picked up his drink and took a sip.

"I may have gone over his uncle's head too," Brent admitted.

Webb choked on his drink and sputtered. "You went to the secretary of the navy?"

"Higher."

Amy reached over and put her hand on Brent's. He wasn't going to admit that she was the president's daughter, was he?

"There's not much higher you can go. We don't have a new secretary of defense yet."

"No, but on Monday, Seth and I were both at the White House. Seth is going to be the new military aide for the president."

"Seriously?" Webb set his glass down with enough force that the contents sloshed over. "You spoke with the president?"

Brent shrugged. "He's a very nice man."

"You spoke with the president." Webb shook his head in disbelief.

"Yes, and he listened," Brent said. "If Gardner manages to push this through, the president will intervene."

"The president may be a nice guy, but he's also a politician," Webb said. "How do you know you can trust him?"

Amy couldn't help but smile. "I promise you, we can trust him."

* * *

Brent followed Amy into the house, still mulling over the events of the day. Would his proposal to Gardner be accepted? And if so, would his squad support the decision to transfer to a new team?

Amy set her purse down on the kitchen table. "I'm going to head to bed."

Brent glanced at the clock on the wall. "It's only eight thirty. Are you feeling okay?"

"I'm just worn out." Amy turned to face him. "I think it's all the stress of dealing with Gardner."

"You sure that's all it is? You look a little pale."

She nodded, her fatigue obvious. "I just need to get a good night's sleep."

Brent studied her more closely. Twice since they'd been married, Amy had suffered from severe exhaustion, the inevitable result of working herself too hard without giving her body adequate rest, but this was the first time her appetite had been affected.

He stepped closer and ran his hand down her arm. "I'm worried about you. You weren't feeling the greatest while we were on leave either."

"Everyone was catching up on sleep after the inauguration."

"That's true, but maybe you should see a doctor."

"I don't have time for that."

"Amy, if this is another bout of exhaustion, you don't have time not to." He leaned in and kissed her gently. "Promise me you'll call tomorrow."

"It's a waste of time," Amy said. "I'm fine."

"Call anyway." He kissed her again. "Please?"

"Okay. You win. I'll call tomorrow." She reached out and hugged him. "Good night."

"Night." Brent watched her as she left the room. The slow footsteps, the relaxed posture, chicken noodle soup instead of a real meal. This wasn't his typical Amy.

A cell phone rang, and he followed the sound to Amy's purse. He pulled it open and fished out one phone and then another. The third was the charm.

He noted Katherine's name on the screen and hit the Talk button. "Hi, Katherine."

"Brent. How are you doing?" Katherine asked.

"Good, but I'm afraid Amy has already headed to bed."

"It's not even nine o'clock."

"That's what I said." Sort of. "I'm sure she's still getting ready for bed. I can go get her for you."

"No, that's okay. I just wanted to see how work went today," Katherine said. "Were things any better with the commanding officer?"

"No. It looks like our whole squad might be transferring to a new team."

"That's extreme. What happened?"

Brent gave her the unclassified version.

"I'm surprised Amy isn't staying up late, staging a coup," Katherine said.

Katherine was right. Problems rarely wore Amy down. Typically, they invigorated her.

"She hasn't been herself for a few days now." Brent moved to the hall and looked down it to make sure Amy wasn't in hearing range. "I'm trying to get her to see a doctor."

"I wish I'd known she wasn't feeling well while she was here," Katherine said. "We could have had one of the White House physicians take a look at her."

"Want to do me a favor?"

"Of course."

"If I give you the number to her doctor's office, can you call in the morning and schedule an appointment for her?" Brent wandered back into the kitchen. "It's not always easy for military spouses to get a same-day appointment, but if the first lady calls . . ."

"I'll call first thing in the morning."

"Thank you. I really appreciate it."

Jim's voice sounded in the background.

Katherine's voice faded when she said, "I'm talking to Brent."

Another rumble of Jim's voice, the words inaudible.

"Jim said he wants to talk to you, but it needs to be on a secure line."

"I'll call him back on my phone." Brent ended his call with Katherine, grabbed his secure phone, and called Jim.

Jim dispensed with a greeting and asked, "What can you tell me about the hideaway by the fortress?"

"It's all in my after-action report." Brent pulled out a stool by the kitchen counter and sat. "Two guards at all times, no one else coming or going in the structure." He described the building and the oddity of the lack of windows on one side as well as the need for guards in such a remote area. When he finished, he asked, "Can you tell me why you're asking about this?"

"Intel is concerned we may have an imminent threat of a cyberattack."

"Any idea what they're after?"

"No. We're still working on when the attack will happen too."

The lack of knowledge created a sense of urgency. "Do you need us to go back in?"

"That option was discussed today," Jim said.

Brent drummed his fingers on the counter in front of him. "Any idea when?"

"Soon." Jim paused briefly before he asked, "How long do you need to adequately prepare?"

Brent ran over the upcoming schedule in his mind. "With Seth transferring to the White House, I'll need to prep for a six-man mission." The thought of Jay's very pregnant wife caused him to amend that statement. "Maybe five. Jay is due to go out on paternity leave around the same time we would ship out."

"Can you manage with only five men?" Jim asked.

"It would be better if we had another squad to back us up. There's one in my platoon who's available right now," Brent said. "Give us a week, and we can be operational. Two weeks would be better, though, especially with the challenges with our CO."

"Still having problems with him?"

"Yeah."

"No matter what his issues are, if the orders come down for your platoon to activate, this commander of yours won't have much choice but to get out of the way so you can do your job."

"One would hope, but it's possible my squad is transferring to SEAL Team Ten."

"I'd better be sure the navy doesn't cut that team, then."

"I would appreciate that."

"In the meantime, I'll have intel pass any new information on to Amy. They're putting a priority on translating the audio picked up from the fortress and the hideout. We're hoping for something that will give us a timeline."

"We'll start putting our mission plans together first thing in the morning."

"Thanks, Brent."

"Thank you, Mr. President."

29

SETH SETTLED INTO A CHAIR by Damian's desk as everyone gathered together for morning prayer. Their early run and workout session had already concluded, and Seth tried to imagine what staying in shape would look like once he was working at the White House.

"Where's Amy?" Craig asked.

"She has some things she needs to do for Webb's unit this morning." Brent closed the door to the large office and stepped to the center of the room. "I'll say it today." He folded his arms and offered a prayer that focused largely on guidance as they entered into the transitions of their future. He also asked for a special blessing on Seth and his family. When Brent finished, Seth had to swallow the lump in his throat before he could manage a muttered amen.

Brent took a moment as well before he spoke again. "We have a lot of things to cover today, starting with the simple logistics. Tomorrow morning, two of us need to help Seth and Vanessa move up to northern Virginia. They aren't taking much furniture, so it's mostly going to be helping with personal effects and rearranging some furniture at Jim and Katherine's house. The rest of us can stay here and help move Damian and Paige into Seth's place."

"An eight-hour round trip or heavy lifting," Quinn said. "Tough call."

"Katherine is sending cinnamon rolls to her house," Brent added.

"I'll help Seth," Quinn said quickly.

"Me too," Tristan said.

A chorus of volunteers followed.

"Sorry, Quinn called it first," Brent said. "He and I will help Seth. The rest of you can help Damian."

"How come you get to help Seth?" Tristan asked.

"I'm the one picking up the cinnamon rolls." Brent picked up a paper off Tristan's desk and handed it to Seth. "This is your checkout sheet. If you can get through that red tape before the end of the day, I'd love to get some help on our mission plan."

"What mission plan?" Seth asked before he caught the telling look on Brent's face. "The fortress."

"We don't have details yet, but a snatch and grab is a high probability," Brent said. "Taking out whatever is in that hideout is also high on the list."

"What do we know so far?" Jay asked.

"Possible cyberattack. When and where, unknown."

As much as Seth hated the idea of inserting back into the fortress, he hated his teammates going without him even more. "Maybe I should ask for a delay on my reassignment."

Brent shook his head. "Webb's squad is already prepping to back us up."

Seth stood. "You sure about this?"

"I'm sure." Brent motioned at the paper in Seth's hand. "Better get that taken care of."

"I'll be back as soon as I can." Seth left the room as Brent began assigning tasks to the rest of his squad.

Seth looked down the long list of offices he needed to obtain signatures from. Commander Gardner's name occupied the line for commanding officer. Too bad personnel hadn't put Brent's name there instead.

Opting to take on the biggest challenge first, he went to Gardner's office. Mei Lien's desk was noticeably vacant. Seth passed it and poked his head through Gardner's open doorway.

Gardner sat at his desk, his fingers typing on his keyboard.

"Excuse me, sir. I need your signature on this." Seth held up his checkout sheet.

"Let me see." Gardner held out a hand.

Seth passed the paper to him.

Gardner gave it a cursory glance, shook his head, and offered it back to Seth. "I'm not signing that."

Seth had expected a lecture or perhaps a rant but straight refusal? He kept both hands down at his sides. "I'm sorry, sir, but the transfer is already approved. Your signature is a mere formality to prove that you are aware that today is my last day here."

"And I'm telling you I didn't agree to this, and I'm not signing."

"Again, my transfer has already been approved. I don't think the president will be very pleased if I'm not there on my report date."

"As if the president has a clue who you are." Gardner set the paper down on his desk. "I'm not signing. That means you can't complete your checkout.

When you don't show up at the White House a week from Monday, the military aides' office will start looking for a new candidate."

"I don't think it works that way."

"I'll get a message to personnel that your transfer fell through."

"Why are you doing this, sir?"

"I was about to give you command of the Saint Squad. Did you know that?"

"I had my suspicions," Seth said. "That doesn't explain why you would block my career growth now. The Saint Squad already has an excellent commanding officer."

"Commander Miller is the type to create discontent within a unit. I want him gone."

"You're the only one creating discontent." Seth struggled to keep his rising temper in check. "You have limited our resources, disrupted our communications, overworked our intelligence officer, and impeded the flow of information. Why? Are you trying to get someone killed?"

Gardner stood, his eyes flashing. "I'm demonstrating that everyone in my unit had better get on board with my program or get out."

"I choose the latter." Seth picked up the checkout sheet. "Sign this, and you'll have one less problem to deal with."

Gardner snatched the paper from Seth again. For a brief moment, Seth thought he was going to sign it. His eyes bulged when Gardner ripped the paper in two and proceeded to tear it twice more.

Seth's jaw twitched. "That was a mistake."

"Oh yeah?" Gardner said in a whine that wasn't unlike when Tristan and Quinn were arguing over food. "What are you going to do about it?"

Seth drew a slow breath and let it out just as slowly. He stepped back. "Have a nice day, Commander." He turned and left the room.

* * *

Amy nibbled on a saltine cracker. Maybe it was a good thing she was going in to see the doctor. Although how Brent had managed to get her an appointment before she'd even called to request one was beyond her.

"Your whole squad is really willing to transfer?" Mei Lien asked from the chair beside her.

"With the tear Gardner has been on, if the option were on the table, Webb and Kaminski would probably volunteer to transfer too," Amy said. "Have you seen any paperwork on it yet?"

"No. I think he's up to something, but I can't tell what it is."

Amy set her cracker down. "What kind of something? What have you heard?"

"It's not anything in particular, but the patterns of the personnel changes is interesting," Mei Lien said. "All the new guys are now in second platoon. Two full squads' worth."

"Did these guys serve together before?"

"Some of them, but it looks like he's creating a specialized task force."

"Specialized in what?"

"Bomb disposal is the common specialty for the Cronos Squad. The Apollo Squad is made up of marksmen."

"He's naming the squads after Greek gods?"

"Fitting, huh?" Mei Lien tilted her head to one side. "Gardner does have a god complex."

"You would know better than the rest of us." Amy pondered this new information. "I don't get why he would cluster people with similar skill sets. It's not like all SEALs aren't capable in demolition or weapons or any of the other specialties, for that matter."

"I know. It's almost like he wants to have the most successful squads in certain areas." Mei Lien shrugged. "I don't know why that would matter though."

"He's trying to make a name for himself by creating squads that will excel in certain situations."

"Seems like most commanders try to balance skills so team members can complement each other's strengths."

"That's the most obvious way of organizing special forces personnel," Amy said. "At least, when you're trying to keep the most tools at your disposal."

"What I don't get is why he went after the Saint Squad," Mei Lien said. "It's one of the most successful squads in all the teams."

"Yes, but Gardner didn't have anything to do with that."

Mei Lien leaned back in her seat. "He wants to be able to take all the credit for any successes."

"I wonder if he'll be as quick to take the blame for the failures," Amy said.

"Highly doubtful."

Amy's office door flung open, and Seth charged inside.

He pointed down the hall. "That man is impossible!"

Amy's eyebrows lifted. Of all the members of the Saint Squad, Seth was the most likely to stay calm in a crisis and to keep his emotions in check. For Gardner to get Seth riled up was quite an undertaking.

"We've already established that we're not fans," Amy said.

"He doesn't know how to command." Seth pushed the door closed with enough force that it rattled. "He's a bully on a power trip."

"What happened?" Amy asked.

Seth moved farther into the room, fury sparking in his eyes and his hands clenching into fists.

Mei Lien stood and edged toward the door. "I should get back to my desk."

"Don't worry about him," Amy assured her. "He doesn't fight with people who aren't the enemy." The memory of an altercation aboard ship with an inept communications officer niggled the back of her mind. "Well, there was that one time . . ."

Seth turned his attention to Mei Lien. "How do you handle working for him?"

Mei Lien straightened her shoulders. "I do what I'm told unless I can find a way around his idiocy."

"I'm adding you to my daily prayers." Seth blew out a breath. "You're going to need them."

"I appreciate the sentiment." Mei Lien looked from Seth to Amy and back again. "Dare I ask what he did this time?"

"First, he refused to sign my personnel checkout sheet. Then he tore it up."

Amy stood. "Is he insane? He can't do that."

"Well, he just did." Seth spread his arms out in a frustrated gesture. "What am I supposed to do now? Technically, I have to clear this duty station before I can move on to my new one."

"I can go down to personnel and get a new sheet for you," Amy said.

"I appreciate that, but then what? Gardner isn't going to sign it," Seth said. "It's bad enough that the checkout process takes most of the day, but I should be helping Brent on his mission plans."

"Go help Brent."

"Amy, I move tomorrow. I can't put this off."

"Give me until lunchtime. I think I can shave a couple hours off the process." Amy turned to Mei Lien. "Any chance you can spare a few minutes to help?"

"I need to get back to my desk, but I'll do whatever I can."

"Great." Amy put her hand on Mei Lien's shoulder. "I need to make a phone call. If all goes the way I hope it will, I'm going to need you to clear a visitor for me."

"Call me with the details." Mei Lien glanced toward her office. "I don't trust email."

"Neither do I."

30

A SNATCH AND GRAB. A search and destroy. A drone strike. Too many options. Brent didn't know where to begin.

The last option would be the most direct and would eliminate any risk to him and his squad. Unfortunately, he doubted intel had sufficient evidence to support deadly force, especially when the target was located within the borders of an ally nation.

Jay plucked two toy army men out of the bucket at the side of the worktable in his office and set them down beside the shoe box that represented the hideout. "Slipping past the guards shouldn't be that hard," he said.

"It's harder than you think," Brent said. "Seth got stuck in the bushes by these windows for a couple hours."

"I say we neutralize the guards," Tristan said. "Two guys go in these windows. Two more in the front door."

"That leaves a fifth to cover outside."

"How are we inserting?" Brent asked. "We have to assume the Z-10 will be flying cover."

Seth walked into the room.

"What are you doing back so soon?" Brent asked.

A muscle jumped in Seth's jaw.

"Gardner?"

"Don't get me started," Seth muttered. He motioned to the soldiers and asked, "Are we using Dixon's toys again for mock-ups?"

"These are mine," Tristan said. "Dixon had so many, he gave me these."

Brent could imagine it too easily: Tristan's three-year-old sharing his toys to help his dad.

"Trying to decide where to insert?" Seth asked.

"We've come by water every time, and it's worked," Brent said.

"There's really no other way in unless we want to fight our way through," Seth said. "The walls are heavily guarded, and it's doubtful we'd make it inside without casualties."

"I want a no-casualty option," Brent said.

"You always do." Seth plucked a piece of paper out of the printer beside Brent's desk and scribbled a rough map. "If we can get satellite images that show us what time the Z-10 is starting its overflights, we could use the sound of the engines to disguise our approach if we have Webb's squad come in at the end of the beach."

"I thought the beach was guarded," Craig said.

"It is, but if we insert at the same spot as last time, one of us can sedate the guard as soon as the helicopter engines start up," Seth said.

"You think we should use the Z-10 as our signal in case our comm cuts out again?" Jay said.

"I do."

"Quinn, check with Amy and have her request satellite images for the fortress," Brent said.

"We may need to ask intel to retask the satellite," Craig said.

"Quinn, ask Amy about that too," Brent said. "If anyone can pull it off, she can."

"Got it." Quinn headed out the door.

"Going off Seth's suggestions, the rest of you work up different scenarios for a snatch and grab," Brent turned to Seth. "And, you, unless you want to have to come back to Virginia Beach to deal with administrative stuff on Monday, you need to get moving on your checkout process."

"Amy said she's taking care of that for me."

"How can Amy check out for you? Everyone has to meet with you to sign off your checkout sheet."

"She's getting me one of those too."

"You already have one."

"*Had* might be a better word." Seth moved closer to the desk. "The Z-10 is going to be a problem."

Brent studied the assortment of boxes and army men on his desk and tried to visualize a successful mission. He glanced at the man beside him. A successful mission without Seth. This wasn't going to be easy.

* * *

Amy was determined to streamline the checkout process for Seth, and she had a pretty good idea of how to go about it. Her call to Sienna had already put the first link of her plan in place. Craig's wife had readily agreed to use her star power to help and had already enlisted the assistance of her costar in her TV show. Now Amy had to work some real magic: getting all the right players into the same place at the same time.

Mei Lien walked into her office. "I put Reed Forrester's name on the list at the gate. Is he really coming?"

"Yes. So is Sienna Blake."

"Sienna Blake? The movie star?"

"Movie star. TV star. Friend." Amy nodded.

"I'll call security and add her name too."

"I already took care of her." Technically, all Amy had done was invite Sienna. Her ID as a military dependent would grant her access to the base. "Is Gardner going to notice you're missing?"

"He's in a meeting for the next hour. I asked Abby to cover for me."

"Is she a Reed Forrester fan?"

"Oh yeah." Mei Lien motioned to Amy's list. "What else can I do to help?"

"We need to call everyone on the checkout list and invite them to meet Sienna and Reed for lunch today."

"We only have three hours, at best. This isn't going to be easy."

"But not impossible," Amy said. "Let's start with the most pressing issue. Where to hold it."

"I can reserve the conference room, but if Gardner walks by and sees what you're doing, he could mess everything up."

"How about the banquet room at the officers' club?"

"It has a reservation fee."

"Do what you can to negotiate it down," Amy said. "Otherwise, I'll cover it."

"You're a good friend."

"Mostly, I'm not willing to stand by and watch anyone get treated this way if I can help it." Amy picked up her laptop from her desk and stepped aside. "Here. You can use my desk phone to call. I'll use my laptop and my cell."

Mei Lien took Amy's place at the desk and dialed the phone.

Amy moved to the worktable on the other side of the room and set down her laptop. Still standing, she made her first call. "Hey, Rose. I need a huge favor."

"What's that?"

"There was a problem with Seth Johnson's checkout sheet today," Amy said. "I was hoping you could email me a new one."

"That's easy enough."

"There's one more thing."

"What's that?"

"We need to find a way to change the commanding officer sign-off to some-one other than Commander Gardner."

"Don't tell me he's trying to block Commander Johnson's transfer."

"You guessed it on the first try."

Fury vibrated through her words. "We aren't going to let him get away with this."

"I agree. There has to be another option," Amy said. "Could Commander Miller sign off?"

"Commander Miller does have to sign off as his commanding officer, but we also need one more at the administrative level."

"What about Admiral Rivera?"

"Go up the chain instead of down?" Rose asked. "Let me check the regs on that real quick." Silence hummed over the line for a minute. Then Rose came back on. "Okay, that will work, but Admiral Rivera isn't going to be easy to catch. He's in a meeting right now, and his secretary said he was plan-ning to spend the afternoon with his daughter while she's in town."

"At least there's a chance with him," Amy said.

"I emailed you the new form."

Amy sat at the worktable and pulled up her email. She scanned the list of individuals and departments that required Seth's signature today—a full page's worth. When she reached the line for personnel, Amy asked, "Are you one of the people who can sign off on the personnel line?"

"I am."

"Great. Any chance you want to join me for a little celebrity meet and greet today?"

"What kind of celebrity?" Rose asked.

"Sienna Blake and Reed Forrester, the stars of *Beachfront*."

"Seriously?" Rose said. "They're coming here?"

"They are."

"Tell me when and where, and I'll be there."

Amy turned toward her desk, where Mei Lien was still on the phone.

Mei Lien grinned and nodded. "Noon is great. Thank you."

"Noon at the officers' club," Amy said into the phone.

"I'll see you then."

"Thanks, Rose."

"Thank you."

Amy hung up and printed off two copies of Seth's checkout sheet. She handed one to Mei Lien. "I already have personnel. I'll start at the top of the list, and you work from the bottom."

"Okay."

Deciding to tackle the most difficult obstacle first, Amy dialed Admiral Rivera's office. As expected, his secretary answered.

Fully aware that the admiral's schedule was likely packed, Amy eased into her request. "Jody, is there a time Admiral Rivera will be in for a few minutes? I need his signature on something."

"I'm sorry. He's in a meeting right now, and as soon as he finishes, he's meeting his daughter for lunch. He doesn't plan to return for the rest of the day."

"I don't suppose he's eating at the officers' club, is he?"

"No. And I'm sorry, Amy, but I'm not at liberty to say where they'll be dining."

"Do you think they might change their minds if they could have lunch with Sienna Blake and Reed Forrester?"

"Sienna Blake and Reed Forrester?" she repeated, wonder in her voice.

"Yes."

"I can ask, but the admiral isn't much into TV," Jody said. "If it were Kendra Blake, that would be different. The admiral's daughter is a huge fan of hers. I think Admiral Rivera is, too, but he doesn't admit it."

Kendra Blake. Amy's sister-in-law was supposed to spend a few days visiting her sister when Charlie went back to work. Was it possible she was still in town? "Let me get back to you."

Amy hung up and pulled out her personal cell phone. She dialed Kendra's number.

Humor flowed over the line. "I was just talking to Sienna. Did you decide you need more star power?"

Amy laughed. "I did. Are you still in Virginia Beach?"

"I am. Should I come with my sister?"

Amy breathed out a sigh of relief. "Yes. Please."

"Should I warm up my vocal cords too?"

"An impromptu Kendra Blake concert? That would be amazing."

"It's better than standing around shaking people's hands." Kendra lowered her voice into a conspiratorial whisper. "That's all Sienna can do, but . . ."

"Hey!" Sienna's protest carried over the line.

"I'll bring my guitar, but if you have someone who's good on the piano, that would be even better."

"I'll do what I can. Thanks so much."

"See you in a little while." Kendra paused for a moment, and Sienna's muffled voice carried over the line. "Oh, Sienna asked where we're meeting you."

"We have the banquet hall at the officers' club reserved."

"Perfect. We'll head over in a few minutes so we can check in with the staff," Kendra said.

"And avoid a crowd," Amy said.

Kendra laughed. "That too."

"I'll see you in a bit." Amy hung up and turned to face Mei Lien.

Mei Lien's eyes were wide, her mouth open. She lifted her hand and tried to form words. It took her two attempts before she managed to stammer, "Kendra . . . Blake? She's coming too?"

"Yes. We need to add her name to the security list at the gate," Amy said, trying not to be amused by Mei Lien's reaction. "If you know how to contact the Fleet Forces Band, make a call. If they have a few musicians who want to be part of an impromptu concert with Kendra, that would be great." Amy glanced at the time on her watch. Nine thirty. "They'd have to leave Norfolk pretty soon in order to have time to set up though."

Her eyes still wide, Mei Lien nodded and picked up the phone.

Amy dialed Admiral Rivera's office again. "Jody, it's Amy. Tell the admiral Kendra Blake will be there too."

31

SETH PARKED IN THE CROWDED officers' club parking lot, his anger from this morning still simmering.

Brent pointed to an open spot at the end. "There's one."

"What are so many people doing at the club this time of day?" Seth asked. "This is worse than when someone's holding a wedding reception here."

"Probably someone's retirement party."

"Is it too much to ask for it to be Gardner's?"

"I wish, but the size of the crowd is about right." Brent chuckled. "Everyone would probably come out to make sure he was really leaving."

Brent was right. Gardner had made plenty of enemies during his short time in his position.

"Do you have any idea why Amy wanted us to meet her here? I've got to get started on my checkout, assuming there's a way to get around Gardner."

"You know Amy will keep working until she finds a solution." Brent pushed out of the car. "Besides, after the time we put in this morning, we all need a break."

Craig and Damian approached from the parking lot next door.

"What are y'all doing here?" Seth asked. "You aren't allowed in the officers' club."

"We're just helping out." Craig continued toward the entrance.

"Do you know what's going on?" Seth asked Brent.

"I got the same text you did." Brent shrugged. "Amy said to meet her at the officers' club and she would help you get your signatures."

Suspicion rose. "Your wife is up to something."

Brent slapped Seth on the back and fell in behind Craig and Damian. "Of that I have no doubt."

"But you don't know what?"

"I didn't ask." Brent cast a glance over his shoulder. "She likes to surprise me."

Notes from a piano carried toward them, the tune recognizable. "Isn't that one of Kendra's songs?"

"Yeah."

Seth walked into the officers' club to a buzz of voices, but the dining area was free of occupants. "Where is everyone?"

"The noise is coming from over there."

Seth followed Brent into the crowded banquet hall. His height allowed him to look over the sea of bodies to where several musicians bustled about on the stage. Kendra Blake stood beside the pianist.

"What's going on?" Seth asked. "There must be three hundred people in here."

Brent shrugged.

Amy stepped onto the stage beside Kendra and looked over the crowd. As soon as she spotted Seth and Brent, she waved them forward and picked up a microphone. "Welcome everyone," she said. "We're going to get started in just a few minutes, but I want to introduce a few of our guests today." Amy waved again, and Craig's wife stepped onto the stage, followed by Reed. "Sienna Blake and Reed Forrester graciously accepted our invitation to come by and meet you all."

Enthusiastic applause broke out, and Amy waited for it to die down before she continued. "We also want to thank the members of the Fleet Forces Band who came by to perform for us with the amazing Kendra Blake."

More applause.

Brent tapped Seth on the back and nudged him forward.

They were nearly to the stage when Amy used both hands to signal the crowd to settle. "Finally, we wanted to congratulate our own Lieutenant Commander Seth Johnson on his recent promotion and wish him good luck as he moves on to his new assignment at the White House. We'll miss you, Seth."

Seth's face instantly heated.

"Now, before we get started, Seth still needs to get all his signatures taken care of on his checkout sheet," Amy said. "For those of you who have been invited to help us take care of this, please step forward. Our guests will happily trade their autographs for yours," Amy said.

Seth shook his head in stunned amazement. He closed the remaining distance between him and Amy. "You organized a concert to get everyone here for me?"

"It started out as a meet and greet and kind of grew from there."

Brent slipped his arm around Amy's waist. "This may be your best surprise yet."

"I'm glad you think so, because I have to leave in two hours for my doctor's appointment. I need you and Seth to make sure someone gets volunteered for cleanup duty."

Seth looked at the line of people waiting to sign off on his transfer. "I don't think that will be a problem."

* * *

Amy approached the receptionist at the doctor's office, a peppermint in her mouth to combat the lingering nausea that hadn't gone away since her most recent run-in with Gardner. She really hoped the doctor could figure out what was making her so tired. Of course, today's exhaustion was well-earned. The send-off for Seth had lasted well past the hour and a half she had scheduled for the banquet hall, but after Sienna chatted with the facility manager to apologize, he not only extended their time, but he also waived the rental fee Amy had expected to pay. The combination of star power and kindness had had more reach than Amy had anticipated.

She printed her name on the sign-in sheet, and the fortyish-year-old woman behind the counter looked up from her computer screen. "Which doctor are you here to see?"

"I'm not sure. I wasn't the one who made the appointment."

"Name?"

"Amy Miller."

The receptionist typed Amy's name. "You were supposed to see Dr. Singh, but she had an emergency at the hospital."

"Is there someone else I can see?" Amy asked.

"I'm afraid we don't have any other openings today, but we'll have the nurse bring you back so we can do your blood work," she said. "I can schedule you with her on Monday afternoon."

Though annoyed she wouldn't get any answers today, Amy nodded.

"Take a seat, and they'll call you back in a minute."

Amy followed her instructions. She'd barely sat down when a nurse called her name. Four vials of blood later, Amy left the office and made her way out to her car.

Her cell phone rang. Rather, one of her cell phones rang. She opened her purse and identified the correct one. Vanessa's name illuminated her screen.

Amy answered. "How's it going? Are you all ready for your move tomorrow?"

"I'm driving up with Talia tonight."

Amy reached her car and opened the door. "Is everything okay?"

"A new transcript from the fortress came through an hour ago," Vanessa said. "We picked up chatter of an electromagnetic strike in DC and New York."

Amy climbed into her car and closed the door. "A pulse weapon?"

"Some of our analysts think it's more than that. The early recordings made it sound like they were working on some kind of cyberattack, possibly on our electrical grid."

"There are safeguards to prevent hacking on those."

"Yes, but we know nothing is foolproof. It's possible Morenta is planning to use the pulse weapons as part of his attack."

"The last time he attacked, he used multiple strategies at the same time," Amy said. "It would fit."

"Yes, but unfortunately, that may also make it necessary for the SEALs to go in and raid the hideout," Vanessa said. "We need to know what's going on."

So much for the drone strike option. Amy let out a sigh. "I was afraid you were going to say that."

* * *

Jim had expected long days in his work as president, but even he hadn't been prepared for this reality. Every minute of every day had been squeezed to allow him to meet with a constant parade of politicians, experts, foreign dignitaries, intelligence officers, and military personnel. Then there were the cabinet nominee submissions, the interview and public-appearance requests, and trying to learn his way around the enormous mansion he now called home. Only it didn't feel like home.

He passed through the West Wing, said his good nights to the outer-office staff, and headed for the exit. His Secret Service agents fell into position behind him after announcing the now-common phrase, "Valiant is moving."

Valiant. He wasn't feeling valiant right now. He was worn out and home-sick.

The kids and grandkids had all returned to their homes, Matt and CJ being the last to leave with their brood only yesterday.

Already, the media had picked up photos of the family of five playing out on the White House grounds. The sheer glee on Spencer's face when he'd chased after his little brother had landed on the front page of USA Today along with the caption First family brings life to the White House.

His grandchildren certainly did that every time they visited him in his real home. Jim shook that thought away. He lived here now. Somehow, he had to find a way to make the White House feel like a real home instead of a glorified hotel.

He entered the mansion and passed the elevator, opting instead for the wide stairs leading to the living area of the residence. He was halfway up when a familiar scent wafted toward him.

"Gray, do you smell that?"

The Secret Service agent sniffed the air. "Smells like something baking."

"It smells like cinnamon rolls." Jim hastened his steps and turned toward the second-floor kitchen. Katherine stood at the counter, a bowl tucked into the crook of her arm and an icing spreader gripped in her hand. Four disposable aluminum pans lined the far counter, all covered in tinfoil. Two more, these of the glass-dish variety, occupied the space in front of Katherine.

Gray took his position in the hall, and Jim passed through the doorway.

"Please tell me one of those is for me," Jim said.

Katherine turned and smiled. "Yes, but you have to wait until I ice these. Those over there are for the squad."

"Four pans?"

"One for Vanessa and Seth. Another for Brent and Amy, and the other two for Brent to take back to the rest of the squad."

"A whole dozen for Brent and Amy is a bit much, don't you think? Seth and Vanessa too."

"Yes, but Quinn's going to eat a half dozen when he helps Seth move in, and Brent will share some of theirs with his men."

"You have them figured out, don't you?"

"In the food category anyway." Katherine finished icing one pan and moved to the last one.

"If you know Quinn is the one making the trip up tomorrow, then you must have heard from Brent or Amy today."

"No. I'm just guessing it will be Quinn." Katherine scooped more icing onto the warm rolls. "You haven't heard from Amy yet, have you?"

"No." Jim slipped his arms around Katherine's waist and leaned his chin on her shoulder. "I'm sure she'll call when she has something to share."

"I was hoping I would hear from her after her doctor's appointment." Katherine finished icing the pan she was on, dished out one of the fat cinnamon rolls, and set the spreader aside. "This one is for you."

"I really love you." Jim kissed her cheek. "I don't know how you found time to bake today, but I'm glad you did."

"It was time to start making this house feel like a home."

"You must have been reading my thoughts." Jim kissed her again, only this time he didn't settle for her cheek. Katherine turned into his arms, and her hands lifted to embrace him. Jim fell into the kiss, the warmth of his love enveloping them both.

When he drew back, he snagged the cinnamon roll and took a bite. "Mmmm. So good."

Katherine laughed. "You always say that."

"And I'm always right." Jim licked some icing off his thumb. "How many of those are you going to save for me?"

"One for breakfast tomorrow. The rest are going to your staff." Katherine called out, "Gray?"

The agent poked his head through the doorway. "Yes, ma'am?"

"Would you like a cinnamon roll?"

Interest flashed across his face before discipline chased it away. "I'm sorry, ma'am, but I shouldn't while I'm on duty."

Jim leaned back and lifted his half-eaten cinnamon roll. "You have two choices: my wife can wrap one up for you to eat when your shift ends, or you can have someone cover for you for three minutes while you enjoy one while it's warm."

The brief debate lasted only seconds. Gray lifted his hand and spoke into the microphone at his wrist. "I need backup in the president's kitchen."

Jim nodded with satisfaction. "You're a very smart man."

32

BRENT PULLED INTO THE GARAGE next to his wife's SUV, his thoughts and emotions churning. It was official now. Seth was leaving. This change was hitting Brent hard, even though he was trying not to let it get to him. Yes, he and Seth had been friends and swim buddies for years, but they were SEALs, for heaven's sake. They were used to change and uncertainty. Brent needed to get on board with his new reality now.

He still couldn't believe what Amy had done today to move Seth's changes along. She was a force of nature, one who couldn't be stopped once her mind was made up. Heaven help Commander Gardner and anyone else who tried to stand in her way.

With the new intel Brent had received today on Morenta's plans, his squad was going to need Amy's tenacity on this upcoming mission, especially with them going in two men down.

He walked into the house to the scent of something cooking. Was that meatloaf? He lifted the lid of the single pot on the stove. Mashed potatoes. His eyebrows drew together. A home-cooked meal prepared by his wife, who rarely cooked? What was going on?

"Amy?" Brent called out.

She walked into the kitchen. "Perfect timing. Dinner is almost ready."

"You cooked?" Brent greeted her with a kiss. "Is everything okay?"

"Everything is fine. I just thought that since I had the afternoon off, I would make dinner instead of ordering it."

"It smells good." Brent shrugged off his coat. "How did it go at the doctor's appointment?"

"It didn't happen. The doctor was called away for some emergency, so I'm going back in on Monday afternoon."

"That's annoying."

"Yeah, but they did some blood work, so hopefully, if there's anything to find, they'll have answers for me when I go in."

"Are you feeling any better?"

"I am. I must have just needed a good night's sleep and some time away from Gardner."

"I hope so."

Amy moved past him to the stove and stirred the potatoes. "By the way, did you get the new intel that came out on the fortress this afternoon?"

"Yeah, but I don't want to talk about that tonight. We need a break from work."

"In that case, go change out of your uniform. I'll get dinner on the table."

"Be right back." Brent changed into jeans and a T-shirt. When he returned, Amy was already waiting for him at the kitchen table.

After the blessing, Brent served Amy a slice of meatloaf and proceeded to cut a second piece twice as thick for himself. "So, are you going to tell me what happened today? That was one incredible send-off you did for Seth."

"I didn't mean for it to get so out of hand, but inviting Kendra was the only way I could be sure Admiral Rivera would be there."

"And Admiral Rivera was your substitute for Gardner on the sign-out sheet."

"He was the only one I could think of that Gardner couldn't go after when he finds out what happened." Amy took a sip of her water. "Does Gardner know what I did?"

"I didn't see him this afternoon, but I'm sure before the day was over, he heard about Kendra, Sienna, and Reed being on base," Brent said. "Everyone was buzzing about it when we went back to the office afterward."

"How long did it take to clear everyone out of there?"

"I don't know. The staff at the officers' club said they would take care of the cleanup for us."

"I need to send them a thank-you note."

"I doubt that's necessary. Kendra and Sienna took lots of photos with them before they left."

They fell into a companionable silence as they ate. Brent finished his second helping before he caught the all-too-familiar look on his wife's face.

"What's wrong?"

"Nothing." Amy scooped some mashed potatoes onto her fork but didn't lift it to her mouth. "It was good seeing Kendra again today."

Kendra. Their pregnant sister-in-law. Brent suppressed a sigh. Though avoidance would be easier, Brent faced the problem head on. "You haven't said much about Kendra's pregnancy. How are you doing with it?"

"It's the same as it always is." Amy pushed her plate away from her. "I want to be happy for everyone who gets to experience parenthood, but the envy is always right there."

"I'm sorry, Amy. Really, I am."

Amy put her hand on his. "I know. It's not your fault."

"It might still be possible to get pregnant."

"We've been trying for over four years." Amy blew out a breath. "Maybe it's time to consider other options."

"Adoption?" Brent asked, a spark of hope igniting inside him. "You've never wanted to talk about that before."

"I know, but I was looking at Doug Valdez and his family at the inauguration. They seemed so happy."

"I think they are happy."

"They adopted two kids, both teenagers. If they can make a family that way, maybe we can too."

Brent turned his hand over and laced his fingers with hers. "Any child would be lucky to have you for a mother."

"Even though I only know how to make about five different things for dinner?"

"Cooking isn't a requirement for motherhood." Brent squeezed her hand. "My mom is proof of that."

Amy laughed. "I guess the men in your family are doomed to cook."

"That's okay. The women we marry are worth the extra effort."

Amy leaned in for a kiss. "I'm glad you think so."

* * *

Amy nestled Talia in her arms and sat on the couch in her parents' living room—their old living room. It was Seth and Vanessa's now.

The baby's dark fingers wrapped around her bottle, and her body relaxed.

Vanessa walked in carrying two suitcases. Her face immediately broke out into a smile when she saw Talia. "Oh yeah. She's going to be out in no time."

"Better tell the guys to get the crib set up first," Amy said.

"I already did."

Quinn walked in holding the end pieces of the crib, followed by Seth and Brent, who had the other sections.

"Are you okay with her for a few more minutes?" Vanessa asked.

"Yeah. Go help the guys set up her room." Amy shifted her position on the couch so she could snuggle the baby closer. "I've got her."

"Thanks." Vanessa grabbed the suitcases again and disappeared up the stairs.

Amy's gaze remained on Talia for a moment before she looked around the room. Her mom had emptied out the built-in bookcases that lined the far wall of the great room, the majority of the contents now stored in the basement storage room along with most of the kitchenware and a few pieces of furniture from the room that would now belong to Talia.

Seth and Vanessa had opted to leave the rest of their furniture at their old house, most of it now stored in their basement to make room for Paige and Damian. It wouldn't be long until Talia's old room would turn into a nursery again, this time for Paige's baby.

What would it be like to prepare a room for a child who would come into her family through adoption instead of through biological birth? How old would the baby be? Would he or she suffer separation issues? Or have health problems? Should she and Brent consider adopting an older child the way Doug and Jill had?

Talia drank the last remnants of the bottle, and Amy snuggled her closer.

Brent, Seth, and Quinn descended the stairs.

Seth's expression softened when he saw Talia. "The crib is set up. You can put her down up there."

Amy nodded, not daring to speak for fear of waking Talia. She scooted to the edge of the couch and stood. Slowly, she crossed the room and made her way up the stairs. When she reached the new nursery, Vanessa was putting a sheet on the crib mattress.

Vanessa finished, then grabbed a quilt from the suitcase that lay open on the floor. "Go ahead and put her down."

Amy lowered Talia into the crib, the baby stirring the moment Amy released her. Vanessa rubbed her hand on the baby's stomach and gently tucked the blanket over her. After plugging in a baby camera and setting it on the dresser, she carried the monitor to the door.

As soon as Amy and Vanessa were in the hall, Vanessa pulled the door closed behind her. "She should sleep for at least an hour."

"With the three guys working together, you should be able to get everything moved in by then." Amy led the way back downstairs.

Brent walked by with a box marked Kitchen.

"I think we should work on unpacking," Amy said.

"Good plan." Vanessa followed Brent into the kitchen and set the baby monitor on the counter.

"Seth asked where you want your books," Brent asked. "The bedroom or the living room?"

"The living room." Vanessa opened the first of two boxes that now lay on the kitchen floor. Amy smiled when Vanessa pulled out her silverware organizer and placed it in the same drawer her family had kept theirs in her entire life.

Vanessa turned. "I still can't believe your parents are letting us live here."

"I'm glad they are." Amy retrieved a few newspaper-wrapped plates from the box and began unwrapping them. "This house needs people living in it. Besides, I kind of like knowing my room is still p retty much the same as it's always been."

"We'll keep it that way for you."

Amy laughed. "Don't feel like you can't use all the rooms in the house. I'm sure your parents and grandmother will want to come visit as soon as you're settled in."

"They aren't waiting that long," Vanessa said. "My mom texted me this morning. They should be here before you leave today."

Amy laughed. "You know that helping you move in is an excuse to play with the grandbaby, right?"

"Oh, I have no delusions about that."

33

SETH CARRIED TALIA THROUGH THE east colonnade of the White House and soaked in the atmosphere. Framed photos hung on one wall of the long hallway; a few images of Jim and Katherine from the inauguration were mixed in with candid images from past presidents. On the opposite wall, a bank of windows invited the White House grounds inside.

He hadn't expected to report to the White House until next week, but when Ted Engel had called to ask him to come in early to pick up his credentials, Seth had faced an unwinnable dilemma: ask his wife to take off her first day of work with the new president or bring the baby with him.

The latter had seemed like the easiest option until he'd tried to explain his plan to security. Of course, once Vanessa got involved, he not only had clearance to bring Talia with him but also a babysitter.

Seth shifted the backpack hanging from his shoulder and entered the East Wing lobby.

A young woman who couldn't be more than twenty-two looked up. "May I help you?"

"Lieutenant Commander Johnson to see the first lady."

The woman picked up the phone, but she didn't have a chance to dial before Katherine emerged from an office down the hall. "Oh, look at her." Katherine approached and reached for the baby. "I think she's grown in the past week."

Seth shifted Talia into Katherine's arms. "Are you sure you don't mind watching her?"

"I'm thrilled to have an excuse to take a break."

"Well, I really appreciate it," Seth said. "I don't know what caused the sudden urgency for me to get my credentials today, but we don't have baby-sitting lined up yet."

"Aren't you starting work next week?" Katherine asked.

"Yes. Vanessa's parents are coming back down this weekend to watch Talia until Vanessa can decide how much time she's going to need help each week."

Katherine turned to the receptionist. "Madison, can you check my personal address book and get Seth the numbers for Jamie Henderson and Carmen Vargas?"

"Yes, ma'am."

"Who are they?" Seth asked.

"Some friends from church. They'll be able to help you find temporary babysitting if you need it."

"That'll be great. Thanks." Seth lowered the backpack and handed it to Katherine. "Everything you need should be in there. I won't be long."

"Take your time. Madison and I are brainstorming today anyway. Talia can help us."

Seth ran his hand along his daughter's arm. "You have my number if you need me."

After pressing a kiss to the top of his daughter's head, Seth left Katherine and went in search of the security office.

The Secret Service agent manning the station by the East Reception Room pointed him in the right direction. Twenty minutes later, he emerged from the security office with his new badge hanging around his neck.

He moved toward Katherine's office. At least she hadn't needed to babysit for very long.

"Commander Johnson!" a man called out.

Seth turned.

Lance Howarth, the US Army military aide, approached. "I heard you were here."

"Captain."

"Do you have to leave right now?" Lance asked.

"I was going to pick up my daughter. Why?"

"If you can spare a few minutes, I wanted to introduce you to a few people."

"Let me make sure my babysitter is okay with that." Seth sent a quick text to Katherine.

Her response came back a moment later. *Take your time.*

Seth looked up from his phone. "I'm all good."

"Great," Lance said. "We'll start with introducing you to the Secret Service agents who work the West Wing stations. If we get lucky, you might even be able to meet the president."

Seth supposed he could mention that he was already on a first-name basis with the president, but instead he simply said, "Lead the way."

* * *

Jim followed his chief of staff down the hall toward the Situation Room. An impending threat. That was all Sawyer had been able to tell him beyond that he was needed in the Sit Room.

They rounded the corner, and Jim's Secret Service detail created a wall between him and the cluster of people waiting to be seated in the White House Mess, the White House's equivalent to an executive dining room.

Sawyer opened the door and waited for Jim to enter first.

As soon as Jim walked inside, everyone stood. Jim focused on the dozen top advisers surrounding the long conference table. "What's the latest?" he asked.

"We have a date for Morenta's attack," Admiral Mantiquez, his new secretary of defense, said. "February 3."

"So we have three days." Jim lowered into the seat at the head of the table. "What else do we know?"

Everyone settled into their seats. The secretary of national intelligence flipped open the notepad in front of him. "We picked up on a conversation that took place on the balcony of Morenta's suite at the fortress. In it, he said to launch the attack in four days. That conversation occurred last night."

Jim focused on Doug, who sat halfway down the long table. "Did he elaborate on his plans?"

"We're still operating under the assumption that it could be a combination of a pulse weapon with an attack on our electrical grid," Doug said, "but we do have a new wrinkle. There was mention of a bombing somewhere in DC."

"So, which is it? A bomb, a pulse weapon, or a cyberattack?" Jim asked, not sure he wanted to know the answer.

Doug's dark eyes flashed with concern. "It could be all three, sir."

"Is there anything on satellite images that can help us?"

"I'm afraid not, sir," Mantiquez said. "Our best chance to find out what they're planning is to go in and raid the fortress."

"Getting someone in there isn't going to be easy," General Browne said. "Not unless Nicaragua grants us permission to use their air space."

"If we involve the Nicaraguan government, we might as well announce our plans," Mantiquez said. "Morenta has people in high places in both Nicaragua and Colombia."

Secretary Hartley lifted his pen in the air. "Mr. President, we have a squad of Navy SEALs who have breached the fortress before. I believe a targeted special ops mission is our best option."

The Saint Squad. Jim forced himself to ask the dreaded question. "Expected casualties?"

"We could lose as many as half, sir."

"I want other options." Jim pushed back from the table.

"Sir, may I suggest we at least deploy the SEALs to the USS *Harry S. Truman*?"

"Permission granted." Jim nodded. "In the meantime, I want you to consult with my new intelligence adviser, Vanessa Johnson."

"Sir, we have some of the top intelligence and tactical officers already working on this."

"That may be, but none of them has ever lived at the fortress." Jim let his comment sink in before he added, "Vanessa has."

* * *

The buzz about the celebrity sightings on Friday hadn't faded when Amy returned on Monday afternoon from the latest briefing with SEAL Team Ten's intelligence officers. Whether the Saint Squad would really be transferred to a different team still remained to be seen, but someone had deemed her presence necessary for the detailed play-by-play of the hot spots around the world.

Amy sidestepped two ensigns exchanging stories about who got to talk to Kendra the longest on Friday. A short distance down the hall, an aide displayed his autographed photo of Sienna and Reed to a coworker.

Amy tuned out the chatter, today's briefing replaying in her mind. Of the six areas of concern mentioned, Amy suspected the Saint Squad would be most likely to deploy to either the Mediterranean off the coast of Abolstan or back to the USS *Harry S. Truman* in the Caribbean. Of the potential threats, Morenta appeared to be the enemy causing the most concern.

Amy's steps slowed when she approached Gardner's office, the commander's voice carrying to her.

"It was good seeing you."

Another male voice followed. "I'll swing back by after I stop by Admiral Rivera's office, and we can get some lunch."

"Sounds good."

A man in uniform appeared in the hall, heading away from Amy. Admiral's stars on his shoulders, salt-and-pepper gray hair. Had Commander Gardner's uncle come for a visit?

Amy continued forward at a slower rate in the hope that the commander would go back into his office. Her hope wasn't realized. She passed by Mei Lien's desk, where Gardner still stood.

"Ms. Miller, I'd like a word with you."

Great. "I'm sorry, sir, but I have new intel reports I need to get to my squad," Amy said. "I can come back after I deliver them."

"That can wait."

"No, it can't." Amy held up the latest surveillance photos. "These are mission critical."

"They don't even have orders to ship out."

"Yet. They will soon." Amy took a step down the hall, but Gardner cut her off.

"In my office. Now."

Amy looked him in the eye, for once appreciative of her height. "I'll be right back." She took another step, but he countered her move.

"Don't you walk away from me." He lowered his voice and leaned in. "I know you were behind the change in Johnson's orders. You went behind my back."

"You didn't give me a choice." Amy fought the urge to take a step back. "Stonewalling someone as part of a power play isn't just low; it's detrimental to the operational readiness of this unit and this country."

"What would you know about what this country needs to be prepared to defend itself?" Gardner shot back. "You're a civilian."

"I'm a civilian who is good at my job."

Footsteps approached from both directions.

Tristan stepped into view. "Amy, is everything okay?"

Amy handed the satellite images to him. "Get these to Brent. I don't know when, but you're shipping out soon." She caught the look of concern on his face and added, "I'm fine. I'll be there in a few minutes."

Gardner stretched out his hand. "Hand those over, Petty Officer."

Admiral Moss approached, a line marring the space between his brows. "What's going on here?"

"Just dealing with a little insubordination problem," Gardner said.

Amy ignored Gardner and the admiral. "Tristan. Go. He needs those now."

Tristan nodded at Amy and repeated the gesture to the admiral. "Excuse me, sir." He skirted around the admiral and made his way down the hall.

"You just earned yourself an official reprimand," Gardner growled.

"Would someone like to explain what is happening here?" Admiral Moss asked.

"Your nephew is more concerned about exercising an iron fist than he is about the well-being of the men in his unit and the missions they need to prepare for."

"She disobeyed a direct order."

"Your order was to deny my squad time-sensitive intelligence," Amy shot back.

Admiral Moss turned his gaze on Gardner. "Is this true?"

"Ms. Miller has a tendency to overexaggerate the importance of her duties here."

"Don't underestimate the value of intelligence officers in the teams," Admiral Moss said. "There's a reason each squad needs one."

"Commander Gardner doesn't see it that way, which is why he has me serving three squads instead of one."

"Three?" The admiral's eyebrows lifted briefly before a scowl crossed his face. "How are you supposed to keep up with the intelligence reports for so many units?"

"Honestly, I've had to bring in some help."

"I knew you were violating security protocols," Gardner spat out.

"I've never violated anything. I only used cleared resources." Amy straightened her shoulders and let the dirty laundry air. "You can cut off my phone service and trade out my computer for a broken one, but I'm not going to let you endanger my men."

"They're my men."

"No." Amy took a step forward, and Gardner took a step back. "A true commander protects his men. You've done nothing but sabotage them."

Amy's cell phone rang. She nearly ignored it until she recognized the ring tone as the one Ghost had given her. Only three people could be calling her: Ghost, Vanessa, or her father. All of them were more important than whatever Commander Gardner had to say.

"Excuse me." Amy took a step back and answered. "Hello?"

Her father's voice came over the line. "Honey, the call should be coming in shortly, but your boys are shipping out in two hours."

"They're going to the fortress?"

"Yes. We have three days before Morenta's attack." Apology hung in his voice when he added, "I'm sorry. I don't have a choice but to send them in."

"I understand," Amy said, a prayer already circling through her head, pleading for their safety. "So will they."

"I need their input on the mission. Make sure Brent knows I want their suggestions."

"I will. Thanks, Dad." Amy hung up and turned to the admiral. "Admiral Moss, it was good to see you, but if you'll excuse me, I need to pass a message on to the Saint Squad before they ship out."

"Of course." Admiral Moss stepped aside. "Best of luck to them."

"Thank you."

"Wait a minute." Gardner stepped into her path again. "Like I said a minute ago, they don't even have orders."

"They will."

"You best get going," Admiral Moss said.

"Sir." Amy started down the hall as Mei Lien's phone rang.

"What are you doing?" Gardner hissed at his uncle.

"You heard her. That was obviously her father on the phone. If he said her squad is shipping out, then they're shipping out."

"What does her father have to do with deployment orders?"

Admiral Moss waited a beat. "Amy's father is the president of the United States."

34

SETH MET SECRET SERVICE AGENTS, two White House physicians, three admirals, and countless aides and administrative types. While he prided himself on his ability to remember names and faces, if Lance gave him a quiz at the end of the day, Seth suspected he would fail.

They passed by the Roosevelt Room and entered the office Jim's secretarial staff shared. Three desks lined one wall, each one occupied.

"The Oval Office is through there." Lance motioned past the line of desks. He stopped at the one nearest the door he indicated. "Sarah, is he in?"

"No." That was as far as she got before Jim's voice carried to them.

"I want options that will bring that casualty rate down," Jim said. He and Doug rounded the corner, and Jim spotted Seth. "I'm glad you're here. We could use your expertise."

"Sir?" Seth asked. "I'm happy to help with whatever you need, but I didn't plan on being here for long," Seth said. "Katherine is watching Talia."

Lance looked from Seth to Jim and back again, clearly confused.

"Sarah, can you get my wife on the line?"

"Yes, sir."

"Come in." Jim led the way into the Oval Office. Seth, Lance, and Jim's chief of staff followed. "Close the door behind you."

Lance complied.

By the time Jim reached his desk, his phone was already ringing.

He picked it up and greeted his wife. "Honey, I need Seth to help me for a while. Are you okay watching the baby a bit longer?" Jim paused. "Great. Thanks." Jim ended the call. "Katherine is going to put Talia down for her nap in the residence. She'll work with her assistant up there this afternoon."

Lance looked from Jim to Seth. "Your babysitter is the first lady?"

Seth shrugged. "She said she needed a break."

"Have a seat, gentlemen." Jim motioned them to the seating area in the center of the room.

Seth chose a spot on a couch, and Lance sat beside him. "What's the situation?" Seth asked.

"I'm sending the Saint Squad to the fortress, and I'm not happy with the expected casualty rates their superiors are giving me," Jim said. "You've been there. What can we do to improve their odds?"

"What's our objective?" Seth asked.

Jim and Doug filled them in on the imminent threat and the plans to capture Morenta and invade the hideout.

"I agree that alerting Nicaragua is asking for failure," Seth finally said. "Our best bet is a repeat of what we did when we went in after bin Laden. What's our timeline?"

"The attack is in three days."

Seth's heart sank. "You want to strike in two."

"I'm afraid so."

Seth's mind raced over the multiple defense measures Morenta had in place. "To bring in a full assault team, we'll have to take out the Z-10 before we insert."

"If we do that, we're announcing the SEALs' presence before they're even on the ground," Lance said.

"What if a couple squads insert a couple hours earlier?" Seth asked. "One can get in place at the hideout, and the other can go after Morenta. As soon as they're in place, you send in a missile to take out the Z-10, followed by reinforcements."

"That could work, assuming the missile can find the Z-10," Doug said. "Morenta's defenses would focus on the incoming threat, which could create a breach in their security on the inside."

"Someone in the first wave will need to take out the guard on the beach and the other by the front entrance to clear the landing zone," Seth said. "And we also have to neutralize any anti-aircraft guns they may have hidden there."

"I'll leave the specifics to you," Jim said. "You can work out of the Sit Room. You'll have access to all the latest intel there."

"Sir, with your permission, I should go in with my squad." Seth stood. "I know the fortress better than anyone."

Jim shook his head. "You wouldn't get there in time. Besides, your squad has been to the fortress before. Having your expertise here will give the rest of us the knowledge we need to make sure this mission is a success."

His squad was deploying without him. Seth felt hollow, but he forced himself to nod. "Yes, sir."

* * *

The phone on Brent's desk rang in the same instant Amy rushed into his office. Brent pushed away from his worktable, where he and the rest of his squad were studying the latest satellite photos. Amy took his place as he snatched up his phone.

"Miller."

"Commander, your unit is shipping out at eleven hundred," Mei Lien said. She proceeded to give him their transportation details.

Brent jotted them down. "Got it."

He hung up the phone. "We hop at eleven hundred. A COD will fly us out to the carrier," Brent said, referring to the carrier onboard delivery aircraft.

Amy looked around the room. "Where's Jay?"

"He's on his way to the hospital," Brent said. "Carina called a while ago. She's in labor." His chest tightened the way it always did when he had to leave his wife behind. Fighting the sensation, Brent turned his attention to the rest of his squad. "Grab your gear and make your calls. Be at the airfield in an hour."

His men didn't have to be told twice. They scattered out the door, leaving the intelligence reports behind.

Amy gathered the photos and the mission notes. "I'm going to grab my go-bag. We can drive to the airfield together."

Amy back on ship with him? It was about time. Brent moved to his computer and opened the email from Mei Lien with his squad's orders. "Amy, I hate to tell you this, but you aren't on the orders."

"Let me see what I can do about that."

"But don't you have your doctor's appointment this afternoon?"

"I can reschedule."

"You sure about that?" As much as he wanted his wife's support aboard ship as his intelligence officer, his concern for her well-being overrode all else. "With the way you've been feeling, maybe it's best you aren't aboard a ship right now."

"I hate not being there with you."

"I know." Brent hit the Print button and crossed to her. He slipped his arms around her waist. "We aren't going to be on board for long before we insert anyway. Maybe you should take advantage of your White House connections and support us from up there."

"Invade the Situation Room?"

"Why not? You have clearance, and all the squads you support will be in the field."

"Webb's unit is going with you?"

"They are."

"I don't like this." Amy's arms tightened around him.

"I know, but you'll be able to do more for us if you have all the intel when it's being created," Brent said. "We can't afford to let red tape impede the flow of information."

"Okay, you win." Amy's gaze lifted to his. "Promise me you'll be careful."

Brent leaned down and kissed her. "Always."

* * *

Amy stood on the tarmac as the aircraft carrying her husband powered down the runway and lifted into the air. She didn't know why the idea of the Saint Squad having only five members had her so rattled, but she couldn't deny the overwhelming sense of fear that continued to push to the forefront of her mind. The Saint Squad had operated as a unit of five for years. Why did the lower number bother her now?

Webb's unit would be there to support the mission. But Seth wasn't with them. Neither was Jay.

The plane ascended over the Atlantic, the sea of blue visible from where she stood. Though she wanted to stay and watch until Brent's plane disappeared from sight, she couldn't indulge in taking that much time. She had only an hour until her doctor's appointment, and she still needed to put in for Jay's leave. If she was lucky, Gardner would still be talking to his uncle and Mei Lien could help her take care of pushing the request through to personnel.

Amy drove from the airfield back to her building, bracing herself as she went inside and approached Gardner's office. Mei Lien's desk was occupied, but Mei Lien wasn't anywhere in sight. Instead, one of the secretaries from reception was sitting in her seat.

"Where's Mei Lien?" Amy asked.

"She's in the conference room with Admiral Moss."

"Why?"

"I don't know. I got a call a half hour ago asking me to cover for her."

"She's been in there with him for a half hour? Is Commander Gardner in there too?" Amy asked.

"No. I think he's out to lunch."

Admiral Moss had mentioned eating lunch with his nephew. Something had changed in the last half hour. Amy would figure it out later.

"I need to get Lieutenant Wellman's paternity leave processed. Is that something you can help me with?"

"Sure. No problem."

Amy passed along the information and checked the time on her watch. "I have to head out for an appointment. Can you tell Mei Lien I'll check in with her later?"

"Will do."

Amy headed back toward the exit. Twenty minutes later, she signed in at the doctor's office for the second time in four days.

She didn't get the chance to sit before the nurse opened the door and said, "Mrs. Miller, we can take you right back."

"Thanks."

The nurse went through the ritual of taking Amy's vital signs. She then led her to a bathroom. "The doctor will want another urine sample. Then I'll take you to your exam room."

"I just did one on Friday."

The nurse shrugged. "Sorry. She asked for one today too."

"Okay." After Amy complied, she was shown to an exam room.

A list of questions followed, along with a conversation about Amy's symptoms.

When the nurse finished updating Amy's chart in the computer in the corner of the room, she stood. "The doctor will be in shortly."

"Thanks."

Again, the wait was mercifully short. A knock sounded on the door, and the doctor walked in. She was nearly a foot shorter than Amy, and her long, jet-black hair was tied back.

"Mrs. Miller, I'm Dr. Singh." Her lyrical voice carried a hint of her Indian heritage. "I understand you've been feeling a bit under the weather."

"Yes." Amy gripped the edge of her chair. "I'm sure it's nothing, but my husband wanted me to come in and get checked out."

Dr. Singh tapped on the computer. "I looked over your blood work, and everything looks good. Your iron count is a little low, but that isn't uncommon in your situation."

Amy's eyebrows drew together. "My situation?"

Dr. Singh offered a smile. "Mrs. Miller, you're pregnant."

Amy's eyes widened, and a tornado of emotions swirled inside her. "Pregnant? Are you sure?"

"Quite."

Tears sprang to Amy's eyes, and she lifted both hands to cover her mouth. So many months and years of hoping and praying. And so many of hopelessness and abandoning the dream of bearing a child of her own.

And now this doctor was telling her that her and Brent's miracle had finally happened.

"Is this good news or bad news?" Dr. Singh asked gently.

Amy lowered her hands. "It's the best news. Thank you, Doctor."

35

SETH PASSED BY JIM'S SECRETARIAL staff, Lance right behind him. He should have stayed with his squad for the extra week. He could have waited to move to northern Virginia until this weekend.

"Okay, spill," Lance said. "How do you know the Whitmores?"

Seth didn't know where to start. The history between the Saint Squad and the Whitmores went all the way back to when Amy and Brent first met. Sticking with the simplest version of the truth, he said, "I guess you could say they're family friends."

"You're friends with the president, and you didn't mention it during your interview?" Lance asked, his voice incredulous.

"It didn't seem relevant."

"Didn't seem relevant?" Lance repeated. "You know that information could have swayed everyone."

"The president got me the interview, and I appreciate his faith in me," Seth said, "but I don't want to be in a job I don't deserve."

"I can understand that," Lance said with respect in his voice.

They reached a spot where two halls intersected.

"Which way?" Seth asked.

Lance motioned him down the hall. "We need to go downstairs."

Seth followed his new coworker's directions. The door labeled Situation Room was in sight when someone called his name.

Vanessa spoke briefly to the woman she was with before approaching Seth.

"What are you doing here?" Vanessa asked. "Where's Talia?"

"Katherine's watching her." Seth motioned to Lance. "This is Captain Lance Howarth. He's one of the military aides."

"Vanessa Johnson. Nice to meet you." Vanessa shook his hand.

"Johnson? You two are married?"

Seth nodded. "She's the real reason the president wanted me to get this job."

"Don't sell yourself short," Vanessa said. "And you still haven't told me why you're here."

"I came in to pick up my credentials, but the president asked me to stay and help with a mission."

"The Saint Squad."

"Yeah." Seth motioned to the Situation Room door. "I need to get in there, but can you give your friend a call and see if he has any new intel?"

"I'll call right now." Vanessa stepped back. "It was nice meeting you, Captain."

Lance swiped his badge across the electronic lock by the door. "You're just full of secrets, aren't you?"

"I'm a navy SEAL." Seth followed Lance into the room, where a large screen took up most of one wall. A conference table stretched the length of the floor, laptops open in front of the occupants, who were mostly high-ranking military officials.

A civilian stood inside the door. "I need to see your badges."

Seth and Lance held theirs up.

The man checked their credentials before he returned his gaze to their faces. "Are you here for the briefing?"

"I am," Seth said. At least, he assumed Jim would want him here for whatever briefing the man was talking about.

"I need to get back to the office." Lance motioned to Seth's badge. "I'll swing by security and make sure your badge is activated since you're starting work earlier than you expected."

"Thanks."

The civilian pointed to a row of chairs on the far side of the room. "Take a seat. We'll be starting any minute."

Seth chose an empty seat that faced the large monitor. Multiple images of the fortress filled the screen, several of which had clearly been extracted from the video taken from his squad's last mission into Nicaragua.

The door opened again, and Doug walked in with Secretary Hartley.

The moment the door closed behind them, Secretary Hartley said, "We have two squads of SEALs en route to the USS *Harry S. Truman*. ETA two hours. They'll be our advance team, inserting using inflatables. Their objective will be to neutralize the Z-10 helicopter at the fortress and take out the guards on the beach. Once they accomplish that, two more squads will insert via helicopter and go after Morenta."

And casualties would ultimately follow. Despite being among the lowest-ranking officers in the room, Seth couldn't help but speak. "Sir, I recommend we make some changes to that plan."

Secretary Hartley narrowed his eyes. "Who are you?"

Seth stood. "Lieutenant Commander Seth Johnson, sir."

"We've analyzed this plan a dozen times," Secretary Hartley said. "One of the squad commanders even recommended this approach."

"If you're speaking about Commander Miller, I believe some details got lost in translation."

Before the admiral could comment further, Doug asked, "Commander, what changes would you propose?"

"First, I would send in the advance team a day early."

"That would mean inserting tomorrow night."

"Yes, sir. That's the only way they'll be able to go after the Z-10. The helicopter is on patrol every night, so if they don't insert earlier, it doesn't give the SEALs adequate time to either disable or destroy the helicopter."

"What else?" Doug asked.

"If they plant an explosive device on the Z-10 that is wired to the motor, the helicopter will explode when the pilot starts it up."

"Like a car bomb," a general sitting at the table said.

"Yes, sir." Seth moved to the front of the room and pointed at the image of the beach. "The explosion would be the signal for the advance team to neutralize the guards and for the second group of SEALs to insert."

"Wouldn't it make more sense to coordinate the attack on a certain time-line?" an air force colonel asked.

"Yes, but having a signal built in if communication goes down is vital," Seth said. "These woods are filled with motion sensors and trip wires. Plus, the Z-10's flight schedule is inconsistent, as are the guard rotations."

Secretary Hartley's gaze lowered to the trident on Seth's uniform, the only outward indication of Seth's background as a SEAL. "You're with the Saint Squad."

"I was, sir. I start on Monday as a military aide to the president."

"We appreciate your insight, Commander Johnson," Secretary Hartley said before addressing the rest of the room. "I vote we make these adjustments and move forward. I want a plan in place before those SEALs get to the carrier."

Nods of agreement followed.

Doug sat at the table and motioned to the empty spot beside him. "Take a seat, Commander, and let's get to work."

"Thank you, sir."

* * *

Pregnant. The word kept repeating in Amy's head. Not only pregnant but seven weeks pregnant. An ultrasound had confirmed the blood test as well as her due date. Her baby would come in September.

She crossed the medical center parking lot to her car as the overwhelming urge to share her news flooded through her.

If only she'd been able to see the doctor on Friday, she and Brent could have celebrated their news over the weekend. They could have shared it with her parents when they had stopped by the White House to visit and pick up her mother's famous cinnamon rolls.

If-onlys and what-ifs. Amy knew better than to let those two phrases invade her thoughts, but keeping the news to herself until Brent got home was going to drive her crazy.

It would be only a few more days. With the short timeline for Morenta's planned strike—whatever it was—Brent would surely insert day after tomorrow.

Her phone buzzed with an incoming text. She pulled it from her purse, and her smile was instant when she read Jay's message. Baby Girl Wellman had made her appearance.

Rather than continue to her car, Amy changed directions and headed toward the hospital that adjoined the medical center. Surely a short detour before going back to work wouldn't hurt anything.

Amy walked into the hospital lobby and approached the information desk, where a man in his seventies sat. "Can you tell me what room Carina Wellman is in?" she asked.

"Let me see." Methodically, he typed in Carina's name. After a moment, he reached for a sticky note and wrote down the room number. "Here you are."

"Thank you." Amy took the elevator upstairs and was halfway down the hall when Jay emerged from a room a short distance away, a large plastic cup in his hand.

"Jay, how's Carina?"

"Good." Jay held up the cup. "I'm just getting her some more ice. She's awake though. Go on in."

Amy reached the correct room and rapped lightly on the open door before she walked in. "Hey, how are you?"

Carina looked up from the infant in her arms, her expression a combination of wonder and pain. "I feel like I got hit by a truck, but she is so worth it."

Amy stepped closer and peered at the scrunched little face. Though little Eva wasn't the prettiest baby she'd ever seen, Amy said, "She's adorable. You did good."

"Thanks."

Jay walked in with the cup of ice water. He set it on the bedside table. "Want me to take her?"

"Maybe Amy wants to hold her," Carina suggested.

Concern flashed on Jay's face. For the first time in years, Amy didn't experience envy when she stepped closer. "I'd love to."

She gently lifted the baby from Carina, careful to support her tiny head. "So sweet." Amy lowered into the chair beside Carina's bed. "I didn't think you would be in a room yet. Jay only left for the hospital a few hours ago."

"He met me here," Carina said.

"Thank goodness." Jay handed Carina her water and put his hand on her shoulder. "She barely made it to the hospital before the baby was born."

"Apparently, I have fast labors." Carina took a sip of her water.

"How long was it?"

"Two hours and twenty-five minutes."

"Wow. That is fast." A little twinge of fear needled through Amy at the thought of going through labor, but she focused on the baby in her arms. Surely a child of her own would be worth it.

The baby stretched her little arms and started to fuss.

"She probably needs to eat," Carina said.

"I should get back to the office." Amy stood and handed the baby back to Carina.

"Has the rest of the squad already left?" Jay asked.

"Yeah."

"What happened with Gardner?"

"Admiral Moss blocked his attempt to get in my way this time," Amy said. "I'm actually going to call Admiral Rivera to see if I can go up to DC and work from there until this mission is over."

"Don't trust your phone to work?"

"I don't want to wait for reports to get forwarded to me," Amy said.

"The front line always has been more your style," Jay said. "Good luck. And let me know if there's anything I can do to help."

"Take care of your wife and baby." Amy adjusted the purse strap on her shoulder. "I'll see you later." She left the hospital and climbed into her car. She debated whether to stop by the office or avoid Gardner altogether. He wasn't going to approve her request to work at the White House. Besides, it was almost three. She had only another couple of hours of work left. If she went home now, she could pack and drive up to DC tonight. She'd prefer arriving at the White House before nine since she could no longer just use her house key to let herself in. Then again, she did have a permanent room assigned to her.

Her cell phone rang, the call originating from the office.

"Hello?"

"Amy, it's Mei Lien. Are you going to be back soon?"

"I can be. Why?" Amy asked.

"Admiral Moss said to tell you he's flying to Andrews Air Force Base at sixteen thirty. He thought you might want a ride to DC."

"That would be great. Maybe if I go with the admiral, Commander Gardner won't write me up for working in DC."

"I'm not sure either of us reports to Commander Gardner anymore."

"What do you mean?"

"Admiral Moss questioned me and a few of the other people in the unit," Mei Lien said. "Then he met with Admiral Rivera."

"And?"

"Commander Gardner was put on administrative leave. I think Admiral Moss may have relieved him of duty."

"Oh wow."

"Not only that." Mei Lien's voice lowered. "Security had to escort him out of the building."

Amy wished she had been there to witness Gardner's removal. It was petty, she supposed, but after the nightmares he had put them all through, if Moss really had relieved his nephew of duty, some celebrations were in order.

"I'll tell Admiral Moss to expect you at the airfield."

"Thanks, Mei Lien."

"Thank *you*," Mei Lien said. "If you hadn't stood up to Gardner, he'd still be making a mess of things."

"Let's just hope we can undo all the damage he's already done."

36

BRENT DROPPED HIS GEAR IN his berthing compartment aboard the USS *Harry S. Truman* and made his way to the board room his squad would share with Webb's unit while on board.

When he reached his destination, a yeoman waited outside the compartment. "Commander Miller?"

"Yes."

The yeoman held out a thick folder marked with the telltale red stripes and top secret stamps on the outside. "This is for you, sir."

"Thank you."

Webb approached as Brent opened the hatch. Brent walked inside and took in the space. It was larger than the board room his squad typically used, a line of five computers along one wall. Three more took up the space on the opposite wall. A rectangular table stretched along the far side of the room, and a scatter of chairs surrounded it. A large flat-screen hung on the back wall, with two smaller ones in the corners.

"You ready to get started?" Webb asked. "I sent my guys to settle in and grab some chow."

"Mine should be here in a few minutes," Brent said. "They'll have some food sent in for us."

"Five-star treatment, huh?"

"We work off the *Truman* a lot," Brent said. "And Craig has a way of finding people who want to help him." Brent dropped the thick file on the worktable.

Webb took a seat. "Should I even ask why people want to help Craig?"

"Sorry," Brent said. "His methods fall under the need-to-know umbrella."

"I had a feeling." Webb jutted his chin in the direction of the file. "What have we got?"

Brent flipped open the file and took the seat beside Webb so they could look over the plans together. He had expected to make adjustments to whatever the higher-ups had sent them, but as he read through the details, he couldn't find fault with any of it. They had even built in a backup signal and taken into account the possibility of being detected by the Z-10's heat sensors.

"The insertion is going to be tricky," Brent said, going over the timeline. "We need to go in in the dark, but if the Z-10 is in the air, it will detect us."

"How about a diversion?" Webb slid an overhead image of the fortress closer to him.

"Got any ideas?"

"We could send a speedboat toward the beach to draw attention away from us."

"That's risky to whoever would be piloting it," Brent said. "There's no guarantee Morenta wouldn't order the Z-10 pilot to destroy it."

"We operate it by remote, then," Webb suggested.

It was an expensive option, but it might work. "We would need something on board that would generate a heat signature."

"I'll have one of my guys check with logistics." Webb tapped on the mission plan summary.

"Which do you and your boys want to take?" Webb asked. "The Z-10 or the guards?"

As much as he hated to do it, Brent chose the more difficult option. "We'll take the Z-10. My men are more familiar with the terrain."

"And the climb to stage Morenta's capture?" Webb flipped through the overhead images. "Any idea which floor he's staying on?"

"Yeah." Dread curled inside Brent, but he forced himself to follow logic. "I'll take that. If I put Quinn on sniper duty, Tristan can buddy up with me."

"And your two new kids will wire the helicopter?"

Damian and Craig weren't exactly new, but they were the most recent additions to the squad. "That's my plan. After they finish with that, they can prep for the takeover of the hideout."

"That'll leave my boys to secure the landing zone and take out any anti-aircraft guns."

"We didn't see any our last time in, but I have to think they have some somewhere."

"That's my assumption as well." Webb flipped the page. "All that's left is picking a spot where we can bed down during the day to stay out of sight."

Brent skimmed over the text, pausing when he reached a suggestion to spend the day in the same spot where he and Seth had slept while waiting for the sun to go down.

"If I didn't know any better, I'd swear a SEAL had planned this out," Webb said.

Seth might not officially be part of the Saint Squad right now, but Brent recognized his handiwork. His deep appreciation for the man who had been his best friend for nearly a decade swelled inside him. On the squad or not, Seth still had his back. "I'm pretty sure one did."

* * *

Amy stopped by her house long enough to grab some extra clothes beyond what was in her go-bag. She pulled into the parking lot of the airstrip and flagged down a ride to take her out to the appropriate hanger. As soon as she reached the plane, she set her backpack on top of her rolling suitcase and approached the aircraft.

Admiral Moss stood at the bottom of the airstair, speaking with a lieutenant.

"Lieutenant, take care of Ms. Miller's luggage."

"Yes, sir." The young man in his midtwenties relieved Amy of her luggage and carried it onto the plane.

Amy closed the rest of the distance between them. "Sir, thank you for offering me a ride."

"Least I could do." The admiral motioned for her to climb the stairs first.

When she reached the cabin, the lieutenant who had stored her luggage motioned her into a seat in the second row.

As soon as she sat down, the admiral settled in beside her.

"I'm ready to hear your side of the story," Admiral Moss said.

Amy's eyebrows lifted. "Excuse me, sir?"

"You heard me. I've already spoken with several members of SEAL Team Eight, but so far, people have only hinted at problems that have occurred since my nephew took command."

Amy clipped her seat belt into place. "You must have heard enough if you relieved him of duty."

He glanced around the aircraft at the few others sitting in nearby seats. His voice lowered. "It's a temporary sit-down unless I have evidence to support a permanent change."

"I'm sorry, sir, but forgive me for being surprised. He's your nephew."

"Yes, he is my nephew. From everything I've heard up until now, he's been moving up quickly because he is bright and innovative."

Bright and innovative. Not exactly the words Amy would use to describe him.

"I don't know why he's had so many issues since taking over command of SEAL Team Eight, but the complaints have been coming in regularly for the past few weeks."

"I'm not surprised. I'm afraid Commander Gardner started planning changes in our team before he even arrived."

"Like I said, he's innovative," Admiral Moss said. "I assume you read through his proposal for the team."

Amy wasn't sure how the admiral would know that, but she wasn't prone to lie. "If I answer yes, are you going to ask me where I got it from?"

He cocked an eyebrow. "I respect anyone who protects their sources."

"Then, yes, I've read it."

"And?"

"And I have some serious concerns, particularly about his proposal to eliminate SEAL Team Ten."

"That's not right." Admiral Moss shook his head as the aircraft began taxiing down the runway. "His whole idea was to streamline administrative costs to cut expenses so more funds would be available for training."

"Sounds like you didn't read all the way to page thirty-eight."

"I hate to admit it, but with the amount of paperwork that crosses my desk, it's not uncommon for me to rely on others to read through reports and brief me on them."

"I believe your nephew was counting on that," Amy said. "I still don't understand his objectives, but his primary focus since joining SEAL Team Eight has been to eliminate the civilians in his command, transfer personnel out to make room for people from his old unit, and to get his proposal approved to get rid of a significant number of SEALs."

Admiral Moss shook his head and let out a long-suffering sigh.

The plane stopped, turned, and, moments later, accelerated. When the admiral remained silent throughout their takeoff, Amy finally asked, "Do you know what Commander Gardner was trying to accomplish?"

"He was trying to eliminate everything that kept him off the teams."

"I thought he was a SEAL," Amy said. "I mean, until he was injured."

"He was only on his second mission when some bad intel put his platoon in the middle of a hot landing zone. He was shot twice. One impacted his vest, the other his leg. The injuries were recoverable, but the PTSD he developed afterward kept him from rejoining his unit."

"That's too bad." Amy suspected there was more to the story. "How is his past trauma playing into all the changes he's trying to make?"

"The intel officer who made the call to send his unit in was a civilian."

"So he holds a grudge against anyone who isn't wearing a uniform?"

"It goes deeper than that. He's always blamed the quick response initiative for the bad situation he was in in the first place." Admiral Moss let out another sigh. "Want to hazard a guess on which team he was originally assigned to?"

The puzzle pieces snapped into place. "SEAL Team Ten."

* * *

Jim dropped into his desk chair in the Oval Office and leaned back. Alone at last. One briefing had run into another today, the situation with Morenta dominating his time and attention.

Jim closed his eyes and leaned his head back. He should go to the residence for dinner, at least long enough to see his wife, but even the thought of walking that short distance was overwhelming. He was going to have to schedule some time to exercise a few days a week if he was going to keep up this pace for the next few years.

The phone on his desk rang. With some effort, he straightened and lifted the receiver. "Yes?"

"Mrs. Johnson here to see you."

"Send her in." Jim stood as Vanessa walked into his office. His office. That thought crashed over him for a brief moment before he focused on the woman before him.

"Did you get your tour today?"

"I did, but that's not why I'm here." Vanessa closed the door behind her. "Ghost called. His colleague in Central America mobilized to Nicaragua. He said there's a lot of movement in and out of the fortress today."

"Any idea why?" Jim asked.

"Nothing definitive."

"I don't think I've met the guardian in Central America." Jim circled his desk and motioned for Vanessa to sit on the couch. "Do you know anything about him?"

"No. Ghost said he speaks the language, and he knows how to stay out of sight. That's all I know."

"Keep the communication lines open with him," Jim said. "Having extra eyes on the ground could make a big difference when our boys insert."

"I will, but is there any chance you can get me cleared to know their names? Or at least their code names?" Vanessa asked. "This is going to be far too confusing trying to describe who is who based on their geographic location."

"Call Ghost. Let's get this sorted out now."

Vanessa retrieved her phone and dialed. After a moment, she said simply, "The president wants to speak to you." Vanessa held out the phone.

Jim took it from her. "Vanessa is in my office. What needs to happen for her to be fully read into the guardian program?"

"She wants to know my name, doesn't she?" Kade asked dryly.

"Guessed it on the first try."

"I'll talk to Hannah and Ace," Kade said, referring to the computer programmer who oversaw operations and the senior guardian. "She is going to stay in this job though, right? You're the first person outside the guardians to know any of our names."

"She's sticking around." Jim made eye contact with Vanessa, pleased when she nodded. "And you know you can trust her."

"Full names and backgrounds will have to remain confidential, but I think Ace will clear her for our first names."

"Same as what he gave me."

"Yes."

"That would be helpful." Jim leaned back on the couch. "And keep me up-to-date on the situation with Morenta."

"You know I will. Just tell Vanessa not to get mad when I call her in the middle of the night."

Jim studied the petite, dark-skinned woman across from him, a woman with a determined stare. "I'll let you have that conversation with her." Jim ended the call and stretched his arm out to hand the phone back to Vanessa.

"He's threatening to call me in the middle of the night, isn't he?"

"How did you know?"

"Lucky guess."

"He'll get back with us on upgrading your access to names," Jim said. "In the meantime, let Seth know the guardian down there spotted a lot of activity at the fortress. He'll want to pass that on to the rest of his squad."

"You mean his old squad."

"Right." Jim pushed to a stand. "That's going to take some getting used to." Vanessa stood as well. "It will for all of us."

"I appreciate your being here. I have no doubt you're going to make a difference."

"Thank you, sir." Vanessa took a step toward the door. "For now, I'm going to pass that new intel on to Seth and then rescue your wife from babysitting duties."

"You know she loves it."

Vanessa's smile warmed her features. "I do. You married very well."

"Don't I know it." Jim walked her to the door. He opened it to the happy squeal of a young child. A grin stole across his face when he spotted Katherine standing by Sarah's desk, little Talia bouncing on her hip.

"Well, hello there." Vanessa laughed when Talia heard her voice and twisted to find her. Vanessa reached for her daughter. "Thank you so much for watching her."

"I can watch her a bit longer if you need me to," Katherine said.

"Are you sure you don't mind?" Vanessa asked. "I just need to pass some information on to Seth really quick."

"It's not a problem," Katherine assured her.

Jim caught a glimpse of Kyle, the White House photographer, down the hall. Ignoring his presence, Jim put his hand on Talia's back. "I think it's my turn to play with the baby."

"If you insist." Vanessa pressed a kiss to the top of her daughter's head before passing him the baby. "I'll be back in a few minutes."

"Take your time," Katherine assured her before turning to Jim. "Are you ready for some dinner?"

"I can have one of the cooks fix me a sandwich," Jim said. "I'm afraid it may be a late night."

"I already have dinner being sent in here." Katherine walked into the Oval Office and set Talia's baby bag by the door.

The photographer moved into the doorway. "Mr. President, do you mind if I get a few shots?"

"That's fine, but anything with the baby in it needs to remain private."

"Yes, sir." He stepped through the doorway. "Just pretend I'm not here." He lifted his camera again and started clicking away.

Jim lowered into what had become his favorite chair and shifted the baby in his lap.

Katherine sat in the chair beside him. "I got a call from Amy this afternoon."

"How's she doing?" Jim asked. He had to remind himself that Kyle had been cleared on both his family situation as well as national security. "Is she still stateside?"

"Yes, and she's on her way here."

"She's coming to the White House?"

"From what she said, she should get here anytime now."

Amy's voice carried from the outer office as she greeted his aide. Then she appeared in the open doorway. Her face instantly brightened when she took in the scene before her.

"Decided to become president so you could sit around and play with the little ones all day, huh?"

Jim grinned. "You caught me."

Amy crossed to hug Katherine and then leaned to kiss him on the cheek. Her hand trailed down Talia's back, a look of contentment on her face. "She is so cute."

"She really is," Jim agreed.

One of the White House butlers approached pushing a meal cart, and the scent of hamburgers permeated the air.

"You're just in time for dinner," Katherine said.

Amy wrinkled her nose. "I'm not sure I'm up for a burger. My stomach isn't feeling the greatest."

The butler set the cart at the front of the room. "Ma'am, would you like me to get you some chicken noodle soup? They're serving some in the mess tonight."

Amy straightened. "I'm sorry. I don't think I've met you yet. I'm Amy."

"Tucker, ma'am."

"Tucker, it's nice to meet you." Amy gave him a friendly smile. "Chicken soup sounds wonderful."

"I'll get that for you right away."

Tucker left the room, and Amy motioned to the food. "You two eat. I can hold the baby."

Jim's eyes darted up to his daughter's face. The smile, the warm glow of her complexion, the queasy stomach, and the air of contentment. He'd seen these signs before in his wife—three times, to be exact. He'd nearly given up hope of ever seeing those signs in Amy, and he couldn't keep his smile from mirroring his daughter's. If he was reading the situation right, he was about to become a grandfather again.

He stood and handed over the baby. "Why don't we bless the food first? We have a lot to be thankful for."

Amy's gaze met his. "Yes, we do."

37

SETH DIDN'T LIKE NOT BEING on the frontlines with his squad. He leaned back in his chair at one of the many desks in his temporary office space and tried to ignore the constant bustle of people coming and going as well as the stuffiness of this particular area that adjoined the Situation Room.

Most of the personnel who had helped him finalize the mission plan had left for the day, and a new group of intel officers—some military, some civilian—now manned the nearby desks.

His squad and Webb's unit would insert at oh four hundred the day after tomorrow. Seth glanced at the five clocks on the wall and focused on the one in his time zone. He adjusted for the time difference in Nicaragua. Thirty hours until the first SEALs arrived at the fortress.

He shifted in his seat, the long hours with little movement catching up to him as he mulled over his work today. The updated mission plan with a secondary vessel as a decoy made sense on the surface, but it could also serve to alert Morenta and his men that an invasion was imminent.

An uneasiness had settled over Seth when Vanessa had stopped by to share Ghost's message. Additional movement at the fortress, an imminent attack. Too many things could change at the fortress over the next forty-eight hours, routines and movement that could both impede his squad's odds of success and increase the likelihood of casualties. It was bad enough that they were going in shorthanded.

The Saint Squad may have started out as a five-man unit, but over time, they had adapted to rely on the strengths of all seven men. Seth knew the fortress better than anyone. Jay was the best lookout on the squad. Would their absence put their friends at greater risk? And was this looming dread a result of being left behind, or was it a sign that something wasn't right?

Doug entered the room, scanned the occupants, and zeroed in on Seth. He crossed the few yards to him. "I thought you would be home by now."

"I could say the same about you." Seth rubbed at his neck to work out the worst of the kinks that had knotted there.

"I heard about the increased movement at the fortress," Doug said. "I hoped to get some satellite images tomorrow to give us a clearer picture, but with the weather moving through, I doubt there will be a big enough break in the cloud cover to give us what we need."

"Weather?" Seth straightened. "I didn't get the report on that."

"There's a storm moving in tonight," Doug said. "Don't worry though. It'll clear out sometime tomorrow, so our units shouldn't have any trouble inserting."

Seth turned to his computer and tried to access the weather intel. When he couldn't, he turned to the woman beside him. "Yvonne, can you pull up the weather forecast for the next forty-eight hours at the fortress?"

The air force lieutenant nodded, then retrieved the report on her laptop and turned the screen to face him. "Here you go."

Seth skimmed over the information, a burst of inspiration flooding his mind. "We need to change the mission plan."

"What's wrong?" Doug asked.

"It's what's right." Seth motioned to the timeline on the screen. "This storm system will hit landfall somewhere around oh five hundred."

"Right, but that's for tomorrow morning, not the next day." Doug pointed. "It's supposed to pass over Nicaragua throughout the day and be gone by night-fall."

"Right, and the wind alone should be enough to ground the Z-10." Seth stood. "If the advance team inserts right before dawn, it won't have to worry about a helicopter spotting them."

"And it takes away the need for a decoy."

"Precisely." Seth motioned to Yvonne. "Can you print that out for me?"

"Yes, sir." A moment later, the printer behind him hummed to life.

"Who do we talk to first?" Seth asked. "Secretary Hartley or the president?"

"The admiral has already left for the day, but we know where the president is." Doug motioned to the door. "Shall we pay him a visit?"

"That's a great idea."

* * *

Amy walked with her parents up the stairs to the residence. Vanessa had returned to the Oval Office and picked up Talia over an hour ago and was now on her way home. A year from now, Amy would be in a similar situation, trying to juggle the needs of a child with the demands of work. Assuming she wanted to keep working.

That thought circled through her head. As much as she loved her job and wanted to be with Brent and the rest of the Saint Squad to support them, would she really want to have to pawn her child off every time national security made demands on them? She and Brent had a lot to talk about, but for now, she'd settle for sharing the good news in the first place.

They reached the main hall of the second floor, and her mom turned to face her. "Do you want me to fix you anything else to eat? Or maybe some herbal tea?"

"No thanks, Mom."

"Your mom made some cookies yesterday. I bet she hid some in the freezer," her dad said.

Amy's eyebrows lifted. "You haven't already eaten them?"

Her dad's eyes flashed with humor. "I saved a few for tonight."

"Smart man." Amy laughed. "Save me a couple. I might be up for some later, but first, I want to call Brent while I have the chance."

"Let us know if you change your mind," her mom said.

"I will. Thanks." Amy went into her room. Her suitcase was no longer in the middle of the floor. She opened her closet, the suitcase and her computer bag tucked into the bottom of it, her clothes neatly arranged on hangers. She had to give it to the staff here. They knew how to keep everything in order.

Amy retrieved her computer and set it on the desk by the window. She took in the view for a brief moment, the Washington Monument illuminated beyond the darkness of the grounds.

She hooked into the White House's secure internet and hit the button on her video chat to call Brent. If he followed his typical pre-mission routine, he should be in his board room going over intel reports about now.

Her call went unanswered. Not easily dissuaded, she ended the attempt and tried again, this time calling Tristan. No luck. Quinn came next, followed by Craig. Still no answer.

Amy's irritation rose. The biggest news since her marriage, and no one was answering the phone. Seriously? She tried one last time.

Damian's face came on the screen. "Hola."

"Hey, Damian, is Brent around?"

"Sí, sí." He turned and rattled something off in Spanish. Amy really needed to take a class so she understood him more often. Craig's voice sounded in the background, his words also spoken in Spanish.

When Damian turned back to the screen and spoke again, Amy said, "In English, please?"

"Brent will call you back in a few minutes."

"Thanks, Damian. Is everything else going okay?"

Before he could answer, Tristan and Quinn's voices carried to her.

"Sorry, Amy. Gotta go," Damian said.

The connection ended, and Amy was left with nothing to do but wait.

Her stomach pitched uncomfortably. Maybe she should take her mom up on the offer to fix her something to eat. She pushed that thought aside. She could take care of her stomach later, after she talked to Brent.

She tapped her fingers on the desk. She skimmed through today's headlines. She played a game of computer solitaire. Badly.

Had Damian even given Brent her message?

Fourteen minutes after Damian ended their call, her computer chimed with a new incoming video call. She clicked to answer it, her smile instant when her husband's face filled the screen.

"Hey there. I heard you called." Brent smiled. "Don't tell me you miss me already."

"Always."

"How did everything go with the doctor today?"

"Everything's good." Amy's smile widened. "Everything's great actually." She drew a breath to share their happy news, but a heavy fist pounded on her door. The urgency of the sound caused her to break off and turn. "Come in."

Seth walked in. "Are you still talking to Brent?"

"Yeah. Why?"

"Are you on a secure line?"

Amy nodded. "What's going on?"

Seth stepped behind her and leaned down so Brent could see his face. "Hey, sorry to interrupt, but your mission is moving up."

Brent's smile disappeared, his expression now serious. "Moving up to when?"

"You leave at oh three hundred," Seth said. "We're sending you in as the storm hits. The ocean will be a bit rough, but it'll let you insert when the Z-10 is grounded."

"How soon will the orders come down?"

"The president just approved the plan. He's making the call now," Seth said. "You should get the new orders within the hour."

"Thanks for the heads-up."

"One more thing. They're seeing extra movement at the fortress."

"Morenta never does make anything easy."

"Good luck."

"Thanks," Brent said before focusing on Amy again. "Amy, I'll talk to you as soon as we get back. Love you."

Though her news burned on her tongue, Amy swallowed it. "Love you too."

The connection clicked off.

Seth took a step back and straightened. "Your folks offered to let me stay here tonight. Do you want to come down to the Situation Room when they insert?"

"Yeah."

"I'll knock on your door when I'm heading back downstairs." Seth moved toward the door. "I'm going to call Vanessa to let her know I'm staying here."

"Thanks, Seth." Amy waited for him to leave before she let her body relax back into her chair. Would it be too much to ask for him to have arrived one minute later? Even two?

She blew out a sigh. She would talk to Brent when he got back. Maybe it was for the best. After all, news of her pregnancy was a big deal. For now, he needed to focus on his mission. And her news would be best shared in person.

38

JIM HUNG UP THE PHONE with Secretary Hartley and went in search of Katherine. He found her in the kitchen, a loaf of bread on the counter beside the toaster.

She looked up when he entered. "Is everything taken care of?"

"I hope so." He motioned to the toaster. "Is that for you or Amy?"

"Amy. Some dry toast may help settle her stomach."

Jim closed the distance between them and lowered his voice. "Has she said anything to you about what's going on with her?"

"Not yet."

"But she is pregnant, right?"

Katherine's lips quirked up, and her eyes brightened. "All the signs are there, but I don't think she found out until she saw the doctor today."

"That explains why she hasn't said anything," Jim said. "Brent left before she went to the doctor."

Amy walked into the kitchen. "Hey."

"Did you get a chance to talk to Brent?" Katherine asked.

"If you count saying hi as talking, then yeah." Her shoulders lifted. "Most of the video chat was Seth talking to Brent."

Jim winced. "Sorry about that."

"It's not your fault." She let out a sigh. "We're kind of used to national security getting in the way of things."

"It doesn't make it any easier," Katherine said. The toast popped up, and Katherine put two slices on a plate. "Here. Try this. It might help settle your stomach."

"Do you have any butter?"

"Yes, but it will probably be better for you if you eat it without." Katherine's gaze met Amy's. "It always worked for me."

Amy's eyes widened. "Don't tell me you talked to my doctor."

"We didn't need to." Katherine's smile bloomed. "We saw the signs. You're pregnant, aren't you?"

Amy nodded, her earlier annoyance giving way to pure joy. "I just found out today. How did you know?"

"I suspected it when you were here for the inauguration. When Brent called about helping you make a doctor's appointment, I prayed I was right."

"Wait, you were the reason I was able to get in to see the doctor so quickly?"

"I just made a call and let them know you needed to get in."

"You're as sneaky as my husband."

Katherine smiled. "The highest of compliments."

"I didn't mean it as a compliment."

"Doesn't matter." Katherine handed Amy the toast.

Amy set the plate on the counter and took a bite. "What about you, Dad? Are you using Mom as a source now?"

"She didn't have to tell me." Jim opened the freezer and dug out the cookies Katherine had hidden there. "When you walked in today, you were positively glowing."

"I planned to tell Brent first." Amy took another small bite of toast.

"Technically, you haven't told anyone yet," Katherine said. "We guessed."

"That's right." Jim fished out two cookies and set the bag on the counter. "Brent can still be the first person you tell."

"Just not the first person to know," Amy said.

"It's up to you when you want to tell him that we guessed," Katherine said.

"We all know our family is capable of keeping secrets," Jim said.

Amy laughed. "No truer words were ever spoken."

* * *

Brent's grip tightened on his seat as the boat pitched with the waves, the stormy ocean fighting against their forward progress. The idea to insert when the Z-10 helicopter was grounded was a good one. He just wished it didn't also involve waves that sent their inflatable boat nearly vertical every few seconds.

Lightning streaked across the sky, and a violent crack of thunder struck right behind it. The boat jerked again.

Their destination came into view through his night goggles streaked with rain. He made a futile attempt to clear the water from the goggles and focused on their landing zone.

Make that their former landing zone. A huge tree lay across the cove, blocking their path.

"You see that?" Quinn pointed, his voice only audible through their comm set.

"Affirmative." Brent turned and signaled to their boat pilot. "Redirect to the alternate landing site."

"Yes, sir."

Brent relayed the order again, this time to the boat pilot for Webb's unit.

The two vessels fought their way through the current until they finally reached the secondary landing spot, the same location where his squad had waited for him and Seth when they had been trapped by the hideout. Unfortunately, with the accelerated mission plan, their contingency plan was greatly lacking in detail.

Wind whipped over them as they disembarked.

Using hand signals, Brent dispersed his men, Tristan and Quinn taking the area to the right, and Damian and Craig the terrain to their left.

Brent took up position beside a tree leaning heavily in the wind.

Webb joined him as his seven men spread out and took a defensive position.

"We aren't going to be able to reach the Z-10 before daybreak," Brent said.

"Is there any way to plant the explosive during the day?" Webb asked. "That area wasn't visible on the satellite photos."

"We'll try." Brent didn't look forward to trying to evade the guards during daylight hours. "If not, we'll try for right after dark before it takes off."

"My men will be ready to take out the guards and neutralize any anti-aircraft weapons," Webb said. "Let me know if you need us to back you up on anything else. You're taking on the lion's share of this mission."

"My men know the lay of the land," Brent said. "Yours don't."

Tristan's voice came over his comm unit. "The area is clear."

Tristan's statement was all Webb needed to dismiss their boat pilots. The two inflatable boats retreated back into the storm so they would be clear before anyone at the fortress could detect them.

Brent focused on his next objective, getting through the woods, past the hideout, and through the jungle to the fortress. One thing at a time.

He adjusted his grip on his rifle. "Move out. We need to get past the hideout while it's still dark."

Tristan took point, and Brent fell in behind him and Quinn, with Craig sweeping behind them.

Webb issued similar orders to his men, his squad taking a parallel path. By this time tomorrow, they would be on a helicopter on their way out of here, but between now and then, both squads had a lot of work to do, including stopping whatever evil Morenta planned to unleash on the United States.

* * *

Radio silence. Standard operating procedure or not, Seth had never before considered the emotional roller coaster for the personnel on this side of the mission.

He stared at the dark screen on the far side of the Situation Room, Amy on one side of him and the president on the other. A computer operator sat at the back of the room, but beyond Admiral Moss, the rest of the senior staff in the intelligence and military community hadn't opted to come back to the White House for live updates. Tomorrow night would be a different story.

To protect themselves from anyone picking up on an electronic signal, the SEALs wouldn't activate their mission cameras until the main event. They would also remain on a closed frequency for communication. Not that there would be much talking. They would use hand signals to indicate any changes from their prearranged plans. How well they had been able to prepare that plan, Seth could only guess.

"How much longer until we get a report?" Jim asked.

Amy glanced at the wall clock. "I hoped we would have heard by now."

"The storm will slow them down." Seth turned to Amy. "Do you always wait for updates before you sleep?"

Amy nodded. "I never know when new intel will pop up after you've already left."

More than once, Amy had relayed information that had prevented disaster for him and his squad. She really was as integral to their success as any of the rest of them.

Amy tapped on her laptop. "With the storm, I doubt we'll get anything new unless something comes over the bugs you planted."

"I haven't seen any new reports from that since yesterday." Jim turned to the intel officer sitting behind them. "Do we have any updates from Fort Huachuca on the fortress?"

"I'll check." The man tapped on his computer. "No, sir. The last transmission received was from two days ago."

"That doesn't sound right," Seth said. "There should have been at least some chatter from the hideout when the guards changed shifts."

"Sorry, sir, but according to the listening post, the fortress and the hideout have both gone silent."

"The last intel report showed an increase in activity at the fortress," Amy said. "That should have resulted in more transmission, not less."

"Unless their security did a sweep and found the listening devices," Seth said.

"What if they did?" Alarm filled Jim's voice. "They would know someone had been there."

"Morenta is known to be paranoid," Amy said. "There's no telling what he would do."

"Best guess?" Jim asked.

"If he thinks we know his plans, he would change his timeline, alter as much as he can."

"Which could explain the extra movement at the fortress," Seth said.

Concern flashed on Amy's face. "This isn't good."

Amy was right. They had been working on options for days, but with the combination of Seth leaving, Amy's increased workload, and the other obstacles Gardner had thrown in their path, the Saint Squad wasn't anywhere near the full readiness state they were accustomed to. Did they have enough prep time to build in backup plans, or was his squad dependent on the mission going off without a hitch? As much as SEALs prepared for the unexpected, Seth prayed his squad would have angels watching over them. Divine intervention could very well be a necessary addition to ensure success.

Static buzzed through the comm line.

"We have the *Truman* reporting," the communications officer said.

Jim nodded. "Put it through."

The captain of the USS *Harry S. Truman* appeared on the screen. His gaze flickered over the occupants of the room and landed on the president. "Mr. President."

"What do you have for us, Captain?" Jim asked.

"The advance team inserted successfully; however, they had to divert to the alternate landing point," the captain said. "The vessels that inserted them returned to the carrier without detection."

Jim turned to Seth. "How will this impact their objectives?"

"It puts an extra five miles between them and their targets."

"Should we push everything back a day?" Jim asked.

If communication were possible without risking the men already on the ground, Seth would discuss the best course of action with Brent. But since he couldn't, he ran through the likely adjustments in his head. "The advance team will expect the second group of SEALs at the appointed time. I suggest moving forward as planned unless we receive communication to indicate otherwise."

"I agree," the captain said. "The other two squads are already on board and ready to go."

"Keep us apprised of any changes," Jim said.

"Yes, Mr. President."

The communication ended, and Jim pushed back from the table. "We should all get some sleep. Tomorrow is going to be a long day."

Amy stifled a yawn. "And a long night."

39

BRENT AWOKE TO THE RUSTLE of leaves. His eyes flew open, and he grabbed his weapon.

"It's just me," Tristan said, his voice low.

Brent willed his heartbeat to steady, and he scanned the thick cluster of trees where he and his men had bedded down for the morning hours. The rain still streamed down steadily, but the thick canopy of leaves above them diverted the moisture and created a relatively dry haven in the storm.

Brent lowered his weapon. "Status?"

"Craig and Damian are doing another sweep," Tristan said.

"What time is it?"

"Fifteen twenty."

Three more hours until nightfall. Time to go to work. If he was right about their current location, the hideout was only a half mile away, and the fortress another mile beyond that. He slipped his communication headset into place.

On the soggy patch of ground beside him, Quinn stirred. "Who's fixing breakfast?"

"Nice try." Brent pulled a protein bar out of his combat vest. "You've got your own."

"I'd rather have pizza." Quinn looked at him hopefully, as though Brent could magically make food appear. "Or bacon and eggs."

"Knock it off," Tristan said. "You're making me hungry."

Craig and Damian emerged from the dense trees.

"We're clear for about a hundred meters," Craig said. "The motion sensors start up after that."

"Can we circle past the hideout?" Brent asked.

Craig shook his head. "Not on the east side. A cliff runs all the way along the ocean. There's a narrow beach below, but in this rain, I wouldn't recommend trying to climb down."

Brent focused on Damian. "What about to the west?"

"*Es posible.*" Damian switched to English before Brent had to command it. "The trees are thick. It's hard to see what's beyond."

Brent turned in search of Jay only to remember he wasn't with them. "Craig, go up that tree, and see if you can get a better perspective."

"Me?"

"Yes, you."

Craig let out a sigh. "I miss Jay."

Brent smothered a grin. "Everyone else, pack up."

Craig climbed the tree while the rest of the squad removed any sign of their presence. Brent took a bite of his protein bar.

"How soon do you want to move out?" Tristan asked.

"As soon as Craig can give us a better lay of the land, we'll move into position," Brent said. "I want Craig and Damian in position to wire the helicopter bomb well before nightfall."

Brent finished his scanty breakfast and tucked the trash into his vest pocket. He spoke into his comm headset. "Craig, what do you see?"

No response.

"Craig? Come in."

Again nothing.

Brent turned to Damian. "Are you hearing me through your comm gear?"

Damian shook his head. "No."

"I'm not either," Tristan said.

Quinn pulled his headset off. "We're batting zero. Mine isn't working either."

"Great," Brent muttered. He took a few steps back so he could signal to Craig.

A few fat raindrops fell off the leaves above. Craig perched above him, one hand gripping the tree trunk, the other holding his binoculars in place. Craig scanned the area again and then one more time. Craig's lips moved. He stopped speaking, pocketed his binoculars, and touched his earpiece. He spoke again before he looked down.

Brent motioned to him.

Craig lowered himself from one branch to another until he joined Brent on the ground. "Is your comm out?"

"Everyone's is."

"Again?" Craig shook his head. "Morenta must have something that's messing with it."

"Good thing we have the backup signal, or we'd be in a world of hurt," Tristan said.

"Thank Seth for that one," Brent said. "You know he was behind it."

"How do you want me to proceed?" Quinn asked. "I can play sniper, but you'll have no way of signaling me if I'm clear to take a shot."

"You'll just have to cover us. If someone is in danger, use your judgment."

"You're trusting Quinn's judgment?" Craig asked. "That's a scary thought."

"We aren't talking about what to have for breakfast," Tristan countered, his words filled with both a touch of sarcasm and his Texas twang. "I think he can handle knowing whether to pull the trigger or not."

"We proceed as planned," Brent said. "Craig and Damian, wire the Z-10. Quinn, pick a spot where you can cover them. They're the most likely to be spotted."

"Got it." Quinn took a bite of his protein bar.

"Tristan, you and I will cover them from the ground level."

"Who am I covering once they're done with the Z-10?" Quinn asked.

"Cover Craig and Damian until they head for the hideout. After that, I want you in position so you can take out any guards who might cause problems for me and Tristan while we make the climb up to grab Morenta." Brent's gaze swept over his men, an uneasy feeling seeping through him. He fought against it with his own determination. These were his men, his brothers. Whether they were a squad of five or seven, it was up to him to ensure they all made it back home to their families. "Who wants to say the prayer today?"

"I'll do it." Quinn folded his arms.

"Let's keep today's prayer focused on the mission," Brent said. "Praying for Katherine's cinnamon rolls can wait until we're back stateside."

Quinn let out a long-suffering sigh. "Fine."

* * *

Amy took a nap. She never napped, but after the middle-of-the-night trip to the Situation Room, her body had been unwilling to cooperate until she'd given it some much-needed rest. Not only had the lack of sleep thrown her system off, but her nausea, which she now knew was morning sickness, had also turned into all-day sickness.

She drew in a steady breath, relieved that her stomach didn't protest against the simple act. She pushed out of bed and headed for the shower. Might as well take advantage of the time she had now because once her squad went into action tonight, she wasn't going to be anywhere but in front of the video feed coming in from her husband's body camera.

After she showered and finished dressing for the second half of her day, she opened the laptop Ghost had given her and pulled up the latest mission notes for the Saint Squad. As she suspected, nothing had changed since last night. The same was true for Webb's squad. She checked the time. Sixteen thirty.

The SEALs would all be hiding somewhere near the fortress now, after working their way through the woods so they would be in position tonight. She prayed everything would go smoothly, both when they went after Morenta and when they went into the hideout. Whatever was going on in those woods could very well be just as important to national security as capturing Morenta.

Amy's secure cell phone rang. Though her caller ID didn't give her a name, the phone number indicated it was from someone at the base. "Hello?"

"Amy? This is Demetrius from supply."

Her eyebrows drew together. Why would he be calling her when all of her squads were in the field? "What can I do for you?"

"I need your help." Exasperation carried over the line. "I've been trying since yesterday to make a call to the *Truman*, but Commander Gardner denied my initial request, and now he's not answering his phone."

Amy gritted her teeth and breathed slowly through her nose in an effort to calm herself. Gardner had been relieved of duty, but the effects of his poor leadership were still being felt. "What's the problem? Not Gardner. I mean, why do you need to call the ship?"

"I checked out some night-vision goggles a couple days ago to a platoon doing some night exercises. Seven of them malfunctioned."

"Okay?"

"I checked the equipment log. All seven of the bad units were ones the Saint Squad used when they were on their last mission."

A streak of panic shot through her. First their comm units and now their night-vision goggles. "Do you know what was wrong with them?"

"Dead batteries," Demetrius said. "I wouldn't have thought anything of it except on the maintenance log, four of them are listed as having new batteries put in only a week before the Saint Squad checked the equipment out."

"And none of the other equipment had a problem?"

"No. Only the ones your squad used." He hesitated. "I know it sounds far-fetched, but Seth mentioned the problem with the comm units. I think they encountered something on their mission that killed the batteries on all of their equipment."

"I hope you're wrong, but that would explain the malfunctions."

"Gardner brushed my concerns aside, but your squad deserves to know about the problem before they go out on their next mission."

"I agree." Amy couldn't share the truth that Demetrius's discovery had come too late. Besides being classified, she didn't want to voice the words. "Thanks for passing this on. I'll make sure it gets into the hands of the people who need to know."

"Thanks, Amy. I didn't know who else to call."

"I appreciate you calling." Amy pushed away from her desk. "Do me a favor though and write up a report of what happened with Commander Gardner and email it to me. I have someone who is going to need that information."

Demetrius's voice lowered. "Any chance this someone will get rid of this guy?"

"I hope so."

40

JIM LIKED IT BETTER WHEN he didn't know the details about his son-in-law's missions. It was bad enough that he had authorized the Saint Squad to travel through a storm front to reach their destination, but finding out they had encountered additional obstacles before even landing only served to increase his concern.

Adding a baby to the equation, a baby Brent didn't even know about, heightened it further.

All day, he had gone through meetings on a dozen topics, but always in the back of his mind, his thoughts turned to Brent and the men under his command, the men Jim had come to think of as friends.

A knock sounded on his door before it cracked open, and his aide popped her head in. "Mr. Valdez to see you, sir."

"Send him in."

Jim stood when Doug walked in.

"Do I need to find you some office space here at the White House?"

"As long as you don't mind me using the Roosevelt Room, I'm fine for now." Doug held up his phone. "We have a situation. The power grid is down in Kansas City, Missouri."

"Okay." Jim lowered back into his chair. "Power outages do happen."

"Yeah, but this one happened on a clear day with no sign of a problem."

"Mechanical failure?" Jim asked.

"We don't know. The word just came in five minutes ago." Doug held both hands out to his side. "I don't want to think someone got through the safeguards there, but the timing is suspicious."

"You're worried Morenta moved up his timetable."

"I always worry when that guy is involved," Doug said. "Just like I worry when people are relying on generators to provide critical care to those in need."

Jim fought the instinct to get down in the weeds to try to help. He needed to trust those who were already on the front line, both in Kansas City and in Nicaragua. "Stay on it."

"I will."

Doug left the room, and Jim picked up his phone. "Sarah, can you please tell Vanessa Johnson and Seth Johnson I need to see them?"

"Yes, sir. I'll make the calls."

"Thank you."

Jim swiveled in his chair and took in the view of the south lawn as twilight approached. Less than five minutes until his next meeting, but before he endured a chat with a senator from Arizona on water rights, he needed the latest on if the Kansas City power outage could be related to anything Seth had observed during his last mission to the fortress.

Another knock sounded.

"Come in." Jim swiveled toward the door.

Rather than Seth or Vanessa, Amy walked in. "We have a problem."

Jim stood. "What's wrong?"

Amy started to close the door, but Seth appeared in the doorway before she had the chance. Jim motioned him inside.

"You asked to see me, sir?"

"Yes. Come in." Jim sat back behind his desk and motioned for Seth and Amy to sit in the chairs across from him. "Doug Valdez came by a little while ago. There's an unexplained power outage in Kansas City. It's unlikely it's related to whatever Morenta has planned, but I wanted your thoughts. Is it possible?"

"I don't know." Seth waited until Amy sat down before he took the seat beside her. "We have no idea what was going on inside the building we found in the woods."

"The hideout."

"Yes, sir."

Jim mulled that over before focusing on Amy. "You said you had something important to tell me."

"I got a call from one of the supply clerks on base in Virginia Beach. All the night-vision goggles the Saint Squad used on their last mission stopped working. All the batteries were dead."

"Like the comm units." Seth straightened. "If Morenta is developing some kind of weapon or device that can zap battery power, who knows what kind of chaos he could unleash if he brought that technology into the US."

"The power outage." Jim fisted his hands. "It could be related."

"I don't know," Seth said. "It's possible."

The phone on Jim's desk buzzed, and his aide announced Vanessa's arrival.

Vanessa walked in. Seth stood to offer his chair to his wife, but Vanessa remained standing. "Sorry it took me so long, but I was talking to Ghost. We have a problem."

"I'm hearing that phrase way too often today," Jim muttered. "What is it?"

"Ghost tried to contact his colleague down in Central America. He's not responding."

Seth gripped the back of the chair in front of him. "Comm went out the last time the Saint Squad was at the fortress."

"Ghost thinks something is interfering with communication."

"A signal blocker?" Amy asked.

"He doesn't think so, but there's no way to be sure."

"At least we built in an alternative signal," Seth said. "Once the helicopter blows up, SEAL Team Ten will know it's time to go in."

"Someone needs to let SEAL Team Ten know we suspect comm is down," Vanessa said.

Seth nodded. "I'll take care of it."

* * *

No helicopter. The camouflage netting that had prevented the satellites from initially identifying the Z-10's presence still remained, but the attack helicopter wasn't anywhere to be seen. And despite the rain, Brent didn't believe for a minute that he and his men had missed it taking off for an evening patrol.

Brent studied the looming ten-story building in front of him. The rain had stopped over an hour ago, and nightfall shrouded them in darkness, though the grounds surrounding the fortress were swathed in light from the security lamps at every corner.

The extra activity he had expected wasn't present. Only two guards circled the base of the fortress while the third remained stationary at the front entrance. No vehicles visible. No extra people milling about. No anti-aircraft guns.

Tristan had taken up position twenty yards away, his gun at the ready, while Quinn climbed up a tree so he could provide cover for the rest of the squad.

Careful not to trip any motion sensors, Brent eased deeper into the woods. Damian and Craig joined him.

"What now?" Damian asked.

"With our comm units down, we need something to blow up," Craig added.

"Like what?" Damian asked. "They don't even have a jeep we can play with."

"Maybe it's time to rewrite the mission plan." Brent contemplated for a moment what he would have done before the higher-ups changed their focus to a snatch and grab instead of an intel-gathering mission. "Craig, you take my place with Tristan. Damian and I are going to double back to the hideout. We need to know what's really going on here."

"What about Webb's unit?"

"They'll cover the beach and clear the landing zone like we already planned."

"And the signal for SEAL Team Ten?" Craig asked.

"You have grenades. Use them." Brent peered through the trees to the base of the fortress. "Blow up a tree if you have to."

"Just make sure it's not the one with Quinn in it," Damian added. "He still owes me lunch from the last time I beat him on the obstacle course."

"Craig, let Tristan know what's going on. One of you will have to climb up and tell Quinn too."

"Great. Climbing more trees." Craig let out a sigh. "I really miss Jay."

"I miss Seth," Damian countered. "He would know where we could find a jeep or something to light up."

A twinge of nostalgia and regret squeezed at Brent. "Seth gave us the layout of the fortress. We need to use that insight now." He slid his night goggles into place, his eyes adjusting to the greenish haze that now sharpened his vision. "Move out."

His men put on their goggles too.

"Great," Craig muttered. "Mine aren't working." He pulled it off and traded out the batteries.

"You good?" Brent asked.

Craig tested his goggles again and nodded. "Yeah."

"Let's pray you stay that way," Damian said.

Brent was already praying. No comm gear and another piece of vital equipment malfunctioning. They couldn't afford for anything else to go wrong.

* * *

Amy scrolled through the latest reports from her seat in the Roosevelt Room. The grandfather clock behind her ticked away, her sense of urgency rising with each second.

Intel had yet to provide anything new that might explain the loss of communication from the Central American Ghost or why the Saint Squad had lost comm during their last mission. Dead batteries continued to be the conclusion, but how those batteries drained so quickly remained a mystery.

Across the long conference table, Doug spread out a combination of papers and electronic devices. Three iPads, a cell phone, two laptops.

"This isn't making any sense," Doug muttered under his breath.

"Want to talk it out?" Amy asked.

"You have your own work to do."

"My work is stalled at the moment. I can't do anything unless new intel reports come through." Amy leaned back in her chair. "What has you stumped?"

"Dead batteries."

"Excuse me?" Amy's gaze swept over the myriad devices in front of them, each screen turned on.

"I'm trying to get updates on the power outage in Missouri, but my people keep losing their cell phone connections," Doug said. "I sent a new person in from the Kansas side. When he called, he said everyone in the office had lost power to their cell phones."

"Any idea what caused it?"

"No, because halfway through our conversation, the call dropped." Doug picked up his cell phone. "I haven't been able to get him back."

Amy's stomach curled uncomfortably, and it had nothing to do with morning sickness. "This is going beyond coincidence."

"Yes, but what's the cause? Even if someone knows what's going on, they have no way to communicate it to us."

Amy pulled out her cell phone and called Vanessa.

"Amy, can I call you back? I was about to call and check on our missing operative."

As in the missing ghost.

"When you talk to your friend, can you ask if he knows about any kind of weapon or device that can neutralize batteries?"

"Batteries?"

"Yeah. Cell phone batteries, batteries in communication headsets, batteries in night-vision goggles."

"That's a stretch, but I'll ask."

"Thanks." Amy hung up and opened her email to send the same request to her contacts at the CIA.

"You think this is connected to Morenta," Doug said.

Amy looked up from her computer. "Don't you?"

"I hope it's not, but I can't deny the timing."

"Time to pray that my husband and his squad can stop whatever they have planned." Amy finished her email to her CIA contacts and pressed Send.

"I only hope Kansas City is the target rather than the testing ground." Doug tapped on the iPad nearest him.

That thought sent another ripple of unease through her. If Morenta really was behind the power outage, what was his objective? And why start in the middle of the country? "Kansas City wouldn't be most people's first choice if they're trying to create mass chaos."

"I know, but if it's the test, why was it chosen?" Doug asked.

Amy fought back a shudder. "And what's the real target?"

41

BRENT'S NIGHT GOGGLES FLICKERED, THE image of the trees in front of him distorting before returning to normal. He held up his hand, signaling Damian to stop. The last thing he needed was to go into the hideout blind.

He pulled off his goggles and quickly changed out the batteries for the spares he kept in his vest pocket. After checking that they were working, he slipped them back in place and moved forward again.

Within minutes, they arrived at the hideout, where a guard stood watch, the same guard who had taken regular smoke breaks the last time Brent had been here.

Brent drew a syringe out of his combat vest and glanced at Damian as he did the same. After signaling to Damian to take the guard who was already visible, Brent worked his way through the trees surrounding the hideout until the other guard came into sight, the floodlights casting an eerie glow through the fog that clung to the ground.

The man held his gun at the ready as he looked over the trees and the clearing that surrounded the mysterious structure he was protecting. Brent faded into the shadows and tucked himself behind a tree to remain out of sight.

Shrouded by darkness, he edged a few feet to his right, where a thick bush and the even thicker fog obscured him.

Brent waited, watching for an opening to approach from behind. It didn't come.

Seconds ticked off in his head. Only twenty minutes until SEAL Team Ten was scheduled to arrive. He didn't have time to wait for the guard to shirk his duties.

Brent lowered his weapon and let its sling hold it in place against his body. He searched the ground for debris, finally settling on a twig. Keeping his hand low, he tossed the twig several yards away. It impacted the base of a tree, and the guard turned, his gun aimed in the direction of the sound.

Brent rushed forward and grabbed the guard around the neck with one arm. With his other, he lifted his hand to inject the sedative-filled syringe. Before he could insert it into the man's skin, the guard threw his weight back and elbowed Brent in the ribs.

The syringe dropped to the ground, and Brent tightened his hold around the guard's neck.

The man tucked his chin to protect his windpipe, kicked backward, and crushed his boot into Brent's knee.

Pain jolted from Brent's kneecap and through his leg. He stumbled back, and the guard broke free and lifted his assault rifle. Brent struck out with his hand, knocking the gun from the man's grip, but the strap hooked over the man's shoulder and torso kept the weapon from falling.

Too close to use his own gun, Brent fisted his hands and punched the guard, first in the jaw and then in the stomach. Again the guard stumbled back, but this time, when his hands went to his rifle, Brent was too far away to counter his move.

Brent's heart in his throat, he dove for cover behind the corner of the building. A spray of gunfire punctuated the air.

The door behind him opened, and another armed guard rushed outside. Brent lifted his gun and fired. The man dropped to the ground, but before Brent could turn, the other guard rounded the corner, gun drawn. With no place to go, Brent dove for the ground toward the gunman. His legs impacted the hard-packed dirt, and a new pain shot through his knee.

He swiveled to strike out with his leg, but the guard backed up and took aim. An image of Amy popped into Brent's mind. He lifted his own rifle, already knowing it was too late.

A flash of movement appeared behind the guard, a blur of a hand knocking the weapon to the side as a bullet exploded. The bullet whizzed by Brent and impacted the ground only inches from him.

Damian grabbed the guard from behind and plunged a sedative into his neck. The guard struggled for a moment before he went limp.

Two more guards emerged from inside the structure. Brent and Damian both raised their weapons and fired. Both guards dropped to the ground.

Brent's breath shuddered out, and his senses heightened. Four guards down. Presumably, that left two more. The sense of someone's presence behind the partially open door caused him to silently push to his feet. He signaled Damian about the potential danger.

Damian nodded his understanding and crept closer.

Brent winced in pain when he stepped forward. He jutted his chin at Damian, a silent signal for him to count off their attack. Both men pushed back their night-vision goggles in preparation for moving into the lighted room.

Damian's hand came up, his fingers ticking off the seconds. The moment his hand fisted to zero, Brent threw his weight into the door. He met resistance, and a man grunted.

Damian burst through behind him, his gun raised. He spoke in rapid Spanish, ordering the two men across the room to put their hands up. One put his hands up, but the other didn't comply, instead reaching for the small of his back.

Damian fired a warning shot and shouted again.

The person behind the door pushed back against the wood, but Brent stepped clear, and the man lost his balance, his grip on the doorknob the only thing keeping him from tumbling to the ground. Using the butt of his rifle as a weapon, Brent struck him in the back and knocked him down. Quickly, he secured the man's hands with a zip tie. Damian did the same for the other two men.

Brent's opponent tried to push to his feet, but Brent took the easy route and sat on him while he secured the man's legs and checked him for weapons. After relieving him of the knife strapped to his calf, Brent took in the long table against the far wall covered with rows of computers, all of them a copper color rather than the more common white or black. On the opposite wall, several truck tires lined the nearly empty shelves, and a hall extended to a dark space beyond the well-lit room.

Though curious why truck tires would be inside what appeared to be a data-mining operation, Brent motioned to Damian to cover him. Time to find out what else was hiding within these walls.

* * *

Amy didn't have to ask to know things were going from bad to worse in Missouri. Doug paced back and forth while he spoke to someone on the phone.

"Get me updates however you can." Doug hung up.

"How bad is it?"

"We have widespread panic. People are trying to get out of the city, but cars are stranded all along the roads and freeways." Doug lifted his hand in a frustrated gesture toward one of the many screens facing him. "Temperatures are dropping, and only a handful of the emergency vehicles we tried to send over from the Kansas side of the city made it without having their own battery failure."

"That's terrible." Amy didn't know what she would do if her power went out in the middle of winter, especially if she had a baby to care for. Fleeing the area for somewhere warm was a logical choice, but that choice was putting many in greater danger than if they had sheltered in place.

"Any updates from the CIA?"

"Nothing that would explain what's going on right now," Amy said. "An electromagnetic pulse weapon would make the most sense, but no one can explain why Kansas City was targeted or where the source is."

"If that's even what we're dealing with," Doug said.

Vanessa walked in. "I found something." She held up the iPad she carried. "Well, my friends found something."

"What is it?" Amy stood so she could see Vanessa's screen. The image of what appeared to be a sonar gun filled the screen.

Doug circled the table and stepped behind Vanessa so he could see too. "What are we looking at?"

"It's the pulse weapon Yago Paquito was working on when he disappeared."

"He's the professor who was kidnapped almost a year ago, right?" Amy asked. "The one from Madrid."

"That's right," Vanessa said. "He had a theory that if this weapon were used in combination with strategically placed magnets, a single person could create a power outage that could cascade into a crippling attack."

"What's the range?" Doug asked.

Amy leaned closer. "And how does it work?"

"We aren't entirely sure," Vanessa said. "Typically, a pulse weapon can only affect a city block, maybe two."

"If this is what caused the power outages in Kansas City, it's a lot more widespread than that," Doug said.

"I know, and intel isn't sure how the signals are being generated to affect batteries even after an initial attack."

Amy took a step back, memories of their last run-in with Morenta repeating in her mind. "Morenta is known for multilayered attacks. What if part of this is cyber? Is it possible they hacked into the electrical grid somehow?"

"I don't know." Vanessa's gaze lifted to meet Amy's. "No one in intel has any updated information. It's possible the only person who can answer that question is Yago Paquito."

"You think Morenta has him."

"I'm afraid so."

An alert chimed on one of Doug's computers, and he moved to open it. He sucked in a sharp breath.

"What is it?" Amy asked.

"I think the FBI found out why Kansas City was targeted."

"Why?" Amy asked.

"Yeah, it's in the middle of nowhere," Vanessa said.

"It's in the middle," Doug corrected. "If Morenta or whoever is behind this manages to repeat the same thing in Philadelphia and Las Vegas, the electrical grid for the entire United States could suffer a cascade failure."

"You're saying the whole country could go dark?"

"About 90 percent of it."

Amy's hand went to her stomach. "We have to find a way to stop this."

"Yes, we do."

* * *

Brent cleared the two empty bedrooms and moved to the third. Unlike the others, this one had a dead bolt attached to the outside of the door. Brent unlocked it, pushed the door open, and led with his weapon as he rushed inside.

The man on the bed in the corner threw up his hands and cowered. Thin, gray-haired, panic in his eyes.

"*Por favor. Por favor. Ayúdame.*"

Help him?

Keeping his weapon raised, Brent checked the single closet and ensured it was empty. He then turned once more to the man. That was when he saw the bars on the window and the chain connecting the man's ankle to the footboard of the bed.

"Who are you?" Brent asked first in English and then again in his limited Spanish.

"Yago Paquito."

The name niggled the back of Brent's mind, but he struggled to recall the details. A kidnapping, maybe? Whatever report he had read with the name had been from months ago.

Brent checked the man for weapons. Once satisfied the man truly was unarmed, Brent retrieved his lockpick set from his vest and freed the man from bondage. He then motioned Yago forward. "Come with me."

Brent escorted him into the main room, where Damian still had his gun trained on their captives.

"Who's that?" Damian asked.

"Yago Paquito. They had him locked up back there," Brent said. "Talk to him. Find out why."

Damian relayed the question and translated. "Morenta's men kidnapped him when he was on vacation with his family in Colombia."

Damian paused while the professor continued his story and again translated. "They forced him to adapt his pulse weapon technology, but he doesn't know why."

"What does his weapon do?"

More back and forth between Yago and Damian, but this time, Damian's expression went from curious to grave when he relayed the message. "They had him working with hackers to adapt his weapon. It uses the electromagnetic current of cell phones to kill battery power of everything within a few feet of it."

Could someone really turn such a useful technology against them? "How do they access the cell phones?"

Damian relayed the question. "The programming is sent through a download when the phones are charging. It can also be used to affect tablets, headphones, and a bunch of other things that use an electromagnetic current."

"How do we stop it? Can we stop it?" Brent asked. He didn't need the translation to understand the answer. The professor nodded and gave an explanation to Damian.

"He thinks he can help counteract the attacks if they haven't happened yet."

"Where are the attacks supposed to happen?"

"Missouri, Nevada, and Pennsylvania."

"Let's get him out of here." Brent led the way to the door. "When our backup arrives, your sole mission is to get him to the helicopter unharmed."

"Got it." Damian checked his wristwatch. "We only have three minutes until they're supposed to insert."

"So we'll be a few minutes late," Brent said. "With this many SEALs, they should already have the area secured when we arrive." Brent moved to the door. "Move out."

Damian communicated their plan to Yago, and the three men started through the jungle toward the fortress. They zigzagged between trees, avoiding the ridiculous number of motion sensors and trip wires planted in their path. A quarter of a mile from their destination, Brent diverted past a ravine, Damian and Yago following a short distance behind him.

Brent glimpsed another motion detector on the ground to his left along with a security camera mounted to the tree above. He circled to avoid them, and the area in front of him went black. Brent stopped suddenly and pulled off his night-vision goggles. His backup batteries were dead too?

Damian's footsteps stuttered, and instantly, an alarm blared.

Shouts echoed toward them, competing with the shrill alarm.

Brent whirled, the evidence of the problem standing right behind him. Damian also held his night-vision goggles in his hand, and he was in the direct line of the motion sensor and security camera.

42

SOMETHING WASN'T RIGHT. SETH COULDN'T explain how he knew it or what was wrong, but the churning in his gut wouldn't stop. He had sent the message to SEAL Team Ten about the communication issues, but despite sending it priority, he still didn't know if they had received it. He hated red tape.

Seth sent up a silent prayer as he moved from the workroom into the Situation Room, where the top military and intelligence officers had gathered.

Every seat at the long conference table was taken except the two reserved for the president and his chief of staff. The chairs at the back of the room and those lining the walls were also filling up fast.

Seth chose an open spot behind where Doug currently sat with a laptop open in front of him.

The door opened, and Jim walked in, followed by his chief of staff.

"Where do we stand?" Jim asked.

"No communication from the Saint Squad since they were dropped off," Secretary Hartley said.

"Doug, anything new on the power outages in Kansas City?"

"We're having a hard time establishing lines of communication," Doug said. "Not only is the power grid down on the Missouri side, but everything with a battery stopped working. Our people are having to drive to Kansas to call from there to give us updates."

"Any sign of what caused this?" Jim asked.

"No," Doug said. "Intel has a theory that it could be some sort of pulse weapon, but we're waiting on confirmation."

"What else do we know?" Jim asked.

"The hospitals are running off generators, but we can't transport patients out of there because the car batteries are all dead."

"What about sending in ambulances from the Kansas side?" Sawyer asked.

"We tried. Those vehicles lost battery power within a half hour," Doug said. "That would be long enough to go in and out of many of the locations, but without reliable communication, it's nearly impossible to coordinate. Not to mention, we have stranded motorists all along the freeway. We're recommending people shelter in place, but we have no idea if our messages are getting through to anyone."

"Stay on it," Jim said.

A computer operator at the front of the room spoke. "Sir, we have an incoming transmission from SEAL Team Ten."

The team commander's voice came over the line. "No word from the Saint Squad. Please advise."

"Any sign of an explosion?" Seth asked.

"Negative," the commander said.

"They only have thirty minutes before fuel status will force them to turn back," Secretary Hartley said.

"Seth? What's your assessment?" Jim asked.

"Comm went out last time we inserted," Seth said. "It's possible something is jamming the signal."

"Yes, but the backup signal hasn't happened either."

"They inserted five miles away from their intended insertion point," Seth said. "They may not have been able to get to the Z-10 before daybreak."

"Wouldn't they find an alternative target?" Doug asked.

That was what he would have done. So why hadn't his squad found another way to send a signal? Had the Saint Squad been captured, or were they simply unable to communicate? Since Seth didn't care for the first possibility, he fell back on the second. "There must not have been a viable alternative."

"You recommend we proceed?" Secretary Hartley asked.

"Yes, sir."

Jim's gaze landed on Seth briefly before he spoke to the admiral. "I concur."

* * *

Gunfire sparked from the tree where Brent had last seen Craig. More sounded in the direction of the beach, but without his night-vision goggles, Brent had no idea who was shooting or if Webb's squad had neutralized the guards.

No sign of reinforcements, no evidence of an explosion or any other sign that his squad had succeeded in sending a signal.

More gunfire rang out.

Brent prayed they wouldn't get caught in the crossfire. Comm was down. He could barely see. For all he knew, the rest of his squad could be as blind as he was.

With no choice but to move forward and hope backup would arrive, Brent pointed at Yago and spoke to Damian. "Keep him covered and get him to the landing zone."

Damian's eyebrows lifted, a nonverbal sign of his doubts, but he nodded and took a path that led his charge through the jungle toward where they hoped a military helicopter would land soon.

More gunfire punctuated the air, again from the beach side of the fortress. Brent worked his way to the tree where he had last seen Craig, his eyes scanning through the fog and the darkness. The gunfire stopped.

Brent reached the base and looked up. Someone was up there, but Brent had no way to communicate with Quinn.

Well, there was one way. Brent slung his rifle over his shoulder and reached for the nearest branch.

Climbing a tree. He was in command, for heaven's sake. He had people for this.

"Who's there?" A hushed voice carried down to Brent.

"Brent." He reached a branch a few feet below where Quinn lay perched across a thick tree limb. "What's our status?"

"More equipment failure." Quinn kept his eye pressed against his sniper scope. "Our night goggles stopped working."

"Ours too." Brent mulled over the information Yago had shared. Was it possible this new technology was somehow in effect here at the fortress? And if so, how was it impacting them? None of them were carrying cell phones.

"Where are Tristan and Craig?"

"They made their climb to the penthouse. They should be outside the balcony now."

"What about signaling our backup?"

"We set an explosive near the main gate."

"And?" Brent asked. "Why haven't you detonated?"

"The batteries in our detonator didn't work." Quinn eased back from his sniper scope long enough to jut his chin in the direction of the beach. "When the alarms went off, Webb's unit moved in. As far as I can tell, they took out two guards, but I can't see much through the fog."

"Damian has a civilian with him, Yago Paquito," Brent said. "We need to get him out of here. He may be our only chance at stopping a major power outage in the US."

The rumble of an approaching helicopter vibrated through the air.

"I really hope that's our backup and not the Z-10 returning."

"You and me both." Brent evaluated their situation and the challenges they faced with no night-vision equipment and no working communication system.

"Do we go down and join them, or cover from up here?" Quinn asked.

"You cover from up here. I'll go down," Brent said. "Don't fire unless it's someone coming out that front door. I don't want any friendly fire incidents."

"Got it. Shoot anyone coming out of the fortress."

"Anyone who isn't Craig or Tristan."

"I figured you'd say that." More gunfire ignited on the far side of the building. Quinn adjusted his grip on his rifle. "For the record, I'm kind of tired of sitting in a tree."

"Yeah, I know. We all miss Jay."

* * *

Seth gripped the arms of his chair. The body-cam image from the SEAL Team Ten commander filled the screen and revealed Seth's nightmare for his men. They had gone into a hot landing zone, and Morenta's men were ready for them.

The rat-a-tat-tat of automatic gunfire carried over the comm unit, and someone reported a man down.

"Sully, get Jackson back to the chopper," the commander ordered. "Rodriguez, cover my flank."

Seth leaned forward and rested his elbows on his knees as more orders ensued and the SEALs pushed forward through the open space between the landing zone and the fortress. Beside him, Amy sat rigidly, staring at the large screen. Jim had given up his seat at the head of the table and now sat on the other side of her.

Gunfire flew from a third-floor balcony. Three men rushed out the front door, their weapons up and bullets flying. One man dropped before any of the Team Ten weapons fired.

Quinn.

Team Ten took out the other two. Seth couldn't tell who shot the next man who emerged. It didn't matter. The immediate threat was neutralized.

Bullets sparked off the railing of the balcony where a sniper had taken position, but Seth couldn't see any evidence that the shooter was successful in wiping out the threat.

Several men dressed in combat gear swarmed in from the beach side of the fortress. Seth studied their movements long enough to know they weren't his squadmates. Probably Webb's unit.

"I don't see the Saint Squad anywhere," Amy said.

"Quinn's playing sniper somewhere," Seth said.

"Yes, but where is everyone else?"

A new voice came over the comm. "We have contact."

"The Saint Squad?" Jim asked. His question was relayed by the communication officer in the corner of the room.

"Yes, sir. He has a civilian with him."

"Put him on comm," Seth demanded, forgetting for a moment that he wasn't in charge.

Secretary Hartley glanced in his direction before speaking to the comm officer. "Do it."

A moment later, Damian's voice came over the speaker. "We lost comm. There's an electromagnetic field that wipes out anything with a battery. Estimate ten minutes before new arrivals experience equipment failure."

Doug swiveled in his chair and spoke to Jim. "If the cars in Kansas City are losing power, that helicopter could be next."

Jim immediately straightened. "Retreat. Get them out of there."

The order was issued, and the new arrivals fell back toward the helicopter. One of the men on the beach side waved his hand to signal to Webb's men.

"The Saint Squad won't get the order." A hint of panic laced Amy's voice. "Their comm is still down."

"Won't they see the rest of the SEALs retreating and follow them?" Jim asked.

"Not if they've spread out to different parts of the fortress," Amy said.

She was right. His squad was tasked with securing Morenta. If the helicopter left without them, it would only be a matter of time before the numbers of Morenta's men would challenge their skills.

"There has to be a way to signal them," Jim said.

"Morse code." Seth pointed at the comm officer. "Have Team Ten fire off shots in morse code to signal retreat."

"Gunfire as a communication method?" someone across the room asked.

Secretary Hartley waved at the comm officer. "Relay the message."

He did so, and a moment later, gunfire sounded in a pattern that represented dots and dashes. Seth prayed his squad would get the message and that it wouldn't come too late for them to flee to safety.

43

THE PATTERN OF GUNFIRE REPEATED in Brent's head, the timing between shots forming into letters and then a single word. *Retreat*. He really hated that word.

"Quinn!" Brent shouted to make sure his teammate had also understood the message.

From the branches above, Quinn waved. He slung his rifle across his body and began his downward climb. Through the fog, Brent could make out the new arrivals and what appeared to be Webb's squad heading for the two helicopters. He studied the forms, searching for any sign of Tristan or Craig. Nothing.

Turning his gaze to the fortress, Brent spotted movement halfway down the building, a limp figure hanging suspended. Had his men captured Morenta?

Two of Morenta's men rushed around the back of the building. One pointed at the suspended body and shouted. Both men lifted their weapons, but before they could take aim, Brent squeezed off a shot and then a second. Both men fell to the ground.

A rifle barrel poked around the edge of the building, and gunfire sounded before another man poked his head around the corner.

Brent dove for cover. Quinn took position beside him.

"Any idea how many men they have inside there?" Brent asked.

"A lot more than we expected."

More gunfire rumbled from the third-floor balcony. A SEAL went down. The man beside the fallen one leaned down and dragged him the rest of the way to the waiting helicopter. Another SEAL returned fire.

Brent focused again on the side of the building. The unconscious man dropped past the second floor and continued downward until his body impacted the ground. A moment later, his body crumpled into the shrubbery next to the fortress, and the rope that had been supporting him spiraled down on top of him.

Despite the low visibility, Brent spotted movement on the top-floor balcony, his two men climbing down the side of the building.

The man by the corner shot again, sending another spray of bullets through the air.

"Cover them. As soon as they get down, all of you head for the chopper."

"What about you?"

"I'm going to sweep behind this guy to make sure you're clear."

Though Quinn's expression revealed his dissatisfaction with the plan, he nodded. "Don't take too long."

"I won't," Brent promised, ignoring the lingering pain in his knee. "I might be older than you, but I'm still just as fast."

"In your dreams."

Brent ignored Quinn's remark and suppressed the chuckle that tried to surface. They could laugh together later. For now, they needed to get out of here before any more SEALs went down.

* * *

Bullets flying in Nicaragua. People freezing in Missouri. Her father had been president for less than a month, yet he delegated tasks to trusted personnel with authority. Amy had no doubt he had a litany of prayers running through his mind as he worked.

Amy sent up her own silent prayers as she fought for calm despite the acid burning in her throat and the weakness that crept into her limbs. Three SEALs down, and she had yet to see any sign of the remaining four Saint Squad members.

On the far side of the room, Doug worked to relay critical information to the power plants in Philadelphia and Las Vegas. The director of FEMA also stood by, taking note of how to protect car batteries from the effect of the electromagnetic field in Kansas City.

In the seat beside her, Seth gripped the arms of his chair. "I should be there."

"There's nothing you could do that they aren't already doing." Amy said the words because they were what Seth needed to hear. At least, she hoped that was the right thing to say. In truth, she wished Seth were there too. Really, she wished Brent and the rest of his men were here.

Doug finished with the translator and turned to Amy's dad. "Mr. President, the team searching the power plant in Philadelphia found the pulse transmitter. They're neutralizing it now."

"Thank goodness."

One crisis averted. With at least one of the critical cities safe, the cascade failure was no longer an imminent threat. Amy wished the same could be said for the scene before her.

A new spray of bullets roared near the side of the fortress, but this time, it was two of Morenta's men who went down. Several figures emerged from the fog. The one in the lead squeezed off another round. Two of the other men dragged a third toward the waiting helicopter. Amy's heart jumped into her throat, closing off her supply of air. Who had been injured? And had he survived?

Several men by the chopper laid down cover fire as the group of four moved forward.

One tall, two shorter. Tears threatened, and Amy swallowed before she managed to speak. "Who?"

"I'm not sure," Seth said, but he didn't lie well.

"Tell me."

"That's Quinn on point."

"And?"

"I can't tell if it's Brent or Tristan helping Craig."

A pilot's voice came over the line. "Estimate three minutes before expected mechanical failure."

"Get everyone out of there," Secretary Hartley said.

One of the comm officers relayed the order.

The Saint Squad neared the helicopter. Only a few more seconds and Amy would know if her husband was still alive.

* * *

Brent offered more cover fire, and, pushing the pain in his knee to the back of his mind, he rushed through the trees toward his ride home. He made it only the length of the building before his foot caught on something, and he stumbled, aggravating his already pulsing injuries. His weapon dropped from his hands, the sling attached to it keeping it close to his body.

Gunfire ripped through the trees above his head, and he rolled behind a thicket of bushes. He gripped his weapon, took aim at the men rushing toward him, and shot off a single bullet.

The man closest to him went down, and his companions retreated back the way they'd come.

Brent glanced at the helicopter and his men loading Morenta into it.

Tristan took position beside the nearest chopper and sent another spray of bullets toward the fortress.

Brent pushed to his feet and ducked behind the nearest tree. A little cover fire from his teammates and Brent would be to the helicopter in another sixty seconds.

A new sound broke through his concentration. Brent barely recognized the hum of the approaching vehicle over the rumble of the helicopters. His gaze swung in the direction of the new sound.

The jeep came to a stop only twenty yards away from the edge of the trees. Brent's heart lurched when a man in the back of the jeep lifted a missile launcher to his shoulder and took aim.

"No!" The word escaped him, but the sound was lost beneath the rat-a-tat-tat of gunfire and the whirr of helicopter engines.

Brent's rifle came up, and he fired. The shooter collapsed and tumbled out of the jeep, the rocket launcher dropping beside him. Brent sighted his next target, the driver, but when he squeezed the trigger, nothing happened. Out of ammo.

Brent quickly changed out the magazine on his semiautomatic rifle. By the time he lifted it again, the driver had taken cover behind the vehicle.

The top of the rocket launcher came into view over the edge of the jeep before disappearing from sight.

Brent's heartbeat quickened. The man had only two targets, and both of them were helicopters filled with navy SEALs.

Brent rushed out of the jungle and circled behind the jeep. He took aim and squeezed the trigger again, but the weapon jammed.

The man lifted the rocket launcher to his shoulder and aimed at the helicopter carrying Brent's squad.

The first helicopter lifted off the ground, and the man redirected his aim.

Brent didn't think. He reacted. He dropped his weapon and dove for the man as he fired.

* * *

Amy gasped when a projectile flared through the air.

"Incoming!" A pilot's shout vibrated through the Situation Room.

"Evade!" someone else shouted.

Amy gripped her hands together.

"Get them out of there," her dad demanded, repeating the order Secretary Hartley had issued only moments ago.

On screen, someone grabbed Tristan's shoulder and hauled him into the helicopter. Tristan stepped into the doorway, but that was as far as he got.

Seth straightened. "Someone's missing."

Her dad turned. "What?"

"We're missing someone." Seth stood and pointed at the screen. "Tristan is still covering."

"Who?" Amy stood as well and spoke to the comm officer. "Who are we missing?"

"And how many?" Secretary Hartley asked.

The comm officer asked the question.

"Commander Miller is still out there," the Team Ten commander reported.

Brent wasn't injured or dead. He was missing. But where was he?

"We're taking heavy fire," the pilot reported.

Automatic gunfire punctuated his words.

Amy's gaze met her father's, his torment visible on his face. Wait for Brent and risk the lives of more than thirty navy SEALs or abandon his son-in-law in hostile territory?

"What's Commander Miller's status?" Secretary Hartley asked.

"He went after the missile launcher," the Team Ten commander said.

Another missile whizzed through the air, this one also shooting wide as well.

Seth stepped in front of Jim. "You have to get them out of there."

A pain ripped through Amy.

"You want them to leave Brent?" Jim asked.

"You have to," Secretary Hartley said. "It's the only way to save the rest of those men."

Apology lit her father's eyes when he looked at Amy and nodded. "Give the order."

Seth put his hand on Amy's shoulder. "We'll go back for him. He's been left behind before."

Amy bit her upper lip, struggling against the overwhelming emotions flying through her. "He's never been left behind without you before. Or without me."

"He's smart, and he's resourceful. He'll get out of there, and we'll go in and find him."

The helicopters lifted off, the pilot's voice cutting out as it came over the line. It then went silent.

"We've lost comm."

The images from the Team Ten commander's body cam switched to the flight camera on the helicopter. The foggy fortress grounds filled the screen across the room, and Amy searched for any sign of her husband. Had he gotten away? Would he be able to hide until they went back for him?

The helicopters rose higher, and more gunfire sounded from below, all of it aimed skyward. Movement near a jeep caught her attention, and Amy strained to make out the figures through the fog.

"Is that Brent there?" Amy pointed.

"I think so." Seth edged closer to the screen. So did Amy.

Two men scuffled, the fog enveloping them.

The SEALs were leaving Brent, abandoning him while he was in the middle of a fight. A half dozen men rounded the corner of the fortress, heading right for him.

The helicopter continued upward, the fog obscuring the men below. Amy curled her fingers into a fist, her nails digging into her palms. Could Brent get away? Would Morenta's men take Brent captive? Could Brent survive?

She fought against the terror climbing through her and the tears flooding her eyes.

Light flashed in the fog, followed by an explosion. The helicopter jerked as the fog turned from misty gray to bright orange. Flames speared into the air from the same spot Brent had been moments ago, the fire expanding to the building in one direction and to the trees in the other. A circle of fire. No movement beyond the flames.

Amy's legs gave way, and she dropped into the nearest chair. The mission that had saved the country from a catastrophic power failure had just cost her her husband—her baby's father.

ABOUT THE AUTHOR

TRACI HUNTER ABRAMSON WAS BORN in Arizona, where she lived until moving to Venezuela for a study-abroad program. After graduating from Brigham Young University, she worked for the Central Intelligence Agency, eventually resigning in order to raise her family. She credits the CIA with giving her a wealth of ideas as well as the skills needed to survive her children's teenage years. She loves to travel and recently retired after spending twenty-six years coaching her local high school swim team. She has written more than forty best-selling novels and is an eight-time Whitney Award winner, including 2017 and 2019 Best Novel of the Year.

She also loves hearing from her readers. If you would like to contact her, she can be reached through the following:

Website: www.traciabramson.com

Facebook page: facebook.com/tracihabramson

Facebook group: Traci's Friends

Bookbub: bookbub.com/authors/traci-hunter-abramson

Twitter: @traciabramson

Instagram: instagram.com/traciabramson